PG

He scarcely see~~~~~~~~~~
of Rose's name he had taken a ~~~~~~
her, as though to shake the story from her, but now
he might almost have forgotten her presence. Sarah
had never seen him so distraught, his face so unguarded. In a single moment he had changed from a
stern, self-assured ruler of family and household to
a man at a loss, fearful and stricken. His helplessness was more·frightening to Sarah even than his
anger.

'Has she said anything to you?'

'No, nothing,' she said in bewilderment.

'You don't know anything about a man, secret
meetings?'

'No!'

'If it is him . . .' He put his hand to his mouth
and bit it. 'My God, my God . . .'

Also by Janet Broomfield

AUSTRALIA LANE

A Song in the Street

JANET BROOMFIELD

WARNER BOOKS

A *Warner* Book

First published in Great Britain
by Janet Broomfield in 1996
This edition published by Warner Books in 1997

Copyright © Janet Broomfield 1997

The moral right of the author has been asserted.

A CIP catalogue record for this book
is available from the British Library.

ISBN 0 7515 2070 5

Typeset in Bembo by M Rules
Printed and bound in Great Britain by
Clays Ltd, St Ives plc

Warner Books
A Division of
Little, Brown and Company (UK)
Brettenham House
Lancaster Place
London WC2E 7EN

A Song in
the Street

CHAPTER

One

Liverpool, 1860

The door opened, spilling a patch of tremulous light across the pavement. A man came out of the house. The brim of his hat, pulled forward across his brows, obscured his face but his clothes marked him out as an alien presence in the dismal, shabby street. His greatcoat, its fabric still dense and unworn, had the fit of a garment made for its current wearer; his shoes, narrow and glossy, gleamed in the pale light from the house. He took a few swift strides along the street, leaning forward in his eagerness to be gone.

'Wait!'

He stopped and turned back. At the door a woman's form was just visible. One hand on the doorpost she leaned out, gazing after him. 'Next week? You will come back?'

'I'll have to see,' he said curtly, his impatience to be away tinged with a more particular irritation at the nature of the delay.

'You will try?'

'I've told you: I will see.' He looked about. There was no one near enough to hear them, only a hunched old woman, her shawl drawn over her head, shuffling her slow way to the beer shop, jug in hand. Reassured, he said less sharply, 'Go inside. You'll catch your death in this rain.'

She stepped back, pleased to take from this some proof of his concern. She began to close the door but stopped, unable to deny herself a last attempt to satisfy her anxious longing. 'Soon, please?'

'Yes, yes . . .'

Before she could make any further plea he broke away, hating her for his own failings. His pace quickened with his fierce desire to distance himself from her. His relief strengthened with every step, yet he knew that she need have no fear. He would return as soon as he could manufacture an excuse. He always did, despite his disgust and his agonised resolves.

The household had retired; the house was dark save for a lamp burning in the hall. As he reached up to bolt the door, it seemed to him that he was not locking out intruders but imprisoning himself. And yet it was a fine house, constructed in accordance with his wishes in every detail, every creature within its strong walls subject to his unquestioned will.

He lit the chamber candle and, once sure that it was burning strongly, for he was a cautious and methodical man, extinguished the lamp. With light, precise steps he climbed the stairs, as careful of disturbance as if he had been a housebreaker.

On the landing he paused. A confused murmur arose from his daughters' room: a voice, Rose's, he thought, raised in an unintelligible cry, its meaning hidden from him as from her waking self, known only in her dreams.

A nimbus of light showed round his wife's door. It was ajar. He closed his eyes, feeling a burglar's dread of discovery in the sleeping house, and more than a thief's guilt.

'William?'

Soft, loving, her voice reached him. He forced himself to move towards the light-edged door.

'Still awake? You will have a headache tomorrow,' he said, looking into the room.

She raised herself on one elbow. 'Come and kiss me goodnight, dear.'

Whatever the changes wrought in her face by time and ill-health, her smile was still that of a girl, trusting and open. He crossed to the bed and bent to kiss her cheek. The scent of lavender rose from the linen. Her nightcap was neat, freshly laundered. Beneath its crisp, lace-trimmed border a strand of hair just showed, thin and grey. As he straightened, memory taunted him: another pillow, its striped ticking bulging from a torn pillowcase; a tangle of thick black hair sprawled across its sour-smelling cotton. He tightened his lips.

'How cold you are, William dear.'

'It's raining.'

'You look so tired. I wish you did not need to work so hard.'

'I'm not complaining.'

'You never do.' She reached out a thin hand and caressed his cheek. 'I hope you managed to finish everything tonight?'

He picked up the snuffer and fiddled with it. 'No . . . I shall have to see Roberts again soon.'

'Just as you say, William. I shall sleep now,' she said, settling herself back against the pillows and smiling up at him.

He put out the candle and by the light of his own went to his room. He shut the door behind him and leaned against it. Greedily, unwillingly, he invoked the memories of a voice, hoarse and uncontrolled in a passion that was almost terror, and of arms clasped desperately about him. Such visions must feed him, until the power of his imagination failed and he was driven once more to their despised source.

'Rose? You will catch a chill, dear.'

The girl sitting on the window-seat, her arms clasped around her knees, answered without turning. 'I am not the least bit cold, Mama.'

'But it's getting dark. There's nothing to see.'

'I like it.'

Mary Brunton sighed. 'Come away, all the same.'

'In a minute.'

'Shall I play for you, Mama?'

Mary Brunton turned to her older daughter and her face lost the faint bewilderment that any dealings with Rose soon induced. Sarah, at least, she could understand. 'If you aren't too busy with your work, dear.'

'Oh, there's no hurry for it. It's just something for the bazaar.'

Sarah put her needle carefully into the fabric, where she would find it easily the next time she picked up her work. With her plainly dressed hair and drab gown she might have been some poor relation, kept out of charity, rather than the daughter of one of the most successful ironmasters in the district.

Sarah went to the piano and was lifting its lid when an impatient gesture from her sister made her pause.

'Listen! That carriage has stopped at our gate!'

'Oh, I don't think so, Rose dear. Your papa is to be late tonight.'

'It did, I tell you!'

As they listened, the crunch of hurrying steps on the gravel of the drive was plain even to Mrs Brunton. Her hand flew to her heart. 'Whatever can it be? Oh, Rose, I do hope nothing has happened to your father!'

'I'll go and see!'

Sarah watched Rose hurry from the room. As the elder by five years, it should have been she who had taken control and put their mother's fears to rest, but as usual Rose's quicker wits had left her feeling slow and stupid. Sighing, she put down the lid of the piano.

In the hall a young man, a stranger to Rose, was talking excitedly to the servant.

'Yes, Betty? What is it?' Rose asked, deliberately ignoring the newcomer.

'This young man—'

'Simon Olivant,' he interrupted. 'I've come up from Warrington, from the works, and I need to see Mr Brunton at once.'

'Thank you, Betty,' Rose said coolly. 'Will you tell my mother that I shall be with her directly?' Although well aware of his restless impatience, she waited until the maid had bustled upstairs before turning to him again. 'Mr Brunton is not at home. I am his daughter. You may explain your business to me and I will see that my father hears of it the moment he returns.'

'I would prefer to see him myself. If you could tell me where I could find him, the cab is waiting . . .'

'He is working and may not be home until late.'

He sighed in exasperation. 'But where is he?' he repeated.

'There is no need to address me as though I were simple-minded, Mr Olivant. I don't know where my father is. His business interests take him to many places and of course he does not explain his every journey to his family. If you will tell me your message I will ensure that he receives it tonight.'

He looked at her doubtfully, but with a little less condescension. A few years older than she, he appeared from his dress to be a clerk rather than a manual worker. Of rather above the average height, slightly built, he was dark-haired, but with strikingly pale skin. The contrast gave no impression of ill-health and was faintly exotic.

'Really, Mr Olivant . . .' She tapped her foot impatiently, awaiting his reply.

'Very well. There has been an accident at the works.'

'An accident!' A gleam of satisfaction showed in his face. Her alarm justified his reluctance to tell her. She was behaving exactly as he had expected. Rose forced herself to regain her composure. 'Has anyone been hurt? Is there any damage to the plant?'

'A wall collapsed in the pattern shop. Two men were trapped in the rubble, but they were pulled out almost at once and don't seem seriously injured. A lot of patterns have been destroyed but that's about all. It could have been far worse.'

She nodded. 'I will tell my father. Keep us informed, please, if the situation changes.'

'Yes, of course . . .' He hesitated, but she could see no reason to prolong the interview and, his earlier arrogance not quite forgiven, she showed him firmly to the door.

Mrs Brunton took the news more calmly than Rose had feared, once assured that nobody had been seriously hurt.

'I am only glad that your father was not still at the works. He would have been the first on the scene, trying to help. You know your dear papa, he never shirks his duty.'

Rose was glad that her mother's fears were so easily soothed. She herself was puzzled by her father's absence from the works. She had understood that he was to be there that evening. She had taken care not to admit as much to Simon Olivant, and did not now mention it to her mother and sister. All the same, when Rose heard her father enter the house she slipped down to greet him alone and give him the news, before he made any comments as to his whereabouts that evening.

He was already closing the door, his back to her as he reached for the top bolt. Not for the first time, it struck her how powerful a figure he still was, compared to her gentle, ailing mother. At the sound of her steps he turned sharply. Usually impassive, his face showed alarm and, she thought, an expression of guilt.

'What is it?' Is your mother unwell again?'

'No, although she won't go to bed until she sees you. A Mr Olivant came from the works, a little before eight. There's been an accident in the pattern shop. A wall fell down, two men are slightly hurt, and they wanted you to know about it.'

He unbuttoned his greatcoat, not looking at her. 'I was seeing a manufacturer in Liverpool. He may be placing a big order, but his specifications are rather unusual. I caught the last train home.'

'Mama was glad you weren't at the works, that's all,' she said, helping him off with his coat.

Rose had never known him give such a detailed account of his business affairs before. It was unthinkable that his actions should ever be questioned. The monolithic source of authority, in the family as at work, his uncharacteristic wish to explain himself was, in its way, even more disturbing than the collapse of the wall.

The following day, William Brunton was able to assure his family that all was well at the works, and that plans were already being drawn up to rebuild the pattern shop. The little flurry of excitement was over.

Perhaps by contrast, the rest of the week was exceptionally flat and dreary to Rose. The weather was too wet even to permit the long walks with Bobby, her father's terrier, that usually lessened her boredom. Instead, she spent as much time as she could in the kitchen. Without any patience for the needlework that occupied much of her sister's day, Rose loved cooking and was proud of the skills she learned by wheedling recipes from the irascible cook.

Saturday, too, dawned wet and overcast, but by the afternoon the sun had broken through. Rose went in search of Bobby.

'You need a really long run, don't you?' Rose said, fondling his rough coat. 'Coming, Sarah?'

'I don't think so. I have a new hymn to practise for the Sunday school . . . but of course I'll come if you want me to.'

'Oh, we'll manage without you, though I don't know how you can bear to sit at home playing hymns on a sunny afternoon.'

Sarah smiled, and picked up her music. Big, awkward, slow-moving, she was ill-suited to match Rose's swift pace on one of her excursions. They both knew that Rose would be happier without her.

The Bruntons lived some distance from Warrington, to the south of the town. A little way beyond their house, a path led to a hill that reared up from the Cheshire plain. The highest point for miles around, it was a favourite with Rose and Bobby.

As usual, on reaching the lane Rose turned left, intending to climb the hill. To her surprise, a young man emerged from the shade of a tree opposite the house and crossed the road towards her.

'Mr Olivant! Is something wrong?' she asked, automatically associating him with misfortune.

'No, not at all.' He bent to pat Bobby, who retreated growling.

'He's suspicious of strangers.'

'I expect he's looking forward to his walk. Mind if I come with you?'

'Well, no,' she said, caught unprepared, 'but what about your business with my father? He isn't home yet but he shouldn't be long.'

'I didn't come to see *him*.'

'Oh . . .' Rose felt that she should protest, and refuse to continue their walk, or that she should put him in his place by some swift, crushing riposte. But she was only seventeen, and so she merely blushed in pleased surprise, even though she had not devoted a thought to him since their brief meeting, and she was far from sure that she even liked him. 'I don't think my father would wish me to walk alone with someone I scarcely know,' she said, but all the same she fell into step with him, and continued along the lane.

'You have an excellent chaperone.' He pointed his cane at Bobby, whose hackles rose.

'Bobby, don't be such a silly.' She stooped and caressed the dog, self-conscious beneath Simon's gaze.

'He is a lucky beast,' he said, in a low voice that allowed her to ignore the remark. She did not look up but her colour deepened. She knew that he would understand the reason for her confusion. The shared knowledge linked them silently together.

Rose stroked the dog's back again and straightened, catching Simon's eye. He was looking at her intently, his eyes so dark that they seemed to be all pupil. His features were good and yet she was not sure that he could be described as handsome. There was a hardness about his face, and particularly in the expression of his eyes, that spoiled the effect of his dark, lightly curling hair, his strong cheekbones and full lips.

'You don't come from around here, do you?' she asked, walking on.

'My accent, you mean? My family are Scottish and I was brought up in St Andrews by my aunts. My father was in the Indian army.'

'What brought you to Warrington?'

'It's a safe distance from St Andrews.'

'Oh?' She was unsure how seriously to take his reply. 'Was that important?'

'It's a stupid place.'

He had not answered her question, but his sullen tone did not encourage her to persist. 'Is Warrington much better?'

'Without money, anywhere is hell.'

'Oh, surely . . . !'

'Have you ever been short of money?'

'My sister and I don't really have any money of our own, but we have everything we need. We don't ever have to think about it.'

'You're lucky.'

'In that respect, perhaps.'

He idly swung his cane and struck down a poppy in the hedgerow, severing its head. 'And in what respect are you not lucky?'

His sarcastic tone piqued her. She wanted to prove to him that her life was not as perfect as he seemed to think. In some way that she hardly understood she wanted to apologise for her easy circumstances, and remove any barriers they set between them. 'Papa doesn't like us to go out much. We don't entertain because my mother is not strong and the worry and fuss would bring on one of her bilious attacks. We aren't even on really close terms with most of the other families around about here, because of Mama being such an invalid and so shy.'

'So you are bored?'

'A bit. Sarah doesn't mind. She's so wrapped up in the chapel and the Sunday school and all the rest of it . . . She's very good,' she added, with faint contempt.

'And you aren't?'

She glanced quickly at him. None of the young men she had met at the chapel events that formed her only, despised, social life would have made such a remark. Simon's cynical tone at once alarmed and fascinated her. She wanted to show herself equally sophisticated.

'I want more out of life than sewing circles and Dorcas societies, at any rate.'

'So what do you want?'

'Excitement, change . . . weeks where every day isn't an exact copy of the same day the week before. I want to travel, and see something of the world, and *do* something.'

He nodded in apparent understanding. 'Some people can only add one day to another, identical, like bricks. They wall themselves in, make their own prisons. What's the point of living, if you aren't free?'

'I know!'

'Most people are such slugs. They crawl on from day to day without daring to imagine that things could be different. They won't take risks, they fetter themselves by petty conventions and laws, just because they are afraid of their own freedom.'

'Yes,' she agreed, a shade doubtfully. In his enthusiasm he was saying things he could not possibly believe. He almost appeared to advocate breaking the law; the suggestion was outrageous. She must have misunderstood him.

'I could tell that you were different,' he went on, his pale face alive with excitement. 'You were so sure of yourself, so bold. Most girls will scarcely look a fellow in the eye but you stared at me as though you'd damn well look at me any way you liked.'

She did not care for his language but to comment on it would be a betrayal of the freedom from petty conventions for which he was praising her. She said nothing, storing away for future reflection the fact that her imperious manner, on which her mother had often passed gentle strictures, had impressed him so favourably.

'You're the first person I've met in this place who's shown a spark of life,' he continued petulantly, 'and the damnable thing is, of course, that your father is who he is.'

'What do you mean?'

'He employs me. He pays my wages, such as they are. Do you think he would approve of your seeing me?'

The question jolted her. She did not want to examine the assumptions underlying it. With conscious evasion, she asked, 'You work in the office, I take it, not in the factory itself?'

'Yes, thank God. I don't suppose you have ever been over the works?'

'Oh, no! Even when we lived in Warrington, Sarah and I hardly knew where they were.'

'He wouldn't want his daughter to go there, right enough. The heat and dust would damage a delicate complexion.'

'I have always heard my father spoken of as a good employer,' she said, with a touch of hauteur.

'There are worse,' he conceded. 'At least he works hard himself. By the way, did you ever find out where he was on Tuesday evening?'

'He had gone to Liverpool, something to do with a special order.'

'It hasn't come through yet, in that case. Our department deals with orders and accounts. There has been nothing recently from Liverpool.'

'Perhaps it hasn't been finally settled,' she said, with a feeling of constraint. To discuss her father's business with one of his employees gave her an unpleasant sense of disloyalty.

'Perhaps not,' he agreed. 'Aren't we at the top of this confounded hill yet?'

'Why? Aren't you enjoying your walk?'

'I would enjoy it a lot more like this . . .' Before she divined his intention, he slipped his arm about her waist. She gasped in surprise, but the sinuous warmth of his arm about her was so pleasant that she made no serious protest.

'You really are a stunner,' he murmured, his arm tightening about her waist.

'That doesn't give you the right to put your arm around a young lady you hardly know.'

'And how am I ever going to get to know you? Shall I call on you and leave my card? Will your father invite me to dinner?'

Her silence was answer enough.

'How else can I see you?' he persisted, pressing home his advantage. 'Can you blame me for making the most of every second we are together when they are likely to be so few?'

She sensed that it was a crucial moment. He was making assumptions that she must either accept or destroy at once. If she put him firmly in his place she suspected that she would not see him again. She hesitated.

'Don't you want to see me again?' His voice sank to a reproachful, caressing tone that she had never heard before.

'I don't know.'

'You are tormenting me.'

'But this is all so sudden . . . how can you expect me to say anything else?'

'And how can you expect me to go away, not knowing if I will see you again?'

'Oh, you will soon forget about me.'

'I have thought about nothing else since we met. If you had not come out when you did, I would have waited under that tree until night fell and I would have been back again at dawn.'

She did not altogether believe him but she was impressed. It was a romantic image and she hungered for some romance in her life. She sighed. 'I have to go to chapel in the morning and again in the evening. There is only the afternoon . . . not before three, probably.'

'I will be waiting.'

They had almost reached the top of the hill, near the graveyard. The trees were thinning out. There were always one or two people there: couples enjoying a stroll together, nannies out with those of their charges old enough to climb the hill. A tall, thin young woman in a glaring magenta gown was admiring the view over the smoke-stacks of Warrington and beyond. Bobby set off towards her at a scuffling gallop. Rose drew back.

'That's Effie, one of Sarah's friends. I'll have to go and speak to her. She'll think it very strange if she sees Bobby on his own. She might say something to Sarah.'

'One minute.' He pulled her back behind a tree and kissed her. She barely had time to register the shock of his lips pressing against hers, the jump to a new awareness of him, as though she had been viewing him through a tele-scope and the lens had abruptly switched to a disturbingly close focus. Before she could react he broke away and, swinging his cane, strode away down the path.

Mercifully, Effie was a talker so indefatigable that Rose's distracted silence was not noticeable. She had her spaniel with her and the dogs jostled together, making a pretence of biting each other's jaws, in the way that showed their playful affection. Rose let Effie chatter on, scarcely hearing a word.

In most circumstances, her first desire would have been to confide in Sarah. Ever since Rose could remember they had shared a room and a bed. The interval between extin-guishing the light and sleep was the time for telling secrets. That night, Rose said nothing After only a few minutes of Sarah's innocuous musings she feigned sleep. She wanted silence to hug her thoughts close, to luxuriate in them. She turned her face to the pillow, pressed her lips against its smooth, starched linen and dreamed.

Her pretence of sleep did not deceive her sister. Sarah

did not mind. She was happy enough with her own thoughts and the eager expectation of the day to come. She loved to lie wakeful, letting her imagination play over the familiar pattern of the Sabbath that, however tedious to Rose, was to Sarah full of interest and even excitement.

The following day, as usual, Sarah attended the morning service with her family. Rose went reluctantly, Mary went whenever her health allowed, and her husband played an active role in the practical activities of the congregation but never spoke of religion in its more personal sense. That area of his life, amongst many others, was hidden from his family. Sarah, a true devotee, instinctively sensed reservations that he never voiced.

Sarah's great delight was the afternoon Sunday school, in which she taught the youngest children. Throughout the week she spent much time and thought on her class and was secretly proud of its attendance record, the highest in the school.

As always, she dressed with particular care on Sunday. Taller and stouter than Rose, she preferred subdued colours and avoided anything that might draw attention to herself, but she liked everything to be neat and in perfect order, however plain.

Rose often teased her for checking her appearance so anxiously in the glass before leaving to teach her infants but today she seemed too preoccupied to notice. Her silence troubled Sarah. At the door she paused and looked back to where her younger sister sat at the dressing table, trifling nervously with her hair.

'Rose? Are you all right?'

'Why shouldn't I be?' she asked, with a laugh that to Sarah sounded forced.

'I don't know . . . you seem on edge, somehow.'

'Don't I look well?'

'Even more beautiful than usual,' Sarah said lightly. It was true. With her deep blue eyes and cloud of dark hair Rose had all the charm of face and figure that Sarah was painfully aware of lacking.

Although she would never have admitted it, Sarah did envy her. Once, many years before, she had heard one of her mother's acquaintances remark, 'You're lucky that Sarah has such a sweet nature, Mary. Any other girl would be jealous of a sister like Rose.' Sarah hated the woman ever after. Who could have forgiven such a compliment? It was a point of pride with Sarah to preserve her love for her sister untouched, but no one knew what a severe struggle it often cost her.

It was a pleasant walk from the Brunton's house to the Sunday school and Sarah soon forgot her vague anxiety about Rose. She arrived early, but the class was already gathering. As children ran towards her, contending for the privilege of carrying her music, her books, she felt a surge of joy. Here, at least, she was loved for herself. Each child was precious to her but some had a special place in her heart: Samuel, with his withered leg, who could never out-run the others in the race to greet her; Michael, one of the few badly cared for children, whose pale, set face hid an inner drama at which she could not guess; Joanna, whose mother had died in childbed only a few months before and whose small hand clung so wistfully to Sarah's. As Sarah moved slowly towards the school, impeded by children, each eager to tell her their news, she felt the most vivid happiness of the week.

It was perhaps not the least of the attractions of the Sunday school that none of the other members of her family were involved in it. Here, free from her father's irritable criticisms, from Rose's impatience with her slowness, even from her mother's well-meant reassurances, Sarah became a different person, confident and capable. It would have surprised them all to see her so poised, so sure of herself, easily holding the attention of even the most restless child.

At the end of the class Sarah remained behind for a few minutes, tidying the room and gathering her things together. Familiar steps sounded along the passage. She looked up, already smiling, as a tall, heavily built man came into the room.

'Good afternoon, Miss Brunton.'

'Good afternoon, Mr Taylor. Did your class go well?'

'A riot, as usual,' Philip Taylor said, picking up her books and tucking them under his arm with his own. 'I wish I had your class. Easily cowed, infants. One glare and they sit petrified, not a peep out of them.'

'Nonsense! They are just as much work as the seniors . . . and anyway, they can't play cricket. Where would the team be without you?'

He laughed. 'Got everything? Come on, then.'

They left the room together. In the year or so since Philip Taylor had begun to teach the oldest class he and Sarah had gradually fallen into the habit of walking home together. At first she had found him a formidable figure. Powerfully built, with dark hair which was beginning to recede at the temples and a thick beard, he had a dry sense of humour which Sarah had taken some time to appreciate. His class adored him, although he maintained a strict discipline, tempered by jokes and a surprising skill in caricatures with which he would occasionally amuse the children.

'Your mother keeping better?' he asked, as they crossed the yard.

'She has had a good week, although I was afraid that she might be the worse for the little excitement we had on Tuesday . . . an accident at the works, though no one was hurt, thank heavens.'

'Has she still not seen a doctor about these bilious attacks?' he asked, frowning.

'She doesn't want to.'

'Your father should make her. She would be seeing one, whether or no, if she was my wife.'

'That's all very well for a bachelor to say. Perhaps your wife might have other ideas.'

'Not where her health was concerned, she wouldn't. Some things are too important to be fooled about with.'

'If you scowled at her like that the poor woman wouldn't maintain her stand for long.'

His face relaxed into a reluctant smile. 'Oh, I'm all talk. Putty in your hands, that's all men are.'

The little exchange left Sarah feeling self-conscious; the conversation had strayed on to difficult terrain. It was not a completely unpleasant sensation, but she struggled to return to safer topics: the coming Sunday school treat, and the bazaar. They were still talking when they halted at her gate.

'Well, until next Sunday, Miss Brunton?'

'Yes . . .' she said, aware, as every week, that it would be natural to invite him home for tea, and that she did not dare. 'Thank you,' she added, taking her books from him. 'It is very kind of you.'

'Oh, I was passing this way in any case,' he said, lifting his hat in farewell.

At the door she looked back a moment to watch him striding down the lane, a little round-shouldered, as he said all farriers were, but strong and confident. With a sigh she turned and entered the house. After the sunshine outside it seemed dark and gloomy, until her eyes adjusted once more to its shadows.

Sarah went upstairs to tidy her hair. She was sitting at the dressing table when, reflected in its glass, she saw Rose as she entered the room, taking off her bonnet.

'Rose? I didn't know you were out. Whatever is it?'

'Nothing. What should it be?'

'I don't know . . . You look as though something has

happened, something to upset you.' Even as she spoke, Sarah realised that this was not quite true. Rose looked flushed and preoccupied, but not unhappy. She seemed to be in a dream.

'I took Bobby out for a walk, that's all.' Rose went to the window, raising her arms to feel for the pins holding her thick, dark hair in place. Her slender figure curved sinuously, like a young plant stretching towards the light. Sarah's vague misgivings strengthened.

'You would tell me, Rose? If there was anything important?'

Rose made no answer but remained, her back to the room, staring out of the window. Sarah wondered if she had heard but she did not repeat her plea. With a sigh she turned back to the mirror and its unsatisfactory image.

Rose did not notice. She was reliving the hour just gone and her walk with Simon, through quiet lanes towards Walton. It had seemed to her that she had never been so vividly herself, so keenly aware of her happiness. Despite the risks, she had agreed to see him again on Tuesday evening. Already she was wondering how she would bear it if the weather were too bad to let her get out.

Her fears were not realised. Tuesday evening was fine and she was able to take Bobby and meet Simon as she had hoped. They chose the least frequented paths and, as soon as they were alone, Simon put his arm about her waist. She made not even a show of protest. How could she, when she had been dreaming of that moment since last they met?

Many such meetings followed, each brief, fraught with the danger of discovery, intense in the need to compress into a few minutes all the emotions of the preceding days. To Rose, part of the intoxicating quality of these encounters was their secrecy and the ever-present consciousness of how little time remained. Even as she hungered to see more of Simon she wondered whether he would be quite such a romantic figure if, an approved suitor, he was a daily visitor to the house and sat at the dinner table making polite conversation with her mother.

If Rose secretly relished the forbidden nature of their love, the snatched kisses and uncertain rendezvous, liable to be thwarted at any moment by a chance caller or a sudden downpour, Simon seemed to find it less satisfactory, particularly when the summer turned into an unusually cold, wet autumn. She became aware that he was increasingly sullen and even bad-tempered.

Matters came to a head one Saturday afternoon in early September, when their courtship had reached its fourth month. It had become obvious that it was too dangerous for Simon to wait for her under the tree close to the house; instead they now met in woods, near the Chester road. They were less open to discovery, although the journey to and from the meeting place consumed precious time. As luck would have it, when Rose was about to leave the house her mother was taken ill. It was over half an hour before she was able to get away and, despite running most of the way, she was still later than ever before in reaching the agreed spot.

Simon was slouching against a tree, his very posture showing his ill-humour. 'Well? What excuse is it this time?' he began, drawing heavily on the cigarette which, to judge by the scattering of butts at his feet, had had many predecessors.

The ungracious greeting brought her to a startled halt. She had been imagining his relief at her appearance, however late; now, he was not even willing to sacrifice his cigarette to embrace her. 'I'm sorry, but I really couldn't help it. My mother was taken ill after lunch. I had to stay.'

'Couldn't Sarah see to her?'

His peevish tone grated on her nerves; she was guiltily

aware that too much was already left to Sarah. 'Sarah was at Effie's for lunch. They had intended going into Warrington together this afternoon but I sent for her to come back and look after Mama, so that I could see you. If I had known that you would be such a bear, I wouldn't have spoilt her afternoon,' she said, more sharply than she had ever addressed him before.

He frowned, but gave way. He threw down the cigarette. 'I was longing to see you, that's all. You can't blame a fellow for being impatient. I look forward to this all week, you know.'

His penitence dissolved her anger. Instantly she saw in his ill-humour only proof of his devotion. She put her arms about him with a sob of relief, appalled at her own harshness to him. 'Oh, Simon, I'm so sorry. I didn't mean to be horrid. I really did come here as soon as I could but I had to stay with Mama until Sarah got home.'

He made a noncommittal sound. 'I suppose she's all right now?'

His tone was less concerned than she would have liked but she told herself that, never having met her mother, it would be difficult for him to show a heartfelt interest in her welfare. 'It was quite a bad attack . . .' she began, but feeling his lips nuzzling her neck she abandoned her explanation, excusing his boredom in view of his overwhelming desire for her. She lifted her hands to his face, all the more tenderly for her few moments of anger.

The wood was deserted and, longing for a perfect reconciliation, she consented to go with him to a small clearing where they could lie close together on the grass. He had often urged this but she had always demurred. Even this concession was not, however, enough for him.

'You are driving me wild,' he murmured, leaning on one elbow and looking down on her. His face had the keen intentness that she never saw at any other moments than these. She felt proud that she alone knew him in this mood.

'Why, aren't you happy?' she asked, teasing him. 'Shall I not kiss you again if it makes you wild?'

'Perhaps not. I often think that would be best. This half and half sort of life is torture.'

His vehemence took her by surprise, although he had hinted at his dissatisfaction with their hurried meetings before. 'I'm sorry if it's difficult for you. I don't like it very much either, but what else can we do?' she asked, hoping to coax him back to a more contented frame of mind.

'Come away with me.'

'Oh, if only I could! You don't know how often I dream about it.'

'I'm not talking about dreams. I mean it.'

'And so do I,' she said, stroking her finger along his brows. They were very dark and straight and when he frowned, as now, formed an almost continuous line. She usually loved their masculine severity but today, for the first time, she found them disturbing: coarse and animal-like with their few bristling hairs in the very centre. She removed her finger. 'One day, perhaps.'

'Why wait?'

'Because we have no choice,' she said, puzzled by his insistence and by a suppressed excitement in his manner. 'It's impossible, you know that.'

'We can make it possible.'

'But . . . we have no money,' she said, seizing at random on one of the arguments crowding her mind. 'You are always saying how little you are paid and I have no savings at all.'

'Don't worry about that,' he said impatiently. 'I will see to it.'

Seventeen years old, hardly aware of the value of money, never having known any deprivation caused by its lack, she did not challenge his claim. No doubt, despite his constant grumbles about his salary, he had other resources. She voiced another, more heartfelt objection. 'My mother and father would be so hurt, and everyone would talk . . . I couldn't do that to them.'

'Is that all you care about? What the neighbours will say?'

'You know it's not!' she said, stung by the sneer, for she liked to think of herself as a free spirit, unhampered by the petty social duties that bound her sister, with her chapel teas and sewing circles. 'If that were true, I wouldn't even be here with you!'

'And what will happen, the first time we are seen together? Your father will forbid you to meet me again: what will you do then?'

'I . . . I won't listen. I will find a way to see you, somehow.'

'He would give me the sack, that's certain. He would probably send you away, perhaps even abroad for a few months. We might never see each other again. Why risk it? Come away with me now and he'll never be able to part us. You do want that, don't you?'

His vehemence softened into the caressing tone she found irresistible. His hand, which had been gripping her shoulder, relaxed and moved to stroke her cheek. 'I couldn't live without you. Rosie. That's why I'm so afraid of losing you. It makes me impatient, when all we need is a little courage and we can be together for ever.'

He had never before come so close to an explicit declaration of love. She was dizzy with pride that he, so handsome, so sophisticated, should be saying such things to her. The sunshine, sifting through the leaves, gleamed on his black, waving hair and dappled his skin in a subtle, constantly changing pattern, as if he were a wild, free woodland creature. It did not seem odd that he should be so impetuous, so scornful of the conventions binding lesser men.

'I shall have to think about it,' she said, with a sense of making an exceptional concession. To her surprise his mouth turned down, sulky as a child denied an expected treat.

'Don't take too long about it, if you want to see me again. I've told you, I can't carry on like this. I won't be kept dangling.'

'But it's such a terrible decision. I must have time.'

'Will a week be long enough?'

She laughed, thinking he was joking, but his eyes were cold. He meant exactly what he said.

The following days brought Rose an anguish she had never before imagined, as she debated the stark alternatives of flight or loss, each with its unbearable consequences: to be with Simon, and hurt her parents grievously; to remain at home, a dutiful daughter, and be parted from him for ever. Each was unthinkable. As she struggled to make a decision, it occurred to her that a third possibility might exist. Without telling Simon, she determined to approach her father.

She went to him as he worked in his study after dinner. As her father's favourite she did not feel the instinctive dread of approaching him that afflicted Sarah when obliged to make even the most trifling request of him. All the same it still required some effort of the will to tap at his door, which always seemed the most forbidding in the house.

'Papa?' she asked brightly, stepping inside the room but still holding the door. 'Is it a bad time to disturb you? Shall I come back later?'

He looked up, frowning, from the ledgers open on the desk before him. 'You may as well come in now. I shall be busy with this all night, I'm afraid.'

He looked so preoccupied that she began to doubt the wisdom of her decision. She hesitated, but Simon had told her with a forcefulness that carried conviction that their next meeting must be their last, if she would not agree to elopement. She went to the desk and stood before her father. She picked up a pen wiper from the little tray beneath the lamp and pleated it nervously in her fingers. It had been one of her early essays at needlework and, clumsily done though it was, had retained its place on her father's desk. Sarah's painstaking offerings, far more expertly worked, languished in whatever drawer he had tossed them.

'Well?' His smile was encouraging but strained. She tried desperately to recall the speech she had rehearsed. It was now disintegrating beneath the force of his actual rather than his so much more malleable, imagined personality.

'I wanted to ask you something, Papa. I was in Warrington last Saturday afternoon and I happened to meet a young man who came to this house once, a few months ago.'

'Oh?' He raised his brows, his face expressing attention but not hostility.

She continued, more cautiously. 'I didn't remember him, but he recognised me. He came over and spoke to me for a few minutes. He was very polite.'

'And who was this polite young man?'

'He is one of your employees so you will know him. A Mr Simon Olivant.'

The glimmering of good humour was gone, leaving his face harsh and intent. 'What did he want?'

'Nothing . . . as I said, he just chatted to me for a few minutes,' she said, hastily revising her intention of further disclosures.

'Good. You were quite right to tell me. Under no circumstances must you let him near you again.'

'Why not, Papa?'

'Do I need to give a reason?'

'I think you ought, in fairness to Mr Olivant,' she said, with a placatory smile to soften her boldness.

'If what I suspect can be proved, you will soon hear about it,' he said grimly. 'Have nothing to do with him, do you understand? He's a bad hat.'

She wavered, half convinced by his sincerity. 'If you would explain why, Papa . . .'

He exhaled noisily, his breath issuing from his nose in an angry hiss, his habit at moments of irritation. 'My word should be enough for you. I can't see why you are persisting, on the strength of a few minutes' idle chitchat. The man's a bounder and may well soon be finding himself in very serious trouble. I can say no more at present. Now, I have a considerable amount of very complex work to do before I can rest tonight. If you wouldn't mind . . . ?'

By her father's standards it was a courteous dismissal but Rose left the room seething with impotent anger. She returned briefly to the drawing room, told her mother and Sarah that she had a headache, and went to her room. Although she pretended to be asleep when Sarah came to bed not long afterwards, the clock in the hall had struck two before she at last drifted into uneasy slumber.

One thing at least she had decided in those hours of conflict and uncertainty. The following morning, while her father was at breakfast, she slipped out to the stables.

'John?'

The coachman looked up, one hand still on the bridle of the bay he was harnessing for its morning journey into town. 'Well, Miss Rose, it's not often we sees you in here at this time of the morning,' he said, with a grin that revealed more gum than teeth. John had been with her father ever since the family had moved out of the town some years before. He still treated her with the teasing affection he had given her as a child.

'I wanted to ask you a favour,' she said, reaching into her pocket.

'Well, look sharp. Mr Brunton won't think much of being kept waiting while you order me about.'

'It's nothing very much, just a letter. Could you see that this is handed in at the office, first thing this morning?'

'Here, you'll be getting me into trouble, you will! I'll get it in the neck if your father finds out I've been passing on love letters for you.'

'It's not a love letter . . . not really,' she added, her conscience pricking her. 'Please, John! It's so important, and it's only this once, I promise.'

'Well . . . I'll see what I can do. I'm not promising nowt, mind.'

'Oh, thank you, John!'

'Now, out of the road, or that young man'll never get his billy doo!'

She knew that she could trust John, but all the same the day seemed interminable as she awaited the hour she had appointed in her letter. She was not sure whether her father was dining at home that night, or whether she would easily be able to absent herself for any prolonged period, so had risked asking Simon to meet her near the house.

It proved a wise precaution, for her father was at home, and in a worse mood than she could ever remember. Throughout the meal he treated her mother with a politeness that barely concealed his irritation. Sarah, as usual, attracted the worst of his sarcasm and even Rose incurred a brusque comment when she announced her intention of taking Bobby out for a walk after dinner.

'I shall expect you back before nine. These long walks at all hours will have to stop, I warn you. It's not fit that a daughter of mine should be rambling through the country-side like a gypsy.'

Rose saw her mother and sister exchange a startled glance at his harsh tone, but she did not stay to argue. She hurried out of the house and up the lane. Simon was already waiting for her. Even in the dusk she could see that he was more nervous, more excitable than she had ever known him. He stepped quickly from the shadows and, gripping her wrist, pulled her towards him.

'What's been happening? Why did you write?'

'Oh, Simon, I didn't know what to do! I spoke to my father last night, just mentioning your name . . . I said we had met by accident and you had spoken to me. He was very angry and said you were somebody really bad and if what he suspected was true you would soon be in serious trouble . . .'

'Were those his very words?'

'Near enough. I asked him to explain but he wouldn't. He said I'd find out soon.'

'Was that all?' he asked, biting his lip.

'More or less. What did he mean?'

He cast a swift, appraising look at her. 'He probably has heard something, some rumour about us. He is trying to turn you against me.'

She frowned. The explanation did not ring true. 'I don't think it was that,' she said doubtfully.

'What else could it be? Do you believe him? Do you think I am a criminal of some sort?'

'No, of course not!'

'Then it must be as I said. He doesn't want you to so much as speak to any man who might take you away from him. He's a tyrant.'

'I suppose so,' she agreed reluctantly, 'and yet he was quite reasonable until I mentioned your name. I don't think he would have minded, if it had been anyone else.'

'That's easy to say. He would have been the same, believe me.'

'If I had known I would never have approached him . . . I'm so sorry, Simon!'

'It's a good thing in a way. It will force us to do something. By the sound of it he may be intending to dismiss
me, on some trumped up charge, perhaps. I don't intend to
wait.' He put his hands on her upper arms and said deliberately, 'I am going back to my lodgings to pack my things.
Tomorrow night I will come here for you. We can go
down to Warrington and catch the first train to Scotland.
Once we are safely married nothing he can say or do will
make any difference. Well?'

'I can't! It's too soon!'

In the twilight his dark eyes glittered in the pallor of his
face. He was leaning towards her, all the power of his will
focused on her. For that moment, she knew, she was the
only thing in the world that existed for him. He wanted to
persuade her, more intensely, perhaps, than he had ever
wanted anything in his life.

'You've got to make up your mind! Are you going to
stay under your father's thumb for ever? He'll never let
you go. There'll always be some so-called reason, but
that's the truth of the matter. It's up to you. Do you mean
to stay here and dry up into a prissy, nervous old spinster?
Or are you going to seize your chance to live your own
life?'

Under his compelling stare all that could have argued
against him faded into nothing. The chapel circle that
formed her sister's world was of no real significance to
Rose; her father had denied her the explanation she
needed, demanding instead her blind obedience; her mild,
harmless mother would forgive her anything; Sarah she
had from infancy treated as little more than an animated
toy, subject to her own, more imperious will.

In her present mood, caution had little power. The self-
preservation that might have checked a more worldly-wise
girl foundered on her very innocence, her inability to
conceive the worst dangers before her. All the same, half

ashamed of her doubt, she ventured to ask, 'We will be married at once?'

'Yes, yes,' he said impatiently. 'That is why we will go to Scotland. You won't need your father's consent there.'

'My father . . . He'll never forgive me!'

'You're his favourite, aren't you? You've said so often enough, at least,' he said, shaking her just a little too roughly. 'Once we are married he will come round. We will be safe then, don't you see?'

'I suppose so . . .'

'Well? What's it to be? Do you come with me, or go back to your cell?'

With the clarity of long experience, Rose pictured the drawing room: the clock whose hands seemed to move more slowly than those of any other in the world, as though in that room time itself became thick and sluggish; the fire that her mother needed in all but the hottest weather, so that the air was always stifling and heavy; her father's covert, pent-up irritation, expressed in the sharp crack of his newspaper as he shook it open, in the tapping of his elegant, gleaming shoe on the carpet though the rest of his body was rigid with self-control; her sister's sprightly, determined cheerfulness; the unendurable hours of boredom, futile and predictable, that somehow must be got through. Even with the prospect of seeing Simon once or twice a week they had been a torment. What would they be, with no hope of ever seeing him again?

'It's not as though it will be for ever,' she said to herself, seeking reassurance. 'I will see everyone again, as soon as we are married.'

'Tomorrow, then? At midnight?'

'But my things! I won't be able to take everything I need!'

'Don't worry about that; I can see to it once we are away,' he said, his lordly disregard for expense an odd contrast to his familiar complaints of poverty.

'I will be back soon, after all,' she repeated.

'A married woman,' he said, kissing her. 'Midnight? You won't fail me?'

Blurred by the twilight, his face was beautiful to her in its pallor and mystery. 'No,' she said proudly, aware that this was one of the crucial moments of her life, 'I won't fail you.'

He released her and, Bobby scudding gamely behind her, she hurried home.

As she crossed the hall, she met her father. On a sudden impulse she stopped. 'Papa, I just wanted to ask you again: is there really any serious charge against Simon Olivant?'

'What is it to you?' he asked coldly.

'I liked him when he spoke to me, that's all,' she said awkwardly.

'Serious enough for me to be considering dismissal.'

'Please, won't you tell me what it is?'

He was standing in the outer limits of the light from the hall lamp. Its shadows emphasised the deep lines that scored his cheeks, the dark hollows beneath his eyes. He was a handsome man still, but his stern, unyielding expression made of his face a hostile mask.

'The matter is under my active consideration. When I have completed my investigation you will hear the results. I may say that it will probably be a matter for the police. Until then I have nothing further to say.'

Involuntarily she took a step back. 'Thank you, Papa. I am just going to say goodnight to Mama and Sarah and then I believe I will go to bed. I am very tired.'

She climbed the stairs, head held high, and did not look back. He watched her go and only when she had vanished from his sight round the turn in the stair did he sigh, and go into his study.

Rose was glad that she had spoken to him. His refusal to explain himself convinced her that his objections were mere prejudice, his threat of police action only a bluff. Simon was right: her father would have found some grounds for damning any young man who sought her company. It banished her last doubt of Simon's innocence.

That night Rose made a start on gathering together her possessions for her departure. She worked quickly and efficiently, choosing only such clothes as would be serviceable in the coming autumn. There was no need to consider summer wear, she reminded herself, for this would be no more than a temporary separation from her family. A few weeks, and she and her husband would be welcome visitors once more.

She examined her jewel box. There were a few good pieces, the most valuable a pearl and garnet necklace given to her on her last birthday by her parents. This, and everything else of any value, she put with her clothes; the trinket box itself she would pack at the last moment. She did not dare to attract comment by removing it until then. There was a carpet bag in the dressing room; she put her clothes into it and replaced it where she had found it.

When Sarah came to bed, Rose pretended to be asleep. She forced her body to lie still but her mind was furiously active, planning the coming day. Now that she had made the crucial decision to cast in her lot with Simon, Rose discovered in herself a new competence, a practicality she had rarely needed to employ before. Romance might have dictated her choice, but a hard-headed realism was ensuring that she carry it out effectively.

Although Simon had said that he would take care of their financial needs, Rose wanted to have money of her own. She and Sarah had only a pound or two of pin money every quarter from their father. The next payment was due in a fortnight and not a penny of the last quarter's allowance remained in Rose's purse. Sarah, she knew, was more frugal. The following morning Rose approached the subject as they sat together over their books. Their father still liked them to study before lunch, although their governess had been dispensed with the previous year.

'Sal?'

Sarah looked up from her German grammar, smiling. 'Well? You want something, I suppose? That's the only time you ever call me Sal.'

'Oh, really, Sal!' Rose protested, blushing. Her sister, mild as she was, had at times a disconcerting acuteness. 'I was only wondering . . . no, I won't ask you, not after what you've just said.'

'I'm sure you will,' Sarah said calmly.

'Well, my allowance is all gone. You know what Papa is like about our keeping to it."

'And you want to borrow from me?'

'I've seen the most adorable pair of gloves in Warrington, lilac kid, they would just match my new gown. I can't wait another two weeks to buy them, I really can't!'

Sarah shook her head reprovingly. 'Then you will be starting off the next quarter in debt.'

'If I'm going to buy them anyway, what difference does it make when?'

'Ask Mama instead. She will probably get them for you.'

This was exactly what Rose would usually have done. Now, she said virtuously, 'Oh, I don't like to bother her. If you could just give me the money . . . I will pay you back.'

'How much?'

'Ten and six . . . could you manage a pound, in case I see something else?'

'Oh, Rose!' Sarah protested, but she gave her the money, as Rose had known she would. She took it for granted that Sarah, reliable and staid, would always do whatever she wanted.

That evening was a torment. Every mannerism of the other members of her family jarred on Rose's nerves, stretched taut by excitement, just when her guilty awareness of the pain she was about to inflict upon them made her wish to treat them with particular affection. She escaped from the drawing room as early as she could, pleading tiredness, and went to make her final preparations. She brought out the carpet bag and added to it her trinket box and one or two other last-minute items, then stuffed it out of sight under her side of the bed. She scribbled a farewell note to Sarah, hiding it beneath her own pillow.

Rose had decided not to undress. Instead, she slipped her nightgown over her dress, and lay down in the bed. An hour or so passed before she heard her sister enter the room.

'Rose?' Sarah called, softly so as not to disturb her if she was asleep.

Rose made no response. Sarah prepared for bed, trying to move quietly about the room but, as usual, the dim light ensured that she more than once bumped into the furniture or dropped something. In the past her clumsiness had infuriated Rose but tonight she felt her tears rise at her gentle, awkward sister's futile attempts at stealth. She wished that she could apologise for all her criticisms of Sarah's ineptness, for her secret contempt that her sister should be satisfied with her limited, blameless life. It was too late. As the bed creaked beneath Sarah's weight Rose felt her heart beat faster, already preparing for her next move. Excitement was crowding out regret.

Sarah was long since asleep when the chimes of the hall clock sounded a quarter to twelve. Rose slipped out of bed and pulled out the letter for Sarah so that it projected from beneath the pillow and would easily be found in the morning. She put a shawl about her shoulders and, picking up her bag, crept from the room.

A light showed from around the door of her father's study. It would be too dangerous to draw the bolts and

leave by the front door. She made her way to the kitchen
and, easing the door shut, went into the scullery. The key
was left in the door. She turned it, inched back the bolts
and opened the door. The night air met her, cold and
unfriendly. She took off her nightdress and left it, folded
neatly, on the mangle. Then, picking up her bag, Rose left
her father's house, flitting like a ghost through the garden
and the orchard and out into the rough, rutted lane
beyond.

CHAPTER

Two

Sarah never knew what woke her but her first impression was of deep anxiety: something was wrong. Her thoughts flew to her mother. Had she been taken ill in the night and called for her? She got up at once, although she could now hear no sound from her mother's room, and reached for the shawl that she kept close to the bed for just such emergencies. She felt her way round the bed, not wanting to disturb her sister by stumbling in the darkness, but as she reached Rose's side she realised that it was empty.

This puzzled but did not unduly worry Sarah. If her mother had called, perhaps Rose had already gone to attend to her although she would more usually prod Sarah awake to go: Rose hated illness and was an impatient nurse. Still, the bedroom door was ajar, suggesting that this was what had happened. With less effort at silence, Sarah crossed the landing to her mother's room.

The room was in darkness but for a night-light that her mother liked to have beside her bed. It had almost burned out but by its humble light Sarah could see that her mother was sleeping and that there was no sign of Rose.

Perhaps Rose had herself felt unwell and gone down to

the kitchen for a cold compress for her head, which Sarah now remembered had been troubling her for a day or two. This now seemed the likeliest explanation. Sarah lit her mother's chamber candle at the night-light and made her way downstairs.

The kitchen was empty but a gleam of white from the scullery caught her eye. She smiled, only in her relief admitting to herself that she had begun to feel alarmed, and went towards it.

'Rose? Are you all right?' She stopped. It was indeed Rose's nightdress that had drawn her attention but it lay abandoned, one sleeve swinging in the draught from the door, which was open.

Sarah stared blankly at the white nightgown, unable to account for her discovery. Had Rose been abducted? Had she thrown it off in a bout of delirium and gone naked into the garden? Each suggestion was more improbable than the last but it was undeniable that Rose was nowhere to be seen.

The obvious course was to find her father and tell him but Sarah hesitated. The instinct to protect her younger sister was deeply rooted. From infancy the two girls had shared an unspoken understanding that their most vital, inner life was not to be revealed to their parents. Whatever their own differences and jealousies, neither had ever betrayed the other. If the explanation for Rose's absence was to her discredit, Sarah wanted to help her conceal it.

Rain was spattering the scullery window and the door was blowing more widely open. It was not a tempting prospect but Sarah knew what she must do. Putting her candle in the window, for it would be useless in the blustery wind, she huddled her shawl about her and went out into the darkness.

As she moved away from the comforting glow of the window her fears grew. The wind stirred the bushes fringing the lawn in sudden, unpredictable flurries; her imagination peopled them with lurking intruders awaiting their chance to leap out on her. She told herself that it was nonsense but it took all her courage to move on, into the orchard.

The kitchen light was now hidden. The creaking of the branches as they tossed in laboured dips and surges, as though reaching out to seize her, reminded her of stealthy footsteps. Her every sense was strained but she forced herself on. At this distance from the house she dared to call her sister's name. There was no answering cry.

She passed fearfully on, into the vegetable garden, and stopped. The gate in the surrounding wall was open, creaking as it swung on its hinges. Her first thought was that it had been blown open by the wind; her second, that it had been forced by some intruder. She glanced over her shoulder and went to the gate. The bolt was undamaged. It had been opened from the inside.

She hesitated in anguished indecision. Could Rose have gone out? It had taken all Sarah's concern for her sister to bring her so far. To venture beyond the confines of their own grounds, in night clothes and slippers, was impossible. She peered out into the back lane. Nothing, except the same restless, suggestive turmoil of branches and foliage. She turned back and ran to the house, barely outstripping the formless fear that pursued her, snatching at her skirt, clawing at her shawl, until she stood once more in the merciful light and warmth of the kitchen.

She was locking the kitchen door when she heard footsteps approaching down the passage. Rose? She looked eagerly towards the door, only to see her father enter, still fully clothed.

'You?' he said, seeming at once suspicious and relieved. 'What are you doing down here at this hour?'

'I'm sorry. I didn't mean to disturb you.'

'I was going up to bed when I heard something. Why did you go out? You're soaked through!'

'I didn't notice . . .'

'Well? You weren't sleepwalking, I don't suppose?'

'No.' She sighed, abandoning the struggle to shield Rose. 'I was looking for Rose. She wasn't in bed and I thought perhaps she was outside, perhaps she had fainted. I don't know what I thought.'

He scarcely seemed to be listening. At the mention of Rose's name he had taken a swift stride towards her, as though to shake the story from her, but now he might almost have forgotten her presence. Sarah had never seen him so distraught, his face so unguarded. In a single moment he had changed from a stern, self-assured ruler of family and household to a man at a loss, fearful and stricken. His helplessness was more frightening to Sarah even than his anger.

'Has she said anything to you?'

'No, nothing,' she said in bewilderment.

'You don't know anything about a man, secret meetings?'

'No!'

'If it is him . . .' He put his hand to his mouth and bit it. 'My God, my God . . .'

She had never before heard him blaspheme. His grief awed her. She could not imagine going to him, offering him any comfort by word or gesture. Even in his suffering he was remote from her.

'Did you see anything out there?' he asked, with some return to his usual decisiveness.

'The gate into the lane was open. That was all.'

'Go upstairs. Check to see if she is in your room.'

She obeyed, glad to have something to do. The bedroom was empty but this time she saw what she must have missed before: a letter beneath her sister's pillow. It bore her name.

She wondered whether she should take it at once to her father but the old childhood loyalty held fast. She opened it and read the few lines it contained.

Dear Sally,

When you read this I will already be far away. I am going to be married to Simon Olivant. I cannot bear to be parted from him and this is the only way. I hope Papa can forgive me. My love to him and Mama, and to you of course. Try not to think harshly of me. You know I could never be as good as you.

Rose.

Sarah went down to the kitchen, clutching the letter. She began to feel that she must be living through some nightmare where impossible, nonsensical events unfolded with their own spurious logic. Simon Olivant? The name meant nothing to her. How could Rose be running away with a complete stranger?

The kitchen was empty but she saw a movement in the scullery. Her father had picked up Rose's nightgown and was clutching it tightly to himself, his hands twisted in its folds. Sarah watched, aghast. As the moment lengthened she could not bring herself to speak and reveal that she had witnessed his grief. At last some tiny sound betrayed her presence. He looked up, staring at her.

'I found this, Papa.'

He read the letter without any change of expression but he let the nightgown drop to the floor. 'Wait here.' He went out, stuffing the letter into his pocket.

He was gone for a considerable time. She went to the range for the last heat in its greying cinders, but it did not stop her shivering. The watching stillness of the house, as though it were holding its breath, awaiting catastrophe; her tiredness; the chill which seeped into her very bones, gave her vigil the binding, crazy reality of a dream. When she heard her father return she started, as though she had been sleeping.

'No sign of her.' He closed and, after a barely perceptible hesitation, bolted the door.

Despite his curt tone he sounded so weary, so desolate that she dared to say, 'Papa, shall I light the range and make you a hot drink? It wouldn't take long.'

'No. Go up to bed. There's nothing more to be done.'

'But what about you? Won't you come up too?'

'In a moment.' He turned his back on her. Dismissed, she could only obey. She did not sleep. Twice more she heard him going out into the garden, searching for his lost daughter.

Mrs Brunton did not come down to breakfast during the week. Sarah forced herself to dress and appear at the usual hour. Her father was alone in the dining room, which the newly lit fire barely warmed. He was dressed neatly as always, his linen a crisp white, his hair brushed smoothly back from his brow. Nothing, it seemed, had changed, and yet Sarah saw at once that he had suffered a mortal blow. His rigid self-control might drive him through his day in a perfect imitation of the man he had been, but Rose's betrayal had broken him.

'Good morning, Papa.'

He inclined his head. She went to her place at the table. He seated himself and held out his teacup. She filled it, apologising as a few drops spilled in the saucer. But it had been his hand, not hers, that trembled. The meal passed in silence but when he rose at its conclusion, evidently with no intention of referring to Rose's flight, Sarah said desperately, 'What will we do, Papa? Have you no idea where we might find her?'

He put both hands flat on the table, leaning forward

with all his weight. 'She would be better dead. To me she is dead. Never let me hear her name mentioned in this house again.'

The vertical grooves in his cheeks were more marked than usual, his lips were set in a narrower, harder line, but when he left the room, his back was straight, his head held high. The wound he had suffered might never heal but it would be hidden.

Rose sat in the hotel bedroom, gazing at the humped figure beneath the tangled blankets. Simon's hair, spread over the pillow, seemed to her the most dissolute sight in the world. Although it was almost eleven o'clock he showed no sign of waking. She had been glad of his continued sleep when, at first light, she had risen and, moving stealthily in the semi-darkness, tidied herself as best she could. Even a week of married life had not accustomed her to performing her toilet in his presence.

In other ways she had begun to adapt herself to her new circumstances, to the strangeness and unpredictability of their shared life. Since their arrival in Glasgow Simon had been lavish in his spending, on himself as well as on her. Remembering his constant complaints of his poor salary she had been puzzled by his prodigality, but the wild extravagance appealed to a vein of reckless enjoyment in Rose which had never before had expression.

The previous night Simon had insisted that they should celebrate the anniversary of their first week of marriage. They had eaten food richer and more elaborate than she had ever imagined, and Simon had drunk what seemed to her to be enormous quantities of champagne and brandy. At his insistence, she had sipped a little champagne, but she had not liked it and, alarmed by his increasing incoherence, had refused to drink more. She had had to support him to the cab which took them back to the hotel and to help him to bed.

He was still sleeping. His helplessness the previous night had disturbed her; she already realised that he was not to be depended on in every circumstance. With a coolness of which she would not have believed herself capable, she went through his pockets. They revealed ample supplies. His wallet was fat with banknotes and even the loose change amounted to almost ten pounds. Following an obscure but compelling instinct, she took four sovereigns and, wadding them in a handkerchief, concealed them in the lining of her jacket, carefully unpicking and sewing up the seam again. The act gave her reassurance.

The quarter hour chimed from a nearby church. She was hungry, bored, restless. She went to the window, making no particular effort to be quiet, and pulled back the curtains. The street below was seething with figures, moving in the apparent confusion which was the sum of so many individual purposes. The sight filled her with exhilaration and a sense of freedom.

The light from the window was falling across the pillow, disturbing Simon. He stirred, muttered, turned over on to his back. She went over to him.

'Awake at last?' she asked, looking down on him. He was wearing his shirt, although she had removed his collar and tie, and the top buttons were undone. She saw his neck and part of his shoulder. It was very white, with an unexpected delicacy. She had not thought that a man's body would be so beautiful.

He sat up, wincing, and passed his hand over his head. 'What's the time?'

'Just gone quarter past eleven.'

'The middle of the night,' he grumbled. 'What was I drinking last night?'

'Champagne . . . brandy . . . a lot of it.'

'I must have been mad. I always suffer for it the next day.' His penitence was encouraging. She sat down on the end of the bed. 'Do you want anything? Shall I see if we can have tea brought up?'

'Oh, in a minute. Come here first. A kiss for your husband.'

She smiled, and moved up the bed to him. His arm snaked about her waist, and pulled her so that her head lay upon his breast. The stale alcohol on his breath was repellent, but she could not resist the temptation to reach up and stroke his neck, fascinated by its blend of fineness and strength.

'Have you seen whether there has been a reply yet?' he asked, ignoring the caress.

'I haven't been down.'

'Slip down and see, will you?' he asked, in the coaxing tone that was already beginning to jar a little, since she realised that he employed it solely to get his own way.

'I don't suppose Papa will have had time to answer yet,' she said, sitting up and lifting her hands to check that her hair was still in order.

'You wrote to him the day after we were married. How long does he need?'

'It's not just a question of writing a letter, though. He will be very angry still.'

'I thought you were supposed to be his favourite. How can he still be angry with you?'

'He is stubborn, I suppose.'

'Like you.' He pulled her to him, his mood changing again. 'What about that kiss?'

There was no letter awaiting Rose downstairs, not that morning or any other for the remainder of the week. Simon was more concerned than Rose. With apparently unlimited amounts of money at their disposal, the excitements of a great city to explore and the new freedoms of a married woman to relish, Rose missed her home and family far less than she had expected. For the first time in her life she was not subject to petty restrictions and an atmosphere in which every act, every thought almost, had some moral dimension. Young, carefree, she was enjoying herself almost as recklessly as he.

'You should write again,' Simon said, when a fortnight had passed without a reply. 'Perhaps your first letter was lost in the post.'

'If you like,' she said, with a shrug, 'but I'm sure he will have received it. He will come round . . . and if he doesn't, is it such a loss?'

Simon was standing at the washstand, his back to her. He had just finished shaving and was raising a towel to his face. He turned, the towel in his hands, an expression of pitying contempt on his face, as though she were an indulged child who had just said something that revealed the depths of her true ignorance.

'Not such a loss? What do you think we will live on if your dear papa doesn't come up trumps?'

'But you said we had plenty of money! We have been living as though we had!'

'It won't last for ever.'

'Well, then you can get a job, can't you?'

'If I'd wanted a job . . .' He broke off suddenly, with an apparent effort. 'Just write to him again, will you?' It was not really a question.

Rose made no further protest and in another moment Simon was smiling once more. Things resumed their normal light-hearted course, but like the first chill breath of winter the brief exchange had warned her what might be to come. She could not quite forget it.

This time, her letter provoked a response. Three days later, in answer to her usual enquiry, the hotel clerk handed Rose a letter. She ran up to their room, where Simon was still in bed, and shook him awake.

'Simon! Simon! A letter has come from Warrington!'

He grunted and sat up, pushing the hair away from his eyes. 'Your father?'

'I don't think so,' she said, scrutinising the envelope. 'I don't recognise the writing.'

'Well, open it, for heaven's sake!'

She tore it open and began to read, and with the first words her excitement turned to horror.

'What does it say?'

'It's from my father's solicitor,' she said distractedly, still reading. 'He says . . . oh, see for yourself.'

Simon snatched it from her and began to read. She saw his face change and realised that there was no mistake.

'It's true, isn't it? You did steal money from my father.'

'That's nice, I must say! A fine example of wifely trust and devotion!'

'Well? Shall I write back and say you deny it?'

Simon was silent, scowling at her as though she was in some way to blame.

'That's where you got the money from isn't it? That's what we've been living off for the past three weeks.'

'So?'

'Aren't you ashamed?'

'No, I'm not. Why should I be? We needed the money and that was the only way to get it.'

'You can't just steal to get what you want!'

'I didn't think he would find out.'

'But that's not the point!' she protested, with a growing sense of helplessness at their lack of common ground. The daring and freedom from petty conventions she had once admired in him were suddenly taking on a sordid cast.

'Of course it is. He's got plenty of money, hasn't he? If I could take it and get away with it I'd be a fool not to,' he said sullenly.

'But you weren't getting away with it! He suspected you,

didn't he? That was what he was investigating. You lied to me; you knew perfectly well that he had found out about your thieving.'

'It was only small amounts, until the last day.'

'Collins says in the letter that you took two hundred pounds from the office then.'

'I needed it!' he repeated, as though that was the sole criterion for any action.

'But surely . . . !' She stopped, realising the futility of any argument based on a moral code he refused to recognise, and cast about for some more effective appeal. 'You must have realised that he would never welcome a thief as a son-in-law. If you wanted him to help us you should not have begun by embezzling money from the accounts that were trusted to you.'

'I thought the last haul wouldn't be discovered until much later. The others were only petty cash, really. He couldn't have proved anything.'

'Not according to Mr Collins. He says my father is considering police action.'

'I'm not worried about that. He will hardly want to prosecute his own daughter.'

'Me?'

'You knew all about it, didn't you?'

'Of course I didn't!'

'Do you think anyone will believe that? Who in their right minds would elope with a penniless clerk, without asking where the money was to come from? Don't worry, your father won't press charges, whatever his solicitor says.'

'But you would never pretend that I was involved!'

'If it got me out of trouble,' he said indifferently. He looked over the letter again. 'Best leave it for a while, until dear Papa cools down a bit. Another month or so and a pathetic epistle from his daughter, destitute and penitent, should do the trick.'

Rose gazed at him. From the depths of her heart the despairing cry silently arose: *What have I done?*

William Brunton might be able to ensure that neither his wife nor his daughter mentioned Rose's name in his presence but he could not prevent them from thinking of her constantly nor from speaking of her when they were alone together, albeit in whispers, with one eye forever on the door.

It soon became apparent that he could not exercise even so much control over the tongues of his neighbours and fellow chapel-goers. The story of Rose's mysterious disappearance was soon known and, since the family refused to confide the truth to anyone, was quickly embroidered with details more or less scandalous, according to the malice of the teller.

That first Sunday Sarah could not face the engagement that in happier times she had loved so much. Although she and her father attended the morning service as usual she begged the superintendent to excuse her from teaching the class that afternoon. The haste with which he accepted and the eagerness with which he urged her not to resume her duties until she felt quite ready, confirmed her suspicions that her absence would be a relief to him.

Loud, tactless and domineering, Effie was the only one of her friends from chapel who seemed neither embarrassed by Rose's flight nor salaciously curious concerning its details. Effie called on Sarah every day, pushing her to resume her normal activities, but met with little success.

'For heaven's sake, Sarah! You're exactly the same person you always were! Why should you go into hiding just because Rose has bolted?'

'When Papa and I went to chapel last Sunday I couldn't bear the look on people's faces. I don't know which was worse, Mrs Marshall's gloating when she saw us, as though she'd like to lick her lips, or the way that Rebecca and Hannah Wilding couldn't look me in the eye. I felt like a criminal, Effie.'

'Don't be so soft! You can't spend the rest of your life shut up here. You're only making it worse for yourself. The sooner you face folk and show them that you've got nothing to be ashamed of, the sooner they'll leave off and find some other poor soul to slander.'

'I know . . .' Sarah said, sighing. She was sure that her friend was right but her courage diminished day by day as her imagination magnified the ordeal before her. That Sunday, for the first time in her life, she deliberately did not go to chapel. Sickness had kept her at home before, but this shrinking from the public gaze was still more incapacitating.

She was sitting with her mother after lunch when she heard the doorbell ring. She and her mother exchanged a glance, half frightened, half hopeful. Ever since Rose's disappearance, any unexpected caller had elicited the same response, which had always met with the same disappointment.

'A gentleman to see Miss Sarah,' Betty announced.

'Oh? Did he give his name?' she asked, surprised.

'He said I was to say he was from the Sunday school.'

Sarah got reluctantly to her feet. 'It will be the superintendent, I suppose.'

'Perhaps he feels it would be better if another teacher took over your class,' her mother said sadly. Nowadays she always seized on the most pessimistic interpretation of events, as though the loss of her younger daughter had convinced her that the worst would inevitably happen.

'We'll see,' Sarah said. She thought her mother was probably right, and paused a moment outside the morning room to steady herself for the coming interview. She entered, and stopped in surprise.

'Why, Mr Taylor!'

'I hope you don't mind me breaking in on you like this,' he said, so evidently ill at ease that her own nervousness increased. Big, powerful, he seemed out of place in the small room crammed with furniture and ornaments, for her mother loved a homely clutter. His heavy boots, polished to a Sabbath gleam, seemed to be making a lasting imprint on the Turkey carpet; his hands, twisting between them the hat he must have refused to surrender to Betty, looked several sizes too big for even his tall, broad frame.

'It's very good of you to call,' she said awkwardly. 'Won't you sit down? Can I get you some tea?'

He dismissed the offer with a distracted gesture and said abruptly, as though he had no time to waste on polite preamble, 'I came to walk you up to the Sunday school.'

'What?' she asked, taken aback.

Her shock must have been all too patent, for he took a step toward the door. 'I'm sorry, I've spoken out of turn.'

'No!' Sarah put out a hand, as though physically to detain him. 'I'm . . . I'm very grateful to you for your kindness. It's just that I won't be going to Sunday school today.'

'Why not?'

Her first thought was that he had not heard about Rose. She said hesitantly, 'My sister, you know . . .'

'Yes. I do know. But that was her, not you. I'll ask again: why aren't you coming to the school?'

'I can't face it. Last week, at chapel, everyone was looking at us. It was horrible.'

'Everyone?'

'Effie Shaw has been very kind. She says the same as you do.'

'She's got a good head on her shoulders. You should take some notice of her.'

'I suppose so.'

'Well? No time like the present. Get your things and we'll walk up together.'

'But Mr Taylor . . . you know what people are . . .'

'They'll talk, you mean? Well, I don't care. Do you?'

'Not for myself, but there's no need for you to be involved in any way.'

'Perhaps I want to be. I don't do much that I don't want to, believe me. Now, fetch your bonnet. I'll wait outside. I'm worried I'll knock something flying if I stay here.'

Suddenly the ordeal before her did not seem so bad. Sarah was ashamed of herself for having given in to the petty malice which, before his calm unconcern, lost half its terrors. She went upstairs, explained to her mother where she was going and collected her things.

Her father was in his study. She knocked on his door and went in. Although a book lay open on his desk he was standing at the window, hands clasped behind his back. He half turned at her entrance and looked at her without smiling. As so often these days, she thought she saw in his manner a bitter resentment that it was she, not Rose, who remained to him.

'I just wanted to tell you that I am going to Sunday school.'

'Oh? What changed your mind? Some new revelation since lunch?'

'Mr Taylor called for me, that's all.'

'The farrier?' His mouth twisted in distaste.

'The Sunday school teacher, yes.'

'I stand corrected.' He turned away, resuming his survey of the flowerless garden. She hesitated, and left the room.

At first the walk to the Sunday school was not too difficult. They met few people and after a week of confinement Sarah found the exercise and fresh air a delight. As they neared their destination, her unease grew. She caught sight of another teacher, Jane Gregory. There was no mistaking her reluctance to meet Sarah: with barely a greeting she scurried past, almost running. Sarah felt her cheeks grow hot. Without any conscious decision, she slowed her pace.

'Tired? Here . . .' Philip Taylor offered her his arm. She looked up in dismay.

'Really, you shouldn't. People will talk.'

'I hope they do.' His arm remained extended. She timidly put her hand within it and walked on with fresh confidence.

Sarah had not prepared her class and it did not pass as smoothly as usual but when the children were dismissed she felt a sense of achievement. The worst was over; next week would be easier.

Philip Taylor rejoined her. 'Not so bad, was it?' he asked, reaching for her books.

'I'm glad you persuaded me to come.'

'The longer you put these things off, the worse they get. The only way is to face up to them straight off.'

'I'm not so brave, I'm afraid.'

'You might be surprised what you can do when you set your heart on something.'

'It doesn't always work out for the best, though.'

'Thinking of your sister?'

Sarah sighed. 'She was always so much more daring than me, so much more lively. And now look what's happened . . .'

'Who's to say it wasn't the best thing for her to do?'

'But she has nearly broken my mother's heart! My father won't hear her name mentioned . . . we are all worried sick!'

'And would your father have let her marry Olivant if she'd waited for his permission?'

'No, I don't think so,' she said, startled by his attitude.

Not for a second had it occurred to her to regard Rose's elopement as anything but a disaster. 'He wouldn't have liked the fact that Olivant was one of his employees. Effie heard that there was some trouble over the accounts, too, although my father hasn't said anything about it at home. He won't talk about it at all.'

'Sometimes you have to take a chance. Your father's likes and dislikes aren't the last word on the subject, after all. It's her life. If she loved Olivant and he loved her she was right to make a stand over it. I admire her for it, to be honest.'

'Well, I don't,' Sarah said sharply. 'She was very selfish. You might see things differently if you knew what my mother has suffered over this. Rose hasn't sent us a word, not a single word!'

'Are you sure?'

'Of course I am,' she said, puzzled by the question.

'Your father wouldn't keep any news of her from you?'

She began to protest but the words carried no conviction. She fell silent.

'Don't blame your sister until you are certain that she hasn't been writing.'

'I had never thought of it like that,' she admitted.

'I should say your father is quite capable of it, wouldn't you?'

'Rose was his favourite. Perhaps that makes it worse, in a way.'

They had reached the gate leading into the Bruntons' drive. Sarah hesitated. She would have liked to invite him in for tea, but she feared her father's displeasure.

'I'll call for you next week, if you like?'

In her mind's eye she saw her father's sneer at the mention of Philip Taylor, the farrier. A lifetime of subservience to his will had instilled the ability to predict his wishes and likely reactions, like the vital understanding by a seagoer of the signs of wind and tides on which safety depends. Her father's domination was so complete that his actual presence was unnecessary. His will, unexpressed but intuited, was now the core of her own, and it told her that he would not wish her to see Philip more than was unavoidable.

'Is there something wrong?'

She realised that her hesitation was puzzling him. She drew a deep breath. 'No, of course not. I should like that.'

'Good. Well, until next week, then.'

There was nothing else to be said but they lingered for a moment, awkward and constrained, yet not wanting to part.

Over the next weeks her walks with Philip were the happiest moments in Sarah's life. She found that she could be more open with him even than with Effie, her oldest friend. Little by little, she told him more about herself and her family, and even admitted how much she dreaded her father's irritation, his scornful comments and his barely controlled anger.

'Men like that are nothing more than bullies,' Philip said. 'There is only one way to deal with bullies: stand up to them.'

Sarah was aware that he was speaking with unusual warmth. 'You seem to feel very strongly about it.'

'My own father was a brute. He beat all of his children, not because we had done anything wrong but because he liked it. I can still remember meals when his eyes would roam about the table, going from one face to the next, choosing the one that he would find fault with. We would be too terrified to eat, and then he'd pick on us for wasting good food. As soon as I was old enough to stand up for myself I gave him a pasting and ran away for good. No, I've not got much time for men who treat their children worse than like slaves and then demand to be respected.'

Sarah did not conceal from her father the fact that Philip now called for her every Sunday. He made one or two barbed comments, but did not otherwise intervene. For her part, although she would have liked to invite Philip home, she did not dare to push her father's tolerance too far. In a state of uneasy truce, Sarah lived from one meeting with Philip to the next.

If Rose was writing to their father, Sarah never knew of it. At times she wondered whether her sister might try to communicate with her directly but as the weeks passed her hopes faded. It was the last thing on her mind when, one morning in January, she saw Effie striding up the drive to the house, one hand raised to secure her bonnet against the wind. Sarah had been confined to the house for a day or two with a heavy cold and she viewed the prospect of a visit from her friend with mixed feelings. Effie's brisk good spirits could be very wearing.

Today, Effie seemed unusually preoccupied. She looked about the parlour. 'Is your mother not down yet?'

'She is never down before lunch now.'

'Of course . . .' Effie said vaguely, still gazing about her.

'Is something wrong?'

'No, not wrong . . .' She went to the door, checked that it was firmly shut, then reached into her reticule. 'This arrived in the first post, with a covering letter, asking me to give it to you. I hope I'm doing the right thing.'

Sarah took the envelope. It was of the cheapest quality, so thin that the writing on the letter within was clearly visible. It bore Sarah's name, in her sister's hand. She tore it open and drew out the single sheet it contained.

Dear Sally,

Since neither you nor Mama have ever replied to any of the letters I have sent you, I am beginning to wonder if you have received them. At least this way I

will know that if I don't hear from you it is because
you are still angry with me. If you could see me now
I think you would pity me, however angry you might
be. I was such a fool and now I am paying for it. The
money has all gone and if you can't help I don't know
what is to become of me. Don't let me down, for the
love of God. We are in Liverpool; send whatever you
can to me at the address above. Be quick. The rent has
not been paid for a month and if the landlady loses
patience she will put us out on the street. Some of my
clothes and things would be useful. I can always pawn
what I cannot wear. I am depending on you . . .

Sarah read the letter over and over again, each time
finding new cause for concern. How could her sister, so
confident, so carefree, have changed so rapidly into the
writer of this letter: desperate, frightened, so consumed by
her own misery that she could not spare a single line to ask
after her ailing mother's health?

'Bad news, I suppose?'

Sarah had almost forgotten Effie's presence. She gazed at
her blankly. 'Rose is in Liverpool. She needs money. How
can I get it to her?'

'A money order from the post office,' Effie said briskly.
'Unless you want to go and see her, that is?'

'How could I? Papa wouldn't allow it.'

'Don't tell him. Let me see . . . I have a cousin in
Wallasey. You could say that we were going to spend the
day with her. How about that?'

'It would be a lie!'

'And if you tell him the truth will you ever see Rose
again?'

Sarah knew the answer. She sighed. 'You will help me,
Effie?'

'Of course. There's one thing, though. You had better

not tell your mother, at least not until afterwards. It would
only worry her and your father might realise something was
going on.'

Sarah had to agree. It would not be fair to involve her
mother in the deceit. Effie's help was crucial. She arranged
everything, even smuggling some of Rose's clothes and
shoes out of the house with her. Since she lived alone she
was freer than Sarah and more independent. Effie found
out the times of trains and bought a map of Liverpool on
which they succeeded in picking out the street where Rose
was staying. It was not far from the docks. Even to Sarah
this sounded ominous.

The train journey passed in a tense silence which Effie,
after one or two attempts at conversation, was wise enough
to leave unbroken. Effie continued on to Wallasey alone.
They agreed that Sarah would meet Effie there later.

The street to which the cab brought Sarah confirmed
her worst fears. As she stepped down on to the pavement
and paid her fare she was aware of broken windows pasted
over with brown paper or stuffed with rags, of the shouts
and screams of a violent quarrel from one of the nearby
houses and of the barefoot, ill-clad children who, drawn by
the spectacle of a cab, were gathering in curiosity and some
vague hope of halfpence.

The door was opened by a small, lean woman in a drab
gown and sacking apron. Sarah was not sure whether she
was the landlady or a servant.

'Is Miss Brunton – I mean, Mrs Olivant at home?'

'In my back room, and the devil a penny of rent I've seen
for it this past month,' the woman grumbled, standing aside
to let her in. 'She'd have been out on the street by now,
only she's a winning way with her, and she's give me her
word that she's wrote to her friends.' As she talked, she led
Sarah through a dark, narrow lobby into a kitchen heavy

with the greasy steam of mutton broth. She pulled aside a
curtain in the corner of the room. 'Up there and to your
right.'

One foot on the stair, Sarah paused. 'Is *he* in?'

'And what would he be doing here while the dram shops
are open?'

The stair was dark and difficult to negotiate. Cumbered
by her baggage, Sarah stumbled, and cried out as she
knocked her shin. As she began to climb once more she
heard footsteps in the room above. The door was opened a
chink, then flung wide. Sarah looked up to the welcome
shaft of light. Rose was silhouetted against the bright
doorway, one hand on the door, the other on the jamb.
And even in the joy of recognition Sarah realised the truth
that, she now understood, she should have suspected from
the first. Her sister was pregnant.

'Sarah! I never expected you to come here!'

Was her welcome tinged with dismay? Sarah thrust aside
the thought as she scrambled up the remaining stairs and,
dropping her bag, flung her arms about her sister. Even in
the overwhelming emotion of the moment she registered
the sour, unwashed smell of Rose's hair and the new
fragility of her body, so thin now but for the swollen belly
pressing against her.

Rose was the first to break away from their embrace. She
wiped her eyes with the back of her fingers, a quick, child-
like gesture at which Sarah's heart ached. 'Come in, sit
down!' Rose threw open her arms in an ironic welcome
encompassing the bare floorboards, the clothes hung from
nails on the wall, drooping as if exhausted, the bed with its
dingy covers, the single chair, its wicker seat torn and
ragged. Hesitantly, yet fearing to give offence by any
indication of her instinctive disgust, Sarah lowered herself
on to the rickety chair. Rose sat on the bed, her arms
propped behind her as a support.

'So, Sarah? Are things as bad as you expected?'

Sarah felt the flickering of an unworthy irritation. Despite her disgrace, Rose was still more self-assured than she. Sarah had sacrificed a good deal to bring help to her sister; she had not expected to be met with such brazen unconcern.

'Worse,' she said tartly. 'Everything is even more squalid than I had expected, although you seem to be quite used to it.'

'You think so?'

Rose's right hand was plucking at the quilt, the nervous trick giving the lie to her careless tone. She looked away from Sarah. Her face was paler than when she had been at home and there was a bitter, disillusioned set to her mouth. Sarah repented her harshness.

'No, I don't,' she said gently. 'Is it really dreadful? What can I do?'

Her sister did not answer at once. Her mouth moved in the way familiar to Sarah from childhood: Rose was struggling against tears. When at last she replied with a shrug, 'Money,' the apparent cynicism did not deceive Sarah.

'I have brought as much as I could . . . here.' She gave her the money, in an old purse of Rose's, which she had found in her drawer.

'Good.' She counted the coins. Effie had contributed generously to the sum but Rose showed no interest in its origins. 'I will be able to settle with Mrs Brady, at least. What else did you bring?'

Sarah lifted the bag on to the bed. 'As much as I could carry.'

Rose riffled through its contents. She showed little pleasure at recognising her things, although she once or twice nodded with approval as she uncovered the more valuable items. 'Some of this will raise a good amount at the pawnshop. You came just in time. Tomorrow I was going to pledge my shoes.'

'Rose!'

'What else could I do?'

'But isn't . . . isn't Mr Olivant working?'

Rose laughed. 'If you call gambling working.'

'He can't support you like that!'

'I don't think he expected to have to support me, that's the trouble.'

'Why did he marry you, then?'

'Why, indeed?' Rose said, her face suddenly vulnerable in its wistful sadness. 'Oh, he's not as bad as you might think. He just doesn't always see things the same way as most people. He wants to be free, that's all.'

'And how free will *you* be, when the baby comes?'

'He is pleased about that, you know. He thinks it may make Papa help us.'

'That's a poor reason to be pleased about a child,' Sarah said, frowning.

'He will love it for its own sake once it arrives,' Rose said, with a show of confidence that Sarah doubted whether she really felt.

'Look, Rose, why don't you come away from here? Come back with me and Effie. We will find you somewhere to stay and at least you will be among friends when your time comes . . .'

'Friends? Would my own father have me set foot inside his house? I have written to him every week, every day at times, and how has he replied? A single lawyer's letter. I know Simon may have done wrong but I don't think I deserve such treatment.'

Despite the note of petulance Rose sounded uncertain, as though she knew very well that she was on weak ground. 'What has Simon done?' Sarah asked gently.

'Oh, he took some money from the office. It was just to

allow us to get away. He shouldn't have done it, of course, but it was the only way he could think of.'

Beneath the bravado Sarah detected a note of desperation, as though Rose were repeating a defence of which she clearly saw the fallacy. She glanced about the cheerless room with its threadbare curtains sagging on a piece of string, its cracked, bulging, damp-stained ceiling. 'Rose, you can't want to stay here with a man who's no better than a common thief. Come away, for heaven's sake.'

Rose's shoulders sagged. For a second her show of confidence vanished and she looked what she was: a frightened, bewildered girl, unprepared to meet the poverty and hardships before her. But even as Sarah drew breath for a further attempt at persuasion, Rose shook her head.

'I'm not coming back. Anything's better than that.'

'But the talk will pass . . . in a month or two everything will be almost the same as before . . .'

'That's what I mean. I've finished with all that, Sarah. I would sooner die here than go back to that half-life. It might suit you,' she added, with the barely concealed contempt that she seemed to imagine Sarah never felt, 'but I couldn't stand it. Those Sundays . . . At least here I am alive, not stifling to death in that drawing room, night after night, with nothing ever happening, nothing to do, nothing new to say or think. I've changed too much. I can't go back, and I don't want to.'

There was nothing else to say. Seeing her set, defiant face Sarah knew that Rose's will, as always, would be stronger than her own. 'You are as stubborn as ever, at least,' she said irritably. 'I need hardly have bothered coming.'

'You thought you would find a penitent sinner, ready to cast herself on your bosom. Well, I'm not. I'm glad of the money and the things but you needn't expect me to beg to come home.'

Sarah struggled to control her annoyance. 'What else can I do to help, then?'

'Papa won't answer my letters or I wouldn't ask, but there is something,' Rose said hesitantly. 'He may believe that I knew about Simon taking the money. I didn't. I wish you could tell him that. And I do think that he might forgive us and do something about helping Simon to make a fresh start. If we had a house and Simon had a job, a job he liked, everything would be so much better. Try and get him to listen, Sal.'

Sarah listened to her sister with mounting disbelief. 'Papa will never do that!'

'I think he owes us something, don't you?'

Sarah got to her feet, biting back a caustic response. 'I can't give you any promises, Rose, but I will think about what you have said. If I see anything I can do, I will.'

'I knew I could rely on you,' Rose said, standing and rubbing the small of her back. 'Don't think too hardly of Simon, will you? All he needs is a start in life.'

'I thought he had one, working for Papa.'

'Oh, he was far too good for that job. That's the trouble, you see. He gets bored when he is doing work that's beneath him.'

Sarah did not trust herself to comment. She wondered whether her sister really believed the excuses she was making for her husband. To see her eagerly parroting Simon Olivant's self-serving view of reality alarmed Sarah. How had he succeeded so soon in erasing her sister's natural contempt for pretence and hypocrisy? Rose's abdication of her own judgement seemed to her even more pathetic than the squalor in which she was living.

That Sunday, Sarah discussed the situation with Philip, as they walked slowly to Sunday school together.

'You should have told me you were going. I would have been glad to help.'

'It all happened so suddenly. I didn't want to bother you.'

'No trouble of yours would ever be a bother to me.'

The warmth in his voice touched her even more than the offer of help. 'I was afraid that it might seem as though I was asking you for money.'

'Effie gave you something, didn't she? Why not me?'

'It wouldn't be right . . .' she said uncomfortably, not wanting to stress the misinterpretation to which, as an unmarried woman, she would have laid herself open in accepting money from a man to whom she was not related.

'Well, we'll see. Come to me first, next time.'

'I wish I could say that there never will be a next time,' she said, sighing, 'but Olivant doesn't seem to be making any effort to find work. With the best will in the world I can't manage to keep Rose for ever.'

'And the baby,' he reminded her. 'It's not your responsibility, in any case. You should think about yourself, for a change. Tell your father what she said and let him deal with it. If he won't help them, Olivant will just have to make up his mind to dirtying his hands with a bit of work, like the rest of us. If he's got anything about him at all, it will be the making of him.'

Sarah doubted it, but she kept her fears to herself. Much as she liked Philip, he sometimes seemed to her to see life in too simple terms. She doubted whether he could really imagine the difficulty she felt in approaching her father, particularly on this subject.

It was Tuesday before Sarah plucked up the courage to speak. Her father was not dining at home that night. Her mother retired early but Sarah sat on, pleading the need to finish a piece of work. She thought her father would be home by about ten but it was almost midnight before she heard him enter the house. She went into the hall and called his name, softly so as not to waken her mother. He was in the act of putting his hat on the stand. At the sound of her voice he turned quickly, looking over his shoulder. His face had a strained, startled look that poignantly recalled her sister. The resemblance strengthened her resolve.

'What are you doing, up at this hour?'

'I wanted to speak to you, Papa,' she said, ignoring his harsh tone. 'I have something to say that I don't think my mother should hear.'

'Won't it keep until morning?'

'I'm sorry, Papa, but I don't think it will.'

He exhaled with the pent-up hiss of irritation that had so often intimidated her, but she stood her ground. For Rose she could do what she would never have dared to do for herself.

'The parlour is still quite warm, Papa.' She led the way and, after a moment's hesitation, he followed.

'Well? What is it?' he asked impatiently, standing astride in front of the cooling embers of the fire, blocking her off from its heat. 'Hurry up. I've had a trying day and I want to get to bed.'

'Last week, I went to see Rose . . .'

'You did what?' He stopped, making a visible effort at regaining his self-control. 'I have made it quite plain. I will not have that name spoken in this house again.'

'My sister, then. Your daughter.' Her voice was trembling but she pushed herself on, despite the fury gathering in his face. 'She is in such trouble, Papa . . .'

'And who's fault is that? Where is she, anyway?'

'In Liverpool, in one of the poorest streets.'

'And when did *you* go to Liverpool?'

'Last week, Thursday.'

'I see. The day you claimed to be spending with Effie.'

'I did go with Effie.'

'And bumped into your sister quite by chance?'

'No,' she admitted. 'Rose had written to me at Effie's. Effie passed on the letter to me. I went to Rose's lodgings.'

'So not only did you deceive your mother and me, not only did you ignore my express orders, but you did all this in conjunction with that meddling busybody Effie Shaw? How dare you stand there and own it?'

'Better this, than stand before my Judge and own that I had done nothing to help my sister when she needed me most.'

The words sprang to her lips unbidden. Her own boldness frightened her but the expected outburst from her father did not follow. He frowned, and dropped his gaze. The silence lengthened. Abruptly, gruffly, he asked, 'How is she?'

'They are very poor. There is a child on the way.'

'Did you see Olivant?'

'No.'

'Is he working?'

'Not at the moment,' Sarah said cautiously. 'Rose is very eager that he should get something. She seems to care for him very much.'

'She cared enough for him to connive at embezzlement, that was certain.'

'No! Rose was very concerned that you should not think that. She wanted me to tell you that she had no idea what he was doing, or where his money came from. I am sure that she was sincere.'

He stared hard at her, then shrugged. 'She has been living off the proceeds ever since, no doubt. She can scarcely claim her hands are clean.'

'By then it was too late.'

'If she had no morals, could she not have had some sense? What will become of her?'

Anguish sounded through the contempt. Try as he might

to deny his younger daughter, he loved her still. Sarah took heart. 'You could help her, Papa.'

'As far as I am concerned, she is dead. I have only one daughter.'

'That may soon be true.' Sarah placed a piece of paper on a nearby table. 'This is Rose's address . . . at the moment. Without help she won't be able to pay the rent for very much longer. Her confinement can't be more than a few weeks away. She will need a doctor, a monthly nurse, expenses of every sort. If you don't help her, I can't imagine how she will manage.'

'A pity she didn't think of that sooner. It is her husband's responsibility, not mine. She's lucky I've not had him charged with embezzlement. They've had enough from me already.'

Sarah could do no more. She wished her father good night and left him. The following morning, the paper bearing Rose's address was gone. Her father made no reference to it and Sarah thought it wiser not to ask.

'You are very quiet tonight?' Susannah made the statement into a question, afraid as always of presuming too far, of seeming to criticise or complain. She gazed up at him, watching anxiously for his response. He made an indeterminate sound, acknowledging what she had said and even perhaps accepting its truth.

She waited, trying to determine whether this was one of the rare evenings when he wanted to talk. The firelight flickered on his face, softening its severe lines. He was deep in thought; it would be better not to disturb him. She was sitting on the floor beside his chair, as he liked. Now she rested her head against his knee, taking comfort from the physical closeness to him that was all he allowed.

She felt his hand move softly across her hair. He always wanted her to wear her hair loose when he was with her, 'like a Magdalene', as he had once said. It flowed down her back, past her waist, for he had forbidden her to cut it.

'Such a child,' he said, as though the words were spoken against his will, his voice sadder and more tender than she had ever known it. 'How could such a child survive alone?'

'There's my brother,' Susannah said hesitantly, not sure whether he had even intended to be heard. 'He would do what he could.'

'A woman without means, not trained for any work,' he went on, as though he was following his own thoughts, not her reply. 'So young, so ignorant of the world . . . and a child on the way, she said. The fool, the fool . . .'

Susannah glanced up at him, bewildered. He was not thinking of her, then. And her amazement grew when, by the uncertain light of the fire, she saw the trace of tears on his cheeks.

CHAPTER

Three

Rose spent the days that followed the receipt of her father's generous money order in a daze of happiness. True, it was transmitted to her in a curt letter from Arthur Collins, her father's lawyer, explaining that this *ex gratia* payment was a final communication from William Brunton, who wished to have no further contact of any sort with her. Whatever Sarah had said to her father, resulting in the sending of the money, it had not succeeded in improving relations between him and Rose.

For the moment, Rose was simply relieved that she need have no worry over the provision of the essentials of life. With Simon's approval, for he liked the sights and smells of poverty as little as she, they left Mrs Brady's lodgings and moved to a rented house in a better part of the city. Although small by comparison with her parents' house, with a tiny front garden and a yard at the back, it was their own domain, not shared with other lodgers or a landlady.

With the better food that they could now afford and the lifting of her anxieties, Rose's naturally buoyant spirits reasserted themselves. She took good care of her health and appearance, and kept the little house fresh and welcoming.

Once the baby was born, she resolved, she would make an effort to ensure that Simon adopted a more regular way of life.

In the meantime, Simon was enjoying the easing of their dire poverty. His good humour expressed itself in extravagant whims: he would return home with an exquisite hat that, he swore, would suit Rose better than any woman in the city, or with a bottle of expensive port wine for her because he remembered hearing that it helped to build up the strength of newly confined mothers. Such gifts delighted her, even though she was well aware that they ought not to be wasting their money on luxuries, and that most of them were in fact for him: elegant clothes and shoes, tie pins and rings.

Rose wrote to Sarah with news of the improvement in her situation. Sarah replied, expressing her relief, but urging Rose to ensure that Simon found work soon, as she knew that their father would not intervene a second time.

Rose received the advice with some irritation, not least because of her uneasy awareness that, generous as the sum had been, at Simon's current rate of expenditure it would not last very long. Seeing her handsome husband, so stylishly dressed, in such high spirits, she could not bring herself to urge caution on him and destroy the carefree mood that made their marriage and their neat little lodgings seem a child's game of playing house. Who was Sarah to pity her, after all? At their last meeting Rose had been the suppliant; now, she thought with all her old, sisterly contempt of Sarah's earnestness, her drab clothes and stout figure.

A letter from her mother was more satisfactory. There was no mention of seeing Rose again in the near future or of any reconciliation with William Brunton, but a great outpouring of thankfulness that she was well and a few kind words for Simon. She sent a little money, too, which Rose concealed from her husband. The instinct born in

harder times had not been eradicated. She had learned that
it was always safer to have a supply of money, however
meagre, that Simon did not know about. With a few
shillings that would melt fruitlessly away in his hands, Rose
could buy a week's shelter, days of food. She did not blame
him; it was a part of the reckless boldness that, at its best,
drew her to him, but Rose had learned that, in money
matters, it was wiser to rely upon herself.

The baby was born several weeks early. The delivery
was rapid and straightforward but the child, a boy, was
alarmingly frail. Dark like his father, Peter had wizened
features which, when he cried, screwed up into an expression of agony. Rose received him into her arms with
dismay. She had not realised that he would be so puny, so
needy. She recognised that the child that Simon had
intended as a bargaining counter with her father brought
with him demands of his own, more pressing even than her
husband's.

Peter's helplessness drew from Rose reserves of tenderness that she had never thought natural to her. The faintest
whimper was enough to send her flying to his side. His
health was poor. To early jaundice succeeded colic and,
during teething, a perpetual cold that often worsened to
croup. When at last he began to crawl and then to walk,
cuts and bruises were added to his ailments, for he was a
clumsy, badly co-ordinated child whose pale skin a mere
touch was enough to mark.

Rose never lost patience. She nursed Peter tirelessly,
fighting for his life during a terrifying bout of whooping
cough, not sleeping for three nights when he contracted
measles. The selfishness of her girlhood now seemed part of
another existence: she devoted herself to Peter without
stint. His total dependence on her, his smiles of radiant joy
at seeing her again after even the briefest of absences were
recompense enough for all her sacrifices.

Simon was not so easily charmed, nor so ready to change his life in any way to accommodate Peter's needs. From the first, his son's weakness irritated him. Accustomed himself to excellent health, he could not understand the careful handling that the baby required.

'You mollycoddle the brat,' he grumbled, when Rose insisted on wrapping Peter up warmly on a bright but chill spring day. 'He needs hardening up, not treating like a hot-house plant.'

'You will be the first to complain if he is coughing all night,' Rose said, not turning, as she tied the bonnet carefully beneath the baby's chin.

'What's the difference? I haven't had a good night's sleep since he was born . . . and damn little else, for that matter.'

The ugly tone in his voice penetrated even her preoccupation. Although her task was completed she remained stooping over the baby. 'I am so tired, that's all,' she murmured. She did not want to turn and face Simon, but she felt his arm about her waist, his lips at her neck. His greedy kisses revolted her; instinctively, before she could stop herself, she shrank from him. He released her at once, so roughly that she almost stumbled and had to clutch at the crib for support. Peter began to whimper.

'Now see what you've done!' Rose cried. 'There, there, love . . . it's all right.'

'As usual! I only have to touch you and the brat starts to howl!'

'It's not that! He was frightened, that's all!' She picked up the baby and kissed his velvety forehead. As his crying ceased she glanced across to Simon. Hands thrust into his pockets, he was scowling at her, his face heavy with the angry sense of his injuries. She sighed, trying to see things from his point of view. 'I'm sorry. Things won't always be like this. Peter is still so tiny, he needs me so much.'

'And I don't count at all, I suppose?'

His mutinous expression haunted her. That night she stayed awake until he came home, although it was so late that she was dazed with fatigue. She could not even feign enthusiasm for his drunken advances, only endure them. The physical intimacy that had been so important in the early days of their marriage was becoming not a bond, but a shackle.

Ominous as this was, it did not disturb Rose so much as Simon's refusal to seek work. 'We've got money. Why are you nagging me?' he would ask whenever she raised the subject. Since he would not say how much of her father's gift remained, she had no answer.

Once, Rose would have accepted their improved financial circumstances with the bland confidence of the well-to-do that money would always, miraculously, be forthcoming to smooth her path. That unthinking assurance, her trust in the essential benignity of life, had been shattered for ever by the weeks of desperate poverty at Mrs Brady's. Her own safety and, what was more, Peter's, depended on her unceasing vigilance.

The responsibility for their child's welfare had changed Rose but not Simon. Had it not been for Peter, Rose might have continued to relish the freedom of a life conducted largely on impulse. At first, it had satisfied in her a longing for spontaneity, for she could be as frivolous, as impetuous as Simon. Now, her craving for financial security became an obsession. She abstracted a few coins from Simon's pockets whenever she could, to add to the rest of her savings, in readiness for a future in which her foresight might be all that protected them.

Despite her unease, in Rose's imagination that future always included Simon. She accepted her husband's weakness much as she accepted her son's frailty, wishing that things could be different, doing all she could to improve them, but not questioning that they belonged together.

The conventions at which Simon mocked so often still held her in this: elopement had been barely conceivable; separation, divorce, were not. And even now there were still moments when she felt all the old excitement in his presence, the admiration for his beauty that could catch her unawares by a single silent glance, by the subtle curve of his lips or the grace of some careless movement. Such times were like the fine days of late autumn, precious not only in themselves but for the memories of carefree summer they evoked, and the dread of winter's inexorable approach.

Sarah had received the news of her father's intervention with mixed feelings. She was glad that Rose would not be subjected to the degrading poverty she had seen her enduring but she wondered whether life with a man such as Simon Olivant could be happy. She hoped that she had done the right thing in approaching her father on her sister's behalf.

Shocking as Rose's elopement had been, as time passed the scandal lost its savour. Life gradually erased the traces of her sister beneath the softly gathering drift of trivial daily events and anxieties. Sarah found that those who had once looked at her askance began again to treat her with their old friendliness. She responded in kind but she never forgot those who had stood by her: Effie and Philip.

Sarah's strengthening friendship with Philip should have been an unmixed good, but life, it seemed, was rarely simple. The pleasure of his company was balanced by her father's growing hostility to Philip. If ever the farrier's name was mentioned, William Brunton would make some sneering comment, or simply allow an expression of contempt to pass across his features. Sarah hated herself for not defending Philip at such moments but her strongest desire was to avoid a confrontation with her father. She trusted to submission and silence. Somehow, she drew the sustenance she needed from the unpromising world in which she must exist, like a plant clinging to life in the interstices of a bleak stone wall.

She could look to her mother for little support. Even where her deepest feelings were involved, Mary Brunton's submission to her husband was complete. Sarah knew how desperately her mother wished to see her younger daughter and her grandson but William Brunton had let it be known that Rose's banishment remained unchanged. There could be no question of inviting her to the house, for Mary Brunton's habit of deferment to her husband's authority was too deeply ingrained for disobedience.

Sarah wondered whether her mother might have tried harder to change her husband's mind if she had enjoyed better health. Since Rose's flight she appeared to have lost what little strength she possessed. Her bilious attacks, which in the past had been severe but infrequent, now afflicted her almost weekly. They could be warded off only by a stringent reduction in the quantity and richness of her meals. For days on end she survived on little more than dry toast and clear soup. Never a sturdy figure, she was almost visibly wasting away.

Sarah constantly urged her to see the doctor but her mother showed uncharacteristic stubbornness in her refusal. She would insist that she was quite well, even when she lay, pale and sweating, exhausted by cruel waves of sickness and pain. Perhaps her husband's intervention might have ensured that she sought medical help but to Sarah's surprise William Brunton made no attempt to force his wife to summon the doctor. Sarah herself, who had the sole responsibility for nursing her mother through her bouts of illness, seemed to be the only member of the family to feel any real anxiety about her condition. Whether from fear or wilful blindness, her parents appeared to be colluding in the pretence that nothing was wrong. So long as her mother had strength to stand she would go down to dinner as usual and maintain the timid, affectionate flow of conversation that William Brunton, as always, received with a mixture of tolerance and barely restrained irritation.

As Sarah's anxiety grew, she turned to Philip for advice. He was sympathetic but forthright. 'She should see a doctor, of course,' he said bluntly, as they strolled slowly home together one evening from a magic lantern show at the chapel. 'Can't you talk her into it, or get your father to see sense?'

She sighed. 'I have tried but neither of them will listen. My mother just insists that she is perfectly well and my father shrugs and says that my mother knows best. I don't think either of them want to face the truth.'

'It's not the only thing they want to ignore, is it?'

His tone expressed more than the words alone. Sarah felt a sudden rush of self-consciousness and a sense that what was to be said was of crucial importance. She remained silent, and half hoped that he would say no more.

'Would you rather I didn't speak, Sarah?'

'No . . . that is, of course, you must say whatever is in your mind.'

'You can't help but know it already, surely? I'm not much of a hand at speeches, but I love you as true as any man could love a woman. I want us to be married. What do you think?'

His slow, matter-of-fact tone could hardly have been more undramatic. There was no impassioned declaration, no pledges of undying devotion such as she might once have imagined in picturing such a scene, and yet she instantly felt a sense of the rightness of it. It was Philip's way to be direct and down to earth, even at such a moment, and she loved him for it.

She gazed up at Philip. She had for so long regarded him with the eyes of love that she could not now tell whether others would think him good-looking; his was simply the face in all the world she most liked to see. 'I think I am the luckiest woman alive,' she said softly.

They were not far from the Bruntons' gate, in a quiet part of the lane. They stopped, and she felt Philip's arm about her. She was overcome by a sudden panic, and buried her face against his sleeve.

'Now, Sarah,' he said, the words so affectionate, so full of humorous understanding that it scarcely needed the gentle pressure of his fingers to raise her face to his. Slowly, as though she were some timid creature that a sudden movement would startle, he lowered his head and kissed her lips, his beard soft against her skin. She stiffened in alarm, but at the same moment she was registering the unexpected pleasure of the contact. At once she seemed to know him in a way that she had not been aware of lacking, through all the months of talk and friendship that she only now realised had been incomplete. She had never thought such caresses would be enjoyable, but already her ignorance belonged to another self.

'I must come and speak to your father.'

Her momentary joy fled as she returned to the intractable reality of her position. With a lifetime's experience of the avoidance of confrontation with her father she said quickly, 'Oh, I don't think that would be a good idea.'

He frowned. 'Why not?'

'He is so difficult . . . you don't know what he's like.'

'I'd best find that out for myself,' he said pleasantly, but with a hint of stubbornness she had not yet had occasion to encounter in him.

'Could we not just wait a while?' she begged.

'What for?'

'I don't know . . . until things are more settled.'

'What else is there to settle? I'd marry you tomorrow. Have you got any doubts? Now's the time to say.'

'No, of course I haven't.'

'Then what's to stop me coming in now and having a word with Mr Brunton?'

'I'm afraid, that's all. You don't know what he's like.'

'So you keep telling me. I never yet met the man could stop me doing what I know's right. If you stick to what you want he can make your life a misery but he can't keep you from marrying me. You're over twenty-one and I don't need his money, if that's what's worrying you.'

'I never gave it a thought,' she said truthfully. 'I just don't want you to be hurt.'

'He couldn't hurt me. Only you could do that.'

'I could?'

'If you let him bully you into giving me up. He doesn't think I'm good enough for you. I suppose that's what you mean?'

Her silence was answer enough.

'It's as well to know what to expect,' he said calmly. 'I'll come round one night in the week, or would Saturday be better?'

'He is often out on business in the evenings during the week,' she said reluctantly.

'Saturday it is, then. I'll write and let him know to expect me.'

It was no use trying to dissuade him. As they parted, a heavy burden of dread crushed the happiness she should have been feeling

Sarah awaited the arrival of Philip's letter to her father with a nervousness so intense that she was hardly able to eat or sleep. It was delivered on Friday morning. She scanned his face as he examined his post, brought to him at the breakfast table. There were three letters. Two he opened and laid aside after a cursory glance but when he began to read the third his expression changed.

'So Mr Taylor wants to come and speak to me on a

matter of some importance, does he?' he said, tossing the
letter down. 'And what do you think that might be?'

Her mouth opened and closed soundlessly before she
found the strength to reply. 'He wants us to marry, Papa.'

He laughed. 'You?'

The contempt burned like vitriol on unprotected flesh.
Sarah seemed to see herself through his eyes: flat hair, pulled
back from a round, well-meaning face; a plain, unflattering
gown with straining seams and too-tight sleeves. She felt
clumsy, stupid. For so long her father had been the mirror
reflecting to Sarah her image of herself that she could hardly
believe, even now, that Philip saw a different picture.

'Philip is coming to see you as a matter of courtesy,' she
said bravely. 'He won't change his mind.'

'We'll see.' He devoted himself to his bacon and eggs and
spoke not another word. At the end of the meal, as he left
the room, he tore Philip's letter in half and threw it on to
the fire.

Saturday was a difficult day. Sarah was glad that she had
arranged to go to Effie's for lunch. Her preoccupation did
not pass unnoticed. After a meal in which Sarah had heard
little of what Effie said to her they set off for a walk with
Rusty, Effie's spaniel.

'What is it? Rose again?' Effie demanded.

'Rose? No, I haven't heard from her for a while.'

'Well, you've got something on your mind, so out with
it!'

Sarah hesitated. A constraint for which she could hardly
account had kept her from confiding in Effie, her oldest
friend, about her feelings for Philip. Now that Philip was
formally declaring himself her suitor, she would have to
know.

'Philip is coming to see Papa tonight. He wants us to be
married.'

Sarah heard Effie's sharp intake of breath, but not the outburst of questions and congratulations she had expected from a talker so indefatigable as Effie. She glanced at her, seeing her friend's face in profile. Her lips were drawn tight in disapproval.

'Why, aren't you pleased, Effie?'

There was a pause before Effie answered, slowly as if choosing her words with care. 'Of course, I am delighted if it makes you happy.'

'Do you think it won't?'

'How can I say, particularly since you haven't said a word about it to me?'

'You knew that we were friends.'

'Oh yes,' Effie said, '*friends*.'

Sarah did not ask Effie to explain the comment. For the first time she felt separated from her by mutual misunderstanding and, perhaps, mistrust. They spoke of other things but the awareness of her unsatisfactory response to Sarah's news lay between them, a burden to them both.

Mary Brunton did not come down to dinner. She was suffering from one of her usual attacks, though more severely than ever, it seemed. Sarah remained with her. She had no wish to face her father over the dinner table. Shortly after eight, the doorbell rang. Sarah felt her heart thump. Her ears caught the murmur of voices, Philip's, she thought, amongst them and, to her surprise, the sound of hurrying footsteps on the stairs. The maid entered.

'Mr Brunton says will you step down to his study for a minute, miss. I'm to sit with Mrs Brunton meantime.'

Sarah could only obey. As she went downstairs she wondered whether the request for her presence was a good sign. A single glance at her father's face suggested the opposite.

'Good. I wanted you here because I have no intention of leaving any excuse for doubt in either of your minds,'

William Brunton said, as harshly as if he were addressing an errant servant. 'This person—'

'My name is Philip Taylor, as you very well know.'

'—has asked permission to marry you,' her father went on, as though Philip had not spoken. 'That permission I absolutely refuse, now and for all time. Is that clear?'

'And why is that?' Philip asked.

'My daughter is at present sole heiress to one of the biggest industrial concerns in the district. It is my duty to protect her from fortune-hunters. I may have failed in the case of my younger child. I have no intention of allowing the same thing to happen again.'

'I am not interested in your daughter's fortune, Mr Brunton. I would marry her without a penny.'

'Fine words. I wish I could believe them, or see any other reason to explain your wish for this match.'

Sarah felt her face grow hot with shame at the sneer. She stepped forward. 'Give us your permission, and we will prove you are wrong. We don't want any of your money, Papa.'

'You would certainly get none, if you were foolhardy enough to continue with this farce.'

'Why do you call it a farce?' Philip asked. 'Sarah and I have known each other for four years or more. We are neither of us rash or foolhardy. We want to marry. Where is the harm in that?'

'Her place is here, as companion to her mother. She is needed at home. It is a simple matter, not open to discussion.'

'But I could see Mama every day!' Sarah said eagerly. 'We would not be far away, after all.'

'You would be the wife of a poor man,' her father said brutally. 'Your time would not be your own. Is this how you repay your upbringing, by abandoning your family when you are most needed? Your sister gave you a fine example. Will you make our name a laughing stock by following it? Was one scandal not enough?'

'There need be no scandal,' Philip said, frowning. 'It is in your hands. We will marry, whether you like it or not. Give us your blessing and no one will think anything of it.'

William Brunton turned his back on him. Leaning forward on his table, he fixed Sarah with the gaze that had dominated her will from her earliest memories. 'Will you marry against my wishes? Will you humiliate me by being the second of my daughters to defy me? Will you leave your mother, sick and in need of your help? Tell me, now, to my face.'

From the corner of her eye Sarah saw Philip make an unfinished movement, as though he had intended to reach out to her, but his hand dropped back to his side. He was too proud to attempt to influence her by an appeal.

'Mama would not suffer,' Sarah said miserably. 'We need not marry at once, there would be plenty of time for her to grow accustomed to the idea.'

'Oh, no.' Her father shook his head. 'If you remain beneath this roof as my daughter you do so in proper obedience to my will. Choose. Leave with him now, or abandon this nonsense once and for all.'

'You can't ask that of me!'

'Why not?' Philip stepped forward. 'He is only trying to bully you, Sarah. Take him at his word. Come on, we are leaving. He has forced you to it.'

'Sarah!' her father said warningly. 'If you go with this man now you will never re-enter this house so long as I live.'

Philip strode to the door and held out his hand. She took a single, faltering step forward, and stopped. Their eyes met. She saw his expression change, his resolution giving way to disbelief, disappointment, anger. 'Sarah?'

'I can't. I'm so sorry, Philip, but I just can't.'

'All it takes is a little courage. Do you want to regret this moment for the rest of your life?'

'She has made up her mind,' William Brunton said, moving swiftly over to the bell. 'Leave at once, or I shall send for the police. You are no longer welcome in this house . . . if you ever were.'

'Is that really what you want, Sarah?' Philip asked softly, as though they were alone. 'Will you throw everything away just because your father wants to keep you at home as an unpaid servant?'

Sarah could not speak for the unvoiced sobs tightening her throat. Silently, she shook her head. He waited for another moment, and left. His swift, angry steps spurning the gravel of the drive and, at last, fading into nothingness seemed to Sarah the most desolate sound she had ever heard.

The silence was broken by the sudden opening of the door. Frightened, breathless, the maid burst in. 'Please, Mrs Brunton is ever so bad. Will you come up and see to her . . . it's terrible.'

Sarah ran upstairs, the maid following. A single glance was enough to confirm the truth of Betty's report. 'Tell my father to send for the doctor,' Sarah said, as she hurried over to her mother. 'Quickly, for heaven's sake!'

While she waited for medical help, Sarah did what little she could to make her mother comfortable. Mary Brunton slipped into what seemed a state of unconsciousness rather than a sleep. Sarah did her best to tidy the room and went to the window, drawing back the curtain to look for the doctor. The lane beyond the garden was deserted, wan and sad in the thin moonlight.

'Sarah . . .'

Her mother's cry was so weak that it was barely more than a whisper. Sarah let the curtain fall and returned to the bed as another spasm seized the sick woman.

'Isn't Dr Millar here yet?'

'He won't be long, Mama,' Sarah said gently.

In the pallor of her face her mother's eyes were desperate and frightened as a child's. 'You won't leave me, will you?'

'No, Mama, of course I won't,' Sarah said soothingly.

'I don't just mean now,' her mother persisted. 'You won't leave me, not ever?'

'I promise,' she said, after barely a moment's hesitation. What else could she say? Relieved, her mother relapsed back against the pillows, still maintaining a weak but surprisingly tenacious grip on Sarah's hand. Even when she drifted into sleep once more her hand still rested on her daughter's, detaining her by her very helplessness. Sarah could not move.

Dr Millar arrived an hour or more later.

'A nightmare delivery over at Walton,' he said apologetically as he entered the sickroom. 'I didn't dare leave until the baby was safely home. Now, Mrs Brunton, shall we see what's causing the trouble?'

Sarah withdrew during the examination. At its conclusion the doctor came in search of her. 'There are one or two things I should like to ask you, Miss Brunton. Quite frankly, I am astonished that I have not been called in sooner. Has she been seeing some other medical man?'

'No. I have begged her but she has always refused.'

He frowned, and asked her in more detail about her mother's symptoms and the course of her illness. Sarah answered as best she could. Dr Millar made no comment but his grave expression told its own tale. 'I think the worst is over, for the moment at least. I will come back tomorrow and see what else can be done. Could I have a few words with your father before I leave?'

Sarah wanted to ask what was wrong with her mother and whether matters really were as serious as she feared but she supposed that, whatever the news, her father must hear it first. She went back into the sickroom, glad to find that her mother was asleep again.

It was some time before she heard Dr Millar leave the

house. Little as she wished to see her father, her anxiety to know the truth about her mother's condition would not let her rest. She called Betty to replace her at the bedside and went down.

Her father must have heard her, for he was waiting at the door of his study. 'How is she?' he asked.

'Asleep. She seems quite peaceful.'

'Come in.'

Sarah was struck by his changed manner. Gone was his confident self-possession, his assumption that he could master whatever challenge life threw down before him. He spoke and moved like a man dazed. As he closed the door behind them he fumbled with the knob; the catch did not engage at the first attempt. The clumsiness, so out of character, made him appear painfully vulnerable to her.

'What did the doctor say?' she asked, as he gazed blankly at her, making no attempt to open the conversation.

'Nothing good. A growth, a tumour in the stomach.'

The terrible word he did not speak filled her mind. 'But he will be able to do something?'

'No. It is a matter of making her comfortable for the time she has left, that's all.'

Sarah gave an involuntary cry, although the full force of the words had not yet struck her. They were both silent for a moment.

'He wanted to know why he had not been called before,' she said dully.

Her father turned away, his hands clasped tightly behind his back. The implied reproach in what she had said must already be echoing in his heart. 'She was always ailing,' he said, with a touch of his old acerbity. 'How was I to know it was different this time?'

Sarah felt that she should reassure him, tell him that, of course, it would have been impossible for him to suspect any serious illness. She said nothing.

'You may need to hire a night nurse to help you, if not now then in a few weeks. See to it, will you?' he asked, as carelessly as if they were discussing a minor domestic rearrangement. It occurred to her bleakly that already he was turning over to her the sole responsibility for the management of her mother's illness.

The following morning Mary Brunton urged her to attend chapel as usual but the undertone of anxiety in her voice convinced Sarah that it would be better to stay by her mother's side. William Brunton went alone. At the end of lunch, a meal passed in almost unbroken silence, he said curtly, 'I spoke to the Sunday school superintendent this morning. I told him that you would not be able to teach your class for some time, under the circumstances.'

'Can't I be absent from the house for a single afternoon?'

'Your mother comes first.'

'Betty can sit with her, and you are here.'

He frowned. 'You know I can't abide sickrooms. Men are quite unsuited to that sort of thing. You aren't needed at the school, in any case. That interfering female . . . the one with the spaniel . . .'

'Effie?'

'Yes. She overheard me speaking to the superintendent and came bustling up. She is to take your class in future.'

'But she hates children!'

'She was keen enough to take over. When I left she was going in search of Taylor to show her the ropes, as she put it. He seemed happy to oblige. They were deep in conversation, the last I saw.'

Sarah did not persist. She retired to her mother's room once more, deeply uneasy.

Mary Brunton's illness now dominated the life of every member of the household except, perhaps, her husband, although even he, despite his dislike for sickrooms, was obliged to visit her there, for her days were now reduced to its narrow confines. He never stayed long and, although he struggled to be patient with the sick woman, Sarah could see the strain in his tense smiles and forced attempts at conversation.

With her mother's increasing weakness came a growing yearning to see Rose again. As her other occupations were closed off to her and her physical powers faded, it seemed that her whole consciousness was reduced to the infinite effort of the struggle to survive one more day, and the passionate desire to be reunited with her younger daughter. At times, Sarah wondered if it was only the strength of her longing that drove her on, so light and frail that her body seemed no more than a husk that barely confined her pining spirit.

At first, the old loyalty to her husband's authority kept her silent, but as the illness progressed even that restraint fell away, like all that was inessential to her. One evening, as Sarah was making her mother comfortable for the night, Mary Brunton raised the subject at last.

'Here, Mama, this is a stronger mixture tonight,' Sarah said encouragingly, as she slipped one arm beneath her mother's thin shoulders and supported her while she put the glass to her lips. 'Dr Millar thought it would give you a better sleep.'

'He is very good,' Mary Brunton murmured. 'So are you, dear, and your papa . . . everyone is so kind, I have everything I could possibly need, except for one thing, you know . . . one person.'

'Rose?' Sarah asked gently. 'You would like to see her?'

'And the little boy, Peter. He must be almost three now. I should so like to see him, if only the once.'

It was a tacit admission of what they both knew but had never admitted: Mary Brunton was dying. Sarah nodded. 'I will see to it, Mama. I will write tomorrow.'

Her mother's hand clutched hers. 'Tonight, Sarah. If you were to slip out and post it she would get it tomorrow. I can't bear to waste a day.'

'I will do what I can. Papa is still out, so I should be able to get to the pillar box.'

'If he really knew what it meant to me, he wouldn't mind,' Mary Brunton said, excusing at once his harshness and her own rebellion. 'He has always been such a good husband . . . always so good.'

Her mother's voice trailed away as the sleeping draught took effect. Sarah lowered her back against the pillows and, despite the fatigue numbing her mind and body, went to carry out her mother's wishes.

CHAPTER

Four

Rose came three days later. Sarah had given the maid the day off and answered the door herself.

'Rose?' she said uncertainly, looking at the thin, shabbily dressed young woman standing before her, a child in her arms. 'Oh, come in, come in, out of the cold.'

As Rose crossed the threshold the little boy tightened his arms about his mother's neck, hiding his face against her shoulder. 'Don't, Peter,' Rose said, but she made no attempt to loosen his grip. 'He's shy,' she explained absently, looking about her at the dim hall with its dark, grained doors. 'I suppose *he* is out?'

'Yes. He won't be home for dinner.'

'The same old story,' Rose said, so apathetically that Sarah felt a stirring of concern.

'Did you have a bad journey? Are you tired? Would you like something to eat?'

'Later, perhaps. Is there a glass of milk for Peter? There was none in the house this morning and he needs to build his strength. He had such a bad cough last month . . . but you're all better now, aren't you, love?'

At the coaxing tone the boy raised his head and smiled at

his mother. Sarah revised her first opinion of him. With his pale face and heavy-looking eyes he had seemed an unprepossessing child, but his smile was so sweet that she now saw in his delicate features something of his mother's beauty.

'Would he come to me, do you think?' She tentatively held out her arms. He gazed at her and suddenly, to her delighted surprise, released his grip on his mother's neck and leaned forward, stretching out his arms towards her.

'Well, you're honoured!' Rose said, relinquishing him. Sarah thought that she was not quite pleased. 'He won't usually go to anyone else, not even Simon sometimes.'

He weighed so little, was so fragile in her arms that Sarah was almost afraid of hurting him by her eager, protecting embrace. Bluish veins showed beneath his skin at the temples; he seemed to have too little flesh to cover and preserve the vulnerable network of blood and nerves. There were deep shadows beneath the blue eyes that regarded her so gravely. He looked tired and, although small for his age, older than his years, as though he had already seen too much of the sorrows of life.

'Go up to Mama, Rose. She might like to see you alone for a few minutes. I'll take Peter down to the kitchen and bring him up to you when he's had his milk.'

'Is she really so ill? I couldn't be sure from your letter.'

'I don't think the doctor can do anything more for her. It's just a question of time.'

Rose wearily put back a strand of hair from her face, the gesture a sad echo of her old girlish vanity. 'How long?'

'He hasn't said to me, and if Papa knows anything he hasn't told me.'

'How is Papa?'

'Oh, you know what he's like. I suppose he does his best, in his way.' She hesitated, then added, 'I don't think he has ever got over losing you. You always were his favourite and you still are.'

'He manages to conceal it pretty well,' Rose said, her mouth twisting into a hard, bitter line. 'He doesn't even open my letters now. He gives them to his lawyer to return to me unopened.'

'You're still writing to him?'

'Simon makes me.' She shrugged. 'Money; what else?'

'You are in difficulties again?'

As she spoke, Sarah realised how foolish the question was. Rose's dress was answer enough. Rose had always been far more interested in clothes than Sarah. She had insisted that everything should be made to the most fashionable designs, culled from magazines and the dressmaker's plates. Now she was wearing a shapeless jacket, baggy with age, of a cut out-moded for twenty years. Her skirt had been extensively darned and was sagging round the hem, which was badly frayed in one or two places. The whole outfit must have been picked up for a few shillings in some slop-shop. In better days Rose would not have touched it with the tip of her finger yet now, Sarah assumed, it was her best.

'Difficulties? You can't imagine.' Rose sighed. 'I had better see Mama now, I suppose. Perhaps we will be able to talk later.'

She went up the stairs, leaning heavily on the bannister. Sarah could hardly believe that this was the same Rose who, not four years ago, had sped up and down stairs so fleetly that she barely seemed to touch the ground. Peter stirred restlessly in Sarah's arms but made no further protest as she took him into the kitchen. The cook had been given permission to go and visit her sister for the afternoon and Sarah was undisturbed as she brought out a piece of sponge cake and a glass of milk for the little boy. She sat at the kitchen table, Peter on her knee, and guided the glass to his mouth.

'Let's see what a clever boy you are, Peter,' she said, stroking the thin hair that hung lankly across his high, bony forehead. 'Can you drink all this milk for your auntie?'

Over the rim of the glass his preternaturally knowing, serious eyes regarded her, like one condemned prisoner silently condoling with another. With her steadying help he replaced the glass on the table.

'Now the cake?' She cut a small piece off the slice and pushed it encouragingly towards him. He made no attempt to pick it up. 'It's nice,' she said, and put it to his lips. His eyes not moving from her face, he opened his mouth and allowed her to feed him.

His fragility, his trust, the light warmth of his small body on her knee moved Sarah. In his grave manner there was none of the fun or silliness of infancy. She could not imagine him being naughty and, strangely, this troubled her. She took a napkin and gently wiped the crumbs and moustache of cream from about his mouth. 'We will go back to your mama in a moment, and you will see your grandmama, too. I will be able to tell them what a good boy you have been . . . but I'm sure you are always a good boy, aren't you?'

He shook his head. 'Papa says I am bad. He says I am a useless little bastard.'

Sarah struggled to conceal her horror at his innocent repetition of the abuse. 'I'm sure he doesn't mean it. Sometimes people say things when they are cross and then they are sorry later.'

'He says it all the time. He shouts at Mama in the night.'

Sarah bit her lip. She did not want to abuse his trust and pry into her sister's affairs but her instinct warned her that something was seriously wrong. 'Does he frighten you, Peter?'

He nodded. 'I like it better when he's not there.'

Still holding him, Sarah got to her feet and, his hands clasped about her neck, carried him up to her mother's room.

Rose was sitting close to the bed, her mother's hand in hers. Mary Brunton had been crying, but Rose's face was impassive. The sick woman's delight in seeing her grandson was evident but soon she turned to Rose once more, gazing at her as hungrily as if she could never weary of the sight. Unregarded, Sarah removed Peter from the bed and, at a nod from Rose, took him downstairs again. Her mother did not notice, engrossed as she was in her younger daughter.

It was five o'clock before Rose emerged from the sickroom and came in search of Sarah. 'I hope he hasn't been too much of a nuisance,' she said, taking Peter from her. 'Mama wants to see him again and then we will have to go. She is very tired.'

'He has been no trouble at all. Oh, Rose, he's a lovely child,' she said wistfully. 'I wish I could see him more often.'

'Yes,' Rose said dully, already turning away.

'Rose . . . is everything all right?'

'It's about as wrong as can be, but that's no concern of yours, Sal.'

It was a rebuff, but so dispassionate in tone that Sarah did not feel hurt, merely appalled at the change in her confident, impetuous sister. Rose was beaten down by life, unable to spare any energy or emotion for anything but her own struggles.

'If it's so bad, why don't you leave? I will do everything I can to help.'

'What can you do?' Rose asked wearily, and hitching Peter more securely on her arm continued upstairs.

The leavetaking was painful. Each of the women knew the unspoken truth: Mary Brunton would never see her younger daughter again. She could not bear to let Rose go. At the last, Rose had to break away, leaving Sarah to care for her heartbroken mother. She had no chance to say anything more to Rose or to give her the small sum, all the money at her disposal, that she had intended.

Sarah noticed that Rose was carrying a package when she left. Later that evening, as she prepared her mother for the night, she discovered what it had been. Replacing her mother's hairbrush on the dressing table, she looked about her in surprise, puzzled by some difference she could not at once identify.

'Mama, did I put your jewel box away in a drawer? I can't remember moving it but it's not here now.'

'No . . .' Her mother hesitated, then added nervously, 'I gave it to Rose, dear. I hope you don't mind, but the poor girl was almost destitute. What use are jewels to me now?'

'You gave her everything? Your cameo, and the pearls Papa gave you?'

'Why, you don't think it means I care any the less for you, do you? Rose needed it more, that's all, and you know you will have Papa to look after you when I am gone.'

'I'm glad you were able to help her,' Sarah said, truthfully enough. And yet, in some dark, secret corner of her heart a seed of resentment germinated. Sown in their earliest girlhood, it found fertile ground in the constant awareness of her mother's hankering to see Rose while her own presence went unremarked, her sacrifice unvalued. As she soon realised, her mother had given every single item of jewellery she possessed to Rose, including her gold watch and every ring but her wedding band. What was more, Rose had taken them, knowing that Sarah would have not a single memento of her mother. She tried to be magnanimous, to understand Rose's need, but the incident rankled.

To Rose, her mother's gift represented money for food, rent, clothes and shoes. She could not allow herself the luxury of sentiment. Since the money from her father had been exhausted, some months before, they had had no regular source of income. Simon's gambling, which had accounted for an unknown proportion of the squandered capital, occasionally resulted in winnings that enabled at least their rent to be paid, although an arrears had begun to accumulate over the past weeks. Sometimes, through contacts in the shadowy world in which he moved, he received what he called commission on financial dealings whose nature was never clear to her. Otherwise, they survived by the pawnshop and credit from sympathetic grocers, by their wits and by Rose's growing talent for making do, and in the last resort, by her secret recourse to her savings from better days.

Rose's visit to her mother coincided with one of the worst times she had ever known. Simon appeared to have exhausted his winning streak; it had been weeks since he brought a penny into the house and her secret hoard was almost gone. It distressed Rose to see her mother so ill but the nagging awareness that there was not a crust of bread for Peter's supper dulled her ability to feel any intense sympathy.

On the way home from the station in Liverpool she called in at the first pawnshop she passed. She pledged her mother's watch, one of the most valuable pieces. The rent had already run on for three weeks and the bill at the local shops ought to be settled. Rose was scrupulous in paying her debts whenever she had the means: she never knew how soon she would again need to appeal to the shopkeepers for time.

The money safe in her purse, she felt the first relaxation of anxiety she had known for months. In a holiday mood, she bought Peter a stick of barley sugar and, tempted by the display in a butcher's shop, she allowed herself the extravagance of good, fresh meat instead of the cheap cuts, purchased at the very end of trading on a Saturday night, that were all she had been able to afford recently.

Rose managed to settle her debts at the local grocer's but Peter was too tired for her to delay further. Burdened by her purchases and by her mother's gift, the child slumped against her shoulder, she trudged home and wearily let herself into the house. A light was burning in the kitchen: Simon was at home. She stopped on the threshold, uncertain how best to conceal the jewellery from him. The parlour was so sparsely furnished that it offered few hiding places and she was afraid to attract his attention by making any noise. She hurriedly stuffed the parcel under the settee and went on into the kitchen.

Simon was sitting by the fire, reading a newspaper. The fire gave out little heat; they were reduced to their last few lumps of coal, eked out with shovels of slack that all but doused the flames.

'What kept you?' he asked sourly, looking up.

'You know I was going to my mother's.'

'I didn't think you'd be so long. Did you get anything out of her?'

'Don't you think you might ask how she is first?' she asked, putting down her purchases and bringing Peter to him. 'Here, take him a minute, will you? I'll get his supper and put him to bed. He's exhausted.'

'Put the brat on the floor. He's not lost the use of his legs, has he?'

Rose knew better than to argue. She put Peter gently down on to a kitchen chair. His eyes were already closing and she was afraid that he might fall off if he grew more drowsy. As quickly as she could, she cut two slices of bread, buttered them and took them to the sleepy child.

'Eat this for Mama, love,' she coaxed. 'Tomorrow you shall have an egg all to yourself, and a nice big glass of milk.'

'Let him alone, for heaven's sake!' Simon grumbled. 'He can eat on his own, can't he? What about *my* supper?'

'I will see to it in a minute. Peter will fall asleep if I leave him, and I want him to eat something before he goes to bed.'

'It doesn't matter if *I* haven't had a mouthful to eat since this morning, of course!'

She suppressed an angry rejoinder. It was not a skill that came naturally to Rose, but the last few years had taught her the wisdom of silence. Tonight it was not enough.

'You still haven't bothered to tell me whether you got anything out of her.'

'My mother is dying,' she said, making no attempt to hide her contempt for him. 'Yes, she gave me a few pounds. She has no money of her own, as I've told you and told you. It will be enough to tide us over another week or two, that's all.'

'Better than nothing.' He threw down the newspaper, his mood brightening. 'Let me have a pound or so, will you? Matthews and Billington and the rest are meeting up tonight and I hear they're on to a good thing. If I can get in on it now it could be worth twenty pounds to me later. It's a certainty, but I'll need to settle tonight.'

As he spoke he was gazing into the looking glass and making the little adjustments to his tie and hair that were always a prelude to his departure. She thought that she had never seen so vain a man. Even at the worst of their difficulties he was never anything but well-dressed. Whatever else might find its way to the pawnshop it was never his greatcoat or the gold hunter inscribed with his name that he now consulted.

'Come on, Rosie, it's nearly eight already! I'll need to hurry if I'm to catch them! I've told you, it's as good as twenty pounds in the bank.'

As always when he wanted something out of her, he adopted a wheedling charm that, she knew all too well, would soon turn nasty if she continued to deny him. 'What about your supper?' she asked. 'I got you a nice chop on the way home.'

'It'll keep until tomorrow. Cough up, there's a good girl! I haven't had a shilling in my pocket for weeks . . . you don't know how that brings a fellow down.'

His self-pity sent a wave of bitter anger surging like uncontrollable nausea through her frame. Afraid of what she might say if he were to remain, she reached for her purse. 'Here, take it!' She thrust two pounds into his hand and, not waiting to hear his thanks, lifted Peter from his chair and carried him up to bed.

By the time Rose had settled Peter down to sleep, Simon had long since left the house. She went downstairs and, with the comforting assurance of her mother's valuable gifts, indulged herself by building up the fire to a cheerful blaze. She made herself tea and toast, tidied the kitchen, and sat down by the hearth, some sewing on her lap. She intended to take in a dart at the waist of a skirt, for she had lost so much weight recently that it was now far too loose. She made a few stitches but soon her hand slowed and lay inert on the worn fabric as she gazed, dreaming, into the flames.

Brief as it was, her visit home had disturbed the resigned apathy into which Rose had gradually lapsed as the easiest way of living with Simon. She had become so used to the burdens of poverty that she had come to accept them as inevitable; she had forgotten what it was to enter a house that was warm and comfortable, in which good, abundant food was readily available. Even Sarah's clothes had impressed her by their relative newness, their fine quality. A flicker of the old sisterly striving for superiority revived: Rose felt her shabbiness more acutely in relation to Sarah than to anyone else.

Her mother's weakness had profoundly shocked Rose. Before seeing her, Rose had accepted that this one, secret

visit could have no successor. Now, knowing that Mary
Brunton was dying, she began to question whether it must be
so. At such a time could there not be a truce, a reconciliation
with her father?

As the warm glow of the flames touched her hair and
skin, awakening colours dimmed by her harsh struggle to
survive, Rose smiled at the future she conjured from the
radiant caverns of the fire: Simon appointed to some
position of authority and prestige, at a salary that would
reconcile him to the drudgery of employment; Peter,
restored to sturdy good health by eggs and creamy milk and
fine white bread, running with Bobby in the orchard,
learning to ride at John's teaching. She imagined herself as
mistress of a prosperous household, her threadbare shoddy
replaced by figured velvet; greys and duns by crimson, lilac,
white. She saw herself sitting by her mother's side, staying
as long as the sick woman wished, not having to hurry
furtively away to avoid her father's wrath.

Rose dreamed on, visions as entrancing and as transient
as the towers and gulfs in the heart of the shifting flames,
until at last her eyes closed and the needle slipped from her
relaxed fingers. Still smiling, she fell asleep.

The following morning she resolved to make some attempt
to realise her dreams. While Simon still slept, she busied
herself in tidying and cleaning the house, bringing to the
task more energy than she had felt for many weeks. She
took Peter out shopping, buying him new boots and, on an
impulse of extravagant happiness, a mechanical toy: a
clockwork bear, which played a tin drum.

Peter's delight exceeded his powers of expression. Arriving
home, he knelt before his miraculous new possession, watching its jerky animation with the wide-eyed adoration of a
devotee for his idol. His fingers were too weak to turn the
key; at the end of every bout of drumming, as the bear's stiff

paws moved more and more slowly, Peter's face drooped in dismay. He remained motionless until the last beat when, released from enchantment, he ran urgently to her, pulling at her skirts until she went to rewind the key and he could settle himself once more to the intent, awed enjoyment of his treasure.

Rose had rewound the bear seven or eight times when their game was interrupted. Furious footsteps thudded across the bedroom floor, so violently that the kitchen windows rattled. Peter barely noticed, but Rose knew what they portended. She snatched up the toy. 'That's enough for now,' she said, intending to hide the bear in the parlour, but Peter howled his outrage and clung to her knees, hampering her escape.

'What the devil's going on?' Dishevelled, unshaven, his hair flopping across his forehead, Simon appeared at the foot of the stairs. 'Can't I get two minutes' sleep without that little fool disturbing me? Hammering, hammering . . . can't he play his stupid games somewhere else?'

Rose had hurriedly concealed the bear behind her back. Peter was silenced for a moment by his father's anger, but his desire for his wonderful toy was even greater than his fear. He began to drag at her hands, trying to prise them open.

'Give it me, Mama! Give it me!'

Simon grabbed her wrist and pulled her hand into view. 'What's that you're hiding? More money wasted on your precious little runt?'

'It's not much, only a toy . . . he has so few. Mama wanted me to get him something,' she said desperately. 'I'm sorry if it disturbed you. I'll make sure that it doesn't happen again. Shall I get your breakfast now? An egg? A couple of chops?'

As she had hoped, the questions diverted his attention from Peter and his toy. 'The chops will do – my stomach's not up to an egg,' he said, sitting by the fire and watching her work. 'How much did you get out of the old lady?'

'Seven pounds,' she said, keeping her face averted from him. She was a poor liar but he appeared to accept her answer. 'I was thinking that this might be a good chance for us to make a fresh start?'

'What do you mean by that?' he asked, his tone barely civil. It would have been worse, she knew, had it not been that she had the money he wanted.

'Now that my mother is so ill it would be natural for us to make another effort to put things right with my father, that's all.'

'You can try to get more money out of him, certainly.'

'That's not what I meant. I was thinking of asking him to help us find work for you.'

Simon laughed. 'Forget it. Not a forgiving sort of man, your papa.'

'But it was so long ago . . . and there is Peter. If my father could see him, it might make all the difference.'

'That?' Simon pointed contemptuously at the child who, nervous as always in his father's presence, sat mute in the corner, clutching the bear and incessantly twirling a strand of his hair round his fingers, a habit most noticeable when he was aware of Simon's eyes on him. 'He looks fit for a straitjacket and you imagine that your father will be softened by the sight of him? By God, I can hardly believe that I spawned such a feeble-minded creature!'

'You know perfectly well that there is no doubt on that score!' she said, with a flash of her old imperious self.

'More's the pity, or I wouldn't be saddled with the two of you!' he said viciously.

Rose bent her head, staring at the chops she was turning in the pan. The frying fat made her nauseous. For ever after, the heavy smell of mutton grease would bring back to her this moment, when her marriage finally died.

There had been other taunts over the years, insults to herself and her family that had hurt her but that she had been able to forgive or ignore, such had been her desire to maintain some pretence of happiness. Perhaps her visit home had woken in her something of the spirit of the young girl who had submitted to no control, who had ruled her docile mother and sister and barely feared her autocratic father; perhaps she had merely grown tired of the effort to excuse his behaviour. Rose raised her eyes from the food she was cooking for him, food she had bought with her own money, food for which she would barely receive a word of thanks. Suddenly, as though she had surfaced from some hallucination, she saw things differently.

'What are you looking at me like that for?' he demanded.

'Nothing . . . it's nothing,' she murmured. Automatically she lifted the pan from the fire and rested it on the oven. She brought him a plate and served him his breakfast, and all the time her thoughts were in seething confusion, a sickening shifting and veering of memories and assumptions that had broken loose and could never again stand in their accustomed relations.

After the meal, most of which he left, Simon went upstairs to change, in preparation for his next drinking bout, she supposed. She did not care. She dressed Peter and, furtively recovering the rest of her mother's things from their hiding place, took him out. They went to the park and sat by the pond. Peter stayed by her side, watching as other, bolder children ran along the paths. Usually Rose chatted to him but today she was too preoccupied to pay him any attention. Sensitive to her mood, he clutched tightly to her skirt, as though to prevent her from leaving him in body as she already had in her thoughts.

In the new, bleak light of her disillusionment she saw the years of her marriage in all their stark hopelessness. Love, and the desire to be loved; the power of the physical bond between them that had blinded her into willing forgetfulness of so much else that was wrong; pride that refused to admit defeat; the inability to face the struggle to support herself and her child alone, all had veiled the ugly truth: Simon had treated her badly almost from the very start. He had no intention of taking his responsibilities to her and Peter seriously; far from being their protector, he would waste every penny that ever came into his hands. She would be better off alone.

'Oh, what a fool,' she said with passionate bitterness. 'How could I have been such a fool?'

'Mama?'

She looked down at her son's pale, pinched little face. 'Don't worry, Peter. Everything will be all right,' she said, wishing she could believe it.

'Are we going home?'

'I don't know . . .' she said absently. In her struggles to recognise the past in its new perspective she had not yet thought of the future. It was all very well to decide that she would be better off without Simon but where else could she go?

The clumsy parcel on her knee could be the means of her escape. Sold or pledged, its contents would enable her to survive with Peter for a year or more, many times longer than with Simon. Alone, she and the child might be able to achieve some sort of reconciliation with her father: with Simon it was impossible. She could walk away with her son, go to the railway station, leave on the next train, vanish from Simon's world.

Rose had never before entertained the idea of flight but now it presented itself to her mind with compelling force. She and Peter could make a new, happier life together. She was never likely to have a better opportunity, with her mother's gifts still almost untouched.

'Mama? I'm hungry,' Peter said plaintively. 'Can we go home?'

She hesitated. The decision before her was so over-whelming, so sudden a change from all that had been familiar to her for the last four years that she found herself seeking some excuse for delay. There were one or two items of clothing at home that might be useful; she could make a parcel of the best of Peter's things and a little bedding; after his travelling and late night the previous day Peter was already wearying. Why exhaust him further when tomorrow they could leave as easily, in better shape and with more resources?

Rose shifted uneasily in her seat. At the thought of returning home some instinct rebelled. She felt again the nausea of that morning, so intensely that she feared she might be sick. Against the reasonable arguments for post-ponement and the residual clinging to what she knew, stood an unaccountable dread, a panic longing to be gone at once.

She got stiffly to her feet. She must have been sitting motionless for hours, for the sun was beginning to set and the damp chill of evening was in the air. She stretched out her hand to Peter.

'Come along, love. Mama and Peter will go for a little walk and then Mama will buy something nice for tea.'

He trailed patiently along beside her, but so slowly that she was obliged to pick him up. It would be better to get a cab to the station but they were far from any cab stand and in a poor area where few were to be hailed. She struggled on, seeing none. Peter began to shiver.

'When will we be home?' he asked, putting a cold hand on her cheek and drawing her face round to attract her attention.

'I was thinking that we might go on another train,' she said brightly. 'You'd like that, wouldn't you?'

His lower lip began to quaver. 'I want to go home.'

'But the train will be such fun!'

'I want to go home! I want my bear!'

'I'll get you another one, don't worry,' Rose promised, trying to forestall the tears already spilling down his cheeks. Sobbing, heartbroken, he was almost choking for breath as his nose streamed and he gulped for air. She stopped, hitching him up higher on her arm, and looked desperately about her. At the end of the street a cab appeared. It approached, and stopped at a house a few feet from them. An elderly couple carefully dismounted from it. Rose ran towards it.

'Are you for hire?'

'It's how I generally makes my living, missus.'

Rose looked down at Peter's miserable face. He was cold, tired, hungry, distressed. She sighed, and gave the man the name of the street in which they lived.

Simon was out. Rose made a light meal of scrambled eggs for Peter and after playing with his clockwork bear with him for a little while prepared him for bed. He insisted on taking it up with him. Her last sight of him, by the gentle glow of the night-light, was of his lids already drooping as he tried to keep his sleepy eyes fixed on the little bear which she wound up and left, still drumming, on the chair beside his bed.

Rose began to work at once, sorting through her few clothes, putting into a blanket what seemed worth the effort of taking. Peter's clothes, most of which she had made herself, were in better condition. They composed the bulk of the burden when at last she secured the blanket at the top. It seemed little enough to have come back for. She already regretted her decision and wished that she had hardened her heart to Peter's misery.

Usually Rose liked to be alone in the house but tonight it oppressed her. She was too overwrought for sleep, her nerves stretched taut as she planned every detail of her movements the following day. At last, having done everything she could to prepare for an early departure with Peter she made herself go up to bed.

Despite her expectations, Rose must have fallen asleep, for she was awoken by the sound of Simon stumbling into the bedroom and cursing loudly. Usually when he came home late he would not disturb her, at least attempting to move with lumbering drunken caution about the room. Tonight was to be an exception: he seemed not to care if he awoke her. She forced every muscle to preserve its sleeping position as she heard him stagger towards the bed.

'Rose? Come on, Rose!'

She made no response, hoping that he would abandon the attempt to waken her.

'Rose!' He put his hand on her shoulder and shook her roughly.

She stirred, opened her eyes, blinking in the light of the candle he had brought up with him, as though she had just woken. She saw him leaning over her and knew at once that he was very drunk.

'Yes? What is it?' she mumbled, slurring the words together as though she were all but talking in her sleep.

'Get up. Make me something to eat. I'm hungry.'

'The fire's out.'

Rose had intended to speak mildly, but years of resentment soured her tone. She sounded, as she was, sullen. He hesitated, still bending over her. She hoped that his brain, dulled by drink, would forget its purpose. Perhaps some change in her face betrayed the contempt she felt for his fuddled condition, for suddenly he shook her again, more violently.

'Get up, I said! You'd make up the fire quickly enough if it was for that little milksop.'

As slowly as she dared, hating him for his bullying, hating herself for submitting, she obeyed. The fire had been out for hours: the kitchen was chilly. Aroused from deep sleep and a warm bed, her body was not yet able to adjust to the changed temperature. Rose had wrapped a shawl about her but she still shivered. She raked out the fire but, clumsy with fatigue, dropped the poker and brushed the ashes on to the floor rather than the shovel.

'Watch what you're doing, can't you?' Simon said irritably, kicking away a piece of clinker that had fallen on to his shoe and smeared with ash its gleaming leather.

On her knees at the hearth, crouched before him, Rose heard in his voice the arrogance of a being who believed himself her superior. 'Never again,' she vowed to herself. 'Not Simon, not any man will ever have such power over me again.'

She looked up at him, wanting to fix this moment of humiliation for ever in her mind, to brand it on her heart. She could feel her hair escaping from its loose plait; the shawl she could not spare a hand to secure was slipping from her shoulders. She must appear to him slovenly, negligible, a drudge. *Never again, oh, never again.*

'What are you looking at me like that for? Get on with it!'

He put out his foot with no particular force, intending nothing more than a warning, perhaps, but it connected with her upper thigh. It was an unpleasant knock; she knew that she would be bruised, but still worse was the recognition of his own power and her vulnerability that she saw in his face. For the first time she was physically afraid of him and of what he might do next. An image flashed through her mind of herself, knocked off balance, and of his shiny, well-fitting shoes driving into her unprotected body over and over again. She wanted to stand up, to escape from her defenceless position, yet to do so might provoke the outburst she feared.

As calmly as she could, she said, 'Why don't you sit down, Simon? It won't take me long to get the fire started. You can be thinking what you would like me to cook.'

The matter-of-fact suggestion deflected his anger. He sat down in the old armchair to the right of the hearth, slumping back, both legs stretched out across the rug. She took care not to bump against them although they were in her way.

'Do you have to make that infernal racket?' he grumbled, as the shovel grated against the fine cinders at the bottom of the hearth.

Rose forced herself to answer peaceably. 'I'm sorry. I've almost done.' She worked on as quietly as she could, crumpling up old newspapers and balancing sticks of firewood on them. All the time she kept an eye on him and soon, as she had hoped, she saw his head begin to droop. She worked on, more slowly, until at last she dared to stop. The fire was laid; it needed only a match.

Rose got to her feet and looked at her husband's sleeping face. In the early days of their marriage it had been a secret delight so to observe him. Then she had loved to trace the straight, fine line of his nose, the complex curve of his lips, the subtle planes of cheekbones and jaw. Now she saw only the marks of self-indulgence and dissolution in the slack mouth, the pouched eyes, the sagging flesh about his jowls. She studied his spoiled beauty with passionate, gloating hatred.

Certain that he was sleeping, she went stealthily upstairs and brought down a blanket. She covered him with a care that mimicked the tenderness it would once have been: now she was simply afraid that the cold might awaken him to trouble her again.

It was two o'clock. She went back to bed, praying for morning. A few more hours and she and Peter would be away. She intended not to sleep, but lulled by the continuing calm of the house she must have drowsed, for when next she opened her eyes the grey glimmer of dawn was filtering through the thin curtains. But it was not the uncertain melancholy of the sporadic birdsong which had woken her; slowly, grimly, heavy footsteps were mounting the stairs.

Rose pulled the covers up to her very chin. She hoped that Simon had forgotten his earlier demand for food and indeed he made no comment on entering the room. He came towards the bed and began to undress. He climbed clumsily in beside her and put his arm around her, pulling her to him. Instinctively, she resisted, her body stiffening in protest.

'Here, what kind of way is that to treat your husband?' he asked, with heavy drunken jocularity which, she knew, was only a breath away from viciousness.

She edged away from him as best she could, sickened by the gusts of alcohol and stale tobacco engulfing her. 'Not now, Simon, please . . . it's the middle of the night and I'm so tired . . .'

'Well I'm not! See for yourself!' He snatched her hand and thrust it against his engorged flesh. She pulled away her fingers as though seared by the contact.

'Simon, I'm sorry, this isn't the time . . . later, when you've had your sleep out . . .'

'It's never the time, is it?' His voice was changing from coarse good humour to the petulant malevolence which had so often won from her what he wanted. In this mood he was unpredictable, as likely to weep in maudlin self-pity as to pour out a filthy stream of abuse. 'I'm your husband. I've got the right to have you any time I want, haven't I?'

She said nothing, not wanting to amplify his anger by opposition. She sought frantically for some means of distracting him.

'Wasn't that Peter?' It was the first thing that came to her mind and as soon as the words were out of her mouth she realised their danger.

'Peter? By God, it had better not be! I'll give the little devil something to cry about!'

He looked up, still bending over her, a jackal disturbed in the act of mauling its spoils. The silence was so profound that the thudding of her heart seemed to pulsate through the room. Satisfied, he turned to her again, yanking at her nightgown, his hand reaching for her thighs to force them apart. She willed herself to submit, as she had submitted to lesser brutalities in the past, but her body rebelled against the conscious decision: the desire to resist, to preserve her bodily integrity obliterated every other consideration. She barely felt the pain as he twisted one hand in her hair to hold her head still; she screamed and drummed her fists against his body as he mounted her. There was no point in further struggle, yet she could not stop herself from sobbing hysterically, until he put a hand about her neck and squeezed her cries to an agonised croak.

And in the silence there came an echo of her screams, as though her panic had possessed her son's frail body, as once her breath, her blood had also been his. From the room across the landing came Peter's terrified shrieks.

Simon grunted, his hand tightening convulsively about her neck as he filled her with the seed of his contempt. The sad grey light was washed away by a sea of darkness as her sight failed; the seething of her own blood in her ears muffled even the screams of her son. As she lost consciousness she was aware that the grip on her throat was slackening, that she could breathe freely. But in her relief was mingled horror at what this sudden release might mean.

Rose was never sure whether she had been fully unconscious, whether there had ever been a moment in which
her son's voice had not sounded in her ears with an urgency
to which her heart but not her body responded. As in a
nightmare from which she was unable to rouse herself she
heard, or thought she heard, Peter's cries grow louder, as
though the boy were coming towards her room; she heard
an indistinct, angry exclamation from Simon, and the
pounding of his feet across the floor. She heard a shout, a
scream, a thud, and a sudden, ominous silence.

Time had no meaning. Rose was never able to say how
long it was before she returned to complete awareness,
and whether to her faint had succeeded sleep. It was full
daylight, and Simon was lying beside her, heavily asleep.
She moved cautiously away from him, as the soreness in
her throat recalled to her what had happened. She eased
herself out of the bed, and made her way to the door, so
weak that she had to place her palm against the wall to
support herself.

At first, Rose thought that her worst fears had been
nothing more than fevered imaginings. Peter was in bed,
the covers tucked neatly about him. The room was still, the
only sounds the heavy rumble of a dray, passing down the
street. She let out a sigh of relief. Everything would be well,
after all. She and Peter would escape that very morning: her
delay would have no consequences, beyond the strengthening of her resolution. She would dress quickly, and at
once come back for Peter.

At the door she paused, overwhelmed by thankfulness
that her nightmare had no foundation in fact. She stole
closer to the child's bed, looking lovingly down on his face.
She frowned. His eyes were not fully closed. Beneath their
lids she could make out a dull gleam. His mouth was slightly
open, the upper lip drawn back a little over his teeth.

Careless now of the risk of waking him she went to the window and pulled back the curtains, although they were so threadbare that the light was barely affected.

She went back to the bed, her concern mounting as she saw how still he lay. She drew aside the covers and gently shook his shoulder. 'Peter! Wake up, love!'

There was no response. His eyes remained half-closed, their cold, leaden glitter showing no flicker of life, his mouth not relaxing into the joyous smile of recognition with which he greeted her every morning. Now seriously alarmed, she lifted him out of bed, calling his name. His head lolled against her, as if he had become once more the infant whose helplessness had summoned all her passionate protective love. And as she anxiously scanned his unnaturally aloof face, she saw on his temple the bruise that disfigured that white, delicate skin and recognised the truth.

Rose laid him down, as carefully as if anything she did could ever hurt him again. As she turned to leave him, her foot spurned the clockwork toy, lying neglected on the floor. The drum beat a single time, a dull, heavy thud, and was silent.

She pounded Simon awake with her fists, not caring what ill usage she would meet with. 'What have you done? You've killed him!'

As he raised his head heavily from the pillow she saw the dawning of some memory of whatever had happened in the child's room as she lay helpless, unable to protect him.

'What do you mean?' he blustered, his eyes not meeting hers. 'Have you gone mad? He was all right when I left him.'

'You know he wasn't! You're not even surprised! You killed him!'

'He'd fallen out of bed, that's all, and I put him back. Perhaps he hit his head somehow and I didn't notice, but don't you start saying I killed him. Why, if he *was* killed, who's to say it wasn't you that did it? So just be careful, because if it comes down to it, it's your word against mine, isn't it?' He pushed her aside and got out of bed. 'I'll go for the doctor. Get me some water for a shave.'

'You'll shave first?' she asked in disbelief.

'No hurry, is there?' Seeing her look of contempt, he added, with a touch of shame, 'I'm sorry. That was a stupid thing to say. Give me some money, will you? I'll need to take a cab, if the local man can't come.'

She went for her purse. He followed her and snatched it from her. 'I'll take the lot . . . you never know what you might need.'

She scarcely cared. Her mind numb from the shock of her discovery, she did not know what to do, or even to think. She tried to recall precisely what she had heard the previous night, but everything was blurred. There had been a thud, but could that have been Peter falling out of bed? Was Simon telling the truth?

Rose dressed and went back to Peter's room. She sat with him until Simon returned with the doctor, a stranger to her.

'This is Dr Forster,' Simon said, with exactly the right note of solicitude. 'He very kindly agreed to come out. Dr Raymond was on a call.'

'A sad business, a sad business,' the doctor said, going towards the bed. He sounded unduly perfunctory to Rose. She told herself dully that it was all in a day's work to a doctor, but all the same she wished that Simon had been able to find Dr Raymond, who knew Peter well.

'It would be better if you went into another room, Mrs Olivant,' he said, kindly enough. 'Less distressing all round, you know.'

Reluctantly, she obeyed. Simon remained. She went into the bedroom and waited. She supposed there would have to be an inquest, but she could not imagine the procedure to be undergone. Could she give evidence against her husband? She thought not. And if she could, if her faltering, confused account were accepted, what good would it do? Nothing could restore Peter to life, nothing could give her the chance she had yesterday, to take him away to safety. A great weariness overwhelmed her.

It was a long time before the doctor emerged from Peter's room. 'Ah, Mrs Olivant, I don't think we will need to put you through an inquest . . . a nasty thing, you know, a postmortem and so forth, the body cut to pieces, most relatives prefer to avoid it if they can. Rupture of a cerebral aneurysm, that would cover it quite satisfactorily, I think. A congenital weakness, you understand, no blame to anyone.' He paused, and added more gently, 'The little lad didn't suffer, you can be sure of that. He would have been gone in a moment.'

She did not argue. Nothing mattered any more. She just wanted to be left to suffer in peace. When the doctor had gone, Simon came back upstairs to where she still sat, staring unseeing at the window. He hesitated, watching her.

'It was the best way, you know. No point in washing a lot of dirty linen in public. I knew you would see sense. I don't mind telling you, this has shaken me up quite a bit. I never thought it would come to this . . . I never meant the little chap any harm, you know, not really . . .'

Her vague eyes suddenly focused on him. She began to understand what he was saying. 'How much did you have to pay him?' she asked, with a fierce contempt which she had never before felt for any human being.

'What do you mean?'

'That doctor. You bribed him to give you a death certificate. That's why you didn't get Dr Raymond. How did you hear of this quack? Is he well known for turning a blind eye to bruises that might need explaining at an inquest?'

'The boy fell out of bed. I told him that.'

'And he believed you . . . for a price.'

'Look, I've told you . . .' He stopped, his angry bluster frozen by her cold stare. 'I'm sorry, right? What else can I say? I really didn't mean any harm. I can't even remember exactly what happened, but I think I picked him up to put him back to bed, and he must have been screaming, the way he does . . . did,' he corrected himself, beneath her stony gaze. 'He annoyed me, wriggling and kicking, and I think I just threw him on to the bed, not knowing my own strength, and he hit his head against the wall. He stopped crying then, so I put him in the bed and tucked him in, and left him. As God's my witness, I never thought he was really hurt . . .'

'Do you think I care what you thought? Do you think I care about your excuses and your apologies?' She stopped, anger choking her.

'Look, things will be different from now on . . . I can see that it was the drink that made everything wrong. We can start again, Rosie, put it all behind us. If you'll help me, I can make a fresh start, we can have another child, that will make things easier for you . . .'

'Get out of my sight.'

'No need to be like that . . .'

She said nothing, but her look was enough. He shrugged, and with the best grace he could muster, went downstairs. She did not see him for the rest of the day. That night she heard him come in late, but he did not attempt to come up to the bedroom.

It was a pattern which was repeated during the two days before the funeral. Rose suspected that his restraint would then be at an end, and that when his son's body no longer remained in the house he would resume his normal demeanour and behaviour. She had no belief in his protestations of change, even though he might believe them himself. But once the funeral was over, it would scarcely matter.

At the end of the brief ceremony, Rose turned to her husband. 'I suppose you will want a drink, now that it is all over?' she asked.

He looked at her doubtfully. 'It was a bit of an ordeal. One or two drinks might help.'

'I'm sure they would,' she agreed. 'I will go home. Don't disturb me when you come in.'

In the house, she collected the few things of value remaining, and left. She went to the station, and bought a ticket for the next train: it was to Manchester, and to Manchester she went.

CHAPTER

Five

Mary Brunton died just over a week after Rose's visit. It was a harrowing time for Sarah. As her mother grew weaker in the last few days, the drugs she needed to dull her pain left her confused: she asked constantly for Rose, and would not be comforted by the explanations for her absence, however frequently Sarah repeated them. Sarah, the child who so closely resembled her, and who had never failed her mother for a moment, could now no longer console her. It was Rose, the errant, the impatient, whose presence the dying woman craved. Try as she might, Sarah could not suppress a sense of rejection when her mother yet again demanded that Rose be brought, and showed no sign of valuing her own devoted attention.

Two days before the end, Sarah sent a telegram to her sister, and was surprised to receive no response. She continued to hope that Rose might appear but even the second message, announcing Mary Brunton's death, went unanswered. She knew that Rose would not be able to attend the funeral, but she had expected some expression of grief and even of condolence for her own sufferings over the past days, as she nursed her mother through her last illness. As time passed and she heard nothing, the grudging thought formed in her mind: She got what she came for, that last time. She took everything; she doesn't care now.

Sarah could not quite silence that sly, mean suspicion. She had found Rose hard, self-absorbed, a stranger, but she would have forgotten all her disappointment if she had received a single word of sympathy after her mother's death. She heard nothing, and her resentment grew. She wrote to Rose; the letter was returned, marked 'Gone Away'. She wrote again, addressing the letter to the landlord, and received a note informing her that both Mr and Mrs Olivant had vacated the premises, giving no notice and owing a week's rent. Sarah settled the debt, and reconciled herself to the knowledge that she could do no more to contact Rose.

It was a difficult time for Sarah. The strain of nursing her mother had been considerable. Her father had remained remote and, although he tried to show the dying woman some consideration, he had none to spare for Sarah. The sacrifice she had made in remaining to nurse her mother went unremarked, a duty for the performance of which no appreciation was to be expected.

William Brunton drew no closer to Sarah in his loss. He gave no overt sign of grief, unless it was that he seemed even more preoccupied than usual during the time they spent together. In the relatively few evenings when her father dined at home, for the demands of his business had not slackened, the meal often passed in almost unbroken silence. If he went with her for a while into the drawing room he might pick up a newspaper and open it, but it soon lay unregarded on his knee as he stared into the fire, his severe, handsome face set in an expression of irritation, as though he were contemplating some baffling problem, some stubborn check to his will.

Once, to her amazement, he said suddenly, after a long silence, 'That Taylor fellow . . . do you still see him?'

'Why, no, Papa. How could I?'

'Go back to the Sunday school. Do you want to live and die an old maid?'

'But you made me stop going!' she said, stung to a tart rejoinder by the injustice of the rebuke.

'Your mother is dead now,' he said brutally. 'You have to make your own life . . . or do you expect to hang like a millstone round my neck for the rest of your days?'

Sarah got to her feet and left the room. The instinct to obey and respect her father was too deeply rooted for open rebellion, but her silent departure was the nearest approach that she could bring herself to make.

Despite the humiliating manner in which William Brunton had announced his apparent change of heart, Sarah determined to take him at his word, at least as regards returning to the teaching that she had always loved. Effie, who had taken on the class, had visited her far less often than she would have expected during her mother's illness. Even when, after two or three weeks, Sarah resumed her attendance at morning service, Effie seemed to be avoiding her as the congregation gathered outside the chapel for their usual exchanges of chat and news.

Philip, after a moment's hesitation, came to speak to her.

'I was sorry to hear about your mother, Sarah,' he said, with a perceptible pause before her name, as though he had considered and rejected a more formal style of address. She took some comfort from that, although his manner was stiff; clearly, he had not forgiven her.

'It was scarcely unexpected,' she said.

'It will take some getting used to, all the same.'

'I hardly know what to do with myself,' she said, encour-aged by his understanding, and by the greater warmth in his voice. 'I was thinking about taking up the Sunday school again, in a week or two, perhaps.'

'Why not?' He broke off as Effie, who had been moving closer, came to join them. 'Sarah is thinking of taking on her class again,' he explained.

'Oh, I don't think that would be a good idea,' Effie said sharply. 'The children are used to me now. Too many changes are bad for them. You can't expect to pick up where you left off, Sarah. There are other people to consider, you know.'

'But, Effie . . .' Sarah began, but Effie was already turning to Philip, a hand proprietorially on his sleeve.

'Do you have a copy of that map of the Holy Land that you were telling me about, Philip? I was thinking of using it this afternoon, but it would be helpful if you could just explain one or two points to me first. Geography was never my strong point.'

'Of course. It's at home, though.'

'We could walk along together, then,' Effie said, her hand slipping through his arm. 'You don't mind, do you, Sarah? I'm sure there are so many people that you want to see, and we don't have long before we need to be back for our classes, do we, Philip?'

Sarah stepped back, and let them pass. She thought she saw a look of apology on Philip's face, but the next moment Effie asked him some question that demanded his full attention; he inclined his head towards his companion and they strolled together to the gate, deep in conversation. Sarah was forgotten already.

The first few days after her arrival in Manchester were hardly real to Rose. While she had remained with Simon, necessity had forced her to keep her wits about her. She had held her agonising sense of loss at bay while she planned her flight. Once she had broken away from him, her sorrow engulfed her. She sought out lodgings; they were cheap but clean, in a poor area of the city, and there she gave herself up to her misery. Sick, wretched, she barely ate for two days, lying in a stupor from which she lacked the will to rouse herself.

Rose had no desire to live, yet some stubborn instinct for self-preservation drove her back to activity. On the third morning she grimly resumed the routines of ordinary existence: washing, eating, planning for the future. And yet, even as she marvelled at her own capacity to present a competent front to the world, she knew that something of herself had died with Peter. She took up the struggle to survive, all the more effectively, perhaps, for the new coldness that made no one in the world now of any significance to her, and yet she knew herself maimed.

All her life Rose had enjoyed vigorous good health; now it seemed to be failing her. A constant nausea made eating an ordeal; she felt a fatigue so great that even the simplest activity exhausted her. She wanted to seek reconciliation with her family, but the effort was beyond her. From day to day she put off the journey, flinching from its physical and emotional demands. She clung to the obscurity of life in the backstreets of Ancoats, where Simon would never find her, possessed by the unreasoning dread that he might be watching her family, awaiting the moment when she went to them for help.

It was a month before she gathered the strength to return to Warrington. She went from the station on foot through drizzling rain to her father's works. She had written to him, but had received no reply. She told herself that he could not have read the letter. No one, surely, could have ignored such a plea. Heartened by the belief that, if he could but hear her story, he would help her, she presented herself at his office.

*

Sarah was standing at the window, gazing down the drive. It was a damp afternoon. Rain was dripping off the leaves of the shrubs in front of the house. Sarah watched it with a blank absorption new to her, whose life had scarcely known an idle or unproductive moment. In the last few months she had often longed for time to herself. Now she had it in abundance, yet she did nothing.

She sighed, and gently rubbed away the moisture clouding the glass. She should do something, anything. It was too wet to go out and where, after all, could she go? Effie would not welcome a visit, she was sure. The unsatisfactory outcome to her attempt to return to her teaching had disheartened Sarah, and she had not yet tried to pick up the threads of her other church activities. Everything was such an effort. It was easier to stay at home, and watch the rain running like slow tears down the pane.

A movement caught her eye. Someone was coming up the drive. The light was poor. Sarah could only make out a vague blur: a woman. Effie? She hurried to the looking glass, wishing that she had taken more care with her appearance that morning. Once, she would not have cared how she looked before Effie, but the old ease between them had gone for ever.

She turned guiltily as the door opened, expecting to see Effie, too old a friend to stand on ceremony. 'Oh, Betty!' she said, surprised to see the maid instead.

Betty seemed nervous. She said in a low voice, 'I don't know what to do. That's Miss Rose at the door, asking for you. I said I'd see if you were at home.'

'Rose?' Sarah looked at the clock. It was only half past three. Her father would not be home for several hours. 'Show her in, please, Betty . . . and bring up some tea, will you? She will be glad of something, especially on a day like this.'

Only when the maid had gone did it occur to Sarah

that she should also have asked her to bring milk, for she supposed Peter would be with his mother. She smiled at the thought of seeing him again, and was still smiling when the door opened to reveal her sister, alone. Her face fell. 'Where's Peter?' she asked, peering into the gloom of the hall to see if he was hanging back, overcome with shyness.

'I'm on my own,' Rose said harshly.

'Oh . . . I was looking forward to seeing him.'

Rose said nothing. She came forward to the fire, hands stretched out to it greedily, as though she could not get enough of its warmth. Betty must have taken her soaked outer clothing, but even her skirt was wet through, its hem sodden and splashed with mud to a depth of almost a foot.

'Would you like some dry clothes?' Sarah asked, moved with pity.

'Yours would scarcely fit me.'

'You are so thin now that some of Mama's things might do.'

'She died, I suppose?'

Rose's indifferent tone shocked Sarah. 'The week after you saw her. I sent you word when she was failing. She longed to see you again: she spoke of nothing else. I wrote to tell you about the funeral, too, but you must have moved house by then. Could you not have left a forwarding address?' she added, with a touch of asperity.

'No. I had to get away from Simon. He must not know where I am.'

'So things are no better, then?' Sarah intended to sound sympathetic, but her voice conveyed a hint of the impatience she felt at Rose's never-ending troubles from which she supposed that she was to provide salvation, as usual.

Rose stretched out her bedraggled skirt to the blaze. She said without turning, 'Peter is dead. Simon handled him roughly. I don't think he meant to kill him but he was drunk. I never want to see him again. No, things are no better.'

'Peter is dead?' It was the only thing Sarah had taken in, the only thing she cared about.

'Soon after we were here. Simon threw him into bed. His head must have hit the wall. Simon said that he must have fallen out of bed, and that was how he hurt himself. Perhaps it was. I don't know. It's all one, anyway.'

'Couldn't you have done something? Weren't you there?'

'Yes, I was there. If I had been able to stop it, don't you think I would have? You can't imagine what it was like. You don't know . . .'

'No, I don't.'

There should have been a bond of shared grief between them, and perhaps they both in their innermost hearts felt its lack and longed for its comfort, but they had moved too far apart. An oppressive silence filled the space between them, heavy with the thoughts and experiences that could not be communicated.

'What does she know about life?' Rose asked herself bitterly. *'What right does she have to look at me like that, as though she blames me?'*

'Surely she could have done something to save him?' Sarah thought. *'Not a tear. I wonder if she really cares at all.'*

'I went to see Papa,' Rose said dully. 'He wasn't at the works; he'd gone to Liverpool for the day, they said.'

'He seems to spend a lot of his time there these days. What did you want from him?'

Rose turned sharply, studying her sister's face. 'That's a strange question. You've changed, Sarah.'

'I'm not such a fool now: is that what you mean?'

'I mean that once you would have understood without asking that I wanted to be reconciled to Papa.'

'Oh? And you didn't expect to get anything else out of it?'

Rose frowned, drawing herself a little more erect. 'Of course I need help. Where else should I turn?'

The frustration, the resentment of years of dutiful, unappreciated self-sacrifice bore Sarah away on an uncontrollable wave of reckless anger. She found herself saying all the things that for so long she had barely allowed herself to think. 'That's the only reason you ever come here, isn't it? To get something! You ran away and did what you wanted, you didn't care about Mama or me or anybody. You left me to bear it all, to look after Mama and ruin my life, and now you come here looking for pity because things haven't worked out the way you expected, although anybody could have seen what would happen. You despised us all, and the decent, boring life we lead, but you aren't too proud to expect us to rescue you from the mess you've made of your own life, time and time again. You'll take whatever you can get, as usual, like the last time . . .'

'What do you mean?'

'Mama's jewels. Do you think I don't know?'

'Mama gave me a few things, yes.'

'A few things? There was nothing left, *nothing*! I haven't got so much as a locket, a brooch to wear that was hers!'

'She knew how badly I needed them, that's all.'

'Didn't I need something to remember her by?'

'I needed it to *live*!'

'You chose that life! Nobody forced you to break Mama's heart by running away – she was never the same again, never!'

Rose's lips tightened. 'You've waited for years for this, haven't you? I thought I could look to you for help, sympathy, but all you want to do is preach at me! You know perfectly well that I have wanted to be reconciled with Papa from the very first. It's not my fault if I haven't been able to help you with Mama, so you needn't blame me for ruining your life . . . what else would you have been doing with it, anyway?'

Sarah's hand rose to her heart. The cruel, unjust taunt struck her like a blow. Not for worlds would she have explained about Philip. 'What can I do with my life, when you have left me to bear all the burdens here alone?' She drew a deep, unsteady breath. 'I think you should leave.'

'I think I should have known better than ever to have come.'

As Rose moved to the door, a gaunt, shabby figure, Sarah was struck by reluctant compassion. 'Wait a minute. I'll see what money there is in the house. I am in charge of the housekeeping now . . . I'll get whatever I can.'

Rose stopped and slowly turned. She regarded her bleakly, with no trace of gratitude. 'Believe me, I would refuse it if I could. I would sooner beg in the streets than enter this house again.'

Rose left soon afterwards, bearing a small sum in cash and a parcel of food and clothing, hurriedly put together by Sarah. Although Sarah made no apology, Rose could tell from her manner that she hated to part on such bad terms and that a single word from her would be enough to bring about some reconciliation. She did not speak it.

Sarah's hostility had taken Rose by surprise, much as if a familiar household pet, docile and disregarded, had suddenly savaged her. From infancy Rose had looked down on her slower, less daring sister, feeling herself to be Sarah's superior in almost every respect. To be thwarted by her now shocked and angered her.

The causes of her sister's animosity were hidden from Rose. Seeing only Sarah's comfortable life, in which violence, drunkenness, squalor and anxiety about money were inconceivable, Rose could not imagine the daily round of empty, thankless duty that constricted her older sister, far less the sacrifice that had been demanded of her. Burdened by her own troubles, she had no energy to spare to seek to understand Sarah's.

Darkness had fallen before Rose reached her lodgings, so tired that she could barely put one foot before another. Her room was on the first floor and was reached through the kitchen. The landlady, Mrs Heeney, was sitting by the fire, a pile of darning by her side, a sock stretched over one hand as she mended it with the other. She looked up as Rose entered.

'You look as if you're about ready to drop,' she said, leaning over and pushing the kettle on to the hob. 'Get the weight off your feet and take a dish of tea with me. The children are all up in bed and I was feeling like a bit of company.'

Rose hesitated, but the prospect of going up alone to her own chill, bare room was not tempting. Mrs Heeney, a widow in her early thirties, with three young children still at home, was always kind to her and Rose had learned the wisdom of remaining on good terms with landladies and shopkeepers. She accepted the offer with a weary smile.

'You must let me do some of that mending for you,' she said, sitting down. 'I used to hate any kind of sewing but I have grown quite good at it over the years.'

'Well, there's plenty to choose from,' Mrs Heeney said, putting the basket between them. She looked at Rose shrewdly. 'A hard day?'

Rose stared into the fire. She had not yet told the landlady anything of her past, too proud to risk becoming the subject of gossip in the streets and courts where the women, standing in their doorways, idled away their few spare minutes in talk of their neighbours. But Mrs Heeney seemed a decent woman and after Sarah's harshness Rose's desire for sympathy was overwhelming. Slowly, she began to talk, and without intending it found herself explaining the whole tragedy of her marriage, and Peter's death.

'I don't know what I am to do,' she concluded. 'I have money enough to last me for several months but after that what will happen?'

Mrs Heeney refilled Rose's cup. 'You'll need to get a place, that's all.'

'A place?'

'As a servant.'

'Oh, but I . . .' Rose began to protest, but stopped. She was not, after all, in a position to object to such a prospect, despite her instinctive horror at the idea. 'I have no experience, no references. I don't think it would be possible.'

'I don't know about that. Miss Rathbone, who used to be the housekeeper for the priests at St Columba's, has had to give up; she's just destroyed with rheumatics, poor woman. She's gone to live with her niece over in Miles Platting and she's looking for a cook-general. I helped her out with cleaning now and again. I could put in a good word for you.'

'I don't know . . .'

'She's a good soul, fussy but a kind heart underneath. It's a nice, quiet household and nobody to bother you.'

Rose sighed. 'I would be very grateful,' she said, and tried to mean it.

Mrs Heeney's advocacy was successful in obtaining an interview for Rose. It was conducted by Miss Rathbone; her niece, Miss Porter, was a pale, nervous-looking woman a little older than Rose, who said not a word throughout. Miss Rathbone herself was a small, elderly lady with a row of precise brown curls displayed beneath her cap. It was an improbably youthful display in someone whose body was so tortured by rheumatism that her hands could barely hold a teacup but, as Rose soon realised, Miss Rathbone was a stickler for keeping up appearances.

'Under normal circumstances, of course, we would not

consider employing a servant without the very *highest* references,' she said, with a glance at her niece, who made a vague murmur of assent. 'Two women living alone cannot be too careful. An unsatisfactory servant can bring a breath of scandal to the most virtuous household. There must be no followers, you understand? There could be no likelihood of your husband presenting himself?'

'There would be no question of it,' Rose said, with a touch of hauteur.

'Well . . . And you are a good plain cook? You can bake? My niece is not strong; there is very little entertaining here, but we often have friends over to afternoon tea.'

'I am particularly fond of baking, Miss Rathbone.'

'Very well.' Miss Rathbone pursed her lips. 'A month's trial. Eighteen pounds a year, all found.' As Rose barely restrained a gasp of dismay, she added sharply, 'Is that not acceptable?'

'No . . . I mean, yes, Miss Rathbone,' Rose said hurriedly.

'Ma'am, if you would.'

It was said kindly enough, but Rose coloured at the reminder of her status. Even in the days of her worst poverty with Simon, she had never felt so keenly the gulf separating her from her origins.

Rose began work the following week, having provided herself with the necessary uniform: caps and aprons, print cotton gowns for kitchen work and plain black for other duties. With Mrs Heeney's assistance she was able to make most of the garments herself, but it still required an alarming outlay.

There was a lot to learn, particularly as Miss Rathbone had very decided views on the correct way to carry out almost every procedure. Rose could not help but feel a secret relief that her rheumatism prevented her from interfering in the running of the house still more. Miss Porter was far more lenient and often saved Rose from difficulties by a quiet word of warning when she saw her in danger of incurring her aunt's displeasure by some innocent mistake.

The work was tiring, particularly in the early days, but this in itself was not a hardship to Rose. She enjoyed the chance to cook in a well-equipped kitchen, trying out once more the recipes remembered as best she could from her days at home. Even the hard physical toil had its compensations. It brought some escape from tormenting memories and she was at least sure of sinking at once into the oblivion of sleep at the end of an exhausting day.

Far worse was the constant awareness that she had lost her freedom, that she was obliged to submit herself to the will of her employers, however trivial or irritating their requests might be. To Rose, obedience was not easy. Both the ladies she was serving were kind, and framed their orders courteously, but nothing could conceal the under-lying truth that Rose was in the position of an inferior to them. She often had to bite back some sharp response, and remind herself that she was no longer anything but Rose, the cook-general.

The month passed satisfactorily and Rose was kept on. Her immediate future now secure, she should have been able to enjoy a period of relative tranquillity, but for a new fear. The nausea that had seemed natural to her in the first terrible days after Peter's death had never quite left her. Now, as other symptoms were added to it, a suspicion she hardly dared contemplate began to haunt her. She hoped desperately that she was worrying unnecessarily and that everything could be explained by the agony of mind she had undergone. She tried to ignore her fears and certainly, after another month or so, the nausea subsided. She greeted the improvement with relief, and told herself that it was only to be expected that her better appetite and the

plentiful food now available should result in some increase
in her weight, so that her new gowns were showing signs
of tightness at the bust and waist. She tried to deny what
every day became more evident.

At last, after a frank question from Mrs Heeney, whom
she still visited almost every week, Rose summoned the
courage to consult a doctor on her next free afternoon and
establish the truth. Mrs Heeney was awaiting her afterwards, as Rose had promised to call in for tea as usual on
her way home from the surgery. The older woman took
one look at her face and turned to her oldest daughter. 'Be
a good lass and take Micky and the baby out for half an
hour, will you, Jessie?' The girl nodded and obeyed. 'Sit
yourself down, love,' Mrs Heeney told Rose. 'You're just as
white as a ghost. It was what we thought then?'

Rose nodded, still almost too shocked for speech.

'Did he say how far gone you are, now?'

'About three months, he thought.' Rose had begged him
to be more precise but the doctor had refused to commit
himself. The question had a significance he could not have
suspected. Rose clung desperately to the recollection of
the nausea that had beset her on the last day of Peter's life.
Better to believe that she had already been pregnant then,
rather than face the birth of a child conceived in drunken
violence.

'Things will work out, you'll see,' Mrs Heeney said.
'They always do, one way or another.' From a widow who
had lost two children in the first year of life and now
supported herself and three others by letting a room and
charring, this was no facile optimism.

'I don't know what I can do now,' Rose said hopelessly.
'I was thinking I could stay at Miss Rathbone's for a good
while, but this . . .'

'Keep your mouth shut for now,' Mrs Heeney advised.
'You'll get away with it for another couple of months if

you're careful, more perhaps. Miss Rathbone doesn't see so well and that niece of hers hasn't much idea. You'd not be the first to give birth in the scullery while the mistress of the house is asleep in her bed, none the wiser of it.'

'And then what?' Rose asked. 'Anyway, it doesn't seem right to deceive her. She's been good to me in her way.'

'Well, I'll tell you this: once she knows you'll be out the door. She'll not tolerate it.'

'You're probably right,' Rose said despondently.

'Sup your tea, now . . . and I've a nice bit of ham for you. You'll need to be keeping your strength up.'

'You shouldn't be spending your money on me,' Rose protested.

'My brother in Canada sent me a pound or two,' Mrs Heeney said, putting the plate before her. 'He's doing well out there. I don't know where we'd have been without our Jim, these last few years.'

Although she had no appetite, Rose made an attempt to eat. She had discovered how useless it was to try to stop Mrs Heeney from feeding her, even though she was able to eat her fill at Miss Rathbone's. As she struggled to finish the food, she became aware that the older woman was unusually silent.

'Is something wrong?' she asked. 'Are the children all right?'

'Oh yes . . .' Mrs Heeney said vaguely, pouring herself another cup of tea and sitting down.

'But there is something?'

She looked doubtfully at Rose. 'I don't know what to do for the best, and that's the truth. I'd made sure I was going to tell you, but seeing you in such a taking I'm thinking that it would maybe be as well to wait . . .'

'Well, you'll have to tell me now,' Rose said, forcing a smile. 'I'll be imagining all sorts of dreadful things if you don't.'

'You wouldn't be so far out, at that. Here, have a look at this. It was wrapped round a few carrots I got from a barrow and the name just caught my eye as I was smoothing it out.'

Rose took from her the sheet of newspaper, dirty and raggedly torn at the edges, which she produced from a drawer in the kitchen table. Mrs Heeney pointed out a short column:

MYSTERY BODY FOUND AT WALLASEY

The body of a young man was recovered from sandbanks at the mouth of the River Mersey yesterday. It is thought that the corpse had been in the water for too long a period to allow of any positive identification. Such clothing as remained was of good quality: a fine gold hunter was found, inscribed with the motto *Sed fugit interea, fugit irreparabile tempus* and the name Simon James Olivant . . .

Rose read the passage over and over again, scarcely comprehending its meaning.

'There now, I knew I shouldn't have told you. You look about ready to faint clean away . . . will I just run and fetch you a drop of brandy?'

Rose shook her head. 'It's just the shock. I shall be perfectly well in a moment.'

'Is it your master, do you think?'

Rose gazed at her blankly. The commonplace local expression had for her a grim connotation. 'He was,' she said, thinking of the years when she had tried so hard to please her spoilt, handsome husband. 'Not another man ever will be, I know that.'

Even to Mrs Heeney she could not admit how great a relief she felt at the news. If her isolation from her family was now complete, she was also free from the fear that had dogged her every time she set foot in the streets, that Simon might suddenly appear. As the first shock receded, she felt a new determination, a grim resolve that, depending only on her own resources, she would make a new life for herself and the coming child. Not for a moment did she consider another appeal to her father. For the first time, she would stand alone.

In the meantime, Rose did not tell Miss Rathbone of her condition. Already a harsh realism was governing her actions: in the struggle to survive, her desire to be honest with her employer was secondary to the need to make some suitable provision for the future. Every week, on her afternoon out, she went to Mrs Heeney and, as she sewed the little gowns and napkins that she dared not work at Miss Rathbone's, she would discuss the possibilities open to her.

'A shop is what you should be thinking of,' Mrs Heeney advised. 'That's the best for a widow woman with a family to keep. If you carry on in service, you'll never see the child for weeks on end.'

At first Rose rejected the suggestion, doubting her ability to manage a business on however small a scale. Still, the idea took root, offering as it did independence and financial security. She began to look about her, to chat to shopkeepers, to make plans.

At Mrs Heeney's urging, she went to see a little shop in Ancoats, not far from the goods station. Mrs Heeney had heard that the present shopkeeper, Joseph Cummings, was desperate to make a quick sale, and would not hold out for a high price. Rose looked around the cramped room, taking in the dust lying thickly on the tinned milk on the shelf behind the counter, the vague but pervasive smell of something rotting somewhere, the shopkeeper's air of defeat, barely concealed by a determined cheerfulness.

'*How* much did you say you take a week?' she asked,

although she remembered perfectly the amount Joseph Cummings had claimed to be making.

He hesitated, and shrugged. 'Three to four pounds . . . a good three, you could say.'

Rose nodded. 'So if we say three; the asking price is usually ten times the weekly takings, isn't it? Thirty pounds, then?'

His shoulders sagged in resignation. He had been asking for forty. They both knew he had been hoping that, young and inexperienced, Rose would not read the telltale smell of failure clinging to the shop like the insidious smell that was turning her stomach. The past few weeks, surveying just such establishments, seeking the best compromise between her limited resources and her exacting standards, had taught Rose many lessons. She was now well able to assess this struggling business at its true value.

Rose went to the door and gazed out over the street. At the beginning of her search she would have dismissed Cummings' shop as she had so many others in the tightly packed streets dominated by marshalling yards and canal, by chemical and iron works, by dye factories, the river and the workhouse. It was dismal, with little natural light, but the surrounding streets were relatively prosperous. Most important of all, she was sure that she could get it cheap.

'It's not bad round here,' Joseph Cummings put in tentatively. 'We've got some good customers . . . course, there's always some that need watching, but you soon get to know them . . .' He faltered into silence, afraid that he might have put her off.

'Why are you leaving?'

'The air doesn't seem to suit the missis. She says it's the rubber works. The smell doesn't bother most folk but she notices it more, being country bred.'

Rose didn't believe him. More likely they were abandoning the struggle to scratch a living from the slow accumulation of pennies, halfpence and even farthings that would form the bulk of its sales. She turned back to him, feeling a flicker of pity mingled with contempt. He was a poor thing, after all. Small, balding, with an anxious, cringing smile, he looked like an eternal failure. She was sure that she could do better.

'How would you want the purchase money?' she asked, and saw his eyes light with relief. As she had thought, he was desperate to be rid of the shop. The knowledge gave her bargaining power.

'Oh, cash on the nail. It's the safest way, I always think, especially if we are going to settle for thirty pounds.'

It was the answer she had been dreading. She frowned. 'I'm not sure. It's a lot of money to find all at once . . .'

He sighed, and she knew that he was weakening. He needed the sale too badly to hold out for the conditions he really wanted. Rose could almost have felt sorry for him. 'How much could you put down, then?'

She pretended to calculate, although she already knew. She had had her mother's remaining jewellery valued. It should fetch sixty pounds. From that she must pay for the cost of her confinement and of restocking the shop, as well as the purchase price. 'Fifteen pounds,' she said boldly.

'That's only half!' he protested, and she knew that she had gone too far. He might have accepted twenty, but now his pride was up. 'For all I know we'd never see the rest. Oh, I can't have that. Twenty-five at least, and the rest within three months.'

She hesitated but her instinct told her that he had reached his limit. 'I will think about it,' she said, turning away.

'Well, don't take too long,' he said, with unexpected spirit. 'It may go to someone else in the meantime . . . someone who has actually got the money to pay.'

As she began the long walk back to Miss Rathbone's,

Rose looked about her in distaste. The desire to support herself and the coming child, the need to find cheap premises, made Ancoats convenient for her to live in, but she did not intend to remain there. She meant to succeed. Money could be relied upon in a way that human beings could not. The love that she had once valued so highly had proved a mirage; the child she had adored had been taken from her. She had sacrificed everything for love; she would do as much for her new god.

She walked slowly, debating what she should do. She sensed that it would be difficult to find another shop with such potential and at such a low price. What was more, in some way she could not define she felt that this was the place for her, and yet she was reluctant to commit so much of her precious resources to the purchase of its lease. It would be a gamble, and with her new sense of isolation she was well aware that there would be no one to come to her rescue if she failed.

She reached Miles Platting tired and a little later than she had intended. She went at once to the kitchen, and was making the preparations for supper when the bell summoned her to the parlour. Miss Rathbone was alone, and Rose saw at once that she was in a state of barely controlled agitation.

'Come in, Rose. My niece has gone out to see poor Miss Evans. She won't be back for half an hour or more. We won't be disturbed.'

'No, ma'am,' Rose said, puzzled by such a reception.

'I had a visit from Mrs Connor this afternoon. She had something most distressing to report to me. Of course I told her that she was mistaken, but all the same I must ask you . . . I mean no offence, my dear, but are you with child?'

Rose gazed at her. A lie would win another few weeks, but explicit denial was beyond her. 'Yes, I am.'

'Rose! I would never have thought you would deceive us in this fashion,' Miss Rathbone said, more grieved than angry, it seemed.

'I didn't know when I took this place. I'm sorry. I was going to tell you soon, but I was so happy here that I wanted to stay as long as I could.'

Miss Rathbone shook her head sorrowfully. 'You will have to leave us at once, of course.'

'At once? You mean tomorrow? The end of the week?'

'I mean this minute.'

'This minute? May I not get your supper for you?' Rose said in disbelief. 'I am a widow, this child is my husband's, there is nothing shameful in the circumstances . . .'

'Who else knows that but you, my dear? People talk, and they don't always care whether what they say is true. My niece's reputation will suffer if any breath of scandal attaches to the household. Go and pack your things, please. I am sorry that you are leaving us. In time I think you could have got into our ways very nicely.'

The old lady's very lack of rancour convinced Rose that it was useless to try to persuade her. She spoke as calmly as if Rose's departure were as inevitable as the operation of the law of gravity, and as inexorable. Rose collected her few things together and, within twenty minutes, had left the house.

That night she spent at Mrs Heeney's, sharing a bed with her oldest daughter. She was made welcome but her old room was now let to two sisters who worked in a nearby mill and Rose knew that she could not stay there for very long. The next day she went again to Joseph Cummings and accepted his terms.

On her return to Mrs Heeney's she found her old landlady in a state of some excitement. 'You'll never guess who's been here!' she said, as Rose entered the kitchen. 'Only Miss Porter!'

'Why did she come?'

'To give you this.' Mrs Heeney handed her an envelope bearing Rose's name. 'She didn't stop above a minute, but she said as she was very sorry you had to leave them and she wished you well.'

Rose opened the letter. It contained a few kind words, and ten pounds. Rose felt a lifting of the anxiety that had clouded her spirits since committing herself to the new undertaking. It was, she was sure, a good omen.

CHAPTER

Six

Sarah was deeply disturbed by Rose's visit. Her own rage shocked her; she had never believed that she was capable of such fury, a physical as well as emotional outburst that had swept away all the restraints of her mild nature and loving ideals. Even in infancy she doubted whether she had given way to such searing anger.

After some reflection, she resolved to tell her father that Rose had visited the house and that she was in need of help. He received the news without apparent emotion and without question or comment. As so often these days, Sarah was left with an uneasy sense that other preoccupations were filling his mind and that even Rose's predicament could no longer touch him.

Little by little, Sarah resumed her former life as best she could, although she had abandoned any hope of taking over her class again from Effie's determined grip. Their friendship seemed to have ended. Philip Taylor still spoke to Sarah whenever they met, and if their conversation lasted more than a few minutes Sarah thought she could detect the beginnings of some return to their former understanding, but if Effie was in the vicinity she always took good care to intervene swiftly and prevent any lengthy tête-à-tête between them.

Some four months after her mother's death, Sarah was surprised by a visit from Josiah Ramage, the superintendent at the Sunday school.

'I won't keep you long, Miss Brunton,' he began. 'I was wondering if you would be willing to help us out with your old class for the next week or two.'

'I would be delighted,' she said in surprise. 'Is Miss Shaw not able to teach?'

Josiah Ramage cleared his throat. 'Miss Shaw is engaged on a work of mercy. She is nursing one of our teachers through a most serious illness . . . pneumonia, I believe.'

'Oh? Who?' Sarah asked, although she could guess the answer.

'Mr Taylor,' he said, with an unconvincing smile. 'He has no family here, you know. Miss Shaw offered her services as soon as she became aware of his situation . . . an example to us all.'

'She certainly is,' Sarah said, rising, her one desire to put an end to the interview. 'You may rely on me to take her class. I should be grateful if you would let me know if you hear any further news of Mr Taylor.'

'To be sure, to be sure . . . If anyone can help him to pull through, it will be Miss Shaw.'

Sarah's thoughts were bitter. It should have been she who claimed the right to nurse Philip; instead, she had heard of his illness only by chance. She considered going to offer her help, but her pride rebelled. She could imagine Effie's response. Instead, she wrote a brief note to Philip, sending her best wishes for his speedy recovery and asking if there was anything she could do or send to help. As she had half expected, she received a reply from Effie, thanking her on Philip's behalf but assuring her that there was nothing she could usefully contribute.

Over the next few weeks Sarah heard reports on Philip's condition from various friends. He was soon out of danger but remained weak. Effie did not return to the Sunday school. Most people spoke highly of her self-sacrifice, but a few of the older members of the congregation were clearly doubtful of the propriety of an unmarried woman taking on the task of nursing a man to whom she was unrelated. Sarah never encouraged such comments. She admired, even while she distrusted, Effie's boldness.

A month after Ramage's visit, as Sarah was preparing to go into town to make one or two purchases, Betty came in search of her.

'Oh, Betty . . . is that the carriage round already?'

'No, miss,' the maid said, so nervously that Sarah turned round swiftly.

'Betty? Is something wrong?'

'No . . . but that's Mr Taylor to see you.'

'Philip?' she said, her heart lurching in the old, painful way.

'I said I would see if you were at home.'

'Yes, that was quite right,' she said absently. Why had he come? She would have said that he would never consent to enter the house again, after her father's contemptuous dismissal. A hope which only a few minutes before she would have believed quite dead stirred to tremulous life. She glanced back at the glass, seeking a reassurance which was now of still greater importance.

'I will come down at once, Betty,' she said. 'Oh, and tell John not to bring the carriage round quite yet.'

As she entered the parlour Sarah caught a glimpse of Philip in the instant before he saw her. He was standing near the fireplace, staring at the worked firescreen which shielded the empty grate. His chin sunk forward on his chest, he was frowning. The marks of his recent illness were plain to see; his face was still pale and gaunt, his clothes hung loosely on him.

Something in his attitude alarmed her; he seemed to be meditating upon some unpleasant task. The fear vanished almost before she had acknowledged it, for as she stepped forward and spoke his name his face lit with the joy of recognition.

'Sarah!' He came towards her, hand outstretched. 'It's good of you to see me.'

'I was delighted to hear that you had come. I hope you really are well enough to be out . . . Sit down, please!'

'I am interrupting you, though.'

'Not at all. I was going to go into Warrington but it really doesn't matter. Shall I send for tea?'

'Thank you, but I can't stay. I won't keep you for long. Only I thought it was right that you should be the first to know . . .'

He paused, reluctant to deliver the blow that her aching heart had already anticipated. 'Effie has accepted me. The wedding is to be in the spring.'

'I am very glad for you both,' she managed to say, all her energy concentrated on the terrible struggle to maintain her composure and conceal from him any hint of the hopes with which she had heard of his visit. Already she looked back on that self of five minutes ago as foolishly, pitiably naïve to have imagined even for a second that he could have come back to her. And yet she thought she saw even now in his face regret, a plea for forgiveness.

'I owed her such a lot. She insisted on helping me when I was ill, even though she knew that people would talk. She sacrificed a great deal for me.'

And I didn't, Sarah thought bitterly. *But it wasn't so easy; Effie is free. I wasn't.* She said nothing, but she was sure that the unspoken comparison was in both their minds.

Philip cleared his throat. 'Now that it's settled, perhaps Effie could drop in and see you? I know she's often wondered how you and your father are getting on.'

'Very kind of her,' Sarah said, with a flash of acerbity. 'I think I'd sooner she didn't.'

'Well, not at first, perhaps,' he agreed.

There was an uneasy silence, weighted with the burden of loss, guilt, regret and, perhaps, love. They stood without moving, neither, it seemed, wishing to break off this last unsatisfactory contact. She wondered what would happen, even now, if she were to reach out and touch him, but it was impossible, a sin even to imagine.

She stepped back. 'Thank you for coming to tell me yourself. I don't suppose it was easy.'

'It was the least I could do.'

Slowly, as though the movement of every muscle had to be consciously controlled, she stretched out her hand to the bell and rang for Betty. She let the maid show him out.

Rose was eager to move into the new premises at once. With the craving for financial security which increasingly dominated her thoughts, time spent idle, eating into her limited resources, was a torment to her.

She threw herself into her new venture with grim determination. The Cummings had clearly lost heart many months before, as the grimy condition of both the shop and the living quarters amply testified. For two days, Rose kept the shop closed and, with the help of a girl, Kathleen Forry, hired on Mrs Heeney's recommendation, began to scour the place as it evidently had not been scoured in a long time. She scrubbed and mopped, as if she was erasing all the humiliations of the past four years. Nothing could disguise the shabby oilcloth on the floor or the ramshackle carpentry of the counter and shelves, but when she stopped working, not long before midnight, she at least had the satisfaction of knowing that the shop could not have been cleaner.

The Cummings had left her such stock as remained, a

depressing collection of rusting tins, damp remnants of sacks of flour, musty broken biscuits and the like. With the money remaining to her she placed generous orders with the salesmen who visited the shop every week, and soon the shelves were sagging beneath the weight of new stock.

The first few months of her career as shopkeeper demanded all Rose's determination simply to survive, far less make a profit. Like all the small groceries in the area, the shop was expected to be open from early morning until eleven at night. Although the surrounding streets were relatively prosperous by Ancoats standards, most families were still barely able to manage, unless they were in the fortunate position of having several older children at work, to supplement their parents' earnings. Few were able to live on a single wage, and rare were the households without at least some clothing in the pawnshop, 'Uncle's', by Monday night.

The consequences for Rose were predictable. Not only were most purchases small in quantity and value, but requests for credit were incessant. The circumstances of many of those seeking 'tick' were tragic, but from the first Rose hardened her heart to even the most pitiable cases. She gave credit, for much of her trade depended upon it, but her sole criterion was the customer's ability to settle the debt at the end of the week. If ever her conscience smote her, when she turned away some mother, infant in arms, who claimed, no doubt truthfully, not to have eaten all day, she reminded herself grimly that she was in business, not a charity. If she failed, through letting her heart over-rule her head, she would soon be in the same position herself.

Rose had begun her business out of necessity but she soon found in it an overwhelming interest. Hard-working, disciplined, she immersed herself in its every detail, seeking escape from the past as much as a way into the future.

Her confinement was almost a week later than Rose had expected, as though the child had been waiting for everything to be ready for its arrival. Labour was brief and uncomplicated, even though the baby, a girl, was much bigger than Peter had been.

The child, whom she named Eva, could not have been more different from him. Peter had been frail and listless, Eva was sturdy, noisy, greedy. He had needed to be coaxed to suckle; she demanded the breast, kneading and pummelling Rose's flesh with her dimpled fist if her hunger was not satisfied. Her appetite was alarming. She grew fatter and stronger every day, and every day her face, opening out from the closed compactness of the newborn infant, reminded Rose more strongly of Simon.

From the first, Rose regarded her daughter with a more complex mixture of emotions than the passionate, protective love that Peter's weakness had inspired. Whenever the little girl's features, drawn down into an imperious scowl at some check to her infant will, recalled Simon's selfish obstinacy, Rose remembered the act of violence which might have given her life. She told herself that the child was not to blame either for her father's faults or the possible circumstances of her conception, but unqualified love for her daughter did not come easily. She dared not give her whole heart again to a child, after the devastating loss she had suffered.

To make up for the spontaneous affection she could not feel, Rose set herself grimly to creating the very best material conditions for Eva. Although she took no pleasure in suckling her she dutifully persevered with nursing the baby herself, as the safest means of feeding the child. Many of the mothers in the area, particularly those who were obliged to work long hours in the mills, fed their babies almost exclusively on condensed milk. Rose stocked the milk, one of her best sellers, but she was well aware of the frequent bouts of diarrhoea which such infants suffered, particularly in summer. The loss of a child to such ailments was commonplace. Her daughter was not to be subjected to such hazards. Eva should have the best start in life that she could provide.

Apart from feeding Eva, Rose had little daily contact with her daughter, given the long hours she worked in the shop. Kathleen Forry would have been quite capable of serving in the shop but Rose preferred to manage alone, and leave the baby with the servant. She told herself that the business demanded her presence, but in fact she was glad to escape from the demands of the child. Eva soon became so attached to Kathleen that she looked to her, not her mother, for comfort when she was distressed. Her devotion to her attendant was further reason to leave Eva to her care, but it did nothing to improve Rose's relationship with her daughter.

When all was going in her favour, Eva was a cheerful, good-natured baby who smiled readily at the customers whenever she was brought into the shop. Her rosy, plump health and friendly nature made her a general favourite. As she grew bigger she was happy to be trusted to the care of the motherly little girls in the street who, unlike richer children, played with real babies instead of dolls. When Kathleen had to get on with other duties, there was never any shortage of nursemaids for Eva.

Engrossed in the concerns of the shop, Rose did not intervene, but she hated to see her daughter playing un-concernedly with the other children on the pavement, her pinafore soon as dirty as theirs. She had no intention of allowing Eva to grow up as a slum child.

However glad Rose was of the relative security of her present position, she was not reconciled to living in the crowded terraces of Ancoats, where the day was governed by the rhythms of factory and mill, by the regular migrations of the workers to and from home early in the morning, at dinner time and at the end of their shift, by the knocker-up's pole and the whistles and hooters of the local works. She loathed the dirt and soot of the district, with its heavy concentration of industry and railways, where washing hung out to dry was almost instantly covered with smuts and every street had its distinctive smell, depending on the nature of the nearest factory and the proximity of the river or canal.

With a fervour which others might have reserved for a religious ideal, Rose came to hunger for a house such as she had in her youth fled so eagerly, for a garden and flowers instead of cobbles, for the discreet self-containment of a substantial detached residence set in its own grounds, and not the enforced intimacy of a terraced dwelling with thin walls, in which she was kept awake at night by the shouts of one drunken neighbour or the noisy lovemaking of another. She, who had once thrown away security, comfort, respectability, on a mere whim, as it now seemed to her, craved the solidity of mahogany furniture, the rich heaviness of velvet curtains, the opulence of marble and brass, of ornate cornices and thick carpets. All her early naïveté sloughed away, she longed to return to a way of life that had once seemed to her no better than a prison.

Eva's existence at once intensified Rose's ambitions and made them more difficult to attain. The wages she paid Kathleen were modest, but Rose refused to dress her daughter in the haphazard assortment of second-hand clothes which was common in the area or, as Eva began to walk, to allow her to go barefoot like other children. She was already determined to send the little girl to a church school, more expensive than the local board school though it was, and even dreamed of sending her away to a private school to complete her education. They were grandiose plans, for a widow who looked for survival to a small shop taking three pounds a week.

As profits slowly increased, Rose constantly devised new means of boosting them still further. There was intense competition amongst the wholesalers who supplied small businesses: she utilised it to extract concessions as to discount and credit, shamelessly playing off one commercial traveller against the next. She wasted nothing, and always gave exact measure. If such precision did not make her popular, the good quality of her produce and its reasonable prices ensured her a steady trade. She was unfailingly polite to her customers, and gave them whatever help she could when asked to read or even write letters for some of the older people in the area, who had had little or no education. This, and the basic advice she was able to give on health matters, went some way to compensate for the reserve that distanced her from her neighbours. She heard that she was regarded as a snob, and at heart she acknowledged that there was some truth in the accusation. Her goal remained unchanged: to make enough money to move out of the district altogether.

The departure of Mrs Heeney and her family from Ancoats strengthened her resolve. Her old landlady had decided to take up her brother's offer of free passage for herself and her children to join him in Canada. Rose urged her to accept, although she knew that she would miss Mrs Heeney. Life in Canada, or anywhere else, she was sure, would be an improvement.

'Miss Brunton?'

Sarah opened her eyes at Betty's voice. The habit of wakening instantly at her mother's call had not left her, though it was more than two years since her death. She sat up in bed, puzzled to see that the maid was carrying her father's shaving water. 'Yes?'

'I didn't know what to do for the best . . . Mr Brunton hasn't been home since last night, miss. His bed hasn't been slept in.'

'He was going to Liverpool, I think,' Sarah said. 'Perhaps he missed the last train and had to spend the night in a hotel. There will be some simple explanation, I'm sure. There is nothing to worry about, Betty.'

'Yes, miss,' Betty said, sounding unconvinced.

Sarah abandoned the struggle to return to sleep and got up soon after the maid had left her. Though not seriously concerned, she was uneasy at her father's absence: such a thing had never happened before. As she went downstairs, she saw her father's chamber candle still sitting on the hall table awaiting his return. The sight was disturbing, a silent witness to the unprecedented overturning of the household routine.

Sarah asked that breakfast be delayed; her father still did not appear in time for the meal. She had little appetite but forced herself to eat and to remain composed. Nothing irritated him more than any display of nervousness on her part and she was determined to greet him calmly.

She had reluctantly instructed that the table be cleared when the sound of a carriage was heard on the gravel. Despite her resolution to behave as though nothing untoward had happened, she hurried into the hall. A man's form was visible through the clouded glass of the inner door. She ran to open it, but her smile of welcome faltered as she recognised not her father but Arthur Collins, his solicitor.

'Mr Collins!' she said, the sense of alarm she had been trying so hard to stifle reviving as she saw his grave expression. 'We don't often see you here so early.'

'I could wish that I were here now on a happier errand, Miss Brunton.'

Sarah stepped wordlessly back, gesturing to him to enter. She led him into the parlour, where a fire had already been lit, although it had yet to warm the room. The chill and her intense nervousness made her shiver.

'Sit down, please,' she said, forcing herself to retain the façade of a calm she was far from feeling. 'Have you come to see my father?'

'Unfortunately, no. I have bad news, Miss Brunton. This morning I received a telegram from Liverpool. Your father died there last night.'

Sarah stared at him. One part of her mind was paralysed by the shock of the announcement; another, in a state of unnatural detachment, was working feverishly, throwing out questions as though the event were of purely intellectual interest to her.

'Who contacted you? How did they know of your connection with him?'

Arthur Collins got to his feet and went to the window. A tall, thin man in his early thirties, shy and fastidious, he was the son of William Brunton's original solicitor. He was so profoundly uncomfortable that Sarah felt sorry for him in the unpleasant task he was required to perform.

'A Mr Paul Risley contacted me. He had some dealings with me in my capacity as Mr Brunton's agent a little while ago and felt that the sad news would be better conveyed by me than by a direct communication from him to you.'

'But who is he?' she persisted, sensing that Collins was keeping something from her.

'Mr Risley is a clerk in a shipping office in Liverpool.'

'A business acquaintance of my father?'

Arthur Collins hesitated.

'Tell me the truth, please,' she said sharply.

'He is . . . was . . . your father's brother-in-law.'

'His brother-in-law?' she repeated. 'There is no one of that name in our family. There must be some mistake, Mr Collins.'

'Believe me, I wish there were, with all my heart. Mr Risley's business with me was in connection with the drafting of a marriage settlement, almost two years ago.' He paused, but as she remained silent, too bewildered to understand what he was saying, he went on brusquely, as though he hated the words he was obliged to pronounce, 'He was acting for his sister, Mr Brunton's second wife.'

'His *second* wife?'

'I am more sorry than I can say that you should learn of it in this way. I begged your father to tell you but he wouldn't listen. You know what he was like.'

'I thought I did, but obviously I was wrong. Perhaps you had better explain,' she said bitterly, her grief silenced by a growing sense of outrage.

'In normal circumstances I should be bound to maintain my client's confidentiality, but the interests of the living must outweigh those of the dead. I'm afraid that your interests, Miss Brunton, have been quite shamefully neglected.'

'In what way?'

'Is this the time to discuss it?' he asked gently. 'You have received a great shock. Perhaps it would be better if I were to come back tomorrow.'

For a moment, Sarah was tempted to agree, but it would be weakness to delay and she was beginning to realise that she must be strong. She shook her head. 'No. Tell me now. I have been kept ignorant too long already. Don't worry,' she added, seeing him frown. 'I won't break down. Sit down, please, and tell me the whole truth.'

'Very well.' He returned to his seat and, after pausing a moment to gather his thoughts, began to speak. 'Mr Brunton married for the second time almost two years ago. It was early in August, I believe, although I would need to consult my papers in the office to be certain.'

'But my mother only died in the June!'

'Quite. It may explain the precipitate nature of the transaction if I inform you that a son was born to their union in November.'

Sarah felt a sudden thud at the back of her throat, as if

her heart had leapt in protest. 'Do you mean that even while my mother was alive . . .'

'I am sorry.' Arthur Collins was not an unfeeling man. He waited until Sarah by a gesture signalled her readiness to continue. 'It was at the house that he had bought for his wife that Mr Brunton died last night. An apoplectic fit, I understand.'

'Why didn't he tell me about her? Was he going to keep it a secret for ever?'

'It was his intention, as made known to me, to sell this establishment at some point in the next year or so and move to the house in which Mrs Brunton is now living, on the outskirts of Liverpool. He believed that this would lessen the inevitable scandal.'

'Sell this house? But it is my home!'

Arthur Collins shifted uneasily in his chair. 'He planned to make provision for your future.'

'Planned? You mean he did not?'

'Not to my knowledge.' He raised a hand, as she gasped in disbelief. 'Some settlement of which I was not informed may come to light in Mr Brunton's personal papers here or in Liverpool. There is even the possibility of a verbal indication of his wishes on his deathbed. While not as desirable from a legal point of view as a probative deed, such bequests *mortis causa* are usually respected, with goodwill from all the parties involved. As you will appreciate, I have not yet been able to investigate the exact circumstances of his death and, in particular, to speak to Mrs Brunton.'

'Have you met her? Do you know what she is like?'

'I have never seen her although, as I said, I have had some dealings with her brother. He appeared to act for her in all things. My impression was that his wishes were paramount. I did not care for the man but he certainly achieved an excellent settlement for her and the child.' He hesitated, then added, 'To be frank, I think he was largely instrumental in bringing about the marriage at all. Blackmail is an unpleasant word, but I don't think it would be ill-applied in this case.'

'But my father . . . he must have wished for the marriage, surely?'

'It was not a simple situation, Miss Brunton. Who can say?'

'But he made a settlement for his new family, and not for me? Why not?'

'Mr Brunton planned to set up a trust for your sole benefit. He often spoke of it and naturally I pressed him to settle the details and execute it in due form. In general I found Mr Brunton to be an excellent man of business, accurate, clear-headed, eager to conclude transactions without delay. In all my connection with him, I do not remember another instance such as this, in which he exhibited such a foolish, a criminal reluctance to do what he knew was necessary.'

'But what was his reason?'

'He refused to face the facts. He made one excuse after another: the business required considerable investment in new plant and he would be better placed to set aside the capital next year; he did not know whether to include provision for future children, or how marriage should affect your entitlement, and so on and so forth. Whenever I raised the question he had some further pretext for inaction.'

'Only a pretext? What do you think lay behind it?'

Arthur Collins shrugged. 'To do him justice, he had no indication of ill health. If he sometimes seemed tired, he vigorously denied any suggestion that this was in any way a warning of organic disease. He often said that he led a life that would tax a man twenty years his junior. In all the circumstances, he was probably right.' He cleared his throat and hurried on. 'He genuinely saw no need for haste. I

wondered at times if he had an almost superstitious dread of
settling his affairs, as though to do so would be in some way
an admission of mortality. Such irrational fears are quite
common. As a solicitor I often encounter resistance to
drawing up wills and the like.'

'But there was surely more than that?' Sarah asked
sharply.

'This can only be my personal impression, you understand. As I said, the trust was to be set up for your benefit.
Your sister was not to be included in its terms. Mr Brunton
more than once said to me that she had already received an
adequate sum and that she had no further claim on him.
Nevertheless, it was my feeling that he could not bring
himself finally to exclude her. While the trust was not
drawn up the possibility remained of reconciliation.'

Sarah nodded. 'You are probably right,' she said wearily.
'In the end, though, his reasons hardly matter, do they? I am
left destitute, it seems, whatever may have been in his mind.'

'Things may not be as bad as that. If we can come upon
even a draft expression of his intentions, I would be able to
argue your case with Mrs Brunton and her brother. If there
is nothing else that you wish to discuss at this point, I will go
to Liverpool this morning and see what can be done there.
You have a strong moral case at least for some provision. I
have stated the situation in its very bleakest terms, Miss
Brunton, but there are certainly grounds for hope.'

Sarah thanked him, but the words seemed empty to her.
Despite his kindness, she was glad when Arthur Collins left
her.

In the next few days Sarah's sense of isolation grew. All her
life had been spent in the comforting security of family and
chapel. A stifling atmosphere to some, it was one in which
she was content. One by one, the supports maintaining that
security had been taken away: her sister, her mother, Philip,
Effie and now her father.

This last loss seemed the severest, despite the harshness
with which he had treated her. As a dutiful Christian, she
had always told herself that she loved him, but the belief
existed in isolation from any real emotion of liking or trust.
And yet, although she had feared him, she was shaken by
her father's death as she had not been by her mother's. She
had scarcely even a memory of him for which to grieve, for
it now seemed that during a lifetime in his shadow she had
never seen his face at all. She had lost a father whom she
had never really had.

He had gone from her, leaving her exposed to a bewil-
dering world of which she had no experience. Arthur Collins
was her mainstay, arranging the funeral and negotiating on
her behalf with her stepmother and Paul Risley. She managed
to write to Rose herself, at the last address she had, care of a
Mrs Heeney, but received no reply. In her shocked condition
Sarah scarcely cared.

Nothing was found in her father's papers that could form
the basis of any claim on William Brunton's estate: he had
died so suddenly that he was unable to speak at all, far less
express any wishes for her future. The business was, in
accordance with his recent marriage settlement, left in trust
for his infant son; his other property and capital were
bequeathed to his second wife and the child. Sarah was left
penniless.

The outcome of Collins's representations to Risley was as
unsatisfactory as she had sensed it would be. Arthur Collins
urged that she be allowed to remain in her old home, at
least for a few weeks. Paul Risley, as his nephew's trustee,
refused. The home was to be sold at once, the furniture
auctioned and the staff paid off.

As news of her position spread, Sarah received several
offers of help from friends. Effie, in the glory of her newly
married status, came to invite her to stay with her and
Philip. Sarah declined. To be a daily witness to the reality of

156 JANET BROOMFIELD

their marriage would be a torment far worse than any of the sufferings of loneliness.

· She saw Philip for a moment at the funeral. At the sound of his voice, murmuring some words of sympathy, longing for him pierced the protective numbness of feeling and thought that was all that enabled her to get through that terrible day. She wanted to rest against him, and cry in his arms, sure of comfort, but all that was possible was a clasp of the hand, a contact that, inadequate as it was, he seemed as reluctant as she to break.

Against Collins's advice, Sarah determined to make a personal appeal for at least a delay in the sale of the family house and even, she hoped, for some sort of financial provision, however small. She was sure that if she could see her stepmother she would be able to persuade her, as one woman to another, of the justice of her case, but when after some difficulty the meeting was at last arranged it was not with Mrs Brunton but with her brother.

Paul Risley came to the house, late one afternoon. Sarah was in her mother's parlour when he arrived. She hurriedly tidied away the references she had been writing for Betty and the other servants and, waiting a moment to compose herself, went to the drawing room to meet the man on whom so much depended.

He did not hear the door opening and she had a few seconds in which to observe him unseen. He was standing in the middle of the room, his back to her, looking about him, legs apart, hands thrust into his pockets. Of less than medium height, slightly built, he was wearing clothes of a conspicuous newness: a braid-edged jacket, trousers of a check pattern, fashionable but slightly too loud. As she watched, he nodded his head and said to himself, 'Very nice . . . oh, yes, very nice.'

Embarrassed, Sarah pushed the door shut with deliberate clumsiness and advanced into the room, hand outstretched.

'Mr Risley? I am Sarah Brunton . . . I am so sorry to have kept you waiting. It's a cold day . . . may I offer you tea?'

He turned, his hands still in his pockets, and looked at her with the same evaluating gaze with which he had been regarding the furnishings. 'Tea? No. Tea parties are not my style.'

Sarah's hand dropped to her side. His rudeness roused her pride. More coldly, she said, 'Well, won't you sit down? I am not accustomed to keep my guests standing.'

'Your guest? I suppose I am that . . . just. You move out at the end of the month, don't you?'

Sarah sat down, struggling for self-control. Whatever the provocation, she would gain nothing by losing her temper. After a moment's hesitation Paul Risley seated himself, lounging back in his chair as though it was his house, not hers. It almost was, she reflected bitterly. He stared insolently at her. His face was narrow and lean but not intrinsically ill-favoured; Sarah suspected that he could be quite a lady's man, with his dark hair and eyes and stylish if flashy clothes. She, clearly, was not to be treated to his charm.

'I'm sorry that your sister did not feel able to accept my invitation, Mr Risley.'

'I handle all her business matters.'

'This is more than just business, surely?'

'Oh, no. Business, pure and simple.'

'In that case I will come to the point. As you are aware, my father's death and the circumstances surrounding it have come as a great shock to me. I am left destitute and, although I have no legal right to his estate, I hope you will admit at least a moral claim of some sort . . .'

'Hope away: I won't admit anything of the kind. Your sort's morals get no respect from me; I've seen too much of them in action.'

Sarah ignored the insult, persevering with what she

increasingly saw would be a hopeless task. 'He intended to make provision for me, as you have been informed.'

'So Collins says. If he's right, all I can say is: too bad. You've had it easy from the day you were born, haven't you? Well, it's about time for you to find out what life's really like.'

'You could at least allow me to remain here for a few months!'

'Why? What would he have done for my sister, if I hadn't forced him to treat her properly? What would *you* have done, if she had come to this house with her bastard, looking for justice? Sent her away to the workhouse or on to the streets, and slept none the worse for it in your bed, I'll be bound!'

'You have no evidence for that,' Sarah said, stirring uneasily in her chair.

'You know damn well you wouldn't have believed a word of it! Some woman from a backstreet in Liverpool comes to you, saying your precious papa has left her with a brat? *Oh, no, not my father! He's a pillar of the chapel, an upright Christian gentleman!*' he said, his mockery uncomfortably close to her own response to Collins's news. 'Where do you think my sister would have been, without me to fight for her? I tell you, I screwed every penny I could out of your dear deceased father . . .'

'I am surprised to hear you admit it.'

'You think I was out for what I could get? Well, you're right in some ways, but it's not the whole story. Yes, I'm glad that I'll benefit. I helped Susie when she needed it and she hasn't forgotten that, but I'd have done the same even if I had to throw every shilling into the Mersey and none the richer for it. For years he used her—'

'I don't want to hear it!' Sarah said, half rising to her feet.

'Well, you will! It's about time that you found out what your father was up to, all those years when he set up as such a model of respectability,' he said leaning forward, his crude insolence swept away by an anger that compelled her by a reluctant sense of its justice. She sank back into her chair and, mollified, he continued more calmly.

'You probably think she was a whore, don't you? A harlot, isn't that what they're called in the Bible? Well, she wasn't. She was scarcely more than a child when she met your decent, God-fearing father. She is still a good-looker, but then she was really something. The kind of girl that catches men's eyes, and whether you believe it or not, a good girl, without a wrong thought in her head. Perhaps you think she must have set herself out to seduce him? She didn't. It was the other way round.'

Sarah caught her breath. Unpleasant as he was, his tone carried conviction.

'Susannah was parlour-maid to one of his business acquaintances. She noticed Brunton giving her funny looks whenever he came to the house but she thought she must be imagining it. He used to tip her when she helped him on with his coat at the end of his visits and she got to like him because of his generosity. Then one night after she'd let him out he came back for a glove that he said he'd dropped. They were alone in the hall and he put his arms around her and kissed her.'

'She shouldn't have let him . . .' Sarah said wretchedly.

'No,' he agreed sarcastically. 'She should have slapped his face, but he was her employer's friend and could have lost her her job. She thought he didn't mean her any harm; just a kiss. And when he asked her when her next afternoon out was she shouldn't have told him, should she? But she did, because she never thought a man like him could mean what he did.

'He was waiting for her in a cab that afternoon, and she shouldn't have got in, but she did. Perhaps she was flattered that he wanted her so badly, perhaps she was so overawed by him so that she gave way to him even when she knew it was wrong. It's a commoner story than you'd like to believe.

'Within a month he had set her up in a house in Liverpool, not far from the station, so that he could come over easily and back again by the last train, and no one any the wiser. And shall I tell you the funniest thing of all? She really loved him. She still does. If you could see her now . . .' He paused, veering away from the first tenderness Sarah had detected in him, and continued more roughly.

'She saw him only when he wanted to, and waited for him the rest of the time, in that house where all the neighbours knew what was going on and most of them wouldn't so much as look at her. He never took her out, never walked down the street with her, never showed her any consideration, unless you count paying her rent and upkeep, as though she were one of his servants now, but she loved him and she was faithful to him.

'They say I blackmailed him into marrying her. Well, I say I was just setting the balance straight. The old hypocrite would have kept her as his mistress, I suppose. She deserved better than that, even if she was only a servant. She was good enough to marry, if she was good enough to—'

He used a word that Sarah had never heard before, although she could guess its meaning. She sat, stunned, incapable of protesting at an outburst that, for all its viciousness, rang true.

Paul Risley got to his feet. Despite his finery, Sarah could see in his sharp, watchful features the still-burning hunger of the dispossessed, the scorned; the resentment of those who learn early that they can expect to be used for whatever in them is of value and, at last, to be thrown away. She was horrified by what she saw, but she was beginning to understand.

She went to the bell to ring for Betty to show him out

but at the last moment she hesitated, wanting to say something but not able to find the words. 'Please, tell your sister . . . Tell her I'm sorry the way things have turned out. Say that I'm glad they married . . . and I wish . . .' She stopped, and shrugged helplessly. 'I don't know. I bear her no ill will, say that.'

He nodded, eyes narrowed in suspicion. They parted without another word.

Sarah doubted whether Risley would convey her message to Susannah Brunton, but she had misjudged him. A few days later she received a letter from her stepmother. Written in the over-careful script of the barely educated, it contained a money order for fifty pounds.

Dear Miss Brunton,

    Paul told me you wished me well. Thank you. I am sorry that you are left as you are but Paul says we would be robbing my son if we went beyond what William's will intended. I could not manage without Paul and he sees to everything for me. I suppose he knows best. This money is from my own allowance so I am not harming anyone, am I? If you are in need, let me know and I will do what I can but please don't tell Paul. He means well but he doesn't always see things the same as me.

Sarah sat for a long time gazing at the letter although she soon knew its contents by heart. Its few, painstaking lines added to the sketch, still dimly described, of a world far more complex than she had ever guessed. The map of an absolute morality, simple, neatly drawn, which she had accepted as her infallible guide in traversing life was, it seemed, inadequate. What warning had it given of the confusion of compromises and unsuspected imperatives which she was beginning to recognise in her father's life, in Rose's and even perhaps in Effie's? She felt like a child again, struggling to interpret an adult world; the experience was painful, baffling, and vital.

After considerable thought, Sarah decided to keep the money. She replied with a letter of thanks but, as she had half expected, received no answer. Even without Paul Risley's hostility it would have been too difficult, too uncomfortable for the two women to continue a relationship of any kind.

She never told Arthur Collins the full story of her meeting with Risley, merely that he had refused her requests but that her stepmother had sent her a generous gift. After further discussions with the solicitor she accepted the solution he proposed. Having spent a week in lodgings kept by an old servant of the Collins's, she went to a post obtained through his intervention, as governess to the family of a lawyer known to him, on the outskirts of Manchester.

CHAPTER

Seven

Rose soon realised that her most ambitious dreams would be almost impossible to achieve on the proceeds of even a successful general shop, work how she might. After almost three years of effort, she now felt confident that the business would pay its way and make a small profit, but not much more. There were so many such shops, each with little to distinguish it from its fellow, that few customers bothered to use any but the nearest. Such money as she made, she decided, would most usefully be invested elsewhere.

The question of the most lucrative investment was one to which her thoughts often turned, as she sat in the shop awaiting the next customer. One afternoon, in the slack period before the rush for food for the evening meal she was so engrossed in her calculations that she failed to notice the door opening.

'Totting up your bad debts?'

She looked up, startled, before recognising the new-comer and relaxing into a smile. 'Mr Finlayson . . . I was miles away. It's not your usual day, is it? I wasn't expecting you until tomorrow morning.'

'I've got special dispensation from head office to attend a

funeral tomorrow, so long as I fit in all my visits as best I
can. I'll be tramping the streets until eleven tonight, I
shouldn't wonder.'

Rose murmured sympathetically. Robert Finlayson was
one of the commercial travellers with whom she dealt on a
regular basis, and one of the few whose visits she enjoyed.

Small and rotund, with an engagingly open expression, he
had an air of health and energy that Rose rarely saw now, in
a district where poverty, poor diet and long hours of hard,
dirty work soon broke even the strongest constitutions. His
teasing manner, she had quickly come to realise, concealed a
good brain and sound business instincts. After trying unsuc-
cessfully to play him off against the other representatives, she
had been obliged to accept that she had met her match: he
gave her good terms, but could not be manipulated into any
deal which was not to the advantage of his firm, Bradley's.
The realisation raised him in her estimation and he became
the only one amongst the commercial travellers whom she
regarded almost as a friend.

'I hope you haven't suffered the loss of a close relation?'
she asked, as she looked beneath the counter for her ledger.

'No, an old aunt of the wife's. There won't be many
mourners, which is why I wanted to do my bit. She was
always good to Minnie and me.'

She nodded, scanning the pages on which she had jotted
down her requirements for the coming week.

'You were lost to the world when I came in,' he said,
leaning on the counter and putting his hat by his elbow.
'Thinking about the business, as usual?'

She looked up sharply at his ironic tone. 'I haven't got
the luxury of a husband bringing in a steady wage. If I
don't make a living my daughter and I will end up in the
workhouse. I *have* to think about the business.'

'There's more to life than making money, though.'

'I'll make my money first, if you don't mind.'

'You surely must be able to relax a bit now? You've built this up to be one of the most profitable little shops in Ancoats . . . you certainly give me bigger orders than anywhere else.'

'That's just your powers of persuasion.'

He laughed. 'Don't bankrupt yourself on my account. Joking apart, are things going well here? They always seem to be, but if you're having difficulties, perhaps I could get the boss to give you credit . . .'

'That's not necessary,' she said, then, repenting her sharp tone, added more warmly, 'If you must know. I was thinking about how I might branch out a little. I've got a small sum laid by and I'm looking for a good investment.'

'Are you, indeed?' he said, with renewed interest. 'I take my hat off to you, Mrs Olivant. You've got a lot more go than anyone else on my round. Most people are satisfied with a few pounds in the bank.'

'But it's not working for you. Money can make more money if you use it properly. A few pounds in the bank won't get me out of here and my daughter a decent start in life.'

'She seems happy enough. I saw her in the street as I passed, giving a bit of a song to the other kids. They were listening to her as if she was Jenny Lind.'

Rose frowned. 'I shall have to see Kathleen about that. She lets her spend too long playing in the street.'

'Oh, Eva was in her element, I wouldn't worry,' he said easily.

'That's exactly why I do worry, Mr Finlayson. I don't *want* a backstreet in Ancoats to be my daughter's element.'

'I see worse places in my job, Angel Meadow for one.'

'To my mother this street would have seemed no better than the worst court in Angel Meadow,' she said bitterly. 'I can't, I won't be content here. You must think I'm a snob. Perhaps I am. But I have to hang on to something, to try to get away from here. I don't belong here, and I don't want to belong.'

He shrugged. 'If that's the way you feel you're as well doing something about it. That investment . . . A nice little cook-shop, maybe? A proper gold mine, if you get the right situation. 'Course, it's a lot of work. It wouldn't suit everyone.'

'I was wondering that, as a matter of fact,' she said eagerly. 'I used to enjoy cooking when I was at home. I'm starting to look about for a good site. Any ideas?'

'I'll think about it,' he said seriously. 'Now, about that order? Double quantities this week?'

She laughed, and gave him a good, though not excessive order. She liked Robert Finlayson, but not enough to override her business instincts.

She had not expected to see him until the following week but to her surprise he called again two days later. The shop was busy. He did not wait for it to empty, but leaning confidentially across the counter asked, 'Are you usually quiet late on? Ten o'clock or so?'

'Yes . . . we take so little some nights that it's scarcely worth staying open, except that everyone would complain if we shut.'

'Do you mind if I look in about then? I think I may have found the very place for your investment.'

'Thank you,' she said, surprised and pleased. 'That's very kind of you. I will look forward to hearing about it.'

He left, and Rose continued to serve the stream of women, who in the late afternoon would come seeking some relish 'for my master's tea' and, if time permitted, for a gossip. She was kept busy, but at the back of her mind, underlying the calculations and the chatter, was a sense of excitement. Already she was relishing the challenge of a new venture.

As he had promised, Finlayson arrived shortly after ten.

She took him through into the kitchen and made tea.

'Now, about the shop you've found?' she asked, sitting down with a sigh of weariness.

'Right. I was in Ardwick the other day and I came across a cook-shop for sale. It's in a good street, near a big cotton mill and a brewery, with another couple of factories in easy reach. I asked what they were wanting for the lease. Fifty pounds.'

'Too much. I can't afford it.'

'Well, how much have you got?'

'Thirty pounds altogether.'

'That should be all right, then. Minnie's aunt left us something. Minnie and me have talked it over and we want to invest some of it. How about a loan, all drawn up legal and proper, at the standard rate of interest?'

'I couldn't . . .'

'Why not? You aren't planning on running off with the profits, are you?'

'No, of course not. It's just that it's such a responsibility. What if the business failed, or you and Minnie needed the money back at short notice? I can't risk it.'

'It really is a promising site. I'm sure you could make something of it.'

'In another six months I will have saved the rest of the money.'

'But it will be taken by then! Where's your sense of adventure gone? Look, we're not treating you like a charity,' he added, as she began to protest. 'It's a sound investment for us – and I'll expect you to buy all your provisions from Bradley's, of course!'

'Only if your price is the best!' she warned, with mock severity.

'So you agree?' he asked, delighted. 'A loan of twenty pounds, terms to be settled?'

She considered. 'Shall we say forty pounds? I will need a

little extra to start out . . . for fitments, equipment and so forth. I mean to do this properly.'

'I can't imagine you doing it any other way,' he said, breaking off as Kathleen, returning from an evening out, came into the kitchen. 'That was a fine concert the little girl was giving to her friends out at the front last week,' he went on, smiling at the servant.

Kathleen looked up in pleased surprise. 'She's a rare voice for her age, and doesn't she know the words of all the songs going?' she said, as proudly as if they were discussing her own child.

'Thank you, Kathleen. That will do,' Rose said shortly. 'You may as well go up. I will see to the tea things myself.'

'A nice girl,' Finlayson said. 'Will you leave her to run this place while you are busy with the new shop?'

'I may do. Where exactly is the cook-shop, anyway?'

'It might be best if I went with you. Let me see . . . tomorrow afternoon? I will be able to juggle things around to make a free hour or so, if that would suit.'

'Very well. Kathleen will see to things here for the afternoon.'

The cook-shop proved to be all that Robert had claimed. It was in a good situation, was clean and showed no sign of damp. It had a range which was provided with oven and boiler, and the proprietor was willing to include in the sale, for another few pounds, all his kitchen equipment and crockery.

'You liked it, then?' Robert asked, as they emerged into the street.

'Very much.'

'So you mean to go ahead? Shall I get my lawyer to draw up an agreement about the loan?'

She nodded, pleased that he made no bones about putting the matter on a businesslike basis.

'You should do well. There will be a good trade from the

mill and the other factories at dinner time, and you should get a certain amount of business from the houses round about for the evening meal. Take my advice, perfect your pastry,' he added solemnly. 'People will travel from miles around to get a good meat and potato pie. I might even patronise you myself.'

'I could make soup, too. Nothing very special, mutton broth. It might sell quite well with the millworkers, during the winter at least. It's cheap to make, but quite tasty.'

He nodded in approval. 'Sell it by the mug, with a couple of slices of bread and butter. I should think you could make a profit if you charged a penny.'

'It would be better if I could bake my own bread, of course,' she said thoughtfully, 'but there is not enough room in the kitchen for that. Later, perhaps, if everything works out, I will look into it.'

'Establishing the new business means a lot to you, doesn't it?'

'Everything,' she said. 'My father began his own business. Perhaps it's in the blood.'

'He must be very proud of your enterprising spirit.'

Rose said nothing. It was not a subject she would discuss, even with him.

Rose took over the lease of the cook-shop within the month. She threw herself into the undertaking with an almost frenzied energy. Its success was everything to her, but she also gloried in the work itself. She revelled in planning, in calculating costs and prices, deciding on recipes and quantities, knowing as she did that it was all for herself and her child. She took a fierce delight in her self-sufficiency, after the years of dependence that now seemed to her so humiliating. To be self-reliant was as satisfying to her as the pleasure another woman might take in being cosseted and pampered by an adoring husband.

During the week that elapsed before she reopened the

shop, and in its first days, Rose spent such long hours at the
new premises across the Medlock that she did not see Eva
for almost a fortnight, for even Sundays she spent in baking
cakes for the coming week. She left Kathleen in charge of
the shop in Ancoats, with a maid of all work to help with
the child and the housework.

It was a happy time for Rose despite the hard work. She
was ambitious, by nature eager to compete, to manage; she
never felt more alive than when she was tasking herself to
the limit with some new challenge. The cook-shop was far
more complex an affair than the general grocery shop in
Ancoats. The profits were potentially higher, but the risk of
wastage was also greater. Rose had constantly to be assessing the balance between supply and demand, particularly of
the most perishable items. Such goods could always be sold
at a reduced price the following day, but it was not a sound
business practice and Rose was always irritated at herself
when she miscalculated.

On the whole, the shop prospered, although the midday
trade was not all that she had hoped. She was making a
profit, but without the help of the Ancoats shop she would
have had difficulty in paying off her loan to Robert
Finlayson as quickly as she had intended. She experimented
with new meals and opened the shop earlier for the sale of
tea and coffee to the workers hurrying to the mill first thing
in the morning. She made sure that she provided particularly appetising food on a Saturday, when housewives were
exhausted by their weekly cleaning, always performed that
day, and the week's pay was still relatively intact, and on a
Monday, when the upheaval of washing might make the
option of a bought-in meal particularly attractive. It was
always a minority of families which could afford such treats,
and many women would have felt ashamed to have recourse
to them, but as the good quality of her food became known
Rose did see an increase in custom.

Things were beginning to improve when, about a year after taking over the shop, Rose noticed a dramatic falling away of business. She was becoming seriously worried as, day after day, she was obliged to sell off cheaply the pies and meat puddings which had once been in great demand. She soon learned the reason.

'Brown's is out on strike,' one of her regular customers informed her, as she waited for a new batch of meat and potato pies to come out of the oven. 'This is the second week . . . a lot of families round here will be starting to clem.'

'They should go back, then,' Rose said, for she was not naturally in favour of such actions.

'No, they're in the right this time,' Mrs Pettigrew said. 'The bosses have been speeding up the machines and cutting back on the rates for piecework. There was an agreement but they just tore it up, no warning to the men or owt. My son-in-law's out, and I don't blame him.'

'I see . . .' Rose said, not fully convinced, for her instincts drew her to support the employers. On the other hand, it was not the bosses but their workers who were her customers, workers who would eventually no doubt go back to their jobs, and who in the meantime had friends, relations, neighbours who worked elsewhere. Rose was not a gambler by nature, but the thought of a bold *coup* appealed to her. She made up her mind.

'Tell your son-in-law that he can come here for a jug of soup every day he's out, and he can tell everyone else who worked at Brown's the same.'

'You can't do that! You'll end up in the workhouse!' Mrs Pettigrew said in amazement.

'I'll risk it. I know it's not much but it will help. It'll be the same soup I always make, too, no cheap rubbish.'

That night, Rose worked until the small hours, preparing extra supplies of soup. She sent an extra order to Robert Finlayson for more barley, dried peas and ham shanks. It would cost every penny of her profits that week, but Rose was thinking ahead.

The following day, there were only a handful of requests for free soup, and one or two of them, Rose suspected, were from those who had no connection to the striking workmen, but who had heard of her offer and determined to chance their luck. She made no attempt to check their credentials. She had no desire to spoil the effect of her gesture.

News soon spread, and every day the numbers of those coming to the shop for the soup increased. After a week, the demand was so great that Rose was obliged to take on another girl to help in the kitchens. Her wage was a further drain on Rose's resources, as the cook-shop was now running at a loss. Robert Finlayson, hearing of what was happening, came to protest.

'I couldn't believe it! You will be bankrupted within the month!'

'Let me worry about that.'

'But I can't stand by and see you throw everything away for some emotional gesture!'

'I am not given to making emotional gestures,' she said coldly.

'I would have said you would be the last woman in the city to let your heart rule your head,' he admitted, 'but what else is this? It certainly isn't business.'

'You couldn't be more wrong. Believe me, in the future I will benefit a hundredfold from every jug of soup I give away now. People won't forget this. The strike will end, probably in victory for the employers, but that doesn't matter. I don't care who wins. All that is of any interest to me is this: when the workers are back at Brown's they will remember that I stood by them. My trade will soar, as soon as they have money in their pockets again. *That's* all I care about.'

His expression changed, exasperation giving way to reluctant admiration. 'I still think you are taking a gamble, but I suppose you may be right. All the same . . .'

'Yes?'

He shrugged. 'I almost wish you were just being generous. It would be foolish, but it would be more human.'

She felt a surge of anger, mingled with the stirring of wistful regret for a long-gone self. That self – impulsive, naïve, softer - had been put aside like a once-cherished, no longer serviceable habit.

'My motives are no concern of yours, Mr Finlayson. I will not fail to repay your loan according to my bond, if that is what you are worrying about.'

'The question had never entered my head. There are more important things than money.'

'Not if you haven't got any.'

'And when you have got all the money you need, what then?'

'When that day arrives, ask me again.'

He took a step back. 'I wonder if it ever will.'

She could see that she had disappointed him, that he thought badly of her, but her pride kept her silent. She could not, would not, pour out to him the recital of her desperate poverty with Simon. She would not beg for understanding, from him or anyone else.

The strike lasted for six weeks and brought the workers and their families to the brink of ruin. Houses were stripped of any item, however essential, that could be pawned: shoes, clothing, bedding, kitchen utensils. It ended, as Rose had expected, in victory for the employers. The strikers were taken back, with the exception of those seen as the ringleaders, but on still worse terms than before. It had been a bitter dispute, and it ended bitterly.

The benefits Rose had looked for were slow to come, but they did at last manifest themselves in increased takings.

It would be many months before she made up the expenses she had incurred, but her business had become known and she was confident that it would ultimately be all the stronger for her support of the impoverished workers. She was pleased with the way trade was developing, although it still involved her in working for sixteen or more hours a day at the cook-shop.

The criticisms Robert Finlayson had made recurred to her mind more often than she liked. She was sure that she was right; she was happy working, earning a future for herself and Eva, planning still further expansion of her business, and yet some part of her, detached from her preoccupations, warned her that all was not well, that she might be paying too high a price for her ambitions.

She was most aware of this uneasy and uncharacteristic self-doubt during the times, increasingly rare, when she saw her daughter. Eva, at four, was big for her age, sturdy and usually healthy. With her rosy cheeks and dark, curling hair she was a striking child, lively and outgoing. Kathleen never had any adverse reports to make, but Rose suspected that, despite her strict instructions, she allowed the little girl to play freely with the other children in the streets. Rose did not like this, but she was well aware that at present there was little that she could do to remedy the situation. Things would be different when, with a comfortable sum in the bank, she could afford to educate Eva as she intended.

In the meantime, Rose did what she could to counteract the effects of Kathleen's laxity. She corrected Eva's language and manners, she ensured that she was always dressed in new clothes of the best quality she could afford, and she bought storybooks for Kathleen to read to her, in preparation for the day when she should be sent to school.

In her presence, Eva soon learned to conform to her mother's wishes but whenever Rose returned home unexpectedly she would usually find her running free in the street, her hair tangled, her pinafore grubby and, often, her feet bare. Once, coming along the street late one winter afternoon, she heard the familiar sound of the hurdy-gurdy. The travelling musician, a tiny Italian with a twisted spine, had set up his barrel organ beneath one of the gaslights and was producing a wheezy version of the popular temperance ballad, 'Come home, Father'. A gaggle of children had gathered around him, drawn despite the cold by the music and the shivering monkey in his red waistcoat and tiny fez sitting hunched on the machine.

Rose felt a wave of revulsion at the shabbiness of the Italian's clothes and the hopeless poverty of his life, cadging halfpence from those who had scarcely enough to keep themselves; at the children's bare feet, blue and swollen with the cold, and the pathetic monkey with its garish outfit. And yet there was a bravery in the music, however sentimental, and in the hunger of the children, starved from birth of art of any sort, for even this faint taste of beauty. She halted.

In the centre of the rough circle of children, Eva was standing, hair wild, her coat slipping from her shoulders. In the sad pool of light her face was unnaturally pale but animated. She was singing, hands flung out in a dramatic appeal to the drunken father to return from the public house to his weeping wife and dying son. She was clearly enjoying herself, and Rose soon became aware that her daughter was literally the centre of attraction. As she watched, the other children fell silent, relishing Eva's act, for so it was, word-perfect, complete with facial expressions, movements, emotions.

Rose was appalled, her snobbery reinforced by the dislike of the theatre, and of the music hall in particular, inculcated by her Nonconformist childhood. The words of the song struck her with ironic significance: but for chance, Eva could indeed have been performing in reality the part she was so relishing. Her daughter's innocent enjoyment seemed almost a mockery of the tragedy from which Rose had saved her. She ran forward, and delivered a stinging slap to her daughter's legs.

'Come in this minute!' she cried, grabbing Eva's hand and dragging her away. 'What an exhibition to make of yourself! I won't have it, do you hear? I won't have it!'

Eva, too shocked by her sudden vengeful apparition even to cry, stumbled along behind her as she strode swiftly away from the pale limelight of the streetlamp and the laboured music of the barrel organ. At home, Rose handed the little girl over to Kathleen.

'Put her to bed at once, and then come down and see me,' she ordered.

'But she's not had her supper!' Kathleen protested.

'She can go without. It will teach her that I mean what I say. I will not have her singing vulgar songs in the street, and the sooner she realises it the better.'

Emboldened perhaps by Kathleen's presence, Eva began to whimper, her sobs soon bringing on a harsh cough that Rose could not recall noticing before.

'Listen to her! This is what comes of letting her hang about the street in all weathers!' she said angrily.

'Sure, she's had that cough a week or more . . . all the children are down with it just now,' Kathleen said, picking up the child. 'Now, now, no need to cry, we'll soon have you nice and snug in your bed, my darling.' As she left the room, the maid flashed a reproachful gaze at Rose. It hurt her less than the sight of her daughter's arms clasped tightly about Kathleen's neck, her head buried for comfort against her shoulder.

Kathleen was long in coming downstairs again and when she did Rose saw at once that she was in no very concilia-tory mood. There were several customers in the shop. Rose served them herself, bidding Kathleen unpack the goods which had been delivered that day. The girl worked with a concentrated energy that hinted at a fine temper, flouncing in and out of the room with a scornful swirl of her skirts. When at last the shop was empty, she called Kathleen to her.

'Yes?' Kathleen demanded.

Rose decided that it would be politic to ignore the challenge in her tone. 'I have told you often enough about this, Kathleen, but it seems I shall have to tell you again. I don't want Eva playing out in the street and I certainly don't want her making an exhibition of herself, singing and dancing. I don't like the sound of that cough of hers, apart from anything else. She could catch anything if you let her run about in the cold like that. You do a wonderful job, but if this continues I shall have to get someone else to see to her.'

'You'd break her heart!'

'That's rather dramatic,' Rose said coolly. 'She would soon get used to another nurse.'

'Nurse? I'm more of a mother to her than anything else!'

Rose stiffened. 'You are getting above yourself, Kathleen. I am her mother, and don't you forget it.'

'You'd never know it from the way you treat the poor mite. Never a kind word for her from one week's end to the next. Her life would be no better than a dog's if it was left to you. It's just a disgrace and I don't care who knows it!'

'Have you taken leave of your senses?' Rose paused, awaiting the apology that would, even now, allow her to avoid the otherwise inevitable conclusion. Kathleen said nothing, staring her defiantly in the face. 'Very well. I will have no more of your insolence. You will take a week's notice.'

'Just as you like. I've only stayed for the sake of the baby, that I've loved like my own. Pity help her now, is all I can say.'

The shop bell rang as another customer entered. Glad of the diversion, Rose left Kathleen to attend to him and went into the kitchen. She was already running over in her mind the possible replacements for Kathleen in the shop. For Eva, she might have other plans.

At the end of Kathleen's notice, Rose installed another local girl, Hannah Swift, to run the shop. Her mother had kept a small shop in Hulme until it had been bankrupted by her husband's drinking. Small, sharp-featured, Hannah would stand no nonsense from even the most plausible or desperate credit seekers. Rose was happy to leave the shop in her hands. Eva, it was true, was wary of her, but that was of no significance, for Eva would not be in Ancoats for very much longer.

The day after her dismissal of Kathleen, Rose had left the girl who helped at the cook-shop in charge and gone to visit the local doctors and the churches, both Anglican and Dissenting. She explained that she was looking for a reliable family, out of the city, in which her daughter could be fostered in a healthy atmosphere. She was sympathetically received and, a few days later, heard from the rector of St Andrew's of a possible foster mother, Mrs Ball, a former servant of his wife's, now married to a farmer in Caddishead, some way to the west of Manchester. She was strongly recommended as a kindly, sensible woman with two daughters of her own, of school age.

Rose wrote at once to Mrs Ball, explaining her wish to have her daughter reared in the countryside, far from the smoke and dirt of Ancoats. She received a favourable response, and went out to Caddishead to see Mrs Ball. All was satisfactory, and the fee she was prepared to offer met with Mrs Ball's approval. Within a week of Kathleen's tearful parting from Eva, the little girl was placed in her new home.

★

John Vaughan gazed at Sarah over his half-moon spectacles. He looked, as usual, as though his patience was being sorely tried. In the time since she had taken up her new position she had never seen her employer smile, even in the brief minutes he spent with his two young daughters. The recent death of his wife might explain his severity, but Sarah doubted it. Tall and lean, with pale, clean-shaven cheeks and tightly compressed lips, he had an air of constantly restraining some outburst at the imbecility of those fools with whom life had seen fit to surround him.

'At six years old, Beatrice really ought to be able to leave these infantile ways,' he said peevishly. 'It ought to be perfectly plain to her that there is nothing to fear in the nursery. She no longer needs a night-light. I thought I had given you your instructions on the matter, Miss Brunton.'

'You expressed your wishes, certainly.'

'Then why were they ignored? Last night when I was retiring I distinctly saw the light beneath the nursery door.'

Sarah sighed. 'These things take a little time, Mr Vaughan. Beatrice is a sensitive child. She is afraid of the dark and has been used to a night-light. To deny her its comfort suddenly will only increase her terror. If you insist that it must be done, I shall have to proceed carefully, by degrees.'

'The sooner she is obliged to face her fears and realise how foolish they are the better.'

'If you were dealing with an adult, perhaps, but Beatrice is a very little girl . . . a girl who has lost her mother only two months ago,' she added, allowing herself a note of reproof. 'She needs extra attention, not unnecessary strictness.'

'You will spoil her,' he grumbled, but she sensed that she had won her point. 'And Louise? Is she making satisfactory progress? She is bright enough, but she *will* fancy herself nervous.'

Sarah chose her words carefully. 'I think that, like any child, she needs to learn at her own pace. At present, while she is still missing her mother so much, I am trying not to drive her too hard.'

'That's all very well, Miss Brunton, but there is no point in allowing them to believe that they can receive special treatment indefinitely because they have lost their mother. I lost a wife, but I was at my desk the morning afterwards. Life goes on, and it is false kindness to protect them from it.'

'Yes, Mr Vaughan,' Sarah said submissively. She had not the slightest intention of acting on such precepts, but she knew that it was wise to pay lip service to them. She had already learned that his interference in his daughters' education did not extend beyond these sporadic criticisms. He had no real interest in the little girls and, although he had delivered much the same strictures to her twice already, he rarely entered the nursery, where Sarah and a nursemaid reigned undisturbed.

Satisfied to have had the last word, he sat back in his chair. 'And you, Miss Brunton?' he asked, condescending to small talk with an obvious effort. 'Do you find yourself at home here now?'

'More than I would have expected,' Sarah said, quite truthfully. 'To be occupied has been helpful to me . . . as well as a necessity, of course.'

'Exactly my point!' John Vaughan said triumphantly. 'One has to carry on, Miss Brunton, whatever one's feelings might be. You are, as I detected at the very first, a sensible woman.'

Sarah supposed that he meant a compliment, and smiled politely.

'Still, I mustn't keep you from your duties,' he said, rising to his feet. 'I have enjoyed our little discussion. It is most important that the girls should be in the charge of someone who can be trusted to continue with the regime to which they are accustomed.'

As she returned to the nursery, Sarah breathed a sigh of relief that her interview with her employer, perhaps the most irksome feature in her new life, was over for another week. As she struggled to remind herself, she must not expect too much. To come to an unknown household in the ambiguous position of a governess, separated from the other servants but not a member of the family, would have been difficult under even the most favourable circumstances. The kindest employers, the most affectionate pupils could have done little to alleviate the shock of her sudden reversal of fortune and the loss of all that was dear and familiar to her.

Things could have been much worse, she told herself encouragingly. John Vaughan, insensitive and humourless, was far from congenial but at least her dealings with him each day were restricted to a brief period when she was expected to bring the little girls down to see him before dinner. At first she had assumed that he would wish to be alone with them, but he had requested that she remain, a silent witness to their stilted exchanges. At times she felt like a wardress, monitoring a visit in some prison or workhouse, although such encounters, she supposed, might display more genuine affection.

Louise and Beatrice were almost painfully polite to her; shy and serious, they had to be coaxed to speak or, when she took them out for their daily walk, to run and play. Thin and narrow-faced, their long, lank hair drawn severely back from high, bony foreheads, they were unnaturally serious, with none of the curiosity or delight in life that she remembered in the children from her Sunday school class. All that was spontaneous or joyous seemed already to have been ironed out of them, an impression now emphasised by the black mourning dresses they wore. Secretly, Sarah had

determined that she would try to persuade John Vaughan
to permit them to lessen their mourning before the year
was out. She was sure that it did nothing to improve their
spirits.

The little girls' unhappiness went some way towards
helping Sarah to overcome her own. She soon found herself devising means to give them a more natural childhood,
in which noise and untidiness were not always checked
with a frown and a cold word. That summer she induced
John Vaughan to permit her to take them to the seaside,
urging the benefits to their health of invigorating sea
breezes. She was successful, largely, she suspected, because
he was relieved to have his daughters taken out of his way.
The girls throve on the greater freedom she allowed them.
After a month in the Isle of Man, they lost the pinched,
anxious look that so distressed her; they even began to join
in the games of other children on the beach, instead of
hanging back nervously and observing them as though they
were the strange rites of some alien race.

On their return home, Sarah won another victory. After
making enquiries, she discovered a dancing class held in
the local town. John Vaughan was reluctant to allow his
daughters to attend, but Sarah argued that it would be a
useful accomplishment: Louise, like many tall children,
had a tendency to slouch. Dancing would improve her
deportment. She persisted and gained the point. One
afternoon a week, she took the girls to the class, held in
rooms above a jeweller's shop, where a dancing master
taught a dozen children country dances and quadrilles to
his wife's energetic piano accompaniment.

As Sarah had hoped, the classes provided Louise and her
sister with the company of other children, from whom they
had until now been isolated. There followed invitations to
tea, to birthday parties and other treats. When Sarah
collected her pupils from such occasions and found them

giggling and whispering secrets with their friends, she could scarcely recognise in these giddy creatures, their hair ribbons adrift and their cheeks flushed, the girls who had once been so lifeless and timid.

Sarah was surprised to find that she too benefited from the girls' wider social circle by meeting other nurses and governesses at the children's parties, while they waited to take their charges home. Their lack of free time limited the opportunities for furthering such acquaintances, but one or two gradually developed into friendships. Slowly, painfully, she was building a life for herself.

With time, Sarah even came to dread less her contact with John Vaughan. She learned to manage him, paying lip service to his wishes and ignoring them in practice. So long as he was able to declare his theories and was not troubled by his daughters he was glad to leave their upbringing to Sarah. They lived parallel lives, in the same household, but never touching. It suited them all. Effectively a servant, alone in the world, Sarah was often surprised to recognise her own happiness.

CHAPTER

Eight

Rose found her life much simplified since the removal of her daughter to a foster home. It was as though a valuable but cumbersome piece of furniture had been put into storage, enabling her to move more freely. Visits proved less than satisfactory; Eva would at first treat her with a wounding reserve, but by the end of the visit would be clinging to her, screaming for her to stay. Rose soon persuaded herself that it would be better to keep away and not disturb her daughter's equilibrium by scenes that so distressed them both. She received regular reports from Caddishead and was confident that Eva was thriving on country food and in country air. Relieved of all anxiety as to her welfare, she threw herself with a clear conscience into what was now the consuming passion of her life: her business interests.

With her unstinted attention, both the little shop in Ancoats and the cook-shop in Ardwick were prospering. She was able to pay off her loan from Robert Finlayson with some ease; she could, indeed, have found herself a house in a better area, her avowed aim. Instead, she resolved to build up her capital. Money was becoming for her something to use to create more money, not to expend on herself. She was already planning another, far bigger venture.

The growing success of the cook-shop, which soon gained a reputation far beyond its immediate environs for the high standards Rose enforced, encouraged her to seek a wider market. The limited space available at the present premises restricted the volume of goods she could produce; she was sure that far more could be sold. She began to look about for a bakery. She was returning from one such expedition when she met Robert Finlayson, about to leave the cook-shop. She was, as ever, pleased to see him.

'Won't you come back inside for a moment?' she added, 'I haven't seen you in an age!'

'I have called in several times, but you have never been here,' he said as he accepted her invitation and stepped back into the shop.

'Come into the kitchen . . . I was going to make myself some tea.'

He seated himself at the kitchen table, scrubbed clean now that the day's baking had been completed, and watched her moving about the small, cramped room. 'Business is good, I take it?'

'It could scarcely be better.' She put the kettle on to boil and, only then taking off her jacket and hat, raised her hands to her head to check that she had not dislodged her hair pins.

'How is Eva, by the way?'

'Oh, very well, according to the last letter from Mrs Ball.'

'Have you seen her recently?'

'No . . . it only unsettles her. It's better if I stay away.' He said nothing, but she sensed his disapproval. 'It's not for long,' she added, 'only until I can afford to move away from here.'

'You are doing pretty well out of the area, all the same.'

'I have made it my business to know what sells and to supply it.'

He shook his head. 'I have never met a woman like you. Most people would have been satisfied with the little grocery shop. What drives you on?'

'I want to make a better life for myself and my daughter,' she said, but even to herself the explanation sounded inadequate.

'It's more than that, though, isn't it?'

'I suppose it is,' she admitted. 'I see opportunities, that's all.'

'Oh? And what opportunities do you have in your sights now?'

She handed him his tea, considering whether to take him into her confidence. 'A bakery,' she said at last. 'With good organisation it could supply bread, pies, cakes to my shops and others, further afield. I was wondering about taking on a market stall as well. It would take a lot of planning, but I think I could do it.'

'It would be a risk. You could find yourself completely out of your depth.'

'I haven't made up my mind yet. It would mean employing a lot of staff. That puts me off; I like to keep everything in my own hands. That way I know it will be done properly.'

'Stay as you are, then.'

She sipped her tea. 'That's the trouble. Once I have had an idea I find it hard to dismiss it. I never could turn down a challenge. To stay as I am seems like stagnation. I soon get bored; if I didn't I would probably still be living at home, sewing cushion covers for the chapel bazaar.'

'I can't imagine it, somehow.'

Rose laughed. 'Well, perhaps not.'

'And have you got enough capital for this bakery scheme?'

'Not yet.'

'Want me to have another word with Minnie?'

It was the offer for which she had been hoping, although she had not wanted to ask him directly. 'Are you sure? I would need a bigger sum . . . a hundred pounds, I should think, depending on what needs to be done to convert the premises and so on. Do you want to risk so much?'

'I'd sooner you had the use of it than a bank . . .'course, it's up to Minnie. She rules me with a rod of iron, you know.'

Rose, who knew perfectly well that the Finlaysons were one of the happiest couples in the country, accepted the fiction with a smile. It would enable Robert to refuse her the loan without embarrassment, if he thought better of it on discussing it with his wife.

'Well, let me know if you are interested. At the moment my main concern is getting a good site for the bakery. Keep your eyes open, will you?'

Suitable premises proved hard to find. On grounds of cost Rose rejected several that Robert Finlayson suggested, for she was cautious over capital outlay. She was content to bide her time, conscious that all the time she was refining her plans. She called in at small shops within an ever-increasing radius, gaining potential customers or at least the expression of interest in taking products from the new bakery.

Such visits, and those to likely sites for the new undertaking, occupied much of her scant leisure. It would have been difficult for Rose to spare time to see Eva, although she had intended to renew her visits to Caddishead once the child was well settled. Now the interval lengthened until she told herself that it was better so, and that Eva was happier undisturbed. It was, after all, a sacrifice demanded for her future benefit. When she had established herself as she wished, the girl could come home, and all would be well.

Shortly before Whitsun, Rose went with Finlayson to look at one of the most promising sites she had yet found, an old dye works not far from Pin Mill Brow. They walked back together slowly, discussing the advantages and drawbacks of the premises, which were cheap but derelict.

'Why save money on the purchase price if you've only got to spend a fortune on making it fit for use?' Robert asked. 'That warehouse we saw last month would have been far better.'

'It was too far away, as well as being too expensive. Besides, I would have had to make structural changes. It would have been financially ruinous.'

'This last place is just ruinous!'

She laughed. 'Oh, you'll see that I am right in the end. It's sound enough, it only needs cleaning up.'

'It's the dirt that's holding it together!'

'We'll have another look next week. Perhaps you'll see it differently then.'

He shook his head. 'Taking it just because it's cheap would be a false economy. You'd be far better waiting for a place in first-class condition . . . and if you can't afford it, then perhaps you're not really ready for such a big step. There's no sense in stretching yourself too far. However carefully you budget, there will always be something unexpected coming up and needing extra cash.'

'I am perfectly well aware of that,' Rose said sharply, Finlayson's warning all the more unwelcome for her uneasy consciousness that she would be pushing herself to her financial limits.

They walked on in silence for a moment. Rose's irritation subsided and she was seeking some conciliatory remark for her old friend when Finlayson forestalled her. 'I was talking to Minnie the other night. She always likes to hear how you're getting on, you know. She said to remind you that we've got that hundred waiting for you whenever you need it.'

'That was very kind of her,' Rose said, genuinely moved.

'I told her not to be so soft, of course, but she would insist.'

Rose laughed. 'I'll give a good rate of interest . . . but I'll still take that dye works.'

'Well, that's up to you. You're the one running the business, not me.'

'I'll make a go of it, don't worry.'

'If anyone can, it'll be you,' he said.

Despite the warmth in his voice she sensed that his doubts remained. It only strengthened her resolve. Stubbornly, determined to prove Finlayson and her own secret reservations wrong, she persevered with negotiations for the empty works. The agent leasing it was eager to conclude an agreement and within a few days, it was hers.

There were to be many times over the next three years when Rose privately acknowledged that Finlayson's initial doubts about the undertaking were justified. The dye works, although she stubbornly refused to admit as much to him, required more expense than she had expected. When the ovens were installed large areas of rot were discovered, necessitating widespread repairs; the roof leaked at the first heavy rain and rats from a nearby market soon discovered the new source of food and proved resistant to the traps and poison of the ratcatcher.

Not only was the initial outlay far higher than Rose had planned, the sheer size of the new business brought problems more complex than anything she had known before. The efficient distribution of the goods was crucial. If the ovens were not heated properly, causing a delay in baking the bread and pies that provided the bulk of sales, they would be delivered too late to the small shops on which the bakery depended. The shopkeepers, whose profit margins were perilously narrow, would refuse to accept goods which had already missed the midday rush; Rose could not risk the loss of their custom by insisting that they should take their full order, whenever it arrived.

As she had feared, the employment of so many workers - bakers, delivery boys, a woman to run the market stall – inevitably led to greater inefficiency than when she was able to attend to almost everything herself. One baker was unreliable, turning up late for work or even not appearing at all. His replacement was careless, burning one batch of pies and undercooking another; the third was a drunkard, tolerated for several weeks because of the excellent quality of his produce when sober, but turned off at last when, in an alcoholic frenzy, he attacked one of the bakery staff with a cleaver.

The delivery boys were as unsatisfactory. Some were too slow over their rounds, others pilfered goods, selling them on their own account. Their misdemeanours were a constant headache and even the most trustworthy rarely stayed for more than a month or two; boys readily found work, at least until they began to need an adult wage.

Rose grimly faced each problem as it arose, rolling up her sleeves when necessary to take over from some absent or useless employee and even, on more than one occasion, taking out one of the carts by which the orders were supplied. She worked harder than ever in her life before, often snatching no more than two or three hours' sleep before dragging herself from her bed before dawn to go down to the bakery and help with the busiest time there. She did not complain, but there were times when she secretly wondered if she had indeed taken on a task which was beyond her.

As far as she could she hid from Finlayson the extent of the difficulties. Her pride made her unwilling to admit that his misgivings had been correct; her independence made her instinctively seek to overcome every problem unaided. It was a relief to her that at least she need not expend time and energy on her daughter's upbringing. She knew that she could not have worked as hard as she now must if Eva was at home. The little girl's return was the goal to which she told herself that she was aiming, but it now seemed further away than ever.

The strain of facing the constant crises and the knowledge that if the enterprise should fail Robert and Minnie Finlayson stood to lose a considerable sum was so great that Rose found her health suffering. She slept badly despite her exhaustion, could barely eat and suffered for the first time in her life from blinding headaches. She struggled on, hoping for better days, but it seemed that no sooner did she surmount one obstacle than another, still greater, loomed before her. She cut expenditure to the bone, sacrificing everything to the ever-increasing demands of the business which she had begun to regard as an insatiable monster.

Matters came to a head after almost four years of unremitting efforts. Rose had risen early to go down to the bakery; it was market day and the bigger order needed by the stall always put a strain on the staff, although after many difficulties she had at last found employees she could trust. It was winter, a bitter February morning. Rose made the familiar journey through the narrow streets automatically, as she had so many times before, weary and shivering in the bleak hours before dawn. Her body protested at being dragged from the warmth of the bed to face the sharp wind and air so cold that it seared the lungs but she drove herself grimly on. She could now barely remember a day which had not been an unremitting test of her powers of endurance.

There were few landmarks in the network of streets through which she passed; she was aware of none of them, her consciousness entirely taken up by the effort of will needed to drive herself on. As she reached the end of the street in which the bakery was sited her eyes sought out the long, low building which had cost her so dear but from which, with stubborn optimism, she still hoped for so much. Usually, however weary and downcast she might be, the sight of its windows glowing with light raised her spirits and this morning, too, her heart lifted with the pride of ownership.

For a brief moment she felt the expected satisfaction, a brave blend of hope for the future and thankfulness to have achieved even so much. But as she fully took in the scene before her Rose's contentment turned to horror. There was something subtly wrong with the radiant oblongs pierced in the blackness of the wall; the light should be a steady, golden glow, not that fierce flickering redness. Rose was fixed to the spot with the terror of the sudden realisation: the bakery was on fire.

The thought that there must be workers already within the building broke through her paralysis of body and will. She began to run towards the bakery and as she ran, another, more selfish consideration flashed into her mind. She had over the past few months allowed the insurance premiums to lapse. If the fire proved serious, she was ruined.

As she neared the entrance to the building her worst fears were set at rest: the baker, Joe Mullen, and two of the youths who helped him were standing outside, apparently unhurt. Their faces were blackened by smoke and the younger boy, Michael Waters, was coughing violently, but they did not seem to have suffered any burns.

'What happened? Have you sent for the fire brigade?' she asked, her eyes desperately scanning the building. The fire seemed to be confined to the left side of the ground floor, although the heat was so intense that without intervention it must surely spread rapidly.

'Billy's gone for them,' Joe said hoarsely. 'They shouldn't

be long. We tried to beat it out but it was no good. We had to get out.'

'Quite right. You are safe, that's the main thing,' she said distractedly, her attention held by the cracking of one of the windows, from which black smoke began to belch forth. 'How did it start?'

'Billy had gone into the store cupboard for salt. As he opened the door a rat jumped down off one of the shelves. It would only have been trying to get past him but he thought it was going for him. He dropped the candle and ran. By the time he'd told us what happened and I'd torn him off a strip for being so soft the candle had set fire to the cupboard. What with all the lard and that, it was roaring like a furnace before we could do owt about it.'

'Well, we can do something now,' Rose said, her initial relief that no one had been hurt turning to anger at the passivity of the men. 'Has anyone roused the people living opposite? They should be warned, in any case, and they will be able to lend us buckets. We may be able to stop the fire from spreading, even if we can't put it out.'

The sound of breaking glass had already awoken several people in the houses across the street; one or two men were emerging, still struggling into clothes snatched up in their haste. Rose and the others ran over and began knocking on doors to alert those who still remained unconscious of the drama. There was, in fact, little danger to the houses since the bakery was surrounded by a good-sized yard, but Rose had no intention of standing idly by and watching the fire work its destruction unchallenged.

By the time the fire engine arrived, enough of the neighbours had come out into the street to establish a chain, bringing water in buckets, pans and other vessels to the blaze. It was enough to restrict the fire to the left side of the building, although not to extinguish the flames. Rose worked with the rest, her clothes soon soaked by water

slopping from the hurriedly passed receptacles, her eyes
stinging at the acrid smoke still billowing from the broken
windows.

While she was absorbed in the need for action she barely
felt the cold but when at last the fire had succumbed to the
greater force of the firemen's hoses and the grey light of
dawn filtered through the smoke, she found herself shivering violently. She retrieved her shawl, which she had
thrown off in order to work unencumbered, and pulled it
closely about her, but there seemed no warmth in it. All
strength suddenly drained from her limbs; she could barely
stand. She leaned against a wall, looking dully about her at
the desolate scene; the smoke-blackened walls, the shattered
windows, the water lying in dirty puddles in the yard,
already beginning to freeze at the edges.

'Mrs Olivant?'

She turned wearily to Joe Mullen who was standing
beside her, twisting his cap in his hands. 'Yes?'

'A bad do . . .'

She nodded.

'I suppose that's it, then? You'll not be needing us no
more.'

She intended to agree, to tell him to inform the other
workers that they would have to seek employment elsewhere, but the words stuck in her throat. In her aching
weariness and misery she could not think quickly, but
something in her that lay deeper than conscious thought
took command and answered for her. 'I am going home
now for a while to rest, but I will be back this afternoon to
see how bad the damage is. I will expect you all here as
usual tomorrow. Tell the others, will you?'

'What, Billy and all?'

She managed a smile. 'Yes, Billy too. He was frightened,
but he's not much more than a boy. He couldn't have
known what a moment's carelessness would do.'

'Well, we'll be here,' he said, looking doubtfully about him. 'I only hope there'll be summat for us to do.'

'We can clean up, if nothing else. If the ovens aren't damaged we may even be able to make a start at baking again.'

Joe nodded, unconvinced, and went in search of the others. Rose slowly made her way home. She tried to keep her thoughts to practical matters, to what would need to be done that day to get the business back on its feet and minimise the damage. She thrust to the back of her mind the more troubling problem of the insurance and of how she would tell Robert and Minnie Finlayson that their money was lost. One step at a time was all that she could manage.

The shop in Ancoats was already open. Rose told Hannah briefly what had happened and sent word to the cook-shop to bake as much extra produce as possible and supply it to the market stall. She could not afford the loss of even an extra shilling, if it could be avoided. Then, chilled and exhausted, she went up to bed.

It was late afternoon when she awoke. For a moment she felt an unfamiliar sense of luxury at waking naturally, having had her sleep out, but her contentment was short-lived. As the memory of the fire returned she groaned aloud, and pulled the covers up over her face. The thought of the struggle before her and the bankruptcy that must almost inevitably follow descended on her like a landslide, sweeping her down in a torrent of mud from the arduous slope she had so painfully begun to scale. It was all, it seemed, to be done again. She was in a worse position than when she had fled from Simon, for then at least she had her mother's gift. Now she would have nothing but debts.

She lay still, the blankets muffling both the sounds and the light that penetrated into the bedroom. As once before, after Peter's death, she had no wish to go on. Life was too much for her. She would lie there, uncaring, and let her creditors sort out the mess, the physical wreck of the bakery and, still worse, the financial confusion. Robert Finlayson: the thought was another crushing weight upon her. She had bought almost all her stores from Bradley's; he had allowed her the last two orders on credit. They were larger than usual, and still unpaid. It might cost Finlayson his job.

She lay inert. Like an animal trapped by a snare that only tightened about her throat as she struggled she saw no escape, no hope. All that she had achieved so painfully had only served to make her downfall still more catastrophic, for she had dragged down the Finlaysons with her. Recovery was no longer within her abilities, however hard she might work. Her confidence had led her to overreach herself. Even with the insurance money to cover the repairs the situation would have been difficult, at a time when they were still struggling to establish the business; without it, it was impossible.

It was an end of some part of Rose's life, as absolute in its way, if not as devastating, as the crisis after Peter's death. She could not go on as she had before. She had surrendered; the fight was knocked out of her. Yet as she lay, not moving, barely thinking, that indomitable instinct to survive began to stir. Slowly, her will reasserted itself, tentatively at first, as though, lying beneath an overwhelming mass of rubble, each limb in turn began to flex itself and test for injury. She still had her youth, her energy, her intelligence, her determination. She still had the responsibility for her daughter, and her pride. She could see no way out, but she would make one.

Money, many hundreds of pounds perhaps, would be needed to restore the fire damage, to replenish stocks and tide the business over the weeks of inactivity. She knew of no way to find such large sums but as her mind adjusted itself to the changed circumstances she began to perceive faint possibilities, the merest chinks of light in the darkness. She would investigate every one, however painful the exploration might be. She would write to her father and Sarah, although her pride baulked at the conclusion. She would visit local banks, and if they refused her, money-lenders. If all else failed, she would sell both shops. The struggle appalled her, but she would undertake it.

Rose lay for a little while longer, gathering her strength, aware of her isolation as she had not been in years of incess-ant occupation. The shop must be quiet, for not even the shrill jangle of the bell broke the silence. It suddenly struck her how sweet it would be to hear Eva's voice in the house that had for so long been not a home but a business. She smiled as she remembered her daughter's singing, her brightness, her pleasure in a life whose harshness had not touched her. For the first time since parting from her, she longed to have Eva beside her, as though the overturning of the edifice she had so painfully constructed had brought to light some precious but neglected treasure, whose exis-tence she had all but lost sight of. All else seemed to her at this moment dross, nothing more.

Rose put back the covers and went to the window. The short winter's day was almost over. The light had gone. There would be no point in going down to the bakery, as she had said she would.

'I will, though!' she said grimly to herself, as she let the curtain fall. Make a start; begin the struggle back.

Rose had expected to find the bakery in darkness; instead, the right side was lit by a steady glow of gaslight and on the left from one or two windows came the paler glimmer of candles or, more likely perhaps, oil lamps. There was a sound of hammering and as she came nearer, puzzled and a little alarmed, that of splintering wood.

A man staggered out of the building, in his arms a tangle of planks and timber. He carried it to the far corner of the

yard and dumped it on top of a heap which she now
noticed for the first time. As he turned back to the bakery
she recognised Joe Mullen and hurried towards him.

'Joe? What are you doing here?'

He stopped, smiling in recognition. 'Me and the lads
thought we'd make a start. I told them you'd be down,
sooner or later, like you said. It didn't seem right to leave
you to it.'

For the first time, she felt tears spring to her eyes. If only
he had known how close she had come to abandoning her
responsibilities and giving the lie to his trust. 'I had things to
sort out,' she said, and saw him nod in understanding. He
took it for granted that she would make everything right.
Her resolve strengthened. She would not let him down.

Despite the work already done by Joe and the others,
including one or two of their friends and relations, the
interior of the building was a dismal sight. In the part of the
building where the fire started the ceiling had fallen in, the
floorboards were partly consumed and would need to be
replaced, every window was broken. Men were at work
boarding up the unglazed apertures. It was a necessary task
but it intensified the gloom and dereliction of the scene.

'A lot of work will need to be done here,' Rose said with
a sigh.

'Oh, we can manage without using this room,' Joe said,
standing aside to let Billy past with another bundle of
charred and saturated timber. 'The sinks and the water
supply is in here. We'll need to rig summat up. We kept the
carts and trays here. They're done for, of course, but otherwise it was mostly food stores and the baking tins and
moulds. Some of them are still all right, and we can easy
keep the flour and that in the other room until this is fixed.'

Rose went through to the other room, which housed
the ovens. The fire had not penetrated so far, but the walls
were blackened with smoke. Soot lay in a thick greasy

deposit on every surface, and the smell of burning was unbearable, although the windows were opened wide, despite the bitter cold.

'We made all the pastry in the other place, being cooler,' Joe said, looking around, hands on his hips, 'but we could as well do it in here in the mean time. We'd be a bit pushed for space, like, but where there's a will there's a way. It's the water that'll be the biggest problem.'

Rose forced herself to think clearly. 'We will need new carts and trays; I will see the joiner who made the last lot and try and get him to supply us with more. If he can't get them to us within the week I'll go elsewhere. I'll see a plumber tonight about the water. I don't want anyone moving around in the other room more than is absolutely necessary until the floor is made safe: it's a long drop into the cellar. When water is available we'll scrub this place down – get as many people to help as you can. I'll pay three shillings a day, but they'll need to bring their own bucket and scrubbing brush. As soon as it's clean and the smell of smoke has gone we'll get stores in and start work as normal . . . a week, say? Once we're back in business I'll see about repairs to the other room.'

'First things first,' Joe agreed. 'You wait, this place will be good as new when we've done.'

His optimism cheered Rose, but she knew, as he did not, that every one of the measures she had outlined so decisively needed money – money that she did not have.

She remained a little longer, helping where she could, but it became clear that she would be more usefully employed in making the necessary arrangements with the plumber and the joiner. She left the bakery, after being assured that Joe would remain until the windows were made secure, and that he and the others would return early the next morning.

It was eight o'clock before she returned to the shop from

her errands, with promises that the water supply would be
transferred first thing the next day and that the replacement
carts and trays could be ready by the end of the week. She
was exhausted, but one task still remained, the most difficult
of all. She wrote to the Finlaysons, telling them briefly that
there had been a serious fire, but that she had made all the
necessary provisions for resuming production as soon as
possible. She hoped that by the time they received it she
would be able to tell them that this was in fact true.

After closing the letter she picked up her pen again,
intending to write to her father and sister. The effort was
beyond her, and what written words could have the impact
of a personal appeal? Her pride rebelled, but the conclusion
was clear. Tomorrow she must force herself to undertake
the journey she had sworn she would never make again.

Rose took a cab from the station. The familiar lanes
were winter-stark, the black branches iced with frost. The
old landmarks aroused in her no nostalgic fondness; she
thought only of the ordeal before her, as she approached yet
again her father's house in the role of suppliant. Even when
she left the cab opposite the tree that had witnessed her first
tryst with Simon she scarcely registered its former significance; it might have happened to some other woman, with
whom her present self had no link.

She walked up the drive, picking up her skirts to keep
them from the snow. Out here in the countryside, on the
higher ground, there had been considerable falls. The lawns
in front of the house were covered to a depth of a couple of
inches. Suddenly she stopped, puzzled. At the side of the
house stood a snowman, complete with a bright muffler
and hat. Around it the snow, where it had not been scraped
clear of the grass to construct the rotund figure, showed
footprints, some of them obviously a small child's. Had
Sarah married, then, and had a child? Rose found the
prospect unlikely and obscurely displeasing. No doubt it

was merely one of the children from her Sunday school, or even some grandchild or younger sibling of one of the servants. She slowly resumed her progress, frowning.

A maid answered the door; Rose did not recognise her. 'Is Miss Brunton at home?' she asked tentatively.

'Miss Brunton? Oh, there's nobody of that name here.'

'She may have married. Miss Sarah Brunton?'

The maid shook her head. 'You must have got the wrong house. The mistress here is Mrs Felicity Mannion,' she said and made to close the door.

'Please!' Rose said desperately, putting out her hand. 'My father and sister used to live here. I need to contact them urgently. Could you ask Mrs Mannion if she has any idea where they live now?'

After a moment's hesitation, the maid stood aside and admitted her. She showed Rose into the room that had been her mother's parlour. 'Could you wait here, please, while I see if Mrs Mannion is at home? What name shall I say?'

'Mrs Olivant . . . I was Miss Rose Brunton.'

Rose looked about the parlour, which she would scarcely have recognised. A fashionable Japanese screen and a paper fan spread open on the wall, the pale green wallpaper and the oriental vases and carvings everywhere displayed testified to a taste far more advanced than Mrs Brunton's.

'I am sorry to have kept you waiting . . . please, do sit down, Mrs Olivant.'

Rose turned quickly as a tall, slender young woman entered the room. 'Mrs Mannion?'

She nodded. 'I understand you are looking for your sister?'

'And my father, William Brunton. This was our family home . . . it was built for my father.'

'Really?' Mrs Mannion smiled politely. 'And you have lost touch with your family, I take it?'

'There was a misunderstanding,' Rose said awkwardly.

'Quite . . . I'm afraid I will be of no use to you, Mrs Olivant. We have lived here for four years, and I know nothing of any previous owners.'

'But you bought it from my father?'

'No. It was a Mr Hewitt who lived here before us. He was a mill owner from Macclesfield, I believe, who bought the place on his retirement. He did not enjoy good health, and his doctor advised a milder climate. He had left for the south of France before we even saw the house. I really have no idea who was the owner before him.'

'I see . . .' Rose got to her feet. 'I'll go into town. My father has an iron foundry; I will be able to get news of him there. Thank you for seeing me, Mrs Mannion.'

'I am sorry not to have been able to help. Mr Brunton's business will be more useful, I'm sure.'

As Rose picked her way down the lane to the main road, she told herself that Mrs Mannion was right. Her father and Sarah would have found the house too big; they must have moved to somewhere smaller and perhaps more convenient for the works. She would have preferred not to have seen her father for the first time at his office, but at least she could be certain to get news of him there.

When at last she came within sight of the premises, she was too preoccupied with preparing herself for the coming encounter to notice any changes in the building. She approached the porter, sentry-like in his box at the gate.

'I should like to see Mr Brunton. Do you know if he is in his office?'

The man, a stranger to her, gazed at Rose in disbelief. 'Mr Brunton?'

'Yes. Your employer, Mr William Brunton,' Rose said sharply. Tired, cold, worried, she was in no mood to be delayed by a halfwit. 'You do know him, I suppose?'

'I know my employer all right, missis.' He jabbed a finger

in the direction of the office opposite his box. 'If you've got eyes in your head there's his name up on that board, nice and plain. And it isn't William Brunton. It wouldn't be, would it, seeing as he's been dead this good nine years?'

'Dead? My father?'

The man frowned, but he answered more mildly, 'If your father was Mr Brunton, yes . . . here, watch out!'

Rose staggered and would have fallen if the porter had not caught her and helped her to a seat in his box.

'Look, I'm sorry . . . if I'd known it was your father I would've tried to break it more gentle, like. Shall I get you someone from the office?'

Rose nodded. The darkness that had suddenly flooded her vision was already ebbing, and by the time an anxious-looking clerk had hurried over from the office she was able to take in what he was saying.

'And everything went to his new family?' she asked, scarcely believing her ears.

'Every penny. Poor Miss Sarah had to go for a governess somewhere. A crying shame, it was.'

'You don't know where she is?'

'Oh, no. Mr Collins might know. I think he helped her a lot at that time.'

Rose thanked him and sat a moment in silence, considering what to do. Go to see Collins? She doubted whether it would achieve anything. Sarah's address she could obtain from him later, when her business affairs were less pressing. As she made her way back to the station she tacitly acknowledged that, now that Sarah was clearly unable to offer her any financial help, her search for her sister had lost its urgency.

Rose reached home too late to begin the round of visits to banks and, a last resort, moneylenders that was now her only hope of raising the money she needed. As she had half expected, Robert Finlayson came into the shop that evening. She had dreaded the interview, but it passed off better than she had feared.

'At least it was no worse. Someone could have been killed, especially if it had spread to the houses. I don't suppose there's any suspicion of arson?' he said, as she concluded a brief and deliberately optimistic description of the damage.

'No. It was an accident with a lighted candle in a store room. There's no doubt about that.'

'So we will be all right with the insurers?'

She bit her lip. There was no point in trying to conceal it from him. 'We weren't insured. I let the premiums lapse.'

'You did what?'

'There were so many bills, these last few months . . . I thought it wouldn't matter, just for a while . . .'

'I never thought you'd be so daft.'

Rose could not meet his gaze. She had no defence to make.

'You said in the letter that everything would be put in order in a week or two,' Finlayson continued mercilessly. 'How can you do that without the insurance money?'

'I thought I could get help from my family; I can't. Tomorrow I'll go to see if I can raise the money elsewhere. Don't worry, I'll pay you and Minnie back in full, even if you have to wait a while.'

'It's not that so much . . . I just never thought you'd play silly beggars over insurance,' he said, shaking his head. 'I don't know what Minnie will say, I really don't.'

'Tell her I've learned my lesson, if that's any consolation,' she said wrily.

'Well . . .' He went to the door, sparing her the reproaches he had the right to make. 'I'll look in again tomorrow night and see how you've got on at the banks. And mind, don't you go near the moneylenders. Nothing but bloodsuckers, the lot of them. Once you get in their hands you've had it.'

'I'll need to get money to pay Bradley's, apart from anything else.'

'Don't worry about that. I'll square the boss, one way or another. No sharks, now!'

The following morning, Rose began her attempt to raise money. It was a sobering experience. As a lone woman, without the backing of husband, father, brother she was received courteously but, as she soon realised, without any serious intention of risking good money. Time after time some bank manager, expressing admiration for her achievements and sympathy for her misfortune, concluded with an apologetic smile, 'Ancoats, you know . . . and these little businesses are so vulnerable . . . I'm so sorry.'

Her final rejection left Rose so downcast that she could not bring herself to face the moneylenders who were now her only hope. She went to the bakery to see how work was progressing and returned to the shop in Ancoats.

'You might as well get your tea, Hannah,' she said wearily, taking off her hat. 'I'll watch the counter for a while.'

Left alone, Rose moved restlessly about the room, tidying the shelves, sweeping up some spilt sugar, anything to avoid the thoughts that awaited her first moment of idleness. It was the quietest part of the day, after the tea-time rush, and there were few customers to distract her. She had almost finished every obvious task when the sound of the bell offered welcome relief. She greeted with a smile the customer now closing the door behind him. A tall, powerfully built man, well dressed, he was a stranger to her. She wondered what had brought him to the area; he looked far too prosperous to belong there.

He came to the counter, looking about him at the shop and its stock with an air of assessing their value. 'Can I help you?' she asked, a little sharply.

'Bradley's,' he said abruptly, concluding his survey and at

last turning to her. He was in his late thirties perhaps, dark haired, with a heavy face saved from dullness by unexpectedly shrewd blue eyes.

'Bradley's?' Rose repeated, a terrible suspicion springing to life. 'But this isn't their day . . . and where is Mr Finlayson?'

'Why do you want to know?'

He was smiling; Rose had the uncomfortable feeling that he was playing with her. 'Mr Finlayson has been Bradley's traveller ever since I began here. I think of him as a friend.'

He shook his head. 'Not always a good thing, you know. It can lead to a salesman letting his heart rule his head. A man might give credit to a friend that he really should refuse.'

'I'm sure Mr Finlayson was always very fair . . .' Rose murmured, her fears strengthening. 'He hasn't . . . Nothing has happened to him, has it?'

'And what would happen to him?'

'He hasn't lost his job? You aren't taking over his round?'

'And if I am?'

'If you are, then Mr Bradley is a great fool and has lost his best representative,' she said hotly. 'Robert Finlayson was honesty itself and if he gave me credit it was only because he knew that I wouldn't let him down . . . and I won't, come what may.'

The man regarded her, still smiling, but now it did not seem to Rose that he was mocking her at all. He put out his hand. 'I had better introduce myself, Mrs Olivant. Michael Bradley . . . and I hope I'm not a great fool, and I certainly haven't lost my best salesman. Finlayson will be in later this week as usual.'

'And why did you not make that plain at the outset? My time is too precious to waste on playing guessing games,' she said, all the more sharply for her relief that Finlayson was not to suffer for his association with her.

'I'm sorry. I meant no harm, I assure you. Please, can't we start again?'

Reluctantly, she gave him her hand.

'Friends?' he asked, retaining it.

'I don't make friends so easily, Mr Bradley.'

'No? Well, we will see. Is there somewhere more private, where we can talk undisturbed?'

Rose frowned, intending to protest that there was no need for privacy, but she thought better of it. 'Come into the kitchen,' she said, drawing aside the curtain. 'Hannah, would you mind watching the shop for a few minutes?'

Bradley looked about the kitchen with the same undisguised curiosity that he had already displayed in the shop. 'You don't do any baking here?'

'No. The cook-shop makes the soup and most of the pies and puddings it sells; the bakery all the bread, and the produce we supply to shops and the market stall.'

He nodded. 'Does that work out well?'

'On the whole. Sit down, please,' she added, her initial hostility dispersing beneath his good nature and her growing sense that there was some purpose behind his inquisitiveness.

'Then why were you in such financial straits that you let your insurance premiums lapse?' he asked, sitting back in his chair and unbuttoning his coat.

He was watching her closely. She knew instinctively that he would respect an honest answer. 'I think I started the bakery too soon. I didn't have enough capital. I've never quite caught up.'

'You were too hasty?'

'Yes. I wouldn't make the same mistake again.'

'Do you think you'll get the chance?'

She responded to the challenge in his voice. 'I won't give up, whatever happens. If I can't find any other way to clear my debts, I'll sell up and start again somewhere else.'

'Will that be necessary?'

'The banks aren't interested. Tomorrow I will try the moneylenders.'

He nodded, regarding her in silence, making up his mind. 'Don't do that,' he said, with as little emphasis as if they were discussing the advisability of taking an umbrella in case of rain. 'I'll put in whatever money you need. We can go into partnership.'

'No!'

'Oh? Why not?' he asked calmly.

'I don't want a partner, that's why.'

'You need one, though.'

'I have managed alone so far.'

'You have done very well, but as you admitted yourself, you didn't have the resources for the bakery. It's always the problem for a small business. You want to expand, but you can't get the capital. The bank won't help you: I will.'

'It's not what I want!' Rose insisted. 'Until now I have had complete control of everything that happens. With a partner everything would be different . . . it would be spoiled.'

'It wouldn't be the same, I agree, but why assume that it would be worse? Your risks would be halved, you would have the funds to get the bakery back on to a sound footing. Do you really want to struggle on alone, never knowing where the next penny is to come from, in hock to the moneylenders?'

Rose stared down at her hands, remembering the despair that had crushed her after the fire. She could not deny that there would be advantages to what Bradley was suggesting. 'But you would want to run the whole thing!' she protested, looking up. 'You would take over; it wouldn't be mine any more, after all the work I have put into it . . .'

'I know what you are feeling. I started out the hard way, like you: a single horse and cart, supplying small shops in Salford. I wouldn't have wanted to have a partner, either.'

'Why are you doing this, anyway? Bradley's is a wholesale business. What's in it for you?'

'I have been wanting to move into supplying bread. With the flour and dry goods at wholesale price and Bradley's delivery system, your business will be cheaper and more efficient. It makes sense, don't you think?' He got to his feet. 'I know it's a lot for you to decide so suddenly. Shall I call again tomorrow? I can see that you are tired and I don't want to push you into something you will regret.'

Rose saw him out. Watching him stride, tall and powerful, down the wet street as though he had not a care or a fear in the world, she felt reluctant admiration, mingled with resentment. 'It's all very well for him,' she thought. 'He needn't think that he can buy me. I would sooner start all over again with nothing.'

Her rebellious spirit did not survive a night of hard thinking, and a single visit to one of the most reputable of the moneylenders, whose interest rates on a loan of the amount she required horrified her. Michael Bradley's offer was her only chance of salvaging the business and, for all her defiant thoughts of starting out again with nothing, she knew that it would be madness to refuse.

Bradley returned the following evening, shortly before ten. He waited while she served a girl, a stranger to Rose, sent by her mother for a penn'orth of Godfrey's Cordial.

Rose leaned over the counter. 'What is it for?'

'Make the baby sleep while mam's at work,' the child answered readily.

Rose gave her back the penny. 'Tell your mother I only sell Godfrey's if the doctor has said the child must have it.'

The girl fumbled with the penny, looking up at her wide-eyed over the counter, as though she suspected that if she could but find the right form of words she would be given what she had been sent for. 'Have you got any other sleeping stuff then, missis?'

'Go home and tell your mother that the baby is better crying than drugged with laudanum.'

The girl suddenly took fright and ran out of the shop. Michael Bradley shut the door.

'You must lose a lot of sales by that. Most of the shops round here sell Godfrey's or Infant's Quietness. She will only get it somewhere else, you know.'

'I won't have it on my conscience. God knows how many babies it sends to eternal rest, from carelessness or stupidity. I don't need money enough to be prepared to make it from drugging infants so that they can't cry for food.'

He shook his head. 'You are a remarkable woman, Rose.'

'I am used to making rules and sticking to them. And one of my rules is that since my husband's death no man addresses me by my Christian name.'

He raised his brows. 'I have rules, too. I make it a rule not to treat women as though they were children, without any real understanding of life or business. If I didn't, I wouldn't be considering a partnership with you now. And another one of my rules is that I only deal with people I trust, and who can trust me. Do you think that I need to be kept at arm's length by silly formality of that sort? Because if you can't trust me enough to allow me to use your name then I see no point in taking our business dealings any further.'

His steady gaze was disconcertingly frank. She hesitated, and shrugged. 'As you wish. I have grown accustomed to formality; I prefer it, but I don't intend to cut off my nose to spite my face.'

'Very sensible. I take it then that you have decided in favour of accepting my offer?'

'Yes . . . subject to some satisfactory agreement being drawn up, of course.'

'I will put it in the hands of my lawyer. In the meantime, some celebration would be in order, don't you think?'

From the breast of his capacious greatcoat he produced a bottle. 'Champagne,' he explained, seeing her frown. 'It's cold enough outside to be chilled still. If you bring glasses, I'll open it.'

Rose stared at the bottle. She remembered the early days with Simon, and the champagne that he had insisted that she try. She hadn't cared for it, and he had finished the bottle alone, and gone on to brandy. It had been the first time that she had seen him drunk. She shook her head. 'No. I'm sorry. I won't have strong drink in the house.'

'Another one of your rules?'

'Not one I am prepared to waive . . . even for my partner.'

'On religious grounds?'

She hesitated. She had only to agree, and preserve the secrecy that she had always maintained about her past life. It would hardly even be a lie: her family had been strict abstainers, from religious principle. Even to Robert Finlayson she would probably have prevaricated, but with Bradley she found herself wanting to tell the truth. 'My husband drank. I can hardly bear the sight or smell of alcohol.'

'Do you think all men are like him?'

'As a solitary woman I can't afford to take chances. I have had my own way to make ever since my husband's death, eleven years ago now.'

'You have made a good job of it,' he said, putting the bottle aside. 'It must be hard for you to give up your independence now.'

She nodded, softened by his ready understanding. For the first time she began to feel that their partnership could be something more than bitter necessity. 'Look, won't you come into the kitchen and sit down? I usually make myself tea at about this time. I know it's a poor substitute for champagne . . .'

'It certainly is,' he said ruefully, but he accepted her invitation.

'I'm sorry about the champagne. It was a nice thought. Take it home. Perhaps your wife might like to celebrate your new venture,' Rose suggested, turning away to put the kettle on to the fire.

'Perhaps she might . . . if I had a wife.'

Rose was glad that her face was averted. She would not have wished her expression to reveal her mixture of emotions, of simultaneous relief and alarm. She was afraid of her own pleasure at his words, and yet she knew that she would not have wished it otherwise. When she turned to him again, her manner was more distant. She confined their conversation to business. She had sensed danger, a threat to the self-sufficiency she had so painfully constructed. She would not willingly surrender it, despite the first stirring of betrayal in her own heart.

Perhaps from some generous wish not to take advantage of the concession he had wrung from her, Michael Bradley did not again address her by her Christian name for the remainder of his visit. She was perversely disappointed by the omission.

CHAPTER

Nine

Sarah picked up the teapot. 'Another cup, Marion?'

'Well . . . if there's a drop left . . .'

Sarah smiled, and poured the last of the tea into her companion's cup. Every Sunday they had much the same polite exchange, but the very predictability of Marion Lewis's response was somehow part of the charm of their cosy afternoon together, the placid culmination to her week. For Sarah, familiarity was never boring.

'Take that slice of seed cake, please. I got the cook to make it specially. I know it's your favourite,' she urged, pushing the plate towards her guest.

As Marion accepted, after a ritual demurral, Sarah got to her feet to poke up the fire into a comfortable blaze. She stood a moment at the hearth, looking about her contentedly at the room that over the past nine years had gradually become her haven. It was crowded with ornaments and mementoes, a homely clutter of no intrinsic value but rich in associations. Louise and Beatrice smiled at her from a dozen photographs; a few of her mother's treasured pieces of china adorned the chiffonier; a sampler sewn in her own girlhood hung on one side of the mantelpiece, balanced on

the other by the only one that Rose had ever been induced
to work.

Marion put down her teacup with an air of finality. At
thirty-five she was about Sarah's own age, a governess in
a large family not far from the Vaughans. The oldest child
of an impoverished clergyman, she had been obliged to
earn her own living from an early age, and was a far more
experienced teacher than Sarah. At first Sarah had been
intimidated by her precise ways and air of authority, but
as their friendship had strengthened she had come to
accept her tendency to dominate and her unyielding
moral code.

Their precious Sunday afternoons together were usually
filled with the gossip saved up from their week, but today
Marion was uncharacteristically silent, though not unhappy,
Sarah thought. She resumed her seat and picked up her
knitting.

'It's for the chapel bazaar,' she explained, for Marion was
a strict Sabbatarian.

'Yes . . .' Marion said absently.

'A penny for them?'

Marion looked at her, as though considering how best to
phrase what she was about to say. Tall, with prematurely
grey hair that Sarah considered gave her a distinguished
air, she looked every inch the governess, strict but fair.

'I had some news this week,' she began.

'Good news, I hope?'

'I scarcely like to call it that. My uncle died, in India. He
was a tea planter. He died some weeks ago, but my father
has only just heard. He had been out in the sub-continent
since he was quite a boy. I don't remember ever seeing
him, although I believe he stayed with us once on a period
of home leave when I was small.'

'I hope the news has not come as a great shock to your
father?'

'He is sorry, of course, but they were never close. Their lives had been so different.' She hesitated. 'The thing is, he has left each of us a legacy in his will. A thousand to the nephews, five hundred to the nieces.'

'Five hundred pounds?' Sarah repeated.

'Yes!' Marion said, allowing herself to express the excitement she had been holding in check. 'Just think, Sarah! So much could be done with such a sum!'

'I can hardly imagine it,' Sarah said wistfully. 'It will be a nest egg for your old age.'

Marion leaned forward. 'It will be more than that. We can do what I have always wanted, and have never thought would be possible. We can start a school together.'

'Marion!'

'Well, why not? Haven't we talked about it, Sunday after Sunday?'

'Yes, but never as a practical proposition. You can't risk so much on a dream!'

'Don't think of it like that. I believe this was *meant*. Just imagine: a small school, in the country, but not far from town; a place where girls can be given a thorough grounding in the essentials of a good education, in surroundings that conduce to perfect health of mind and body.'

'Yes . . .' Sarah agreed, a little doubtfully. More practical, less given to enthusiasm than Marion, she found her thoughts turning to difficulties with staff, recalcitrant pupils, parents who declined to pay their bills. 'It would be very nice, of course, but there would be such a lot of responsibility, wouldn't there?'

'Nothing worthwhile is ever easy,' Marion said, with a note of reproof. 'It would be a challenge, certainly, but one that we are well qualified to meet.'

'I suppose so . . .'

'I thought you would be so pleased. Something is wrong, isn't it? Be honest, now.'

Sarah sighed. 'I would be sorry to leave Louise and Beatrice, of course, but I had been thinking for some time that they might be beginning to need more than I can give them. They would benefit from going away to school, and I don't suppose Mr Vaughan would object. The real problem is the money. I have almost nothing to contribute. It would be risking your inheritance, and I wouldn't be able to help. There is the money I got from my stepmother, of course, and a few pounds I have been able to add to it, but it still doesn't amount to much.'

'Really, Sarah!' Marion said, eyes widening in amazement. 'As though that matters!'

'But it does! I don't want to feel . . . I don't know, like a poor relation.'

'And if I say that your support will mean more to me than hundreds – thousands of pounds? If you won't join me, I will forget the whole idea.'

'But, Marion . . .'

'But nothing!' Marion said, in the firm tone that had quelled so many girlish rebellions. 'Now, are you with me or are you not?'

'If you are sure . . .' Sarah said, her reservations not quite dispelled, but with the first stirrings of excitement.

'I would not have proposed it in the first place if I weren't. Now that's settled, we can make a start. Where shall it be? Have you any ideas? What do you think about somewhere like Altrincham? It's not far from Manchester by train and the air is good . . .'

The winter afternoon faded into dusk, and still they talked, breathing life into what had seemed nothing more than an impossible dream. As it grew more real to Sarah, she found herself for the first time since her father's death imagining a future in which, by her own efforts, she could attain real independence. It was unexpectedly exhilarating.

★

Rose intended to make enquiries after her sister once the repairs to the bakery were in train and everything had returned to normal. The thought nagged her from time to time, like the twinge of a tooth requiring attention, but it always seemed to be when she had too much to do. She put it off from day to day; the twinge grew fainter and at last ceased. She forgot all about it.

She remained determined to bring Eva home, or at least to send her to a school nearby, so that she might see her more often. Rose still had no intention of allowing her daughter to grow up in Ancoats, and until the bakery repaid all the money now being poured into it there was no question of buying a house of the sort for which she longed.

The bakery was soon back in production, but Michael Bradley wanted more than the essential repairs to be done. Rose had installed old ovens; he wanted them replaced by the most up-to-date equipment, capable of an increased, faster output. At first, Rose had her doubts, but she was soon fired by his enthusiasm. The renovated premises were brighter and more efficient than the old makeshift accommodation; as a final, triumphant gesture Rose had the name Olivant painted in large white letters on the roof, witness to her pride at its resurrection from the ashes.

'It should be Olivant and Bradley, you know,' Michael Bradley pointed out as they walked away together from one of their frequent visits to the bakery.

'There wasn't room on the roof,' she replied disingenuously. 'You don't mind, do you?'

'Keep it as Olivant for now. It's an unusual name.'

'My husband was Scottish.'

'Were you happy together?'

'It doesn't matter now, does it?'

'In other words: mind your own business. You don't give much away, do you?'

'I see no reason to drag my private life into everything, that's all.'

'And I see no reason why you dole out information about yourself as grudgingly as if every word hurt you. We are partners, after all. Isn't it natural that we should get to know each other?'

Rose felt suddenly breathless, as though she had been transported to some high altitude, where the air was too thin for her. She had not faced such questions in years; she had told Mrs Heeney something of her life with Simon, but this was different. To tell Michael would be to admit him within the first line of her defences; her very yearning to do so strengthened her sense of danger.

'We will find out all that is necessary in the course of our business connection,' she said stiffly. 'Anything else is irrelevant.'

'It needn't be. Finlayson told me today that you have a daughter. I don't think I have ever heard you mention her name?'

'Eva.'

'She doesn't live with you?'

'I sent her away, into the country, for her health,' Rose said, half truthfully. 'I am thinking of bringing her back to a school where I will be able to see her a little more often.'

'How old is she?'

'Eleven.'

'Where is she, exactly? Do you manage to find time to see her often?'

She glanced at him sharply. 'She's out at Caddishead. No, I don't see her very often. It used to distress her, in any case. I found it was better not to unsettle her by frequent visits.'

He smiled. 'Spring is coming early this year,' he said, with apparent inconsequence. 'Nice weather for a drive, wouldn't you say?'

'I don't have time for drives.'

'You can make time, if you want to. Next Sunday? I will hire a gig and take us out to Caddishead. We can make a day of it.'

She wanted to refuse, to put him firmly in his place, to keep him out of the life she had made so safe, and so sterile: she could not bring herself to utter the words.

They had reached the shop. 'Sunday, then, about ten?' Before she could protest, he was gone.

For many years before Simon's death, Rose had worn only the cheapest, drabbest of clothes; since then, her gradually improving circumstances had been reflected in dress of better quality, but she had never regained her girlhood interest and pleasure in her appearance. There was so much to do, so little time to spare, that she had come to adopt a plain, serviceable style: dark bodices, cut loose enough about the arms and shoulders to allow her freedom to work, stacking shelves and lifting heavy baking trays; sensible skirts, without too much fullness to catch on obstructions. Her hair, too, she had worn in the same simple knot at the back of her head which could be dressed in a few minutes. She was always neat and presentable, but she gave no thought to showing herself to her best advantage.

That night, Rose was restless. After supper, leaving Hannah in the shop, she went up to her room and scrutinised her wardrobe, flicking with mounting dissatisfaction through the few, well-worn items it contained. Nothing was new, or designed to flatter. She did not, she told herself, wish to impress Michael Bradley, but he himself was always well dressed, and she had no intention of sitting by his side in shabby, old-fashioned clothes.

The following morning, Rose went to a local dressmaker and, after a lengthy discussion, ordered a costume, to be ready by the weekend, and a white blouse, finely pleated at the breast, with a high collar. To compound her extravagance, she visited a milliner's and selected a matching hat.

The new outfit was delivered at the last moment, on Saturday night. Rose went upstairs to try it on. The dressmaker had done well; it fitted to perfection. In the palest grey that Rose had been able to persuade herself was practical, the jacket had the sleeves, puffed at the shoulder and tapering to a close-fitting cuff, that were the latest word in fashion. It was short, with a curved edge, bound with braid of a darker grey, and met at the front without fastenings, showing the crisp white blouse beneath. The skirt, cut on the bias, fell smoothly in front with added fullness at the back. Not since her early frivolous days with Simon had she possessed anything so stylish.

Rose turned this way and that in front of her pier glass, craning her neck to check each angle. She saw a woman still almost as slender and supple as that ardent, headstrong girl had been, but slower and more deliberate in her movements. The freshness and naive charm that the years had marred had been replaced by greater strength and confidence. She looked, as she was, a woman who had survived great sorrow. Suffering had left her beauty all but intact, and only the hardness in her eyes, the tightness about her mouth, her guarded expression, showed what had been lost. Rose turned reluctantly from the glass and with a sigh resumed her workday clothes.

Sunday was a perfect spring morning. Even in Ancoats the lightness and promise of the season could be felt in the air, free for one day from the worst of the smoke and fumes from the works that jostled for space with railways and housing. Instead of the clatter of the daily rush to and from the mills and factories, the streets were quiet, the piercing urgency of hooters giving way to the melancholy clang of bells as the churches summoned their adherents. Apart from those hurrying to church, few women were to be seen;

Sunday dinner demanded the labour of all but the poorest during most of the morning. Men were more in evidence, chatting together at street corners, enveloped in a cloud of pipe smoke, lounging at their ease before strolling on to the pint or two that whet, and occasionally ruined, their appetite for the best meal of the week. Newly shaven, they were smart in the boots and white mufflers and billypot hats that appeared on a Sunday, even if the boots at least might be back in the pawnshop on Monday morning.

'Glad to be out?' Michael Bradley asked, as the streets began to give way to the silence of the suburbs, where the houses sprawled at their ease amidst grass and trees and spring flowers.

'Oh, yes,' Rose said, smiling, 'but I almost feel uneasy to be doing nothing, as though I have forgotten something important.'

'You have. You've forgotten how to enjoy life.'

'Perhaps I haven't had much to enjoy for the last ten years,' she said sharply.

'There's always something, if you look for it.'

'What do you . . .' She broke off, unwilling to begin their outing with a quarrel.

'What do I know about it, you mean?'

'I suppose so.'

He was silent for a moment, and she thought she had offended him, but just as she was about to apologise he began to speak, more slowly and gravely than usual. 'I was brought up in the country, by foster parents, an elderly couple. They took me from the workhouse because they wanted help on their farm. My parents were Irish. They died on the road between Liverpool and Manchester, of starvation, exhaustion, fever. I was only three or so at the time. I didn't know my surname, and my parents had no papers bearing it, so I was given the name of the couple who adopted me.'

'Were they kind to you?'

'In their way. They worked me hard, but they fed me as well as they fed themselves and they sent me to school whenever the farm work was slack. One way and another, I learned enough to get by. When I was fifteen, Joe Bradley died. His wife had been failing for some time; she didn't last long afterwards. The lease went to a young couple. They would have kept me on but I fancied a change. I came into Manchester and got work as a carter. I knew how to handle horses and I had the strength for the loading. I liked the work, but I didn't take kindly to being at the boss's beck and call.'

'No,' Rose said, 'I can imagine.'

He laughed. 'In the end I made my mind up that I'd sooner give the orders than take them. I got work navvying, up on the Settle to Carlisle line. I thought I knew what hard work was, but I soon found out different. It was getting on for a year before I could put in a day's graft with the best of them. To start off I'd have to down tools about three; I could scarcely drag myself back to the shanties for tiredness.'

'It must have been terrible for you.'

'Well, it was and it wasn't. I wouldn't like to do it again, that's for sure. I stuck it, though, because the money was good. I was able to save it; a lot of the navvies drank it away but heavy drinking was never one of my vices . . . not even champagne.'

Rose coloured at his ironic tone. 'I'm sorry. I judge all men by my husband, I suppose.'

'It's hardly fair, is it?'

'It's safer.'

'Sometimes you need to take a risk.'

'It depends on how much is at stake. I have long since decided that it's not worth it,' she said, meeting his eyes steadily.

Beneath his gaze, so direct and frank, she felt unprotected; he seemed to detect the confusion behind the façade of strength and decision she wished to present to the world. It was unnerving yet reassuring, as though she were facing a doctor who perceived symptoms she had long concealed, and who could promise health. Nobody else had ever questioned her front of self-sufficiency and invulnerability; perhaps with others she really was what she appeared to be, or perhaps only he cared enough to look so far. She wondered whether he was so with everyone he met; the thought was not pleasant to her.

'Perhaps you will change your mind, given time,' he said, with the good-humoured smile that gave him an appeal far greater than his features warranted.

Some people, she supposed, might consider Michael Bradley ugly. Certainly, there was nothing fine in his face. His brow projected in a heavy ridge over his eyes; his nose appeared to have been broken at some time and was not quite straight. Almost childishly full, even so early in the morning his cheeks showed a bluish haze of stubble. A fleshy curve blurred the jaw; his chin was deeply cleft in the centre. His mouth was not particularly well shaped, setting in repose in an irregular line that hinted at a mind generally finding cause for amusement in the world about it. The only aspect of his face that might attract attention was his eyes, though not by any beauty of size or shape, for they were of pleasant but unremarkable blue. Penetrating but humorous, they indicated a man who had seen enough of humanity to be without illusions, yet who retained an unquenchable interest and delight in life. It was a kind face, yet its strength made her feel that even his most obstreperous employee would not care to incur his displeasure.

'I don't usually change my mind, particularly not about things of importance.'

'Anything worth waiting for takes time. I'm a patient man.'

'So you were telling me,' she said, glad to return to safer territory. 'You left navvying?'

'The moment I had enough money behind me. Navvies don't often make old bones and I wasn't taking any chances. I came back to Salford, bought myself a horse and cart, and touted for custom. Things were hard at first. I gave myself a year to make a living. After that I would have gone on the tramp, navvying again. The year was all but up when I had a stroke of luck. I met one of the gangers on the Settle line who'd made his money and set up in the wholesale line, fruit and vegetables that he sold to market traders. He gave me a contract for old time's sake, carting potatoes mostly. The money wasn't good but it kept me going and it made me think. When the contract was up I bought a cartload of potatoes from him and went around the small shops, selling them for what I could get.'

'It must have been a struggle to get started.'

'I couldn't have done it if I'd had anyone to think about but myself. It was worth it, though. Bradley's is one of the biggest wholesalers in Manchester now,' he said, with a pride she could well understand.

'And you're your own boss.'

He shrugged. 'And human nature being what it is, now that I've got what I want I've started to wonder if it's been worth it. Everything comes with a price, and I've paid it . . . just like you.'

'Oh? And what price do you think I've paid?'

'A daughter that you never see?'

'I am seeing her now, aren't I?' Rose replied, frowning.

'You're right,' he said equably, 'it's none of my business. Now, have you any idea where we're supposed to be going?'

They reached the farm in the early afternoon, having stopped for lunch at a country inn, where Michael Bradley ordered a private parlour. He had a pint of beer with his meal. Rose reflected sadly that in all the years of her marriage she had never seen Simon have one drink and be satisfied.

Alerted by the barking of the dogs that raced to the gate as the carriage approached, Mrs Ball came out to greet them, wiping her hands on her apron. A small, wiry woman with dark hair drawn back in a neat bun, she regarded Rose coolly.

'The lad'll see to the horse,' she said, beckoning to a young boy who was hauling the dogs back by the collars. 'Come in, you'll be feeling the cold after coming all this way.'

Mrs Ball opened the door of a stiff, dismal room. 'The parlour's in here.'

'Can't we come into the kitchen?' Michael asked, rubbing his hands vigorously together. 'It's good and warm in there, I'll be bound.'

Mrs Ball looked at him approvingly, and led them down the stone-flagged passage to the room that was the heart of the house. Rose admired Michael's social ease; by the time they reached the kitchen, he was chatting to Mrs Ball as though they were old acquaintances.

'Sit down and I'll get a drink of tea,' she said, going to fetch cups from a dark old dresser. She paused as she placed them on the table and called into the scullery, 'Maria! Go and get Evie, there's a good girl.'

The casual use of the affectionate diminutive, which Rose thought particularly ugly, affected her unpleasantly. Although Rose had been relieved not to have to concern herself about her daughter's welfare, the reality that another woman had been mothering Eva had not until now fully struck her. Her nervousness grew, and with it a resentment she could neither justify nor quell.

'Where is she?' Michael asked.

'Out in the dairy. I kept her in all morning, seeing as we

were expecting you,' Mrs Ball said, with a pointed glance at Rose, 'but when you hadn't come by two o'clock I let her go and help Winnie with the churning. She loves it, bless her.'

'She must be looking forward to seeing her mother again,' Michael said, with an encouraging smile at Rose.

'I don't know that it meant that much to her, to tell you the truth. Not after all this time.'

Rose was spared the necessity of answering by the sound of steps crossing the yard behind the kitchen. A thin, anxious face peered round the scullery door. For a moment Rose felt her heart constrict in disappointment. Could that pale, puny creature be her child? She arranged her features in a welcoming smile, only to realise her mistake as Mrs Ball asked impatiently, 'Well? Couldn't you find her?'

'She's outside, she won't come in,' Maria said timidly.

Rose looked helplessly at Michael. He got to his feet. 'I'll go and say hello, shall I?'

Rose was glad of his intervention, but she felt herself close to panic as she watched him leave the room. She tried to make conversation with Mrs Ball. 'It must be difficult for her, I suppose . . .'

'Stands to reason,' Mrs Ball said, setting down the teapot with a bang.

'Is she usually shy?'

'Evie? Happy as the day's long.'

'Good,' Rose said weakly. It was a relief to hear Michael's voice outside the door and to see him enter once more, holding a dark-haired child, her daughter, she assumed, by the hand.

'Here's your mama now.' Michael led Eva forward. She was a sturdy, well-grown child, red-cheeked, her hair a frizzy mass of dark curls. She could not be described as pretty. Her features were strong, almost coarse, her mouth over-large, set now in a sullen pout; Rose saw in her little of the resemblance to Simon that she had remembered. If anything, she had a look of Sarah, with perhaps some promise of later beauty if her heavy features and lumpen build should ever be refined.

'Don't you know me, Eva?' Rose asked, with a nervous laugh.

'I suppose you're my mam. I can't rightly say for sure.'

'I hope you've been a good girl for Mrs Ball?' Rose continued, thinking it wiser to ignore her ungracious tone.

'Good as gold,' Mrs Ball put in. The girl shot her an affectionate glance, the sudden animation transforming her face.

'Won't you show us the dairy, Eva?' Rose asked, and saw her daughter's expression relapse once more into discontent.

'Is that what you like best?' Michael asked.

'No. The pigs,' Eva said readily, directing her answer solely to Michael, 'and the horses and all, especially Blossom. I give her a carrot this morning.'

Rose winced at her daughter's slow, broad accent. It was only to be expected, but it was yet another proof of how different Eva had become from the child Rose intended. It was partly Rose's fault, no doubt, but it really would not do.

'Can we see the animals?' Michael was asking. Eva nodded shyly. Although Rose shuddered at the prospect of trudging through mud and manure in the farmyard, a further tête-à-tête with Mrs Ball was even less appealing, and so she braved the cold and dirt. Absurdly, she began to feel a twinge of what might almost be jealousy as she saw how eagerly Eva chatted to Michael, telling him every detail of the hens' diet and the pig's vast appetite.

'She likes to be scratched,' Eva informed him and Michael obediently leaned over the wall of the sty and obliged.

'Come on, give her a tickle!' Michael said, turning to Rose with a smile.

Rose recoiled. 'I've never liked pigs,' she said coldly. 'They are so dirty.'

'No, they aren't,' Eva said, looking to Michael for confirmation.

'That's right. They're as intelligent as a dog, I always think.'

Rose shook her head in distaste and moved away, feeling still further excluded from the easy companionship that was so rapidly developing between Michael and her daughter.

It was the same story for the remainder of their visit. Eva and Michael chatted and joked together; Rose and her daughter remained stilted and wary of each other, a barrier between them that neither could break down.

On the return journey, something of the same stiffness afflicted Rose and Michael. They sat in silence, each wrapped in their own thoughts. At last Michael said, looking towards her, 'A lovely child. You must be proud of her.'

'She needs to learn a little more refinement.'

'She is friendly and natural. What more could anyone ask?'

'She charged around the farmyard like a heifer,' Rose said sourly.

Michael paused before answering, and when he did speak Rose suspected that he was controlling his irritation with some effort. 'How long is it since you last visited her?'

'Too long, obviously,' Rose said, unwilling to admit that she had not seen her daughter since she was five. 'I will need to see that she goes to a school that will cure her of her low tastes.'

'Take care that you don't spoil her.'

'I am hardly likely to do that.'

'You will if you make her awkward and unsure of herself by criticising her every move.'

'I am her mother, for heaven's sake!'

He said nothing, but every line of his face expressed the disapproving rejoinder he did not make. The remainder of the journey passed in near silence, so uncomfortable and disappointing that Rose wondered if even a quarrel could have been worse.

CHAPTER

Ten

'Sarah?'

'In the linen room!' Sarah called, inserting one hand in the pile of sheets she was counting. She looked over her shoulder as Marion Lewis peered round the door, a neat bonnet surmounting her hair. 'Going out?'

'That's what I was coming to tell you: I forgot I was expected in Manchester this afternoon, to see the bank about the loan for the annexe. You will be all right here on your own, won't you?'

'I expect so,' Sarah said, smiling. Even after three years together, and a success which was already necessitating the purchase of a second building to house the large numbers of boarders at the school, Marion persisted in believing that her own continual presence was all that fended off disaster. 'Is there anything I should do while you are away?'

'I don't think so . . . oh, a possible new parent may be coming. She wrote and said she would like to look us over, today or tomorrow. I can't remember the name; the letter is in my desk somewhere.'

'Don't worry about it. I will show her over and give her

tea if she does turn up. Now, off you go. You'll miss the train if you're not careful.'

Marion hesitated a moment, but as Sarah deliberately turned back to her counting she reluctantly took her leave.

Sarah breathed a sigh of relief. Fond as she was of Marion, she at times found herself resenting her assumption that Sarah was capable of little more than obeying her instructions. On the whole their partnership worked well, and Sarah had never regretted her decision to throw in her lot with her friend, but she was always glad of a few hours' peace, without Marion's anxious fussing.

Sarah had completed the inventory of the linen and was beginning to check the stationery cupboard when the bell rang. She hurriedly removed the coarse apron she wore for such tasks and, patting her hair nervously into place, hurried to the parlour in which they received visitors. On the way through the hall she passed the maid who was going to answer the door.

'Oh, Jane, that will probably be a lady interested in seeing over the school. Show her straight into the parlour, will you?'

Sarah had barely time to seat herself behind the businesslike desk which Marion had insisted upon installing in the otherwise cosy room before Jane opened the door, ushering in the visitor, a tall, slender woman, the upper half of her face shaded by a pretty, spotted veil. Sarah rose to her feet with a welcoming smile.

'Mrs Olivant to see you,' Jane said. 'Shall I bring tea now, Miss Brunton?'

Sarah made no answer; she had heard nothing but her sister's name. She stared at Rose, frozen in shock and disbelief. Jane hesitated, and left the room, shaking her head at her mistress's strange ways.

Rose recovered first. She gave a brief laugh and came forward, pulling off her gloves with decisive little movements.

232   JANET BROOMFIELD

'Well! this is a turn up for the books, isn't it? How long have you been a schoolteacher?'

'What? Oh, three years,' Sarah said mechanically. 'I was a governess before that, but then I got the chance of this . . . Rose, I really can't believe it's you! And you look . . .'

'Yes?' Rose said, seating herself unbidden and fastidiously smoothing the skirts of her gown into a becoming drape. 'What do I look?'

'So well,' Sarah said weakly, taking in her sister's dashing little hat and the close-fitting costume that emphasised her trim waist and the swan-like curve of her bosom.

'Better than when you last saw me?'

'You look as you used to look when you were a girl, before . . . before everything went wrong.'

Rose smiled. 'I hope I have a good deal more sense now, however I may look.'

Sarah gazed at her visitor, wondering how to phrase the questions she longed to ask. Clearly, Rose's fortunes had made a remarkable recovery, and with her new prosperity had come a return of the old ascendancy: she was once more in control, of herself and, instantly, of Sarah.

'I tried to tell you about Papa. I wrote to you at Mrs Heeney's but I never heard from you . . .'

'She had left, gone to Canada. I always meant to try and get in touch with you, but what with one thing and another . . . I scarcely have a minute to myself. You know how it is.'

'Yes,' Sarah agreed doubtfully. 'But I don't understand: Marion – Miss Lewis – told me to expect a lady looking for a school for her daughter. I thought you had left Simon? Has there been a reconciliation, after all that happened?' She broke off in confusion, struck by a dreadful conjecture. Surely even Rose could not have formed some illicit liaison?

'When I last saw you I was already carrying a child, although I didn't realise it. Don't worry, she's Simon's daughter all right,' she added sardonically. 'He was found drowned. I am a widow.'

'So you have had to bring up your daughter alone? I can see that it must have taken up a good deal of your time.'

'Eva? Oh, not really,' Rose said, as though the suggestion surprised her. 'I sent her to a foster mother. I was running two or three businesses, you see.'

'Successfully, by the look of things?'

'I have had my ups and downs, but everything is going very well now. No, the problem now is Eva. I have tried one or two schools for her but . . .'

'Things haven't worked out?'

'No. She runs away.'

'She misses you, it's quite natural . . .'

'She doesn't run to me,' Rose said sharply. 'She goes back to her foster mother, on a disgusting farm in the middle of nowhere.'

'Perhaps the schools haven't been suitable?' Sarah suggested, tactfully avoiding any comment on Eva's choice of refuge.

'I selected the best schools in the area,' Rose said, glancing disdainfully around the homely parlour. 'I would not normally have considered a place as small and untried as this, but I saw that your prospectus puts more emphasis than usual on music and drama. Is that right?'

'We wouldn't advertise it if it weren't,' Sarah said tartly. 'Miss Lewis has a great interest in music. She takes the older girls into Manchester for concerts at the Hallé.'

'That won't hold much appeal for Eva. What else?'

'We have a music master who comes to the school three days a week to teach singing and pianoforte, and another who visits on a Monday for violin. I'm sure Marion would be happy to consider engaging another tutor, if your daughter wished to study some other instrument. What is her particular talent?'

In Sarah's experience, such a question usually produced an enthusiastic answer from the fond parent. To her surprise, for the first time since entering the room Rose looked ill at ease.

'It's singing. Popular songs. Vulgar songs, I think them.'

'Well, it's a start, I suppose,' Sarah said encouragingly. 'I'm sure that Marion will be able to lead her on to more serious work.'

Rose looked unconvinced. 'I really don't know . . . and with you being here, too. If I had known that I might have looked elsewhere . . .'

'Oh? Why?'

'You may be too indulgent with her. She needs a firm hand.'

'I have been earning my living for over ten years by teaching and caring for children. I hardly think *you* need to give me instructions on the art, Rose.'

The barbed comment found its mark. Rose was silent, looking down at the pretty, lilac gloves that lay in her lap and putting them meticulously together, finger to finger. At last she said, less confidently, 'It is very important that this time Eva should be happy. Every time she runs away it causes me a great deal of inconvenience . . . and distress, of course.'

'I'm sure it does. Have you considered letting her return to the farm for another year or two?'

'That is out of the question. She would grow up no better than a milkmaid. What is the point of all I have done for her, the position I want to give her, if she doesn't know how to comport herself in polite society?'

'Well, could you not keep her at home? Engage a governess and a singing master?'

'At present I am still living in Ancoats. I am planning to move out to the suburbs in the near future, but until then

I have no intention of having her with me for more than a few weeks of the year.'

The picture was beginning to become clearer. Sarah nodded, and got to her feet. 'I can't say whether we will be able to make your daughter happy here. We would certainly try. Come and see the rest of the house. It's a pity that you have come during the holidays. You would have been able to judge the atmosphere of the place better if the girls had been here. Still, you can get some idea.'

The tour was, on the whole, successful. Rose left without making a firm commitment to send her daughter to the school, but as she returned home she felt herself more and more inclined to do so. She took a cab from the station, first to the cook-shop, to check that a disputed bill with a small music hall nearby had been settled satisfactorily, then to the general shop that had been her first venture. She had often thought that it would make sense to sell it, but somehow she never did. It was an almost superstitious clinging to the place that had given her so much and was even now the visible proof that, if all else failed, she could still support herself.

'Where is Eva?' Rose asked Hannah as she passed through the shop.

'She went to her singing lesson.'

'But that was at two o'clock! She should have been back by now!'

Hannah shrugged. 'I wouldn't know owt about that, Mrs Olivant.'

Rose said nothing more. Hannah was a good and reliable worker but she was an inveterate gossip. Rose tried to keep her in ignorance of her family affairs, although she was aware that her difficulties with Eva were common knowledge.

It was almost six o'clock before Eva returned. Rose, in the kitchen, heard her daughter's voice as she entered the shop. 'Is my mother home yet?'

Despite her anger, she felt a pang of loss: even to

Hannah, for whom Eva had no special liking, her daughter spoke in an eager, friendly tone that she never used to Rose. She swept to the door and said grimly, 'Yes, Eva, I'm afraid I am. In here, please.'

Eva turned. Her face, which the instant before had been open, glowing with pleasure and excitement, suddenly changed to the sullen discontent Rose knew so well. Rose watched with distaste as her daughter walked heavily towards the kitchen, shoulders slumped, dragging her feet gracelessly in the way that always infuriated her. Big for her age, at almost fourteen she was physically as mature as many far older girls. Clumsy, surly, disobedient, in Rose's eyes Eva managed to combine the aspects of her own sister's behaviour she had always found most irritating, with Simon's wilful selfishness.

'Where were you?' Rose asked, when they were alone together in the kitchen.

'My singing lesson.'

'That would have finished at half past three. It's all but six now.'

Eva looked down at the floor, her expression mutinous and, it seemed to Rose, deliberately obtuse. 'Well?'

'I went to the Folly.'

'The Folly?'

'The Theatre of Varieties. In Peter Street.'

'And why did you go to such a place, for heaven's sake?'

'Just to look.'

'At what?'

'The programme for this week.' For the first time, Eva raised her eyes, in her face something of the excitement Rose had seen when first she entered the shop. 'Chirgwin's top of the bill! Oh, I wish I could see him!'

'At a music hall?' Rose said scornfully.

'All the other girls are going. Some of them go with their mothers,' she added.

It might almost have been an appeal, but Rose was too angry to notice it. 'By *all the other girls* I suppose you mean the mill girls? The girls from the dye works? The rubber factory?'

'Why not? They're my friends,' Eva muttered, dropping her gaze.

'They shouldn't be.'

'I like being with them.'

Rose made an effort to keep her temper under control. 'They are not suitable friends for you. I'm sure there isn't much harm in them, but you don't belong with them.'

'Where do I belong?' The question was barely audible.

'Your grandfather was a rich man,' Rose said impatiently. 'He would never have believed that his granddaughter would be consorting with mill girls and wanting to go to the music hall.'

'I like them,' Eva repeated stubbornly. 'I like them better than the girls at school.'

'Well, you'll just have to get over that. You will be starting at a new school in a fortnight. You will enjoy it there, I'm sure.'

'Why?'

'Because it is in a nice area, and there is excellent music teaching . . . and your aunt teaches there.'

'I didn't know I had one,' Eva said, showing more interest than Rose would have expected.

'We lost touch,' she said, with the reluctance that she always felt to discuss the past with her daughter. 'Wash your hands, please. Your dinner is almost ready.'

Eva made no move to obey. 'The girls are always asking me about my father.'

'He's dead. You know that perfectly well.'

'But what was he like? Why do you never tell me anything about him?'

'There is nothing you need to know. Now do as I ask, please.'

Eva stared at her, and went slowly into the scullery. As so often, Rose was left with an obscure sense of failure.

Late that evening, Michael Bradley came into the shop.

'Just as I was thinking of closing,' Rose said, greeting him with a weary smile. 'Lock the door behind you, will you? I don't suppose anyone will turn up now.'

'A hard day?' he asked over his shoulder, as he stretched to the top bolt.

'Oh, not really. Eva was a trial, as usual. Come through into the kitchen.'

'What was it this time?'

'She seemed to want me to take her to see some music-hall performer, Chegwin, or some such name.'

'The Great Chirgwin? Well, why not? We could all go. I'll stand you a treat.'

Rose gazed at him doubtfully. He appeared to be serious. 'Really, it would hardly do.'

'You might enjoy it.'

'A music hall? They have a terrible reputation.'

'Don't be such a snob, Rose.'

As ever, the use of her name, even when he was criti-cising her, gave Rose a sense of intimacy that pleased and alarmed her. 'Eva's not fourteen yet,' she temporised.

'Most girls her age are earning their own living. She's old enough to go to the music hall.'

'It's not suitable,' she said firmly. 'Would you like tea? Or whisky?' she added self-consciously.

'Whisky?'

'I bought a bottle. I thought you might like a glass.'

'Rose . . .' he said, looking at her in amazement. 'I know what it must have cost you to do this.'

'Far too much,' she said briskly, 'so make it last.'

'You didn't need to sacrifice your principles, you know,' he said, turning the bottle in his hands as though he could not bring himself to open it. 'It has never mattered to me.'

'That's why it seemed pointless to make such a fuss about it. I began to feel that it was a way in which . . . the past was still influencing me' she said, avoiding as usual Simon's name. 'So I went out and bought it, and laid that ghost to rest . . . Come on, open it. Don't spoil my grand gesture.'

He poured himself a small drink. 'The finest whisky I ever tasted in my life,' he said softly, and pushed the glass aside. He leaned forward towards her. 'And what other ghosts still remain?'

She sighed. Michael reached out and touched her hand. Instinctively, without thinking or willing it, she pulled away. 'I'm sorry,' she said helplessly, as he took away his hand.

'Don't be,' he said gently, although she could see that the rebuff had hurt him. 'I'm not such a brute as to force myself on a woman who doesn't want me.'

Rose was silent, unable to explain to him feelings that she scarcely understood herself.

Sarah was not sure what she had been expecting of Rose's daughter, but it was not Eva, so different from her slender, spirited, headstrong mother. Despite her initial surprise and, perhaps, disappointment, she found herself increasingly drawn to the girl, who was obviously unhappy at her new school. During the walks on which it was part of Sarah's duties to conduct the pupils she tried to chat to her and, after the first shyness had worn off, found her eager to please, unsure of herself but capable, Sarah felt, of great affection. She could barely recognise in her niece the sullen, disobedient child of whom Rose had complained when viewing the school.

As far as she could without showing undue favouritism, Sarah did everything possible to make Eva feel at home at the school. She sensed that she was succeeding, and that the girl was settling down well, but complaint came from an unexpected source.

One evening, when the boarders had retired for the night, Marion Lewis came to Sarah's parlour. This was not uncommon; the two women often met at that time to talk over the day's events, but Sarah saw from her friend's expression that this was not to be their usual relaxed chat.

'Come in, Marion. I was just about to make myself some cocoa. Will you join me?' she asked, getting up to fetch the cup and saucer that had come to be regarded as Marion's on these occasions.

'I don't think I will, thank you,' Marion said stiffly. 'I'm sorry to say that I am obliged to raise an unpleasant matter with you, Sarah.'

'Oh?' Sarah said, setting down the cup. 'Well, won't you at least sit down?'

Marion complied, sitting on the very edge of the chair. 'It's Eva,' she said, as though the name left an unpleasant taste in her mouth.

'She has been settling in well, hasn't she?' Sarah said, ignoring her friend's sour expression.

'You *would* think so . . . but I will come to that in a moment. I was passing the senior girls' dormitory on my way to bed and I heard . . . really, I can hardly describe it.'

'I'm sure you'll try, Marion.'

'Singing. *Eva* singing . . . and such songs! They would have been out of place in all but the *lowest* gin palace, but to hear them in a room of innocent girls!'

Sarah felt a surge of indignation. Marion had always been stricter than she in most ways, but she had never before thought her quite so sanctimonious. 'Really, aren't you exaggerating a little?'

'You didn't hear her . . . or see her,' Marion said grimly.

'And how did *you* see her?'

'I felt it was my duty to ascertain all the possible facts before I intervened.'

'You peeped through the keyhole, you mean?'

'I opened the door, the merest chink. They were so engrossed in the disgraceful spectacle that I doubt they would have noticed if I had flung it wide.'

'I hardly think you are being fair,' Sarah said, struggling to control her mounting anger. 'I know perfectly well that the girls are not supposed to make any noise after lights out, but there can be little harm in singing a few songs.'

Marion pursed her lips. 'Not even a song entitled "Every pub we saw, we went inside of it"? Or "Four Ale Sal?" And the words were still worse!'

This was far beyond anything Sarah could have imagined. 'You seem to have been able to hear remarkably clearly,' she said, determined not to allow Marion to see how shocked she was.

'Your niece has an extremely *carrying* voice, and besides, I was able to confiscate several song sheets in her possession. I have locked them in my drawer, if you can bear to view them.'

'It was very remiss of Eva, I will admit, but I'm sure she was not fully aware of the nature of the material . . .'

'I might have agreed with you, if I hadn't seen her performance. The gestures! The knowing air! She looked . . . she looked *no better than she should be!*'

'Marion! That is a shocking thing to say about a girl of not fourteen!'

'Girls from her background are not like the gently reared children we have here,' Marion said primly.

'Her background? Her mother is my sister!'

'I am well aware of that fact. Indeed, I may say that it has contributed to this whole fiasco. If you had not been so culpably lenient with Eva, showing her a quite disproportionate amount of affection, cosseting her and coddling her at every turn, perhaps she would have behaved more properly.'

'You have no right to say such a thing! I have been most

careful not to show her any favouritism. I only treated her as I would any homesick girl . . . as you yourself have said so often, we are *in loco parentis.*'

'I should never have taken her! I never would, had it not been for your persuasion! I might have known that she would be a bad influence . . . A girl who had run away from other schools . . . a girl from one of the lowest areas of Manchester—'

'That is quite uncalled for! Her mother has struggled to support her, in the most respectable way possible! I never thought you were such a snob, Marion!'

'It isn't a question of snobbery; it's a question of decency! The girl must leave the school, at once!'

'If she leaves, so do I!' The words were uttered before Sarah had known that she would speak them. She gazed at Marion, appalled at the level of animosity they had somehow reached, and saw her own shock mirrored in her friend's face.

'If that's what you want . . .' Marion said slowly.

'You know it isn't.'

They were silent. The threat had sobered them both. At last Marion sighed. 'Talk to Eva tomorrow. Tell her that any repetition of this will mean certain expulsion. We will do our best with her, so long as the other girls are not harmed.'

'Thank you,' Sarah said, forcing herself to ignore the final insult. 'I'm sure that she will see sense.' As Marion got to her feet she cast about for some way to repair the damage their quarrel had caused. 'Won't you stay and have some cocoa, after all?'

'No, Sarah dear,' Marion said, with a touch of wounded pride. 'I shall go and destroy those song sheets at once. I would hate to think of them falling into any other hands. I feel as though the house is contaminated by their presence.'

'Oh . . . bosh!' Sarah muttered under her breath, as the

door closed behind her stately back. For the first time in her life, she wished she had stronger language at her disposal.

The interview with Eva the next morning was not easy, torn as Sarah was between her fondness for the girl and the duty that was imposed upon her.

'I was so sorry to hear what happened last night, Eva,' she began. 'Miss Lewis was very distressed by what she heard.'

'She shouldn't have been listening, then,' Eva said in an undertone.

'Look at me, not the floor, please. You know perfectly well that Miss Lewis and I are duty bound to inform ourselves of all that concerns the pupils in our charge.'

'She was spying on us, creeping about and listening at keyholes . . .'

'Eva, please! You are not making your situation any better, you know. I had great difficulty in dissuading Miss Lewis from expelling you at once. Do you want to be sent home in disgrace?' The girl was silent, but Sarah saw her mouth working in an attempt to hold back tears. 'Do you?'

Eva shook her head.

'There must be no more of these performances, if you are to say.'

'But the other girls like it! They ask me to sing for them! It's the only thing I'm good at, the only time I feel that I am somebody. Where's the harm in it?'

'You are too young to understand . . .'

'Everyone always says that to me. My mother is always saying it. She will never tell me anything. She just sends me out of the way.'

There was a real distress beneath the girl's rebellious outburst, a distress that went far deeper than the present occasion. Sarah hesitated, out of her depth. 'What do you want her to tell you, Eva?'

'About my father. She says he died. Other girls have fathers who have died, but at least they know something about them. I've never seen anything of his, or heard how he died, or anything. Sometimes I wonder if I even had a father.'

'Everyone has a father, dear. Yours was a man named Simon Olivant. Your mother fell in love with him when she was a very young girl. They married without your grandfather's consent.'

'She ran away with him?'

'Yes. I'm afraid they weren't well matched. They became very poor. There was a little boy . . .'

'I had a brother?'

'Peter. I saw him once. He was a lovely child, but . . . he died,' Sarah said, unable to bring herself to tell the whole truth. 'Soon after that, your father was found drowned. Your mother had to support herself and you without any help. That was why she had to send you away to a foster mother. She only wanted the best for you.'

'She could have come to see me sometimes. At first I wanted to see her, but after a while I didn't care any more. When she came for me in the end, I didn't know her.'

Sarah sighed. 'It hasn't been easy for her, Eva. Don't make it any worse, will you?'

The girl was silent. Sarah could see that she was struggling to make sense of what she had heard. 'I know that your mother would be very disappointed if you were sent home from here. I have promised Miss Lewis that there will be no more of these songs. I hope you won't let me down. Now, go back to your class.'

'Thank you,' Eva said absently, as though she had forgotten all about lessons. As she moved to the door, slowly but with the beginnings of a new self-possession, Sarah wondered if she had been right to say so much about Olivant, although she could see that the information seemed to have lifted a burden from Eva's shoulders. She hoped that Rose would forgive her, if she ever found out.

There was no repetition of the scene that had so horrified Marion Lewis, or at least, none that she ever discovered. Sarah was relieved to find that her niece was obviously intent on making the best of things. She made friends, and was soon one of the more popular girls at the school, although she remained indefinably set apart from the others, holding herself naturally aloof from the petty feuds and passions that were the plague of her age group but that held no interest for her.

Marion, Sarah could see, never liked or trusted Eva, but she did her best to foster her undoubted talents by giving her leading roles in the dramatic productions, carefully selected for their moral content, that were one of the showpieces of the school. On first seeing Eva in one such play Sarah was amazed by her niece's ability. Eva's awkwardness seemed to vanish the moment the play began: she was by far the most confident of the participants, and dominated every scene in which she appeared. A melodrama with a strong temperance message, it required her both to act and to sing. Her lines were mere bombast but she delivered them with such flawless timing and power that, absurd as she knew the piece to be, Sarah felt a lump in her throat. At the end of the work, even Marion Lewis lifted a handkerchief furtively to her eyes.

Sarah and Marion were carefully polite to each other after their quarrel. Within a week or two they had, on the face of it, resumed their normal friendly relations, but although neither said a word that could be taken amiss Sarah knew that things were not as they had been. All spontaneity had gone: the differences between their personalities began to be more apparent, and in a dozen tiny ways Marion left her feeling conscious of her inferior standing as she had not before.

When, the following year, increasing success necessitated the employment of a third teacher, Sarah saw how Marion subtly enlisted the newcomer as her ally. In insignificant ways at first, then more openly, Sarah was excluded from their companionship and given all the least attractive work in the school. She began regretfully to recognise that, sooner or later, she would have to move on.

It was a relief to Rose that she had at last found a school in which her daughter could be happy. She was pleased by the way Eva had changed over the last three years. By sixteen, she had fined down physically. Eva would always have a big frame, with large hands and feet, but the mere heaviness of her figure was now becoming voluptuous; no longer blurred by puppy fat, her features were revealed as bold, sensual, unlike Rose's delicate beauty but striking in their own way.

In other respects, too, Rose found her daughter improved. She was more amenable during the weeks that she spent at home in school holidays, and although she still enjoyed going back to Caddishead for a time each summer, she never showed any reluctance to return to Ancoats. Eva was always eager to help Rose in the shops and was popular with the customers. She had far more patience than Hannah with the old women who would spin out the purchase of a penny mix of tea and sugar to last for an hour of gossip and company. Rose suspected that some of her customers waited until Eva was alone in the shop to come for the single ounces of cheese and ham that Hannah steadfastly refused to sell.

'You lose so much in the cutting, there's no profit in it,' Rose explained for the hundredth time, when she caught her daughter supplying one of her customers with the paltry quantities. 'Mrs Chalmers knows that perfectly well. She's taking advantage of you, Eva, and indirectly of me.'

'Oh, we can afford it, can't we?'

'Where do you think your school fees and your music lessons come from?' Rose asked sharply.

'Not out of the pockets of widows and mothers of ten like Mrs Chalmers, I hope.'

Rose wanted to check her for her insolence, but there was increasingly a quality in her daughter that very nearly cowed her. Eva was too old for her age, she told herself irritably; she mingled with working girls and expected to be given the same freedom they enjoyed, in the brief period of their relative affluence and lack of responsibilities, between starting work and marriage.

Rose often found herself complaining about some example of her daughter's growing independence to Michael Bradley when, as had become his almost daily habit, he called in to see her at the shop towards the end of the evening.

'It suits you, though, doesn't it?' Michael pointed out. 'When she's at home she's more use to you than Hannah. I've seen her in the shop. She's pleasant and takes trouble with people; she can give a bit of backchat, too, and that goes a long way with the troublemakers. How would you manage if she was the hothouse plant you seem to want? Could a shrinking little miss handle a drunkard and coax him out of the shop with no damage done? Eva's a fine girl, and I wish you could see it.'

'Perhaps she is, but she's not . . . I don't know, she's not a young lady.'

'And all the better for it,' he said, frowning. 'And where would *you* be now, if you'd been some genteel creature, too fine to roll up your sleeves and get down to work when you had to?'

'That's the point. I don't want her to have to live as I have. I want something better for her. Is that so unnatural?'

'Have you ever wondered what Eva wants herself?'

'She's only a girl. She doesn't know enough about life to make up her mind about anything important.'

'Well, all I can say is that she will give you a surprise one day. If ever I saw a young woman with a mind of her own, it's your daughter.'

'All the more reason for caution. I don't want her making the same mistakes that I have done.'

'Oh? What mistakes were they?'

She gazed at him sharply. 'Nothing I want to go into now. Ancient history.'

'It's not, though. There's not a day goes by that whatever it was that happened to you during your marriage doesn't affect you. I can see it, if you can't.'

'I don't know what you mean,' she said, with the sense of panic that any mention of the past always aroused in her.

'You're not much of a liar, Rose. How long have you known me now?'

'Six years, I suppose.'

'Six years, and I doubt whether I know a single fact of any importance about you . . . except one, of course.'

'Oh? And what's that? she asked, dry-mouthed with fear.

'That I love you and I want to marry you.'

She gazed at Michael, allowing herself to imagine the closeness to him that, she now realised, had tempted her from the first moment she met him. He was as unlike Simon as it was possible for any man to be: strong and for-bearing, where Simon was weak and bullying; hardworking and ambitious where he was lazy and dishonest; loving where he was selfish. He might not be handsome, as Simon was, but she had come to find a charm in his face that had gradually exercised its appeal over her. She liked to look at him. She liked his plain speaking, and the fact that their frequent disputes never intimidated her, unlike Simon's threatening outbursts. Michael was a match for her, in every sense, a man she could trust and love. And yet, slowly, with a sigh, she shook her head.

'I'm sorry . . . I can't.'

'Why not?' he asked, and she could see his disappointment.

'If ever I could have married again, I would never have wished for a finer man than you—'

'Oh, spare me the compliments,' he said roughly. 'Why not? I'm hardly love's young dream, I know. Is that it?'

'No, no!'

'What, then? Is there someone else?'

She shook her head. 'I can't bring myself to take that step again, that's all. If I could, it would have been you, believe me.'

'That's not much consolation. I want you, living with me as my wife, not some sweet, fond memory of what might have been.' He leaned forward across the table, catching her hand. She made an instinctive movement of recoil, but he did not release her. 'I want to wake up in the morning and find you in bed beside me; I want to see you at breakfast, still sleepy and cross; I want to quarrel with you, and kiss and make friends again. I want to tell you everything that happens to me every day, every boring little detail, and to hear the same from you. I want your face to be the last thing I see on this earth. Is there nothing I can say or do that will make you want this too?'

'Michael, please, I can't. I'm sorry, I just can't.'

He sat back, still holding her hand. 'Your husband was a brute?'

She nodded.

'Tell me about it. At the very least it will help me to understand. Who knows, it might be a help to you, too.'

'I don't want to talk about it. Not now.'

'Will you ever?'

'I don't know. I need time, Michael.'

'I wish that I could say that we had all the time in the world, Rose, but we haven't. I love you. I will do anything I can to persuade you that you can trust me to try and make you happy, but I'm only human. There is a limit to how much I can take of wanting you and facing a blank stone wall in return.' He lifted her hand to his lips and kissed it. It was not a decorous or formal gesture, but the expression of a passionate yearning that must try to satisfy itself with such crumbs of physical contact.

Rose was shaken. He got to his feet, releasing her hand.

'Will I come round again next week?' he asked.

It was the first time he had asked permission for one of the visits that, she now realised, she had almost come to expect. The responsibility would no longer be his alone. If she wished to see him, she must admit as much. She sensed that nothing would be the same again and, reluctantly, she acknowledged that he had a point. For so long she had been taking from him, relying on his undemanding affection and support. Her life over the past five years had been richer for his friendship, but she had given him little or nothing in return, accepting his visits as her due.

'Next week?' she said, with a rueful smile for her own inconsistency. 'That seems like a long time to wait.'

'I shall be away from Manchester for the rest of this week, as it happens. The new warehouse in Bolton needs to be set to rights, so I'll be there until Saturday.'

'Come for your Sunday lunch, then. You know how glad Eva will be to see you again.'

'And you?'

'And me.' Rose put a hand on his sleeve. 'I will miss you.'

He reached out and passed his hand over her hair in a brief caress. As the door closed behind him, Rose stood motionless, poised in a balance between her fears and her

desires that could not, she knew, hold for very much
longer.

The following morning Eva surprised her by broaching
the subject of Michael's visit. 'He was here for a long time
last night, wasn't he? Any special news?'

'No, why should there be?' Rose said, annoyed to feel
herself blushing.

'You've known him such a long time, that's all, and he's
always here for one reason or another. He isn't married, is
he?'

'No.'

'He should marry you. I like him.'

'That's hardly a reason,' Rose said, getting up to bring
over the teapot.

'Well, I wouldn't want you marrying someone I *didn't*
like. Will you marry Mr Bradley, do you think?' she asked,
as carelessly as if she were enquiring about Rose's choice of
a hat.

'We will have to see.'

'Has he asked you?'

'That's none of your business,' Rose said heatedly.

'I suppose that means he has,' Eva said composedly. She
laughed. 'You'll have to change the name on the roof.'

'The roof?'

'Of the bakery. Olivant's. I can see it when I come home
on the train. It always seems funny, in a nice kind of way. I
know I am back where I belong when I see it.'

Rose was touched, although she merely said briskly,
'I'm sure that would be the very last thing on anybody's
mind.'

'He's all right,' Eva conceded, taking another piece of
toast. 'Was my father like Michael?'

Rose moved away. Her back to her daughter, she said
curtly, 'No.'

'Why will you never tell me anything about him?'

'There is nothing you need to know. Will you take over from Hannah in the shop for a moment so that she can come through for her breakfast? I don't want her to get cold tea.'

Eva did as she was asked. The moment of danger passed. Rose had preserved the secrets that, every day, were weighing more heavily upon her.

CHAPTER

Eleven

The week passed more slowly than any Rose remembered, as though to prove to her how much she had come to depend on Michael's company. She thought constantly of his insistence that she should describe her life with Simon. She could see that he had a claim to know and tried to bring herself to a resolution that she would, at the right moment, tell Michael everything, including the circumstances of Peter's death.

Not only was Rose reluctant to revive painful memories; she was ashamed of having to admit her own gullibility in having been seduced by a charm that had never been more than superficial. She was ashamed of having remained with Simon so long, when love between them had died and only fear of the unknown tied her to him; she was ashamed of the need to confess to Michael that, had she acted more courageously and left him sooner, her son would not have died. Although she told herself that she bore no guilt for Peter's death, she could not quite believe it; she blamed herself. To tell Michael and see him shrink from her, as in her worst moments she imagined, or even to sense that she had been reduced in his eyes, was more than she could bear.

Simon was much in her thoughts. She often awoke, heart pounding, from nightmares. In some, she relived the terrors of the night of Peter's death; others, vaguer but no less frightening, remained just beyond the recall of her conscious self. In the years when she had struggled to survive she had forced herself to put aside the tragedy and the grief she had barely allowed herself to feel. It seemed cruel that now, when a new, happier life might be opening up before her, such wraiths should float to the surface of her mind from the depths of her memory, to which she had thought they were safely consigned.

Rose knew that these chilling reminders of the past were making her uncertain in temper with Hannah and Eva, now home for the summer holidays. When Eva was not helping her in some way, she tended to spend much of her time out of the house. Rose suspected that she was going to matinées at the music hall with the young women who, liberated from their work in mills and factories, looked forward to Saturday afternoons with almost religious fervour.

Rose made no move to intervene. As so often before, she sought in work salvation from both her preoccupation with the past and her uncertainty about the future. On Friday evening, as she and Eva were finishing their dinner, Hannah called Rose into the shop to receive a message from Josie Martin, who ran the cook-shop. Rose went back to the kitchen and read the letter, frowning.

'Anything important?' Eva asked.

'Josie's mother's been taken ill. Josie won't be able to come into work tomorrow.'

'That still leaves the new girl, doesn't it?'

'Peggy only started work this week. She can hardly be left in charge.'

'I'll go down, if you like.'

'Oh, I wouldn't mind doing it myself. I haven't had a day

there for a while. I like to keep an eye on the place, although Josie's very good. Could you help Hannah here?'

'All day?'

'Why not?'

'Nothing. It's just that it's a Saturday . . .'

'I know that perfectly well,' Rose said sharply. Eva did not say any more.

In the cook-shop the early part of Saturday was, as usual, quieter than the rest of the week as the factories worked only a half day. The early evenings were busier, as this was both the pay day in many industries and the traditional day for housewives to scour the house. Many, at least temporarily solvent and exhausted by their scrubbing and polishing, took the opportunity to treat themselves and their families to a shop-bought tea.

Rose was kept fully occupied from four o'clock or so by the constant stream of children sent by their mothers for the pies and puddings with rich gravy which were becoming famous throughout the district. By seven o'clock, custom had slackened. From the back kitchen came the clashing of pots and crockery as Peggy washed up.

Rose totted up the contents of the till, debating whether, just this once, she might close the shop early. As she put the last coppers into the pouch of strong canvas which, buckled about her waist, always conveyed the takings home, the doorbell rang out once more. She looked up quickly. At this time of day there was a considerable sum on the premises and she never liked to be seen handling large amounts of money. But when she saw who was standing before her, swaying slightly like a corpse hanging from a gibbet, she wished she had only a thief to face.

'Not know me, Rose?'

Her face felt frozen and distorted with shock but she summoned the presence of mind to close the door into the back kitchen, though Peggy was making so much noise that she would never hear. Wordlessly, she pointed to the shop door. He nodded, and went to turn over the sign. They should not now be disturbed, although she could not bring herself to ask him to bolt the door, as she usually did on closing the shop. To be shut in with him was more than she could bear.

'Not pleased to see me again, after all these years?' he asked, picking his way towards the counter with the studiedly careful gait that was so horribly familiar to her.

'I thought you were dead,' she whispered, recoiling from the counter although without its support she feared that she would fall. She backed away until she was pressed against the wall, her fingers, splayed against its rough plaster, making tiny, desperate movements as though seeking some escape. But the wall remained impenetrable, harsh and unyielding, as undeniably real as the leering face thrust towards her.

'Now, why would you have thought a thing like that?'

'They found a body in the Mersey. Your watch was in its pocket.'

He burst out laughing, although it quickly turned into a fit of coughing. His breath was tainted with alcohol, the nauseating smell of spirits that had accompanied the worst moments of her life. She thought that she would be sick, but made a desperate effort at self-control. She could not afford a single moment of weakness, of inattention.

'I sold my watch for the price of a bottle of whisky and a train ticket,' he said, as proud of himself as if he was describing some noteworthy achievement. 'It didn't bring its next owner much luck, by the sounds of it.'

'Where did you go?' she asked automatically, not really caring but wanting to keep him talking until her mind, still paralysed by shock, could begin to suggest what she should do.

'Back to Scotland. Back to my ain folk,' he said mockingly.

'You never would take me,' she said, the old bitterness emerging even now.

'Sometimes a wife can be an encumbrance,' he said, and laughed again, so loudly that she glanced fearfully over her shoulder. The back kitchen was suspiciously quiet. Gesturing to him to remain silent, she opened the door a fraction.

'You may as well just go, Peggy. I will see to everything else.' She turned back to him. 'What do you want?'

Simon leaned more heavily on the counter. He looked like an old man. Beneath his eyes the skin sagged in heavy folds; his hair was greying and dull; his skin had a yellowish tinge. 'You're my wife, aren't you? What do you think I want?'

She closed her eyes as a hot tide of disgust, so strong an emotion that it was a physical sensation, washed over her. 'You can't mean that,' she said.

'I've got my rights. Nothing can take them away. Conjugal rights.' He paused, dropping each phrase in turn, like acid onto unprotected flesh. 'Rights to your property. Rights to my daughter.'

'What?'

'Think I didn't know about her? I've been asking about, these last days. I've come up with a lot of good news, too. A rich wife, not bad looking still, and a nice little daughter to complete the picture. She *is* mine, I suppose?'

Rose nodded, too shocked to lie.

'Of course, if you were to drive me away, I could always take her with me. The law would be on my side. She's mine by rights. My property. But you wouldn't do that to me, would you?'

'I don't know . . . I can't think.'

He shook his head slowly. 'You're on your way to finding

yourself another husband, too, from what I hear. I turned up just in time, eh?'

'Why did you come here? *Why?*'

'It wasn't convenient for me to stay in Scotland. Let's put it that way.'

'How did you find me?'

'It must have been fate, Rosie. You could say you advertised your presence. I didn't mean to stay in Manchester; I was just passing through, when I looked out of the train and saw my name staring at me from a roof. It's an unusual name, especially down here. I thought it would be worth a look, just in case. You're a well-known figure, you know. Nice to see you've done so well for yourself . . . for us, I mean.'

Rose was so intent on what he was saying that she was aware of nothing else, and when the bell rang she started as though at some sudden violence. She stared blankly at the door as Michael entered. His smile of greeting faded as he looked in surprise from Rose to the man turning with slow, reptilian deliberation to face him.

'What is it, Rose? Some problem?' he asked lightly.

'No, nothing,' Rose said, forcing a smile.

'A particular friend, I take it?' Simon asked, the sneer in the words evident despite his slurred speech.

'Who is this?' Michael demanded sharply.

'I will explain later,' Rose said, watching Simon to see if he would intervene, force a confrontation. To her relief he said nothing, intimidated perhaps by Michael's obvious physical power, or not yet certain what he wanted from her. Blackmail would be very much his style. 'I didn't think you would be back yet,' she went on, struggling to maintain some pretence of normality before Michael.

'I got back early and came to see you home. Are you about ready?' Michael asked.

She forced herself to answer naturally. 'There are still

one or two things I need to see to before I can lock up. Don't bother to wait for me. I will be home as soon as I can.'

Michael looked doubtful, but he turned reluctantly away. As he closed the door he looked over his shoulder, scanning Rose's face for any silent message. She remained impassive. It would be better if he could remain untouched by the contagion of Simon's presence.

'You told him you were a widow, I suppose?' Simon asked, leaning now against the counter for support.

'Of course. I believed it was the truth,' she said wearily.

'You wanted to believe it.'

'Yes. I wanted you to be dead.'

'Still do, don't you, Rosie? I can see it in your face.'

'You killed my child. You deserved to die.'

'It was an accident,' he said sullenly, 'and nobody can prove any different.'

'No.' It was part acquiescence, part denial.

'Not very good at letting bygones be bygones, are you?'

'No. Not after Peter.' She stopped, making a deliberate effort to remain calm. 'What do you want?'

He gazed at her, calculating how far she could be pushed. 'A bed for the night, for a start.'

Rose thought of the little terraced house, already filled to capacity. He could hardly stay there, unless she took Eva into her bedroom. She could give him money for a night in a lodging house, but could he be trusted not to brag about who he was, why he had come back? That might be the greatest evil.

'What else do you want?' she asked, still undecided.

He nodded at the canvas wallet, lying unregarded on the counter. 'Plenty of money there for a bottle of whisky.'

'You've had enough already.'

'That's not for you to decide. Not for the bloody doctors either. What do they know about anything? I'll drink what

I want, when I want it, liver or no liver. Getting the money, that's the only problem.' He laughed, as though this was a joke he had often repeated to his bar-room cronies.

'A bed for the night. A bottle of whisky. Then what? You can't want to stay here? There's nothing for you.'

'You couldn't be more wrong, Rosie. I could be very comfortable here. Fallen on my feet all right. We can take up where we left off, eh? Quite like old times.'

'You would be better somewhere else. I will give you enough money for a train ticket to wherever you like, and something to start you off. You could leave tomorrow . . .'

He shook his head slowly, with drunken emphasis. 'I'm not leaving. Not tomorrow. Not ever.'

There was clearly no arguing with him while he was in this state. She bit her lip, trying to find some other solution. She could not. She opened the money bag and took out two florins, which she pushed towards him across the counter but did not relinquish.

'Very well. You can come home with me . . . on one condition. You are my brother-in-law. If you dare to tell a living soul any different you won't get another penny out of me. Do you understand?'

'We'll see about that . . . but I'll go along with it for now,' he added, as she made to take away the money. She removed her hand, and he gathered the coins up with greedy, shaking fingers.

They left the shop together. It was raining, a cool night for July. As they began to walk along the street he staggered and would have fallen in the gutter had she not instinctively reached out to catch his arm. Even through the cloth of his jacket she could tell how wasted his muscles were. Simon had never been strongly built, but this emaciation was new. She examined him more closely by the pale glow of the gaslight. Although his features were puffy his neck was scrawny, the collar of his shirt standing away from it as though he were a child whose clothes were bought too big, to allow for growth.

'Are you ill?' she asked, with grudging concern.

'I need a drink, that's all.'

'When did you last have anything to eat?'

'I can't keep food down much. Drink, that's what keeps me going.'

At Simon's insistence, they called into a licensed victuallers and bought a bottle of whisky. It was not far from the cook-shop but she was obliged to lend him her arm to enable him to reach it. She hailed a cab for the remainder of the journey. Simon slumped in the corner, his head drooping forward on his chest, the bottle cradled in his arms. Within the cramped carriage, the streetlamps and the bright windows of the public houses they passed cast an ever-changing pattern of light and shade. Sometimes Simon appeared a grotesque humped figure, a monster, and sometimes nothing more than a useless heap of rags, an abandoned and broken puppet.

The little shop was still open when they arrived home. The brave glow of its windows, her sanctuary for so long, had never seemed so precious to Rose as now, when all she had achieved was threatened once more. She opened the door and stopped in alarm. Michael was in the shop, serving old Mrs Power, who often came in late on a Saturday night to beg for the scraps of ham and cheese that had fallen from the block in cutting. Rose was glad that there was no sign of Hannah, or of Eva, although the girl should have been at home.

'I let Hannah away early,' he said, frowning at the sight of Rose's arm about Simon's waist.

She steered Simon past him, hoping that he would not notice the bottle of whisky. 'It was good of you,' she said abstractedly. 'I will see you in a moment, Michael . . . and if Eva comes in, tell her she will have to sleep with me tonight, will you?'

Simon lurched heavily up the stairs. She pushed him into Eva's room, and hastily set about gathering the few things she thought her daughter would need for the night. She took them to her own bedroom and returned to find Simon sitting on Eva's bed, the bottle of whisky lifted to his lips. Rose opened her mouth to protest, but instead the bitter thought formed itself in her mind; *let him drink himself to death. It's the best thing he could do.*

'Do you want anything else?' she asked coldly.

He put down the bottle. 'You,' he said, reaching clumsily for her.

She evaded him without difficulty, although her heart quickened with fear. 'Don't be such a fool. You are my brother-in-law, remember? I will see you in the morning. We can talk again then.'

Before he could make any further attempt to detain her she slipped away from him and closed the door behind her. She waited a moment but all was silent. He would be drinking again.

The shop was empty. Michael was in the kitchen, attending to the fire. He looked up, frowning, as she entered. 'I have made us some tea. Do you want anything to eat?'

'I couldn't . . .'

'Sit down, for heaven's sake. Who was that fellow? I take it he is staying the night?'

'I'm afraid so. It's my brother-in-law. I couldn't turn him away, could I?'

'Your brother-in-law?'

'Paul.' She dared not meet his gaze to see if he believed her.

'You never mentioned him before.'

'He didn't have much to do with Simon. He was a heavy drinker, even then.'

'Seeing him again has upset you, hasn't it?'

She shrugged, trying to appear indifferent. 'He is very like Simon. It brings back memories.'

'Unpleasant ones?'

'All my memories of Simon are unpleasant.'

The answer seemed to satisfy him. He came and put an arm about her shoulder. 'I couldn't bear to wait until tomorrow to see you. All week I have been looking forward to being with you again . . . I have scarcely been able to give a thought to business.'

She smiled, but her nerves were stretched taut with the effort of listening out for any alarming sounds from Simon. She could make no other response, although she, too, had longed for their reunion.

'You look exhausted,' he said, his arm leaving her shoulders as she gave no answering sign of affection. 'Why don't you go up to bed? I will see to the shop.'

'Oh, that's not your worry. I need to wait up for Eva, anyway. I told her to help in the shop today. Did Hannah say where she was?'

'Eva asked if she could go out for a while, about six. She said she would be back before you got home. The shop was quiet, so Hannah let her go.'

'Haven't I got enough on my mind—' She broke off, seeing his suspicions revive.

'Rose, won't you tell me what's really worrying you?'

'A shortage of staff, a drunken relation and a wayward daughter aren't enough? I'm sorry, Michael, I'm not very good company tonight. I shall be myself again tomorrow.'

'You don't have to be good company. I only want to be sure that I know what's on your mind.'

'And how many times do I have to tell you, before you believe me?' She stopped, aware that her self-control was wearing dangerously thin. 'I'm sorry. I don't want us to quarrel. Perhaps it would be better if you went.'

Hurt, more nearly angry than she had ever known him, Michael left. Simon's presence hung threateningly over the house as it had in the last weeks of their marriage – in what she had thought were the last weeks of their marriage, she reminded herself drearily, as she climbed the stairs with a fearful caution she had never known since those days.

Outside his door she paused, scarcely daring to breathe. All was still, but as she strained to hear any sound from within she thought she could detect a faint snoring. He must have drunk himself to sleep. Was he in bed? Even in summer, the room could be chill. He really should not be left in a drunken stupor, perhaps only partly dressed. She put out a hand but could not bring herself to open the door to see that all was well. As silently as a ghost, she moved away.

She was in the shop when Eva returned, flushed and happy, a look of dreamy contentment on her face that vanished as she saw Rose.

'And where do you think you have been to this time?' Rose demanded, her voice cracking with the intolerable strain of the past hours.

'It's not late,' Eva said, with a conciliatory smile.

'It's almost ten.'

'I meant to be back before now. I'm sorry.'

'You were supposed to be helping Hannah. Can't I rely on you for anything?'

Eva glanced at her sharply, as though she detected something more than the usual irritation in her mother's tone. 'Is something wrong?'

'Nothing that's helped by having a daughter who runs wild at all hours. And where were you, in any case?'

'I was with Peggy Richardson and the others. They were going to the first house at the Queen's. They came and asked if I'd like to go with them . . . it was Jenny Hill,' she said, with some return of her first excitement, 'and Hannah said she could manage without me. I thought I would be back not long after nine . . .'

'And why weren't you?'

Eva lowered her eyes. 'Oh, we met some people, and we took longer than I thought walking home.'

'Some people?' Her daughter made no response. 'Men, I suppose you mean?'

'It was just some boys that Peggy knew from the mill and . . . and one or two others. We got talking, and all walked home together. There was no harm in it.'

'No harm? You pick up men in a common music hall, no better than the sluts that haunt these places—'

'No! It wasn't like that!' Eva raised her gaze to meet Rose's, deference swept away by a passionate outrage at her accusation. 'What do you know about it? You are such a snob you have never even been to a hall. Just because—' She faltered, as if her own defiance frightened her.

'Yes? Don't stop now!'

'Just because you ran away with my father and ruined your life – and probably his—'

Before she well knew what she was doing, Rose reached out and slapped her daughter's face. It was not a very hard blow, hampered as she was by the counter between them, but it was the first time Rose had struck her since she had smacked her chubby legs for some infant misdemeanour. She gazed at her, almost more shocked than Eva by what she had done.

'Go upstairs,' she said, lifting the flap in the counter. 'You will be sleeping in my room tonight. I will explain why tomorrow.'

Without a word, Eva obeyed, her head held high in tearless pride. As she passed, Rose could see the marks of her fingers on the girl's cheek. She wanted to stop her, and beg her pardon, and make all well, but she too had her pride. She said nothing, and the moment passed.

When at last Rose was able to close the shop and go to bed her daughter was huddled on the far side of the bed, shunning any contact with her. Rose feigned a sleep that was long in coming. Almost until dawn she lay wakeful, tormented by memories of the past, as raw as if its wounds had never healed in all the past years of tranquillity, by dread of what the future held and of what she must tell Michael.

The following morning, Sunday, she got up early despite her fatigue and made breakfast, leaving Eva still asleep. Choosing a moment when the shop was quiet, she slipped upstairs and knocked softly at Simon's door. There was no reply. She opened it a fraction. The room smelled unpleasantly stale, like the cage of some ailing, neglected animal. As her eyes adjusted to the gloom she could make out the figure of Simon, slumped across the bed. He was fully clothed but for his jacket which sprawled beside him, one sleeve hanging drunkenly down to the floor.

Rose moved silently across the room. As she drew nearer to the bed she realised that at some point Simon had been sick. She felt a spurt of anger, and shook his shoulder roughly.

'Simon! For heaven's sake!'

He stirred, and lifted his head, his hair sticking to one side of his cheek. He stared at her without recognition; she wondered if he even knew his own name, far less hers. With a movement of impatient disgust she strode across the room, flung back the curtains and pulled up the window.

'I am going down for hot water. When I get it you can clean yourself up,' she said angrily. He did not reply. His head had already fallen back once more on to the soiled bedcover.

Simon was still lying as she had left him when she brought back the water, a good half an hour later, for she was detained by one customer after another. She had difficulty in rousing him, and could barely extract a coherent word from him. His eyes, even when open, were without any understanding. Unnaturally bright, they seemed to be focused on some other scene invisible to her.

Overcoming her repugnance at touching him, Rose took a flannel and wiped his face and crusted lips. His skin was hot, but he was shaken by tremors. It occurred to her, without any sense of sympathy, that he was ill. She managed with some difficulty to drag the counterpane off the bed; the remainder of the covers seemed untouched.

'Come on, you'd better get into bed.'

He grunted, but made no move to obey. With a mounting sense of anger and revulsion, she knelt to remove his boots. They were old and ill-fitting, with holes worn in the sole, the uppers cracked and marked with a white bloom from their last soaking. He had always been so careful of his appearance; however poor they had been, his footwear had always been highly polished, beautifully fitting his slim feet, of which he was inordinately proud. She eased off his boots. His socks were damp from the water seeping through the holes in his soles. She peeled them off. His feet were white, except where the water had dirtied them. They were cold, so cold that he might indeed have been that unknown corpse, the drowned man she had been so willing to take for Simon.

Automatically she began to chafe his inert chilled feet, calloused now, the toenails thick and yellow, but still slender, their innate elegance not quite destroyed. An unexpected lump rose in her throat: for all the health and beauty Simon had once possessed and had so profligately squandered; for the love there could have been between them; for the pointless waste of his life and Peter's and the destruction of something in herself, some generosity and innocence that she could never recreate. She brushed the back of her hand roughly across her eyes and, rising awkwardly to her feet, went into the other bedroom for a pair of bedsocks for him.

When, after a struggle, Rose had got Simon into bed she stood a moment, frowning. His breathing, quick and shallow, suggested fever, perhaps a chill that had settled on his lungs. If Eva were in such a condition she would certainly send for the doctor, but what did she owe Simon? No tenderness, certainly, after all that had happened. She felt no loyalty to him, and not even the compassion that a stranger would have roused in her.

Would it not be for the best if he should sicken and die? Michael need never know who he was, or that she had unwittingly deceived him as to her widowed state. She need not ill-treat Simon, simply let him succumb to the consequences of his own neglect of his health. Drink, indirectly, would kill him as it had killed Peter.

Rose heard the shop bell ring. She gladly turned away to answer its summons, the decision deferred. As she hurried down the stairs the thought crept into her mind that, if she delayed for long enough, the problem would be solved without the need for her intervention.

For the remainder of the morning Rose made herself keep busy. She flitted between the shop and the kitchen, preparing the vegetables for the Sunday meal to which she now regretted inviting Michael. She tried to concentrate her thoughts solely on what she was doing, but not for a second could she forget that upstairs lay a sick man who should be receiving help.

When her uneasy awareness became overwhelming, she unwillingly went up to the bedroom, drawn by a conscience she wished she could silence, and did what she could to make Simon comfortable. She wiped his face, offered him water, brought him another blanket. He scarcely seemed aware of anything. She was glad of the interruptions of customers, although Eva, sullen and with-drawn, had come down unasked to the shop to help.

The meal was a strained affair. Simon might be upstairs, silent and unseen, but he dominated Rose's thoughts as if he were sitting at the table with them, his sardonic smile reminding her that a single word from him could destroy the harmony she had so painfully constructed.

'How is he?' Michael asked, as he seated himself. 'You had a bad night with him, by the looks of it.'

'He has a fever of some sort, I think.'

Eva, who had been maintaining unbroken silence, looked accusingly at her. Rose forced herself to speak naturally. 'Your uncle has turned up, quite out of the blue. He isn't well and we will have to put him up for a few days, I'm afraid.'

'My uncle?'

'Your father's brother,' Michael supplied, looking to Rose for confirmation. She nodded. 'A very sick man, it appears.'

'Shall I take him up something to eat?' Eva offered, already rising from her place.

'No!' Rose was aware that Michael and Eva exchanged a glance of surprise at her cry of panic. 'It isn't suitable . . . I will see to everything myself.'

'That's all very well, Rose, but you can't do everything,' Michael pointed out, frowning. 'You will be ill yourself next.'

'Don't worry. I will manage,' she said, more sharply than she had intended. Michael sighed. After an awkward pause, he turned to Eva with some joking enquiry. The subject of the sick man was not raised again.

As soon as the meal was over, Rose made an excuse and returned upstairs. In the hour or so since she had last seen him, Simon had clearly worsened. There was a catch in his breath now that made her suspect that breathing was painful for him. He seemed to have grown less confused, however, and even managed a word of thanks when she lifted his head from the pillow to help him to sip some water.

'You could have some soup, if you like,' she said stiffly, her dislike and distrust of him struggling with her unwilling compassion.

'No, nothing to eat. You could give me that whisky, though. I'll feel better for that.'

'That's the last thing you'll get. I should never have let you have it last night.'

'Come on . . . a glass or two won't do me any harm. Where is it?'

'I've put it away.'

'You don't know what it's like . . . just a drop, that's all. I can't do without it, truly I can't.'

'It's poisoning you!'

'Look, just get it, will you?' He moved his head fretfully on the pillow, looking about the room.

'It's not here.'

'You don't understand, I have to have it. It will put me right.'

She got up abruptly. 'On your head be it, then.' She left the room and returned in a moment, bringing a glass of whisky. 'Would you like hot water with it?'

He shook his head. She helped him to drink, and even she did not know whether she gave it to him out of pity or the hope that it would kill him.

At intervals throughout the rest of the day Rose went upstairs to see to Simon. Michael offered to help but she refused, on the pretext that 'Paul' was too confused by his fever to be nursed by anyone but herself. Michael acquiesced, but he was clearly not happy.

'What's wrong with him, in any case?' he demanded. 'Shouldn't he be seeing a doctor?'

'Oh, I don't think there's any need for that. It's just a chill.'

'How can you be sure? He could be infectious: it might be typhus. From the look of him last night he's been living rough. God knows what kind of lodging houses he's been staying in.'

'I don't think it's anything like that,' she said uneasily.

'You can't afford to take the risk, with Eva here. If he's not better tomorrow I'm calling a doctor, if you won't.'

Rose knew there was no point in arguing. Michael was easygoing, but when he had made up his mind there was nothing more to be said.

Simon had a bad night, crying out in his delirium. Rose spent much of the night in his room trying to calm him. For the most part she could make no sense of his ramblings.

Michael was due to return to Bolton the following day. The firm's area of activity was expanding, and he had been devoting much of his energy recently to visiting outlying towns and solving problems of distribution there. He called at the shop before leaving, and Rose promised to send for the doctor. He was reluctant to go but she made light of his fears and insisted that he honour his arrangements.

It was a relief to have Michael out of the way, as she was afraid he realised. She sent a message to the cook-shop; the staff there would have to manage as best they could with Eva's help. With Hannah looking after the shop, Rose could take care of Simon herself, not from any sense of devotion but from the fear of what he might let slip in his ravings. All that had seemed so important only two days ago now held little interest for her, beside the desperate need to conceal the truth of Simon's identity.

Rose remained in the room while Dr Nesbit saw Simon. The sick man was barely conscious of what was happening and, to her relief, spoke only to answer the doctor's questions. At the conclusion of the examination she followed the doctor out on to the tiny landing.

'Well?'

'A very difficult case. He will need careful nursing, and even then . . .' He shook his head doubtfully. 'Your brother-in-law, you said?'

'My late husband's brother, yes.'

'Quite . . . Does he have any other relatives?'

'I don't think so.' Seeing his surprise she added quickly, 'We never saw Paul from one year's end to the next. I think he has been in Scotland. Since my husband's death some years ago my brother-in-law and I have lost touch completely.'

'You would know if there was a wife to be contacted, though?'

'Oh, he certainly isn't married.'

'He would have let you know that much, at least? Well, if there was any close family they would need to be contacted. I'm afraid Mr Olivant is gravely ill. It is pleurisy. That alone is serious enough, but to make matters worse his liver is all but done for. From the looks of it he has neglected his health for years. He has no reserves to draw on.'

'Will he . . . I mean is he likely . . .'

'I doubt if he will live for more than a few days, even with the best of care.'

Rose leaned back against the wall, closing her eyes. 'It must be a great shock to you, of course,' the doctor was saying, but she could scarcely comprehend his words for the intensity of her relief. She suddenly became aware that he had fallen silent.

'I'm sorry?'

'I was asking whether you would be able to manage the nursing alone? I can recommend a very experienced woman, or I might be able to get him into the infirmary . . .'

'No, that won't be necessary. He is better here.'

'He is fortunate to have you.'

His approval made her uneasy. She turned away, glad

that in the dim light of the landing he could not see her face clearly. 'I will do my best.'

'Who knows? He may pull through yet. No alcohol, of course. Spirits would be as good as poison in his present state. Apart from that, it's just a question of keeping him comfortable. Plenty of fluids, no use in trying solid food. I'll give you a line for something to bring down his fever.'

'And the pain in his side?'

'I would like to do something to ease it, but I always think the use of opiates is dangerous in lung disorders. They slow the breathing and lessen the natural cough reflex. I only allow them in the most hopeless cases, when it is simply a question of soothing the patient's last moments.'

'And this isn't?'

'Well . . . not at this stage.'

Rose hoped that he was only attempting to comfort her. After the doctor's departure she set herself grimly to the task of implementing his instructions in every detail. Little as she wanted Simon to survive, she intended to abide by them to the very last.

Michael looked by that night, tired though he obviously was. 'I will have to go back to Bolton tomorrow but I couldn't rest, not knowing how you were and what the doctor had said.'

'A lung disorder, complicated by his poor health and chronic liver disease. He thinks it unlikely that he will survive.'

He scanned her face, seeking some clue to her feelings. She looked away. 'You will need help with him. It is taking its toll already.'

'I have taken on a girl to help Hannah in the shop. That frees me to nurse him myself.'

'It would be easier for you to hire a nurse.'

'I prefer to do it this way,' she said sharply.

'It's too much for you, Rose. I can see that, even if you won't admit it,' he said, his patience worn thin by her stubbornness and his own fatigue.

'Let me be the judge of that, please.'

'I don't know whether you are in any position to make a sound judgement. You are near to breaking point. Every time I see you now you are more remote, more irritable, more wrapped up in this Paul fellow. I can't stand by and watch you destroying yourself from some misguided sense of duty to a man without any particular claim on you.'

'Then don't,' she said wearily. 'I know you mean well, Michael, but perhaps it would be better if you didn't come round again, until this affair is settled one way or another.'

'You are sending me away?'

'Yes, I suppose I am. It's just too much for me to cope with, on top of everything else.'

He shook his head in disbelief. 'Rose, this isn't fair to me. You say that you scarcely know this man; he could as well be nursed by any woman in the city as by you, and yet you insist on martyring yourself for him. Can you blame me for thinking . . .?'

'Thinking what?'

'That you are using this as an excuse; that you have decided that you don't want to have any more to do with me, but can't face saying so.'

'That's not true!'

'What else am I to think, when you tell me so little? Don't you trust me, even now, Rose?'

She stared at him speechlessly, paralysed not only by the horror she still felt of telling him anything about her first marriage, but by the lie she had told about Simon's identity. She could not bear to admit that she had deceived him. If Simon were to die, Michael need never know. She watched the eager appeal in Michael's face fade to angry resignation.

'So I am to take it that you still want me to keep away from you?'

'Until all this is over, anyway,' she pleaded.

'And if I say that if I leave now I won't return? That in future I will confine all communication with you to business affairs, conducted by letter?'

'I can't make that choice, Michael . . . please, don't try to make me.'

'Do you think I have no feelings . . .' He broke off and, turning on his heel, strode to the door. 'Let me know what you decide. If I don't hear from you by the end of the week, I will take it that you wish to be left alone, permanently.'

The door banged shut behind him with an impact that set every bottle in the little shop rattling. Automatically, Rose glanced along the shelves to check that all was well. As her eye fell on one particular rank of bottles she turned hurriedly away, pushing aside the thought they suggested.

As she wearily climbed the stairs she felt only relief that Michael had gone, with the demands that she had no energy to satisfy, however reasonable they might be. To that extent, the sickening confusion of her life was simplified. The events of the next few days would decide whether she was in a position to renew the relationship that had offered her so much, or whether she would be bound again to the man who had all but destroyed her.

CHAPTER

Twelve

Simon was not an easy patient. Although she explained to him that he must not drink any more alcohol, he persisted in begging for whisky. When she refused he would weep, tears trickling weakly down his cheeks, or try to catch hold of her skirts, clinging to her like a child and imploring her not to be cruel, to save him from the torments he was suffering.

Rose never gave way to his demands. She followed the doctor's orders faithfully. It was a point of honour with her to do nothing that could possibly damage Simon's chance of survival. It gave her a grim satisfaction to reflect that for his own sake she was obliged to deny him what he most craved. It was an ironic revenge for all the sufferings he had inflicted on her and her son. Drink, that had hurt them so badly, was now her weapon against him, wielded in his own best interests.

She did not spare herself, allowing no one else to relieve her of her burden of nursing. She kept Eva and the other members of the household out of the sickroom, snatching sleep whenever she could in an armchair beside Simon's bed. By the rules of the deadly game she forced herself to observe she fought for his life, even as she daily hoped for its extinction.

Her will was now stronger than his; perhaps it always had been, if she could but have known it. And slowly, inch by inch, it prevailed. Her loveless devotion pulled him back from the abyss. Each day the doctor's report grew more optimistic. At the end of ten days, Dr Nesbit could assure her that their patient was out of immediate danger.

'I've never seen such a remarkable improvement,' he assured her, beaming his approval. 'Between you and me, I thought at first he was a hopeless case. I hardly expected him to last another night. You are an outstanding nurse, Mrs Olivant.'

'I only followed your instructions,' she said wearily.

'It just goes to show what miracles can be worked by the most dedicated and selfless care. He never would have survived under the ministrations of a hospital nurse, however skilled. It's the family tie that made the difference, you see. Keep him off the whisky, and he'll be out of any danger in another week.'

In a daze, Rose thanked him and automatically returned to the sickroom. It had been the centre of her life for so long that she scarcely knew what else to do. Every other duty, to Eva, the house and the business, had been abandoned while she fought a quixotic battle for an unwanted victory. She looked down at the bed where Simon was sleeping, his breathing now almost normal. His fever had gone and, although his features were gaunt, his colour was better than when she had first seen him. He would live, to destroy her life and happiness once more. She sank down into the armchair, and buried her face in her hands.

She had not seen Michael since their angry parting. She wondered now whether there would be any point in resuming their friendship and whether she could face describing to him the hopelessness of the situation in which she now found herself. Better, perhaps, to let me believe that it was merely her stubborn pride that had driven them apart.

In the lonely watches of the night she thought of what the future now held. Divorce was expensive and difficult; she did not even know whether she had sufficient grounds, since it would be impossible for her to prove any adultery by Simon during the years they were apart.

Of one thing Rose was certain: she could not live with Simon again. If she could not pay him off to go away, leaving her and Eva in peace, then she and her daughter must themselves begin a new life far away, where he could never find them. It was a frightening prospect.

Permanently exhausted from lack of sleep and from the anxieties that barely allowed her to eat, Rose was in no state to devote any but the most cursory attention to Eva. The girl faithfully carried out all that Rose asked, but when she was not needed in either shop or, less frequently, in the bakery, she spent little of her time at home. Rose was too relieved to have her out of the house to worry what company she was keeping. Above all, she feared that the girl might discover the truth from Simon. It would be safest to tell her herself, yet day after day she put off the evil moment.

Simon's progress was slow but undeniable. As the danger to his life receded he became ever more troublesome and the strain on Rose grew more intolerable. His demands for alcohol were now voiced so loudly that it was all she could do to prevent him from disturbing the household. He began to threaten her with exposure if she did not give way; only by keeping him from any contact with Eva and Hannah could she withstand him. At the same time, the other responsibilities that she had put aside during the crisis were reasserting their claims. She could not abandon her usual commitments indefinitely.

Ever more frantically she clung to the hope that Simon

would agree to leave and never return. And yet, as she was forced to admit, the restoration of his health only renewed Simon's apparent determination to establish himself as her rightful husband.

Inevitably, Rose could not for ever remain at Simon's beck and call. One afternoon an urgent message summoned her to the bakery. William Dewey, owner of several small groceries throughout the city, had come to enquire about a contract with Olivant's to supply his businesses with bread. Dewey was one of the most important shopkeepers in Manchester, who had hitherto refused to stock Olivant's goods, as he had always dealt with an old-established firm run by his cousin. To gain his custom would be a major advance, but he was demanding especially favourable terms. Rose was needed to negotiate with him.

Under normal circumstances, Rose would have gone at once to meet him. Dewey was known as a quirky, irascible man impatient of delay. That morning, however, Simon had been particularly difficult, even struggling to get out of bed and go out in search of drink himself, despite his enfeebled state. Rose was afraid to leave him.

'Can't Mr Bradley see him?' she asked Billy, glancing fearfully upwards at the sounds of movement from the bedroom.

'I went there first. He's away to Carlisle, not due back till this evening.'

'I don't know if I will be able to see Mr Dewey today. Maybe tomorrow . . .'

'He'll not wait, Mrs Olivant. You know what he's like.'

The boy was disappointed; he had obviously run full tilt to get her. As he turned away, wiping his brow with the back of his hand, she was struck with compunction. It was the most important contract they had yet been offered.

'Just a minute, Billy,' she said uncertainly. 'I'll go upstairs and see how things are.'

In the bedroom all was peaceful. Simon was lying still, apparently asleep. She must have been mistaken in thinking she had heard him moving. He had had a disturbed night; surely it would be at least an hour before he awoke? She would probably be back by then. She closed the door softly behind her and stole downstairs on tiptoe.

'Hannah, I think it will be safe for me to go out for an hour or so,' she said, pulling on her gloves. 'If Mr Olivant wakes up, just leave him. I will be back as soon as I can.'

Hannah nodded impassively, and continued with her interrupted task of replenishing a shelf of washing soda.

'Right, Billy . . .' The boy replaced his cap and opened the door. As she set off at a brisk pace along the street Rose was already calculating the best terms she could offer Dewey, and praying that he would not be in a mood to wrangle over every detail.

'You're back early,' Hannah said, as Eva came into the shop.

'I had a headache and Josie said she could manage without me.'

'You do look a bit pale, at that.'

'Where's my mother? Upstairs with him as usual?'

'No. Billy come for her. She's away to the bakery.'

'Oh . . . When did she go?'

'Not five minutes since. I'm surprised she never saw you on the way.'

'Did she say how long she'd be?'

'Not long. It was summat about a big order.'

'Do you mind if I just go upstairs and lie down for a bit?' Eva asked, rubbing her head fretfully. 'You can always shout if you get busy.'

'Up you go,' Hannah said, not unkindly. Dour and taciturn though she was, she had a liking for the girl.

'Thank you. I'll be fine after half an hour or so.'

Eva had reached the door into the kitchen when she stopped. 'Did you hear that?'

They exchanged a glance. There it was again; a definite thud from the bedroom.

'She said if *he* woke up to leave him.'

'Oh, but Hannah, what if he's feeling ill, or wanting something? Don't you think I had better just look in and see that he's all right?'

'Your mam won't like it,' Hannah warned.

'She needn't know.'

'You'll get me into trouble, you will.'

'It's not your fault if I happen to look into his room, when you're busy down here, is it?'

'You're a cute one,' Hannah grumbled. 'I don't know owt about it, all right?'

Eva nodded, and climbed the stairs with a sense of growing excitement. For three weeks now she had speculated about the mysterious uncle whose arrival had thrown the household into such turmoil. She had longed to see him, and ask him about his brother, the father of whom she knew so little. Her offers of help had been rejected with what she had sensed to be something close to fear on her mother's part. Why should she be kept from him? There must be some secret, she decided, and she was determined to discover it.

Outside the door she paused, her courage failing. She listened and thought she heard faint sounds of movement. 'Hello?' she murmured, trying not to disturb him if he was in fact asleep.

The sounds ceased abruptly. A voice called out tentatively, 'Rose?'

Eva took a deep breath and opened the door a chink, conscious that she was now definitely breaking her mother's express instructions. 'No. She's out. It's me, Eva.'

'Eva?' He sounded pleased. 'Come in, let me see you.'

For a fleeting moment, Eva drew back, with a sudden sense of disloyalty to her mother, but her curiosity was too strong for her. She stepped inside the room.

'Close the door. Go and draw the curtains back. I want to have a good look at you.'

Puzzled, intrigued, a little alarmed, she did as he asked. By the better light she could make out the details in the figure she had at first seen only vaguely. He was sitting on the bed, wearing a strange assortment of garments: his nightshirt; a jacket that was half on, half off; a pair of trousers that appeared far too big for him, and loose, fluffy bedsocks. His face was pale and so thin that she could see the bones close beneath the skin. She supposed he must have been her father's older brother, for he looked almost a different generation from her mother.

'Mama didn't say the doctor had said you could get out of bed yet,' she said, unnerved by his intense gaze. 'Does she know that you are up?'

'Your mama doesn't know everything,' he said, grotesquely contorting his cadaverous face in a conspiratorial wink.

Eva smiled uncertainly. 'Can I get you anything?'

'Well, perhaps you can. I was going to slip out myself but your dear mother has taken away my shoes. You could go instead, I suppose.'

'What for?' she asked uneasily, already beginning to wish that she had not ventured into his room.

'The only thing that will help me to get better. A bottle of whisky. She won't let me have it, you see, although the doctor has recommended it.'

'Has he?' she asked doubtfully.

'Oh, many a time. She pretends she is giving it me, but she won't.'

'But I am sure Mama wants you to get better.'

'I don't know about that. It would suit her just fine to have me six foot under at last.'

'You are my father's brother?' Eva asked, trying to distract him from a demand that she was sure she should not satisfy. 'I wanted to know about him. That's why I came in, really. Mama has never told me anything.'

He laughed. 'You've come to the right man for that. I tell you what: be a good girl and get me a bottle of whisky and I'll tell you all you want to know, and more. How's that?'

'I've got no money,' she said desperately.

'Get some out of the till.'

'Hannah is in the shop. She would be sure to tell Mama.'

He thought a moment. 'Nothing of your mother's lying about you could pawn?'

'No!' she said, backing away.

'Here, I was only joking! I tell you what: go to the licensed victuallers and tell them you want a bottle of their very best whisky for Mrs Olivant, on the slate. She's well known around here; they'll let you have it all right.'

'I don't think I should . . . Mama would be very angry.'

'That's nothing new, is it? You'll regret it for the rest of your life if you don't find out now, while you can.'

Eva hesitated. 'The doctor did say that you were to have it?'

'Medicinal purposes only,' he assured her, 'but you know what your mother's like about drink.'

She nodded. 'I'll see what I can do,' she said, turning to the door.

'Be sharp about it. She's never out for long. You might not get another chance like this.'

Eva left the house the back way, through the yard, rather than go through the shop and explain her journey to Hannah. She obtained the whisky without difficulty, although she was sure her guilt must be written all over her face, and within twenty minutes was back in his room once more.

'You got it?'

She produced the bottle from beneath her shawl. 'I haven't got a glass . . .'

'I'll make do, don't worry.'

She watched, fascinated and repelled, as his fingers scrabbled feebly to open the bottle. He raised it to his lips, his hands shaking so much that the liquor dribbled down his scrawny neck. The smell filled the room. Her mother would notice it at once.

'You said you would tell me about my father,' she said, not far from tears.

'I don't need to tell you,' he said, taking another mouthful.

'You promised!'

'You can see him for yourself.'

'But he's dead!'

He shook his head with exaggerated slowness. 'That's what she told you, but I'm not dead yet.'

'You? You're my uncle!'

'Oh no. Simon Olivant, that's me, your father, her husband. I never had a brother. She put it about that I was her brother-in-law, and never let anyone near me in case I told them the truth. She's got a nice little berth here and she didn't want me turning up to claim my share. Well, I married her for better or worse, didn't I? And this is a damn sight better than anywhere I've been in the last few years, believe me.' He laughed, and took another swig. 'Not bad, this. Want a nip? No? You look like a bit of the right stuff, not like the first brat. Should have drowned him at birth, like a kitten. Saved me a lot of bother . . .'

The detail, confirming what her aunt had told her, convinced Eva that he was telling her the truth. She gazed at him, horrified. 'Did my mother know you were alive?'

'No. She says she thought I was drowned. It was a nice surprise for her, eh? Not that she seems all that pleased.

Neither do you, for that matter.' He stooped to put the whisky on the floor and, in straightening, reached out and grasped her hand. 'Not got a kiss for your papa after all these years? Come on, don't be shy!'

Caught unawares as he pulled her towards him, she staggered forward on to the bed. He toppled over, pinning her beneath him. As she felt his lips pressing against hers, she turned her face away, screaming hysterically, all thoughts of secrecy gone. After what must only have been a moment, though it seemed an eternity, hurried steps rang up the stairs, and Hannah burst into the room.

'In the name . . .' Hannah pulled her free, and turned her attention to Simon as he lay slumped on the bed. She seized Simon's shoulder and shook it. 'You should be ashamed of yourself! A man your age . . . and her uncle! And what's this? A bottle of whisky? How did you get this? When Mrs Olivant hears . . .' She turned, at the banging of the front door. 'That'll be her, back now. Eva?' she called, going to the door. 'Where are you, love? That's your mother now . . .'

But after a thorough search, Hannah was forced to conclude that the sound had not been that of Rose's return, but of Eva's terrified flight.

Rose was away for almost two hours, during which her impatience to be back struggled with the desire to make the best bargain she could, however lengthy the negotiations this entailed. She entered the shop, still feeling some glow of satisfaction: the deal she eventually struck was a good one.

A single glance at Hannah's face and her contentment fled. 'What has happened?' she asked, the anxiety she had so briefly evaded falling once more, a leaden cloak about her shoulders.

'Oh, Mrs Olivant, if I had known, I never would have let her . . .'

'Eva? What has she done now?'

'We heard him upstairs, banging. She says: "Maybe he's ill." I says to her: "You know your mam won't like it." She says: "I'd better go in, my mam won't know." So she must have gone in, and the next I hears is her screaming fit to burst. I runs up and there he is, on top of her and the room reeking of whisky. I pulls her away and when I turns round she's gone, and I've never seen no more of her from that minute to this.'

'She has gone? When was this? Did she say anything?'

'An hour or more since. I turned round and she was gone, with never a word . . . if you'd seen the taking she was in . . .'

'Yes, yes . . . And did he say anything?'

'What could he say? And him her uncle?' Hannah said in disgust.

It was something that she had not realised the full horror of what had happened, Rose reflected, as she stared sightlessly at the window, forcing her tired mind to devise some way to cope with this, the disaster she had been expecting in one form or another since first she saw Simon again.

'Shall I make you some tea? You look done in,' Hannah said nervously.

'No. I had better go up to see him. Why did you let Eva near him?' she added, as she made her way to the stairs. 'God knows where she has gone.'

'She wouldn't be told. You know what she's like . . .'

'I should,' Rose said wearily. 'It wasn't really your fault, I suppose. It was bound to happen, sooner or later.'

There was no sound from Simon's room. Rose pushed open the door. He was lying on his back in the bed, one hand resting on the neck of the bottle of whisky that Hannah, in her distress at Eva's disappearance, must have forgotten to remove. As Rose approached, his eyes opened.

She wrested the whisky from him before he could divine her intention.

'You have done well today, Simon. I hope you are proud of yourself.'

'I didn't mean any harm. She started to scream, silly bitch . . . A kiss for her father, that's all.'

'You told her?' Rose said, her last hope fading before his vague, mindless gaze.

'Why not? She asked. Got a right to know my own daughter.'

'You have terrified her. She has run away,' Rose said, and stopped, as his eyes drooped shut once more. She took the whisky and went downstairs.

It was still only four o'clock. There were one or two customers in the shop, chatting in the relaxed way that indicated a pleasant half an hour to spend between the end of the day's housework and the beginning of the making of tea. Hannah was slicing bacon, frowning in concentration. It was probable that Eva would return before long, but Rose was not easy in her mind. She waited until the shop cleared, then reached a decision.

'Do you know any of Eva's friends, her closest friends, I mean?'

'Well, there's Peggy Richardson and Margaret Downs, and another couple of lasses that work beside them in the mill.'

'Do you know where any of them live?'

'Peggy, aye. She'll still be at work, though.'

'Yes . . .' Rose tried to think, but the facts slid away from her exhausted mind. 'I don't want to give rise to talk, but on the other hand . . .'

'Do you want me to go round to Peggy's and tell her mam there's been a bit of bother here, and you're worried where she's got to? I don't need to say no more than that.'

'Perhaps we should wait a while,' Rose said indecisively.

'There's Mr Bradley, too. I suppose she might have gone there. She was always very fond of him.'

'I could go there and all.'

'He probably won't be in yet, but you could leave a message. I'll write a note. That might be best. I would go myself, but I want to be at home in case she comes back.'

While Hannah put on her bonnet and shawl, Rose scribbled a few hasty lines to Michael, telling him merely that Eva had left the house in great distress and that Rose would be grateful to know where she was and that she was safe.

Left alone, she could not rest despite her fatigue. She served customers as rapidly as she could, not wanting a shop full of curious eyes to watch Eva's return, and when the shop was empty she roamed constantly between the window and the stairs, listening out for Simon. All was quiet.

Hannah returned soon after six. Nobody had heard anything of Eva's whereabouts, although Hannah had visited several addresses suggested by Peggy's mother and had gone back to the Richardsons' at the end of Peggy's shift, to see the girl herself.

'Thank you, Hannah. I am very grateful. I don't suppose there is much more we can do.'

'She'll come home when she's hungry,' Hannah said, folding her shawl. 'Let me get you summat to eat. There's no sense in you making yourself ill.'

'I couldn't face food . . . tea, perhaps . . .'

Hannah busied herself in the kitchen while Rose maintained her vigil. She told herself over and over again that she should never have let the news of Simon's identity be broken to Eva so brutally. She had not been able to face her daughter's questions; was it any wonder that she should have sought information from him?

One thing at least she resolved: Michael must be told the truth, at once, if he had not already learned it from Eva.

She was sure that, whatever their recent differences, he would come to her on receiving her note and yet, as the hours wore on, and nobody entered the shop but the usual scattering of customers her certainty faltered. He, too, it seemed, had abandoned her.

It was almost nine when she heard sounds from Simon's bedroom. Calling Hannah into the shop, she went upstairs. He was sitting up in bed, one hand incessantly scratching at his neck and torso, as though his skin was unbearably itchy. He seemed to have slept off some of the effects of the alcohol, but his face was a worse colour than she had seen for some time and his temper, she soon realised, was vicious.

'What have you done with that whisky?' he asked belligerently.

'It is well out of your reach.'

'Who do you think you are to tell me what I can and can't do? I will have it, do you hear?'

'The doctor forbade it.'

'To hell with him, and you too!' He picked up a candlestick from the table near his bed and flung it at the window, shattering a pane of glass, which fell into the yard below.

'Mrs Olivant? Are you all right?' Hannah called anxiously from the kitchen. 'Shall I come up?'

'No . . . It was just an accident, Hannah,' Rose replied, with a warning glance to Simon. She closed the door. 'I won't have you disturbing the household, Simon.'

'You won't, won't you? You'll damn well bring me that whisky or I'll do more than disturb it!' He swept the medicine bottles from the table, and hurled a jug of water directly at Rose. She dodged, but the water hit her full in the face. As she stood, her hair soaked, it was as though the past sixteen years had never been, and she was once more at his mercy, victim of his drunken rage. She wept with weariness and impotent fury, tears mingling with the moisture running down her cheeks.

Downstairs, she heard the bell above the shop door clang and the muted murmur of voices. Was it Eva? She must not be greeted by scenes such as this.

'All right. I'll get you the whisky. Just wait a minute, will you?'

He lay back against the pillows. 'Be quick about it, or it will be the worse for you.'

She stumbled downstairs, leaning heavily on the handrail, her strength suddenly leaving her. At the foot of the stairs she took off her sodden apron and used it to wipe her face and hair as best she could. Hannah was in the kitchen, alone.

'Mrs Olivant! In the name of goodness!'

'It's nothing . . . an accident. I heard voices . . . I thought it was Eva?'

'No, only the little lass from next door. Her mam heard the window smashing and sent her to see everything was all right.'

'Good,' Rose said vaguely. 'Is that water hot, Hannah? I will make him a toddy. It may make him sleep better than neat whisky.'

She took a glass and went into the shop, where she had hidden the whisky beneath the counter. As she straightened, her eye fell on the row of bottles on the topmost shelf. She hesitated, and looked round her. The door to the kitchen was closed; the shop was empty; nobody was passing by in the street beyond the window. Slowly, fearfully, she reached out her hand.

CHAPTER

Thirteen

It was the end of a hot August day, the sky a dull, louring red like a great furnace. Even the approach of night brought little relief from the stifling heat that, mingled with the dust and smoke of the city, made the air thick and oppressive, but Rose was shivering. Her hands were shaking as she clutched the balustrade of the bridge. She tried to hold them steady, but they were out of her control. She gazed blankly at her trembling fingers. She, who had worked so hard, achieved so much, who had prided herself on her independence and self-reliance, was now unable even to command her own muscles, her nerves. Her weakness appalled her.

She looked down to the river, its sluggish waters tinted an improbable rainbow of colours by the effluent disgorged from dye factories along its bank. Once, she supposed, many years ago, over a century perhaps, the river had been clean and pure. Children could have bathed there, cattle could have been driven to its margin to drink, women could have washed their clothes by its stream. Now, polluted and poisoned, it could offer nothing.

Rose was not sure how long she had been on the bridge,

or why she had come. She could not even remember how she reached it. She remembered nothing but Dr Nesbit's visit, and her overwhelming need to escape. She leaned her cheek on her hands, pressing them against the rough, rusting metal of the rail, and stared into the dirty waters with their veins of vivid, unnatural colour, and wondered how she could carry on.

'Rose?'

She had not heard his approaching steps, but without turning she recognised Michael's voice close at hand. It was what she had longed for, and dreaded. She remained motionless a moment, gathering her strength, then slowly raised her head and looked at him without speaking.

'You're shaking . . . here.' He took off his jacket and draped it gently about her shoulders. 'I only got back half an hour ago. I stayed an extra day in Carlisle. I came as soon as I got your note.'

'How did you know where to find me?'

'I met Hannah on the way. She was worried about you. She said someone had seen you coming down here.'

She took her right hand from the railing and tugged his jacket close about her, holding the lapels together over her breast. She must decide what to say. It was important, but her mind was numbed, the normal processes of thought choked and sluggish. Michael reached out to touch her arm.

'Look, Rose, I'm sorry. I shouldn't have spoken to you so harshly, that last time. I couldn't understand why you insisted on putting yourself through such an ordeal, but I still shouldn't have left you to bear it all alone. I wanted to come back but I was too pig-headed. I was waiting for you to make the first move. I never stopped loving you, not for a moment.'

'No, no . . .' she cried, shaking her head over and over again. 'Please, don't . . . you don't know!'

'What don't I know?'

'My brother-in-law . . .' Rose said, and stopped. The lie had become second nature. She could brazen it out, telling Eva that Simon had been confused by his illness, that of course he had been her uncle. Michael need never discover what had happened. She would be safe, the only person in the world to know the truth. Her first marriage, and the manner of its final dissolution, could again be locked away in the dark shadows of her mind. She could begin afresh with Michael, never allowing herself to remember what had happened, what she had done.

Rose gazed at him, a big, bulky man, in his waistcoat and shirtsleeves looking like the navvy he had once been, as he worked for his independence. Never before had she needed him so much or seen him so clearly: honest, patient and loving, a man she could trust. And yet she had now to choose to deceive him, or to tell him what might make him turn from her for ever.

'Your brother-in-law died this afternoon, Hannah said?' he prompted, as she remained silent, struggling between her fear and her disgust at the endless deceit. Suddenly she found herself speaking, blurting out the truth before she was aware that she had made a decision.

'I killed him.'

'You mustn't blame yourself,' he said, not understanding. 'The doctor said at the very beginning of his illness that your brother-in-law might not survive. I'm sure it was only owing to you that he lived so long.'

'No, no . . . you don't understand . . .'

'Tell me, then, if you want to,' he said, putting his arm about her shoulder.

Rose could see that he believed that her distress was merely a natural reaction to the loss of the life she had struggled so hard to save. She forced herself on, destroying his illusions and, perhaps, his love.

'He wasn't my brother-in-law. I lied to you. He was Simon.'

'Your husband?'

Rose felt him recoil a fraction from her and even though his arm almost at once tightened again about her shoulders she knew that her worst fears were about to be realised. When he knew all, he would leave her.

'I'm sure you are wrong to blame yourself for his death, whoever he was,' Michael said steadily.

'It was Simon, I told you. I was so shocked to see him that night when he came to the cook-shop that I didn't know what to do, what to tell you. Then the doctor said he was dying, and I thought perhaps you need never know. But he lived, and it was the same as it always had been . . .'

'And what was that?'

It was a long time before Rose could bring herself to answer. Slowly, often halting before she could steel herself to some new disclosure, she began to tell him the story of her married life, with its sad litany of dishonesty and disillusionment, of poverty and drink, of gambling and, at the last, violence.

'And he had not changed?' he asked, as she fell silent.

'Yesterday, while I was out, he frightened Eva. He got her to bring him drink and tried to kiss her. Hannah had to go to help her. Eva ran away. When I refused him more whisky he began to smash whatever he could reach. He was shouting and I was afraid that if Eva came back to find him in such a state she wouldn't be able to bear it . . .' She faltered, before the last, the worst truth.

'Yes?'

'I went down to the shop. There was nobody there. I got the whisky and I saw . . . I saw the bottles of Godfrey's. I thought the laudanum in the mixture would make sure he went to sleep, and didn't disturb us again that night and frighten Eva when she came back. I made him up a hot toddy with the whisky and the Godfrey's.'

'Didn't he notice the taste?' ·

'He made some comment but I said I hadn't known how much sugar to add so I must have overdone it. He grumbled but he drank it and even asked for another. I made it, just the same as before, but by the time I took it up to him he was asleep, and snoring. I waited up until past midnight but he didn't stir, just went on with this horrible snoring.'

'And Eva?'

'There was no sign of her. I lay down in bed but I didn't sleep, listening out for her. I got up early and went to see Simon. He was still asleep but somehow . . . I can't explain it, but he didn't look right. I left him a while longer, then I tried to waken him but I couldn't. I didn't really care. I was so worried about Eva that I was just glad that he wasn't causing trouble.'

'Has Eva come back yet?'

'I got a telegram from my sister, Sarah, this morning. Eva's in Altrincham. She's well, Sarah said.'

'Thank God for that!'

'I went to check on Simon again but he was still the same. I knew that I ought to get the doctor but I didn't. I told myself that I would have an hour or two's sleep and then I would be fit for anything, and it wouldn't make any difference to Simon, but I should have sent for Dr Nesbit, I know I should . . .'

'I'm sure you are right,' he said, trying to calm her mounting agitation. 'It would have made no difference. Nobody could think any ill of you for waiting.'

'When I woke up, about five, I went to his room again. He was dead. I had killed him with the laudanum.'

Michael frowned. 'But you got Nesbit out then? What did he say?'

'He seemed a bit surprised, but he said there had always been a chance of a relapse even though Simon had been doing so well. He gave me a death certificate without any problem.'

'Then why not accept what he said? Simon was only alive at all because of your devotion. It was his own craving for drink that killed him . . . as it would have killed him sooner or later, whatever you did. Nobody can ever know how important the laudanum was, beside the effects of the pleurisy and his ruined constitution.'

'But that's not the point!' she said, with an impatient gesture. 'When I gave it to him . . . I was so confused, I didn't think straight, but I wished he was dead. I wanted him to go to sleep and never wake up. I wanted him to stop frightening Eva and making my life the hell that it was the last time. I didn't care whether the laudanum killed him. Perhaps, deep down, I hoped it would, and I'll never be sure that it didn't.'

'No, I suppose you won't. And you'll never be sure that it wasn't the whisky that Eva got for him. Do you think she should blame herself, too?'

'No! She didn't know what she was doing!'

'And did you? You were afraid for Eva, you were trying to protect her. You were at the end of your tether.'

'But it doesn't alter the fact that I may have killed him.'

'You may have. I can't lie to you and say it's impossible, although quite honestly I doubt it had very much effect. You will have that doubt in your mind for ever, I suppose. Neither I nor anyone else can say or do anything to take it away. What matters is whether you are going to let it destroy you: Simon didn't succeed when he was alive. Will you let him do it now?' He took her hand in his, squeezing it tight. 'You've been such a fighter, Rose. That's what I first loved about you.'

'And now?' she asked, dreading the reply.

'And now?' He gently put back a stray tendril of hair from her face. 'Nothing has changed, except that I know you better, and love you more than ever.'

Rose rested her head against his chest, feeling despite all her exhaustion, her horror and her guilt the beginnings of a sense of great peace.

'Hannah will be wondering what is happening,' Michael said gently. 'Shall we go back to the shop?'

Rose looked up in alarm. '*He's* there . . .'

Michael considered. 'The Finlaysons, then? They would be glad to have you.'

Rose nodded.

'Come on. We'll go back to the road and I'll find us a cab. Lean on me,' he added, as she staggered when she tried to walk after so long a period of immobility. Supported by his arm, she slowly covered the short distance to the main road. Within minutes of entering the cab, she was asleep.

The arrival of her niece, late one night, exhausted and distraught, shocked Sarah. Still more horrific was the story Eva had to tell her when, the following morning, Sarah gently questioned her as to what had occasioned her flight. At first she was inclined to believe that Eva was lying.

'But your father is dead! Rose told me so!'

'He told me he never had a brother and his name was Simon Olivant,' Eva said stubbornly. 'I can see you think I'm making it up, Aunt Sarah, but I'm not. He was a horrible, disgusting old man and I'll never, ever go back home if he's there. I will run away if you try and make me.'

Sarah was sure that her niece was quite capable of carrying out her threat. She sighed. 'I'm sure you do believe that he said he was your father but perhaps . . . perhaps he was joking? Perhaps he was too drunk to know what he was saying?'

'He said it before he started drinking,' the girl said,

moving her head impatiently against the pillows. As a special treat, Sarah had brought her breakfast in bed. 'He told me about my brother dying and everything. He said he was a sickly child and he should have drowned him at birth.'

'Well, Peter was never strong,' Sarah admitted. 'I just can't imagine . . . surely Rose wasn't trying to deceive me when she said she was a widow?'

'He said that she thought he was dead. I'm not sure, though. She didn't ever speak about him, and when he turned up she wouldn't even tell me the truth. I think perhaps she did know and I'll never forgive her, Aunt Sarah, never.'

Sarah bit her lip. She hoped that Eva's intransigence would soften as the shock of what had happened receded, but for the present it certainly seemed advisable to keep her away from home.

'I sent a telegram to let Rose know that you were safe, first thing this morning, while you were still asleep,' she said, taking the breakfast tray from Eva's knees and putting it on a table near the door. 'I will have to write as well, of course, and I was wondering . . . there are still another three weeks to go before the new term. I am on my own here . . .'

'Where are Miss Lewis and Miss Rutherford?'

'They went on a walking tour of the Highlands together.' Sarah did not add that since Joyce had joined the school, she and Marion had not gone away together for their usual fortnight's holiday by the sea. 'To be quite honest, Eva, I have begun to find time dragging a little, being here on my own with only one or two of the household staff to keep things going. Would you like me to ask your mother if you can come away with me for a week or so, to help you to get over what happened? We could go to St Anne's, somewhere nice and quiet . . .'

The glimmer of enthusiasm in Eva's face was suddenly dimmed. 'Not too quiet, Aunt Sarah. What about Blackpool? There are two piers there!'

'But there are so many excursionists!' Sarah protested. 'Still, just this once, I suppose . . .'

'Oh, thank you!' Eva said, sitting up. 'We will have such a good time, you can't think!'

As Sarah went to write the letter that was to win Rose's permission for the treat, Sarah was already beginning to wonder if Eva's idea of a good time was entirely compatible with her own peace of mind.

Rose replied at once, giving her consent to the plan and enclosing a generous money order to cover Eva's expenses. She also informed Sarah that Simon Olivant had died the day after Eva had run away, and that she and Michael Bradley were to marry in a small, private ceremony as soon as it could be arranged. Since Eva would be safe in Sarah's hands, they would take the opportunity to go away for a few days together.

After some hesitation, Sarah told Eva both pieces of news. To her relief, the girl seemed pleased about Rose's plans. Mr Bradley, she informed Sarah, was a good sort.

With the aid of Rose's contribution, Sarah was able to organise the holiday on a grander scale than she had at first intended. She booked a room for a fortnight in a small but eminently respectable hotel, recommended by one of her friends in Altrincham, and took Eva shopping in Manchester for new clothes to supplement those sent on by Rose.

Eva had quickly recovered from her shock and threw herself into the purchase of her holiday outfits with enthusiasm. It was not merely a question of the resilience of youth, Sarah realised. Perhaps as a result of her unsettled upbringing, her niece had developed an enviable self-reliance, a toughness that carried her unscathed through life.

It was on returning with Eva from one such outing that

Sarah had an encounter that disturbed her more than she cared to admit. She and her niece were entering the station in London Road, Sarah at least weary and jaded from hours of walking around the shops, although Eva's appetite for trying on hats and shoes seemed insatiable. Suddenly Eva nudged her.

'That man's staring at you, Aunt Sarah.'

'I doubt it very much, dear,' Sarah said wrily.

'No, he is!' the girl insisted. 'Look near the ticket office . . . he's coming over!'

Reluctantly, Sarah turned in the direction Eva indicated. A tall, bearded man, heavily built but with a slight stoop, was walking towards them. Sarah stopped abruptly, dropping her parcels to the ground, heedless of the bustle of hurrying travellers around her. She did not hear her niece's whispered questions, no longer felt her own fatigue. Her entire consciousness was filled by Philip Taylor who stood before her, hand outstretched.

'Sarah . . .' She smiled, unable to speak, content simply to see him and feel his hand tightly gripping hers. 'Won't you introduce me . . . your daughter, I suppose?'

'Oh, no! I have never married . . . My niece, Eva . . .' she said in confusion, wondering if she had imagined the look of relief that passed over his face. 'Philip Taylor, dear. An old friend.'

Philip shook Eva's hand, barely glancing at her, and at once looked back to Sarah, as though he could not bear to lose sight of her for a single moment. 'What brings you here?'

'Shopping. I am taking Eva to Blackpool and we are getting a few things for the holiday.' She paused. 'Is Effie with you?'

'No. She doesn't keep well, these days.'

'I'm sorry to hear that.'

'There was a child, four years ago . . . it was a difficult

confinement. The baby died, and she has never been the same since.'

'Tell her that I was asking after her, please.'

'I will. She has often said how sorry she is to have lost touch with you.'

'Yes . . .' she said awkwardly.

'Won't you come and see her? She would so like it. We both would,' he added, in an undertone.

'I don't know . . . I am teaching now, and it isn't easy for me to get time away from the school,' Sarah said slowly. It was true enough, but they both knew that it was not the real reason.

'Where is the school? At least Effie will be able to write to you. She has often wanted to be able to contact you again but nobody seemed to know where you were.'

'I have lost touch with the old crowd. Quite honestly, I could never bear the thought of going back, after all that happened. Even to see the house belonging to another family would be bad enough . . .' She broke off, hoping he did not realise the still greater pain that would have awaited her: a visit to Effie and him.

'Please! I can't let – that is, Effie will be so sorry if I don't at least take her your address.'

'Miss Lewis's Academy, Altrincham will find me,' she said reluctantly.

'Thank you. You don't know what it means to us both to have found you again. To have let you walk away, and not be able to contact you again would have been more than we could bear.'

The sentiments were clumsily phrased but she was left in little doubt as to his feelings, and the impossibility that they could be more openly expressed. Sarah felt a moment of exultation and, instantly, of guilt. What was she thinking of? She forced herself to pick up the parcels that had lain tumbled about the floor, utterly forgotten.

'I'm sorry, I really must be going,' she said, turning to Eva who had moved a few paces away and was apparently engrossed in studying a timetable on the wall. 'Eva? We will miss our train, dear . . .'

'But you will write to Effie? Come to see us, if you can find the time? You must!' he said urgently, putting out a hand to detain her.

Only Eva's presence gave Sarah the strength to remain calm. 'I will see,' she said hurriedly. 'Goodbye, Philip.'

At the ticket barrier she could not deny herself a backward glance. As she knew he would be, he was gazing after her, a big, shabbily dressed man, his hat held between his hands. His hair was thinning, his beard was streaked with grey, but to her he was, as he had always been, precious beyond all telling.

'Who was he?' Eva asked, when they had settled themselves in their compartment.

'I told you. An old friend, from when I was a girl.'

'Your beau?'

'I suppose so,' Sarah said, sighing.

'He looked as if he wished he still was.'

'That will do, Eva,' Sarah said, with unaccustomed severity. The girl raised her brows, but said no more. Sarah stared out of the window as the train passed slowly through the city, above the monotonous furrows of rooftops glistening in the light rain. Smoke drifted above them; women would be at work preparing the evening meal for their husbands and children. Why had life denied her that common fate? To be the ordinary wife of an ordinary man, extraordinary to her alone: what more would she have asked?

Sarah closed her eyes. She allowed herself to recall her last sight of Philip, trying to imprint it on her memory. If Eva had not been with her at the station, how would she ever have found the strength to leave him? What would

Effie have mattered to her, beside the imperative she had then felt to remain with him, to cling to him and never be parted? She moved her head fretfully, sickened by her own thoughts yet unable to relinquish them. She thought of her father and for the first time came near to understanding his behaviour.

Rose stood at the window. The hotel was on the cliffs, overlooking the bay far below. The moon had risen; its light silvered the restless sea. It should have been a romantic setting, but she was barely aware of it. She stared before her, her thoughts returning, as they had all day, to Simon: to the day of their marriage, on which she had first given herself to him, a loving, foolish girl; to the night on which he had brutally possessed her for the last time.

She shivered. The room was growing chill. She must prepare for bed, for Michael would soon be joining her. She turned away from the window. They had come to north Wales immediately after the simple wedding ceremony at which the Finlaysons had been the only witnesses, arriving late that afternoon. They had unpacked their cases, moving constrainedly about the room, bumping into each other, apologising with painful formality. She had sensed his longing for her but had remained aloof. It was too soon; their marriage was too soon. It was this that she must tell him, that she ought to have told him before.

Their night things were laid out on the bed. For the first time in almost seventeen years, Rose saw a nightshirt next to her nightgown, shaving gear on the washstand, a masculine array of brushes, combs, collar studs on the dressing table.

She had wasted too long at the window, paralysed by memory. She began to hurry, dragging the pins from her hair and tossing them in panic-stricken haste on to the table. She did not want Michael to find her half-dressed, defenceless.

She unbuttoned her bodice and pulled it off, her fingers, clumsy with fear, fumbling the simple task. She was standing in front of a long looking glass; her own face, taut with nervous apprehension, was strange to her.

Behind her, the door opened. Michael came in. Instinctively, she pulled the bodice close to her, protecting herself, clutching its flimsy cloth tight. She dared not turn round to greet him, but watched his reflection in the glass. His features, flawed and heavy, were transfigured by a tenderness she had never seen in Simon's face.

'Rose?' He came softly up behind her and put his hands lightly on her naked shoulders. 'You're cold, love.'

Warmth radiated from his hands, seeping into her chilled flesh. He rested his cheek against her hair. She felt his breath against her skin; it was unusually rapid. She realised how much he wanted her. She reached up and touched his hand.

'It will be all right, you know,' he said. 'You mustn't worry.'

She studied his face in the glass and saw that she did not need to explain her fears. His love for her gave him understanding; it made him generous and patient, as Simon never was, because Simon, weak and selfish, had been incapable of love. The ghost of Simon's cruelty, that had haunted her for so long, began to fade at the first dawning of a forgiveness that at last would bring her peace.

She smiled. 'I am not worried, not about anything at all.'

He wrapped his arms about her. She saw him close his eyes, his face intent and vulnerable as a child's as he pressed his lips against the curve of her neck and shoulder. She leaned back against him, her bodice falling, forgotten, to the ground as her hand relaxed its needless grip.

It was a relief to Sarah to get away with Eva to Blackpool. Despite her initial reservations about the resort, she soon began to enjoy her holiday. The weather favoured them, the hotel was everything she could desire and the North Pier at least was free from the more boisterous element, who patronised the cheaper South Jetty, the People's Pier, with its German band playing popular melodies, its open-air dancing and its pierrot shows.

Eva's unaffected delight in all the resort's attractions was all that was needed to complete Sarah's pleasure. At times, it was true, the girl would plead for some treat that Sarah would have preferred to forgo. She begged for a trip on one of the crowded steamers that plied their trade from the South Jetty, until at last Sarah gave way, only to find, to her surprise, that she enjoyed the experience just as much as Eva. On one thing alone Sarah remained intransigent: she refused to take Eva to any of the music halls in the town. As she reminded the girl, Rose had trusted her to her care, and she would certainly not wish her daughter to frequent such places.

The second week began as pleasantly as the first. After church on Sunday morning Sarah and Eva joined the 'fine feathers' parade' on the North Pier, taking the air in the company of a respectable throng of well-dressed townsfolk and visitors. Sarah caught more than one admiring glance directed at her niece, who was wearing one of her new outfits, a cream skirt and close-fitting jacket and a broad, extravagantly trimmed hat. With her dark hair and vivid colouring, and a figure whose curves were all that fashion decreed, Eva would have been striking under any circumstance, but as Sarah was aware, she also possessed an indefinable quality that drew her still more attention. She had a poise, a self-confidence, a certain way of looking about her that at times Sarah feared was uncomfortably close to boldness. Much as she enjoyed the girl's company, Sarah occasionally felt that she would heave a sigh of relief at returning her to her mother at the end of the holiday, her duty fulfilled.

Eva, it was clear, felt that there would be no compensatory blessing attached to the end of their stay in Blackpool. As the days rolled inexorably onward, she stubbornly refused to discuss with Sarah her return to Rose and her stepfather, who were to live in Michael Bradley's house at Cheetham. However beneficial the holiday, it had not changed Eva's resentment against her mother.

Towards the end of the week, the weather grew still hotter. Sarah was too stout to enjoy much activity during the hottest part of the afternoon, which she preferred to spend sitting in the cooling breeze on the North Pier beneath her parasol, listening to a selection of airs played by a small orchestra there and, from time to time, allowing herself the pleasant luxury of a brief doze.

On the Thursday afternoon, Sarah awoke from one such nap with an indefinable sense that all was not well. It must, she realised, have been a longer doze than usual, for the sun appeared to have moved round and had eluded the protecting parasol to beat directly on one side of her face, which felt unpleasantly hot. Her head was aching, and she longed for a cool drink and the chance to lie down in a darkened room. It was when she turned to Eva to suggest that they should return to the hotel that she realised what was wrong. Her niece, who only a moment ago, it seemed, was sitting peacefully beside her, was gone. Sarah stared in amazement at the empty deckchair, then looked around her. There was no sign of the girl.

'Looking for your daughter?' an elderly woman in the next row of deckchairs asked her. 'She went away about an hour ago. I expect she'll be back any minute.'

'I expect so,' Sarah agreed, sitting back. It was quite natural, after all, that Eva should not have wanted to waste a moment of their few remaining days. The girl could come to no harm in the broad daylight. She closed her eyes, trying to ignore the pounding pain over her eyes and, still worse, a faint but growing sense of nausea. At last the symptoms grew too pronounced to be neglected. Sarah got up and, asking the helpful old lady to tell Eva on her return that she had gone back to the hotel, made her way slowly along the pier.

In the dim cool of her room, lying on her back with a cloth soaked in cold water on her forehead, Sarah soon began to feel better. She began to feel drowsy and, despite her concern at Eva's absence, must have slept, for she was awoken by the sound of the door opening. She turned her head.

'Eva? Is that you, dear?'

'Yes, Aunt Sarah,' the girl said, carefully closing the door and coming across the room to her. 'Are you all right? I met Mr Harrison and he said that you seemed to have caught a touch of the sun. Can I get you anything?'

Eva's solicitude was welcome, but its very warmth excited an unworthy suspicion in Sarah's mind. Was the girl trying to divert her attention from her absence, which must by now have lasted for several hours? Sarah struggled to sit up, wincing as the change in position revived her headache.

'What time is it?'

'Oh, I suppose it's about six o'clock,' Eva said self-consciously, 'but are you sure there is nothing you want? A drink of lemonade? Tea?'

'Never mind that now. Where have you been?'

'Oh, just strolling about, nowhere in particular. When you fell asleep on the pier it seemed a pity to disturb you but I was getting cramp. I just had to get up and move about and, what with one thing and another, I lost track of the time. You know how it is . . .'

Sarah relapsed thankfully against the pillows. She was not entirely happy with Eva's explanation. A certain suppressed excitement in the girl's manner hinted at more than the vague stroll that she described so casually, but after all, she had come back safe and sound. If she had got into conversation with some boy or other, as Sarah was inclined to suspect, there could be no real harm done, now that they had only another full day in Blackpool.

Certainly, for the remainder of the evening Eva's behaviour was beyond reproach. She devoted herself entirely to Sarah, a gentle and willing attendant, and was with difficulty persuaded to go down to dinner with the Harrisons, a family with whom Sarah had struck up a friendship during the past week. Sarah herself remained in her room, unable to face food.

It was a hot night, which increased Sarah's discomfort. After dozing during the day, she was unable to sleep deeply and found herself tossing fretfully from one side to another or, at best, falling into troubled dreams in which she was endlessly hunting something that remained forever elusive.

After such a night, Sarah had little inclination to go very far the following day, although her headache was better. She and Eva took a short walk along the promenade together in the morning, which promised to develop into another hot day.

'It has been such a good holiday, Aunt Sarah,' Eva said unexpectedly, after a period of silence. 'I am so grateful to you for everything, I really am.'

'I have enjoyed it too, dear,' Sarah replied, pleased by the girl's appreciation. 'It's hard to believe that in only another week I will be teaching again. I wonder whether your mama will want you to come back to school for another year. Now that she is married again she may want you at home with her, to be a proper family, you know.'

Eva said nothing, but Sarah saw her pull a face, which she thought it tactful to ignore. It was, after all, Rose's problem.

That afternoon, while Sarah rested, Eva asked permission

to go out alone. Reluctantly, Sarah agreed. It was their last day, and there could surely be no harm in it.

Eva returned after two or three hours. Her mood seemed to Sarah more than usually excitable; during dinner she laughed almost hysterically at Mr Harrison's somewhat laboured puns, but when she and Sarah went back to their room to complete their packing, she burst into tears.

'Whatever is it, Eva?' Sarah asked, putting her arm about her niece's shoulders.

'Nothing . . . I've been so happy, that's all.'

It was not a satisfactory reply, but Sarah thought it wiser not to probe more deeply. 'We can come back next year, if Rose agrees,' she said comfortingly.

'Next year everything will be different,' Eva said, brushing away her tears. 'I'm sorry, I'm just being stupid. Don't think badly of me, will you?'

'Of course not,' Sarah said, puzzled by the question, which seemed out of all proportion to the cause of Eva's tears. 'Do you want me to finish your packing for you?'

'No, thank you. I'm over it now,' Eva said, hugging her, and indeed her normal liveliness seemed completely restored. For the remainder of the night she was as cheerful and affectionate as Sarah could have wished.

After her previous broken night, Sarah was tired when at last, everything packed away for an early departure, she was able to retire to bed. She soon fell into a deep sleep. She half woke once, sitting up in bed at hearing Eva move about the room but, still fuddled by sleep, lay down again after a few reassuring words from the girl. The whole incident might have been a dream, and when she fully awoke in the morning she really could not say whether it had actually happened or not. Eva would be able to tell her.

Sarah looked about the room. There was no sign of Eva. Her luggage, which had been left with Sarah's by the door, was gone. Sarah frowned. Her own case was still there. She hoped the girl had not taken her things down to the reception, instead of waiting for the porter to collect them. She got up and dressed, expecting at any moment her niece to re-enter the room, after some early morning pilgrimage to her favourite spots, perhaps. But even when the gong sounded for breakfast, Eva had still not returned.

By now becoming seriously alarmed, Sarah went down to breakfast, hoping that Eva would meet her there. As she took her seat at their usual table, beside the Harrisons, she was surprised to be given an envelope by Robert Harrison. It bore her name, in Eva's hand.

'This was pushed under our door this morning,' he said. 'Somebody must have mistaken the number, I suppose.'

Sarah scarcely heard him. She was already reading the letter, her expression changing from bewilderment to alarm.

Dear Aunt Sarah,

When you read this I will already have left Blackpool. I am not on my own, so don't worry about me. I will let you know from time to time that I am all right but I can't give you an address in case people try to find me.

Could you tell my mother, please? You mustn't blame yourself, it wasn't your fault. Whatever happened, I couldn't have stood going back home so it's better the way it has worked out. Thank you for the wonderful holiday, I enjoyed every minute. I am so sorry to do this to you. I wish I could have told you and spared you the shock. Everything will come out well in the end, I know . . .'

Sarah was trembling as she put the letter down. One thought filled her mind: *Whatever will Rose say?*

It seemed best for Sarah to follow her original plan and

leave by an early train. She reached Manchester before noon and took a cab out to Cheetham. Rose was at home, although Michael Bradley was away on business.

It was not a pleasant interview. Sarah was left in no doubt that, whatever Eva might have said in her letter, her sister held her very much to blame for the girl's flight. She questioned Sarah over and over again as to Eva's actions in the last days of her holiday, and the friendships she had struck up. She appeared to be convinced that some boy must be involved, despite Sarah's assurances that Eva had barely had a chance to meet one. The more Sarah protested that the girl had scarcely been out of her sight, the less inclined Rose appeared to be to believe her. They parted on poor terms, Rose evidently considering that Sarah was entirely responsible for what had happened, Sarah hurt by her sister's lack of understanding and devastated by her own sense of guilt. There was nothing more to be done, it seemed, but wait for some further communication from Eva that might give some clue as to her whereabouts.

A fortnight after her return to Altrincham, Sarah received a brief letter from Eva, bearing a Newcastle postmark. She wrote that she was well and happy, but little else. There was no address.

Sarah forwarded the letter to Rose, who replied with a cold note of thanks and the news that she had herself received a letter from Eva, postmarked Birmingham.

Eva's letters proved to be the beginning of a one-sided correspondence carried on by the girl from most of the major towns of England, it seemed, and some in Scotland. The letters, never more communicative than at first, arrived regularly each week, in no particular geographical sequence that Sarah could determine.

Sometimes she wondered if Eva really was moving so erratically about the country, or whether she had managed to find some way of arranging that her letters should be posted from a different town each week. Occasionally, the postmark would remain unchanged for two or three weeks, and once there were no less than six letters from London, leading Sarah to speculate that this might be her actual home. But the mystery remained, for the next week's letter appeared to be from Bristol. Sarah tried to be thankful that her niece seemed to be safe and happy, and not to be in any financial difficulties.

Still more distressing were the letters Sarah received at regular intervals from Effie. Her health was poor, as Philip had said. The confinement had been difficult and had left her with several troublesome ailments. More serious was a heart condition that severely limited her activities. Sarah read with real compassion that the friend whom she remembered as bustling with energy, taking her dog for long rambles every day, now had to spend a large part of her time resting on a sofa.

Sarah wrote often but never accepted any of Effie's frequent invitations to visit her. She was sure that it would have given pleasure to the invalid, but she knew her own weakness. The very strength of her longing to see Philip again, to be alone with him, prohibited her from seeking out an opportunity.

And so she continued, a plump, inoffensive spinster, writing to Effie letters as cheerful and sympathetic as she could make them, and struggling against a temptation that never seemed to lessen. Her only consolation, and it brought her as much pain as pleasure, was the stilted sentence or two that Philip usually appended to Effie's letters. In those few lines she sometimes saw nothing more than common civility, sometimes a coded message of affection as heavy with un-expressed love as her own formal enquiries after his health.

Two years passed with no explanation of the puzzle of Eva's whereabouts when, at the beginning of the autumn term, Sarah received a startling letter from her niece. She was to be in Manchester the following week and asked if Sarah could meet her on Sunday afternoon at London Road station.

It was not easy for Sarah to arrange to have an afternoon of liberty at such a stage in the term, when the school was full of new pupils, still homesick and unused to the school routine. She steeled herself to approach Marion with the request, telling her, after a severe struggle with her conscience, that she had been summoned to see Rose on urgent family business.

Marion agreed to her absence, though with very ill grace; Sarah doubted whether her consent would have been forthcoming if she had told her the true reason. Marion never referred to Eva without a shudder of abhorrence. She made no secret of her belief that there was certainly a discreditable explanation for Eva's continued silence as to her whereabouts and occupation.

Sarah could not have said what it was she expected when, at the appointed time, she alighted from her train and walked nervously to the barrier at the end of the platform. Her recollections of Rose's troubles with Simon were vividly present to her mind as she looked about for some downtrodden, bedraggled woman, a mere shadow of her strapping, lively niece or perhaps, still worse, some abandoned creature, flaunting her ill-gotten finery, whose gaudy dress proclaimed her shame.

'Aunt Sarah!'

Sarah barely had time to register Eva's undoubtedly stylish and prosperous appearance before she was engulfed in her niece's enthusiastic embrace. To her surprise, she found herself close to tears.

'Eva, dear, is it really you?' she asked, drawing back to scan her face. 'You look so well!'

'Of course I do,' Eva said cheerfully, slipping her arm

through Sarah's. 'Can you come to my lodgings for a while?
We can have tea there and I have a cab waiting.'

'Well, if it isn't far away . . . Marion didn't want me to be
too long . . .'

'Oh, let her manage without you for a while. You
deserve an afternoon off every now and again, don't you?'

'Yes, but . . .' Sarah protested, without much conviction,
as Eva swept her away to the cab. Her niece's confidence
amazed her; she could hardly believe that only two years
ago this competent, self-assured young woman now
giving her instructions to the driver had been a schoolgirl
in drab pinafore and plain straw boater, subject to the
petty restrictions of a boarder's life.

Inside the cab, Eva sat back, regarding Sarah with an
affectionate smile. 'You can't think how much I have
looked forward to seeing you again, Aunt Sarah.'

'You could have seen me any day you chose in the past
two years – and your mother, too, for that matter,' Sarah
pointed out. 'You have worried us all very much, you
know.'

'You got my letters, didn't you?'

'They were hardly very informative.'

'I didn't dare to be. I was afraid my mother would find
me and try to make me come home.'

'She certainly would have. Have you told her you are in
Manchester?'

'Well, I was wanting to talk to you about that,' Eva said,
avoiding her gaze and looking out of the window, ill at ease
for the first time since their reunion. 'I would like to see
her, but do you think she would still try to force me to
come home?'

'I suppose that would depend on what you are doing,
wouldn't it? Are you married?'

Eva laughed. 'I should think not. Here, wait a
minute . . .' She pulled aside the little flap in the roof of the

cab and called to the driver to stop. 'Look at that, Aunt Sarah.'

'What?' Sarah asked, staring out of the window. They had stopped at a large building, a theatre by the look of it; it did not seem to have any bearing on what they had been discussing.

'Look at the bill . . . the fourth from the top.'

'Eva Oliver?' Sarah said, making out the writing with some difficulty. 'I don't understand . . .'

'It's me.'

'You?'

'I changed my surname a bit. It's more catchy, don't you think?'

'But do you mean you're *appearing* here? Oh, Eva!' Sarah said in dismay.

'It's quite a good spot, you know. Lots of artists would give their eye teeth to be so high on the bill,' Eva said, calling to the driver to move on.

'And is this what you've been doing since . . . since Blackpool?' Sarah said, trying to conceal her disapproval.

'Well, not solo at first, of course. I was one of the Three Graces to being with.'

'The Three Graces?'

'That's how it started, you see, that day when you fell asleep in the sun,' Eva said, smiling at the reminiscence. 'I got bored, so I went for a stroll. I thought I'd see what was going on at the South Jetty. It was a sort of talent contest, mostly children. I was watching, just standing in the crowd, thinking how much I'd love to have a try myself, when the master of ceremonies caught my eye. When the next turn finished there was nobody else willing to go up and he shouted down at me to come on the stage and try my luck. I said no but he must have seen that I really wanted to, because he kept on teasing me so in the end I just went forward and gave them "She was poor but she was honest".

I was nervous at first, but once I got into the swing of it I really started to enjoy myself.'

'Did you win?'

'Oh, no . . . it was a set of clog-dancing children from Rochdale, I think. I didn't mind that, but as I was coming away this young woman said to me, "Have you ever thought you'd like to take it up professional?" I was surprised, but she seemed friendly so I said I didn't suppose I'd ever have the chance. She laughed and said she could offer me work that very night.'

'Singing in a music hall?'

'Her name was Polly Soames. She and her two sisters had been touring for quite some time as the Three Graces. They were what's called a serio-comic singing turn. They'd done pretty well, but the youngest sister, Lily, had been unhappy for a while. She was engaged to a publican in Bradford and she wanted to settle down there with him. Things had been getting worse during their run at Blackpool and they came to a head the night before I met Polly. They had a flaming row and Lily had stormed off and, as far as they knew, gone away to Bradford. If they couldn't replace her the whole act would have to be altered and perhaps even scrapped.'

'And she thought that you would be suitable?' Sarah asked. 'But you had no experience! You weren't the sort of girl who would think of going on the stage!'

'I had thought of nothing else for years. I just never imagined it would ever be possible and there it was, the chance of a lifetime. Can you see why I had to take it?'

'You should have asked your mother for permission, all the same.'

'She would only have said no.'

'In that case you would have had to tell Miss Soames that it was impossible.'

'And miss a chance like that? No. I'm sorry, Aunt

Sarah, but you just don't know what it meant to me. I wasn't prepared to put my mother's wishes before my own – I couldn't. I have my own life to lead. I know what I want and I intend to get it. I suppose things were different in your day . . .' Eva concluded, with a kind smile that proclaimed more loudly than words her belief that Sarah could never have experienced such a dilemma in her tame, blameless existence.

Sarah was silent, remembering a time when she, too, had a decision to make, her own wishes against her parents'. Should she, like Eva, have boldly chosen to follow her own desires? 'No, Eva,' she said at last, sighing. 'Some things never change. I'm surprised that Miss Soames was prepared to take you without your mother's permission, in any case.'

'Well, I'm afraid I stretched the truth a bit. I told her and the other sister, Dorothy, that I was an orphan, in Blackpool with a friend. I said I was eighteen, too. They were so glad to get me that they didn't ask very many questions. I was just the person they needed for the part, you see: the same build and colouring, the right kind of voice. They couldn't believe their luck, any more than I could.'

'So that's where you've been for the last two years? Touring the country?'

'And loving every minute of it. We didn't have a single week without a booking.'

'But you have left them now?'

'I think I can do better on my own. Our routines were getting stale but Dorothy and Polly weren't interested in changing anything as long as we were getting the bookings. Anyway, when we were in London I saw to it that I got myself a good agent. Once he had come up with some interest from one or two big halls I told the other girls that I was off.'

'Didn't they mind?'

'Well, they didn't like it very much, but too bad,' Eva said calmly. 'You don't get very far by considering other people's feelings all the time.'

'I suppose not,' Sarah admitted, taken aback by her niece's brutal realism. 'So is this your first appearance alone?'

'Yes. I have worked on my act for weeks, of course, but you can never really be sure how it will take . . . whether it will fizz.'

'Fizz?'

'Like champagne; whether it will hit the right nerve in the audience,' Eva explained. 'To be honest, I think I'm dreading tomorrow night more even than when I first went on with the Soameses. That was one reason why I wrote to you. Of course, I didn't want to come to Manchester without seeing you, but the thing is . . . it will be such a help to know there are some friendly faces in the audience tomorrow. Can you come, Aunt Sarah?'

'Me? To a music hall? Oh, Eva!'

'I know what you're thinking, but really, they're not the sort of place you imagine. Lots of perfectly respectable women go now, and the drink isn't nearly as important as it used to be.'

'But what would Marion say? And I don't know if I could get away, not so early in the term,' Sarah said, truth-fully enough, but clasping at the excuse with a sense of relief. 'I will try, of course . . .'

'I do hope you can manage it. It would make such a difference . . . and that's the other thing. I would love my mother and Michael to be there. Do you think if they knew they would try to stop me?'

Sarah considered. 'I really can't say. I have never met Mr Bradley at all and I have only seen Rose once since she married. She was quite angry with me for letting you . . . for what happened in Blackpool.'

'You see, I was wondering whether, after tea, you would possibly be able to go over to see them, and tell them everything, and how much I would like to see them again, and for them to be there tomorrow night,' Eva asked, leaning forward, her eyes fixed pleadingly on Sarah. 'It would mean so much to me if you could.'

Sarah hesitated. She had almost promised Marion that she would be back by six at the latest, and yet would such an opportunity for reconciliation ever occur again?

'Please, Aunt Sarah . . .?'

'Well, I will see what I can do,' Sarah said, resigning herself to a frosty reception from Marion on her return. 'I will not be able to stay long for tea, though, if I am to go out to Cheetham afterwards.'

Eva readily agreed, but in fact it was almost five o'clock before Sarah left her niece's room. There were so many things that Eva wanted to tell her, photographs to show her, costumes to display, that time, it seemed, had never passed so quickly. As they talked, Sarah found her curiosity about her niece's world increasing. As she kissed Eva goodbye and settled herself in the cab that was to take her to Rose's new home, Sarah found herself wondering wistfully whether it was, after all, impossible for her to attend Eva's performance the following night.

CHAPTER

Fourteen

Rose was smiling as she opened the gate. She paused a moment before going up the path to the house, savouring the pleasure of return. Even after two years of marriage, the prospect of reunion with her husband after the very briefest of separations could revive in her an excitement, a delightful sense of nervousness that made her feel herself a girl once more, though happier than she had ever been in her girlhood. She closed the gate and, still smiling, went towards the house.

'Michael? Did Mrs Pearse give you your tea?' Rose asked, closing the door of the drawing room behind her. She crossed the room and, as usual, greeted her husband with a kiss. 'I meant to be back hours ago but you know what old Mrs Jamieson is . . . Is something wrong?'

'Why should it be?'

'I don't know. You seem very thoughtful, that's all.'

'It's a pity you had to go out this afternoon. You missed your sister.'

'Sarah? She came here? Whatever for?'

'Eva asked her to.'

'Oh.' Rose turned away.

'There's no need to turn to stone as soon as you hear your daughter's name.'

'I wasn't.'

'Well . . .' Michael sounded unconvinced. 'Come and sit beside me, Rose.'

She obeyed, ill at ease. 'So? What is Eva after now?'

'I don't think she has been *after* anything in the last two years, has she?'

'Why is she so eager to get in touch now, then, if you prefer it?'

'Is it so unnatural?'

'Was it natural behaviour for her to run away in the first place?'

Michael sighed, and took her hand in his. 'Come on, Rose. Don't you think it's about time to let bygones be bygones?' Rose said nothing. He squeezed her hand, shaking it from side to side, as though to chide her stubbornness. 'Eva is in Manchester. She wants to see you, but she is afraid that you will try to force her to come back home. I told Sarah that you wouldn't.'

'Did you, indeed?'

'Well? Would you?'

'I should think that's for me to decide, isn't it? I am her mother, after all.'

'And I'm not her father, you mean?'

'I suppose so. Anyway, there's no point in falling out over it. You've seen fit to tell Sarah what I will and will not do and that's that.'

'You aren't very pleased about it.'

'Of course I'm not! I like to make my own mind up about things and not have them decided for me by someone else . . . even you,' she said, struggling to avoid what threatened to be their first quarrel since their marriage. 'Well, what is Eva doing in Manchester, anyway?'

'Singing at the Folly, in Peter Street. She wants you to

be there, tomorrow night. I told Sarah that we would go

'To a music hall? No, that's really too much!'

'Look, I know what you feel about it—'

'You clearly don't, or you would never have said that
would go. How *could* you?'

'I was sure that, when you really thought about it, yo
couldn't let Eva down.'

Rose sprang to her feet, her mounting anger demandin
some physical outlet. 'I don't suppose you think *she's* eve
let *me* down, do you? Oh, no! It's always been Eva this an
Eva that; she can do no wrong, and I can do no right! Sh
worries me to death by vanishing without trace; she sink
to performing in places that are little better than brothel
she reappears when she chooses and expects me to roll ou
the red carpet – and I am to smile sweetly and applaud
Well, I won't! You had no business speaking for me.
certainly will not be in the audience at the Folly tomorrov
night or any other night and that is my last word on th
subject.'

'She's your own flesh and blood!'

'That doesn't mean that she can walk all over me! I'r
amazed that you can imagine that I would stoop to ente
such a place . . . there will be drunkenness and vulgarit
and the very lowest elements at their worst—'

'Now, look here, Rose! There will be people of ever
sort, including some roughs, I'll admit, enjoying themselve
Is that a crime?'

'Enjoying themselves? Drinking like fish!'

'God forgive me, you're being nothing but a narrow
minded snob!' Michael said, rising to his feet in his tur
and looking angrier than she had ever seen him before. 'S
there'll be drink? Is that the end of the world? A bit of
drink's not always a pact with the devil. I'm going, tomor
row night and every night of Eva's run if I choose. *And* I'
have a drink or two if I feel like it – I'll have a rare old time

for a change!' He crossed the room to the door in a few swift strides and paused. 'I'm going over to see Eva at her lodgings and wish her well. I was only waiting for you to come home before going, just in case you wanted to come with me. Do you?'

'I certainly don't intend to go anywhere with you while you are in such a mood!'

If Rose had hoped that this might bring Michael to his senses she was disappointed. He banged the door behind him and, a moment later, she saw him striding from the house.

'Well!' Rose said to herself, with a little laugh. It was not quite successful; although she prided herself on her self-control she felt not far from tears. Beneath her righteous confidence in her handling of the episode an unpleasant sense of dismay was spreading, washing away her earlier happiness. Eva, of course, she thought bitterly. As usual, she brought trouble.

Michael returned home late, and in no very concilia-tory mood. He volunteered no information about Eva, and Rose, though she was consumed with curiosity about her daughter, stubbornly refused to enquire. For the first time since their marriage they retired to bed without a goodnight kiss. Although Michael soon fell asleep, Rose lay wakeful, fluctuating between a proud resolve not to surrender her principles and a growing sense of misery.

It was much the same story at breakfast. Michael was polite and willing to chat with his usual good humour about everything but the one question that filled both their minds, making everything else seem empty and of no importance.

Only when he was putting on his coat and hat did he raise the subject of Eva. 'So? Will you be coming tonight?' he asked. Rose hesitated, reluctant to part from him on poor terms. Seeing her doubt, he smiled, with what seemed to her an odious assumption of superiority. 'Seen sense at last?'

'I saw sense from the very first,' she retorted, her good intentions shattering at the teasing comment. 'No, I won't be coming tonight. You may do as you please.'

'Oh, don't worry, I will!' At the door, he paused. 'Do you know something? You are treating Eva in exactly the same way as your father treated you! What's wrong with you? Can't you accept the way she wants to live, and be happy for her? Why do you have to be so stiff-necked? You have learned nothing, have you? Forgive her, for heaven's sake, and make a fresh start.'

Before she could protest he was gone. The day stretched before her, empty and comfortless.

Restless and unsettled, Rose decided to take a stroll in the garden to recover her composure. The comparison of her behaviour with her father's was one of which she had at times been uneasily aware, but voiced by Michael it became more difficult to thrust aside. It was different, of course, she told herself, but all the same . . . As her sense of justice painfully asserted itself, she was forced to admit that, if anything, her crime had been greater than Eva's, its consequences far more serious.

It was not merely a question of Eva's choice of a life of which she disapproved. As she roamed to and fro, seeing nothing of the garden's beauty in the intensity of her struggle, she looked back over the years of Eva's childhood, and the banishment she had been so ready to tell herself was necessary and in the child's best interests. Already, things had been going wrong, and it had not been Eva's fault. From the start, Rose had given her a love that was hesitant, circumscribed, based upon an inner reservation, the nature of which Eva could never have guessed although she must have felt its effects.

Rose stood still, seized by the importance of the truth

she now saw so clearly. She had never been able to forgive
Eva for being alive when Peter was dead. She had wanted
her son, who had been taken from her, and not the daughter whose very conception might have been the moment of
his death. She had never given to Eva the love she had felt
for Peter. It would have been too painful to risk; she
dared not trust life again. Only now, having so slowly, so
hesitantly drawn close to Michael, had her capacity to give
herself without stint been restored. Because of him she
might, as he had urged, make a fresh start. She had the
chance to give Eva, as an adult, what she had denied her as
a child.

As she walked to and fro, Rose struggled for honesty.
Would a single visit to a music hall, however distasteful,
really cost her so much? Was it worth hurting Eva and,
perhaps, causing lasting harm between Michael and herself?
She prided herself on the strength of her will; to back
down would be painful, but as the long hours of silent self-
questioning wore on she began to see that it might, after all,
demand greater courage than a stubborn persistence in her
refusal.

Michael was usually home for dinner early. Rose,
determined to make her surrender gracious, dressed in a
flamboyant gown that she rarely had occasion to wear.
When at last she regarded the finished effect in the glass, she
had no reason to be dissatisfied. If Michael thought her too
much of a Puritan to have a rare old time, she would prove
him wrong.

She went down to the dining room to check that all was
as she had ordered, down to the champagne which she had
decided would be a suitable peace offering. Everything was
ready. She sat by the window, smiling in excited anticipation
of his delight on seeing her, dressed to go out.

As the time for his usual arrival came and went, a chilling
doubt began to steal across Rose's happiness. He surely

would not go straight to the music hall, without one last attempt to persuade her? Her angry pride, so laboriously subdued, began to rebel once more, and with it came murmurings of more insidious doubts. Did he care so little whether she went or not? Did he prefer to go alone?

The dinner had already been put back by half an hour when a cab drew up outside the house. Still at the window, Rose looked eagerly for Michael to jump out, but she was disappointed. A boy got down, clutching an envelope, and looking uncertainly at the house number, opened the gate.

He brought a letter from Michael, explaining that an emergency at the warehouse had prevented him from coming home for dinner, but that he would go straight to the Folly, where he hoped to see her. The tone was, to Rose's eyes, curt and unfriendly. She set her lips in a stubborn line and, tearing the note into a dozen pieces, rang for dinner.

She ate alone, without appetite or enjoyment, deliberately spinning out the meal until it would be impossible for her to reach the music hall in time. Proud but wretched, she went upstairs to change into an everyday gown. He would never realise that she had been intending to give way after all. But as she approached the glass to unfasten the aigrette from her hair she paused, her hands still raised, struck by a sudden recollection.

Staring into the glass, she remembered their wedding night, in the little hotel on the north Wales cliffs. She seemed still to see his shadowy form bending over her as they stood, clinging together in an embrace that neither could bear to break and so be parted, even for a second. More than anything, more than her pride, or consistency, or the sterile principles on which she had so stubbornly insisted, she wanted again to be at peace with him; she wanted to see again that look of tender love on his face, and feel his arms around her.

She glanced at the clock on the mantelpiece, and her hands dropped to her side.

Sarah's late arrival back at the school did not go unnoticed. Marion came into her room before she had well taken off her outdoor things.

'I expected you back before now, Sarah. Miss Rutherford and I were intending to discuss tomorrow's meeting while you saw to the girls' supper.'

'Tomorrow's meeting?'

'Really, Sarah, you can't have forgotten! The headmistress of St Martha's is coming!'

'Oh, of course,' Sarah said absently. St Martha's, a small school at the other end of Altrincham, and their chief rival, had suffered such a drop in the roll since the opening of their school that the headmistress was considering closure, with the recommendation to parents that they should transfer their children to Miss Lewis's. A certain number of the staff at St Martha's would be taken on by Marion, and it was planned that the existing buildings should be retained as a preparatory school.

'You *will* be here, I take it?' Marion asked sarcastically. 'Heaven knows, Joyce and I seem to have to bear the brunt of most of the work these days.'

Sarah had increasingly become accustomed to such comments over the last few years. She had learned to accept Marion's spitefulness, but now, preoccupied with Eva's situation, she felt a sudden spurt of anger at the injustice of the jibe. 'I don't know, really. Eva is to appear at the Folly in Manchester tomorrow night. I was thinking of going,' she said, although she had told Michael Bradley that it was out of the question and, even a moment before, would have denied the suggestion.

'The Folly? A music hall?'

'Yes. Eva is to sing, you know,' she said defiantly.

Marion's eyes were bulging. 'You cannot mean to say . . . you don't imagine that you can go?'

'Why not?'

'You are – I thought you were – a gentlewoman, a *Christian* gentlewoman, responsible for the education of children entrusted to us by some of the best, the most respectable families in the area. You are engaged here on that understanding.'

'And are you saying that I am not?' Sarah asked, with a mixture of irritation at Marion's pomposity and anger at the slur she appeared to be intending.

'If you can even seriously contemplate attending such a place, on whatever pretext, then you can make no claim to gentility or religion.'

'Nonsense. It is a place of entertainment, that's all.'

'The resort of streetwalkers and drunkards? The setting for debauchery and vulgarity? No, I can't believe it! How can you, a total abstainer, even pretend to be considering such a visit?'

'I am not pretending, I am not considering, I am going!'

'If you do, don't bother to return here! How can I permit a member of my staff to frequent such places, and present herself as a model for innocent girls to follow? If it came out, how many of the parents at St Martha's would allow their daughters to walk past our gates, far less enter them?'

'I should be surprised if most of the fathers at least have not *frequented* far worse places in their time,' Sarah said, too reckless now to care for Marion's outrage.

'How dare you! Just because *your* father—'

'Marion!' Sarah said, angrier than ever in her life before. In a confiding moment she had often regretted since, Sarah had once told Marion about the circumstances of her father's second marriage. 'That really is too much! I think you had better go and leave me to pack. I take it I may remain until tomorrow morning?'

'Suit yourself . . . you usually do,' Marion said, and swept, tight-lipped, from the room.

Despite her brave words, Sarah could not keep back her tears. She made no attempt to do more that night than have her trunks brought up from the lumber room, in readiness for the morning. She rose early, her head aching from her fit of weeping, and began the melancholy task. It took far longer than she had expected, for she was constantly disturbed by callers. The news of her impending departure must have leaked out, and every member of the domestic staff slipped up at one time or another to wish her well, and most of the girls, in ones and twos, some in tears. Sarah was greatly touched. She had not expected any particular displays of affection from them, although she had often tried to soften the effects of Marion's more rigid authority.

It was late afternoon before Sarah had at last finished packing her trunks, ready for the carrier the following day. Her furniture would have to be collected at a later date. She exchanged a frosty farewell with Marion, who informed her with a martyred air that Joyce Rutherford was unable to be present, having taken over Sarah's duties.

Carrying a carpet bag containing all she would need for the next day or two, Sarah made her way to the station. She had intended going first to Rose's, and continuing on to the Folly with her sister and Michael Bradley. Unfortunately, by the time she reached Manchester it was already seven o'clock. If she was to reach the music hall before the performance began, she must go there directly. She hesitated. She had never envisaged entering alone a place that, despite her defiant words to Marion Lewis, she secretly regarded as little better than a den of vice.

'Why shouldn't I, after all?' she said to herself, lifting her head a little higher, in the black straw, trimmed with wax grapes and cherries that she had thought most suitable for her venture into the unknown. Now that she had come so far, a certain relish for her adventure began to make itself felt. She was surprising herself, and rather enjoying the experience.

The response she received from the cab driver whom she approached at the station to take her to the Folly was not encouraging.

'The Folly?' he repeated, looking her up and down. 'Here, you one of them temperance crusaders you hear about?'

'No, certainly not. My niece is appearing there . . . singing, you know,' she said, making the announcement with unexpected pride.

'Hop in, then. I wouldn't have took you if you were. They only goes to be disgusted and complain to the authorities afterwards and spoil other folk's pleasure . . . miserable old biddies,' he said, helping her in with her bag. 'Who is she, any road?'

'Eva Oliver . . . she's very good.'

'I'll probably look in myself one night later in the week and see how she shapes up.'

The music hall appeared to have been built as a chapel. The interior, with its gallery, still showed some trace of its original purpose, but the resemblance did not extend very far. No chapel in the land would have flaunted such ornate decor, such a plethora of glass and red plush, of gilt and of elaborate plaster. It was well lit, but the flaring gas jets added to the smoke from pipes and cigars that almost every man in the audience was enjoying, to make the atmosphere almost unbearably hot and stuffy.

Despite its inordinate price, Sarah chose a box, partly as an extravagant gesture in keeping with the momentous nature of the occasion, partly in the hope that she would feel more comfortable away from the body of the hall, where waiters carrying trays of drinks and food wove their way deftly amongst the tables. Although she felt alarmingly open to the public gaze, she was glad to be above the clouds of tobacco smoke that drifted over the stalls, and not to be part of the rowdy crowds in the gallery, who were awaiting the opening of proceedings with good-humoured but noisy impatience. She sat alone in her box, bolt upright, as though she were awaiting a popular preacher in church.

Although the gallery was packed, and the tables that seemed to form a large part of the ground floor were almost full, no other box was taken. On the opposite side of the hall, however, there were signs that one was booked; though empty, it contained a bottle of what Sarah thought must be champagne and two glasses on a small table. Not until the orchestra was filing into the pit did the door into the box open, admitting a burly figure whom Sarah recognised as Michael Bradley. She leaned eagerly forward, looking for Rose, but sat back, disappointed, as she realised that he was alone.

Michael looked far from cheerful, and was frowning as he scanned the audience. Sarah waved shyly, too nervous to dare to draw attention to herself by any bold gesture. He did not notice her, for he gave no sign of recognition. Once or twice, he turned and gazed expectantly at the door to his box, as though some sound had led him to believe that he would soon be joined by the companion, Rose, she assumed, for whom the second glass was intended. Once he even got to his feet, his face lit by such delight that Sarah, watching, felt her own heart sink in sympathetic disappointment when he sat once more, shaking his head in answer to the waiter whose enquiry had momentarily raised his hopes. Clearly, Rose had remained obdurate.

An overture lasting only a few minutes, played in a slapdash fashion at breakneck speed, was largely ignored by the audience which continued to talk and laugh, to eat and drink and stroll about the promenade area as though the performance had not yet started. To Sarah, used to attending the concerts at the Hallé, such behaviour was shocking but the chairman, a balding, red-faced man seated at a table in front of the orchestra, seemed to expect no better. At the end of the overture he arose and, after bawling out the name of the next turn, banged his table with his gavel like an auctioneer and sat down to take a long draught out of the glass before him.

The first act, whom he had announced as Alf George and Lily Grey, the great London sensation, did little to hold Sarah's attention, distracted as it was by the unfamiliar surroundings in which she found herself. She glanced constantly over to Michael Bradley who sat, still alone, gazing sombrely at the stage, and at the packed gallery where the noisiest of the audience were crammed. Most seemed to be young lads, errand boys and apprentices, Sarah would have said, who despite their youth were smoking and drinking with a freedom that horrified her. The smell of oranges mingled with that of tobacco; they seemed to be a popular treat amongst the patrons of the gallery although at the tables on the ground floor baked potatoes and pies were more in evidence.

Women were in a minority as far as Sarah could see. Those in the gallery were for the most part as young as their male companions, and as raucous in shouting their approval at the end of the turn. The stalls and the tables at the front of the house boasted a more respectable clientele and what appeared to be some family groups, solid citizens who would not have been out of place in the Folly's original manifestation. In the promenade area, one or two of the women looked even to Sarah's inexperienced eyes to be of doubtful status; something in the boldness of their gaze as they exchanged backchat with the men lounging near the bar suggested an easiness that hinted at no good although she tried charitably to assume that this might merely be a harmless mannerism. Marion, she was sure, would be scandalised by their freedom.

Although she was feeling far from comfortable, Sarah valiantly set herself to ignore such misgivings as a comic vocalist, Barry Phillips, came on to the stage. He appeared to be a favourite, and sang a number as a railway guard that had the gallery roaring its approval. The noise was deafening, as many of the lads stamped their feet, setting a sound like thunder rumbling through the building. Sarah had never heard anything so loud in her life but it was so clearly good-humoured that she found herself unexpectedly exhilarated by the explosion of enthusiasm. Despite her reservations, and her underlying nervousness at the prospect of Eva's first solo performance, she was beginning to enjoy herself.

The next act, the last before Eva was billed to appear, was less well received. A plump Irish tenor, who varied his routine by an attempt at dancing that was almost as embarrassing to watch as his strained top notes were to hear, he was very evidently both past his prime and, as even Sarah realised, so drunk that he could barely stand.

She now saw the gallery in another mood. As the tenor struggled on, forgetting his words, repeating himself, almost falling into the orchestra at one point, loud hisses began to resound throughout the building. Mocking shouts, and comments that ranged from the humorous to the obscene, were soon followed by a hail of missiles: pennies, oranges and even eggs. The uproar swelled in volume, spreading to the more respectable parts of the auditorium. To Sarah's horrified eyes it was little short of a riot but the singer, too drunk or too hardened to such scenes to care, battled on, breaking off from time to time to shake his fist and yell back abuse, which intensified the clamour.

At last the tenor reeled off the stage to a storm of derision.

The chairman, who appeared unmoved by the anarchy, got to his feet.

'And now, in her first solo appearance, one of the celebrated Three Graces . . . Miss Eva Oliver!' He banged his gavel perfunctorily as though knocking down a not particularly interesting lot to a poor bid, and devoted himself once more to his beer.

For some reason, there was a moment's delay before Eva appeared. To the audience, still excited and unsettled, it was an opportunity for further catcalls. 'Come on, let's be having her!' 'Plenty eggs left up here!' 'Grace, Disgrace and Candle Grace, which one's she?'

It was a daunting introduction for Eva and, when at last she came on to the stage, Sarah could see that her confidence was shaken. She was dressed in character, in the cotton print gown and clogs of a mill girl, with apron and shawl, and looked uncharacteristically nervous. 'Lost your master? He went that way!' 'He's in the pub!' and other, cruder witticisms rained about her ears as she stood, apparently paralysed by nerves, waiting for a lull in order to begin her act.

Sarah shot an agonised glance at Michael Bradley, with some vain hope that he might intervene in some way to help Eva. He was not looking at the stage, for at that moment the door into his box opened. Resplendent in a décolleté gown of crimson and black, Rose entered. His face alive with joy and admiration, Michael stretched out a hand to her, rising in his seat. For the moment at least, neither of them had a thought for Eva, in the delight of their reconciliation.

The shouts from the gallery were becoming uglier, changing from teasing to insult. Eva made an imploring gesture, and suddenly Sarah could stand it no more. Without thinking, without knowing what she was about to do, she got to her feet and, gripping the edge of the box, leaned out to face the gallery and the worst of Eva's tormentors.

'Fair play!' she cried. 'Let her have a chance! It's not right! Shame!' As she realised the absurdity of what she was doing, she hastily sat down again, her face as scarlet as the cherries on her hat. Feeling for her handkerchief, she burst into tears, scarcely able to believe that she could have made such a spectacle of herself, at her age.

Few of the audience could make out her words, but most could see the surprising sight of a stout, middle-aged woman in a sober, schoolmistressy costume and a ridiculously inappropriate hat berating the entire gallery.

A gale of laughter swept through the hall, but it was not entirely unkind. Despite all the uproar and confusion Sarah's essential decency had somehow made itself felt. The bravery of her quixotic protest appealed to the basically good-natured audience. The less rowdy participants began to calm down and then to call for silence from their noisier companions. The tide had turned; with surprising speed, those who a moment before had been shouting insults settled down to listen, all the more sympathetically, perhaps, for their growing sense that the young girl on the stage had not deserved such a rough reception. Eva at last was able to begin her act.

Rose sat close to her husband, holding his hand tightly. In the drama of her reconciliation with Michael, she was not at first able to grasp what the ripples of laughter from the audience soon informed her: Eva was, after her initial setbacks, proving a success.

'My master's out of collar,' she confided to the audience, leaning forward, one hand holding her shawl close about her, the other at her back, rubbing away the permanent ache of incessant toil. It was, Rose realised, the attitude of any one of the women in the streets near the shop, as they stood gossiping at their doors in a rare moment of snatched leisure. Eva's intonation, her expression, her sigh and her shrug, the wry set of her mouth, all fleshed out the humour and the grumbling and the courage of the women she had observed, it was clear, with an affection that Rose had never been able to summon for her neighbours. Eva was presenting no caricature, but a portrait, complete with the robust turns of phrase that were drawing appreciative laughter from the audience.

Rose's enjoyment of her daughter's performance was tinged with unease as the turn progressed. Eva recounted a visit to the local shop to get tick, acting both the wheedling customer, pleading her husband's unemployment and her children's hunger and the unsympathetic shopkeeper who, at last, is talked into concessions. The encounter had an authentic ring to it; Rose wondered how often Eva had observed such scenes, storing them up for this moment.

The monologue ended to enthusiastic applause. As the orchestra struck up a tune new to Rose, Michael leaned closer to her and said softly, 'She's got them eating out of her hand. You wait, they'll not want to let her off the stage.'

Eva began to sing, her voice clear and strong. It was a sentimental ballad with a simple, catchy refrain, sung as a mill girl, looking forward to the end of her shift and the boy who was waiting for her at the gates. Each verse saw a new stage in the girl's life: marriage, motherhood, widowhood, old age.

The final verse, as the girl awaits death and reunion with her love, brought a lump to Rose's throat. It was, as Michael had predicted, a triumph. Most of the audience seemed to join in the final chorus and Eva was twice called back by the applause.

'Well?' Michael asked, turning to Rose with a smile.

Rose sighed. 'She's very good. I only wish that her talents could have lain elsewhere.'

'Look at the pleasure she's given so many people here tonight. Every woman in the hall will go home humming that song. Eva has touched them, given them something. Why wish her any different?'

'Give me time, Michael,' she said gently.

'Well, have a glass of champagne to toast her success, anyway.'

Rose frowned. 'Two glasses with the champagne? You were very sure of me, weren't you?'

'Of course. I knew you wouldn't let me down . . . although I never thought you'd cut it so fine.'

Rose smiled, and accepted the glass he offered her. Every marriage has its secrets. He would never know how close she had come to disappointing him.

'Now, what do you think about going round to see Sarah? Eva has just gone into her box, look. We can all go on for a supper somewhere, if you like?'

'Yes,' she said, rising to her feet and smiling as she put her hand in his arm. 'Let's make a night of it, all of us.'

Sarah approached Rose's gate with a feeling of relief, tinged with faint apprehension. Rose must have been looking out for her, for she was at the door before Sarah reached it.

'Come in . . . here, let me take that,' she said, reaching for Sarah's valise. 'Tea straight away?'

'Please,' Sarah said gratefully, unfastening her mantle.

'A good journey?'

'Not too bad. Do you know, it was the first time I had ever crossed the Pennines?'

Rose laughed. 'And how was Eva?'

Sarah followed her into the parlour. 'Very well. She sends her love to you and Michael.'

'Did she go down well in Hull?'

'They were very enthusiastic. She is more confident

already, you know. She was quite looking forward to York.'

'Didn't you feel like going there with her?'

Sarah sat down with a sigh of relief. 'I would have gone if she had really wanted me to, but between you and me after a fortnight living in lodgings I'd had enough . . . and the late nights! I never liked to go to bed until Eva was back, of course, and sometimes it was one or two in the morning before she came in! Not that she was any the worse for it, but I'm too long in the tooth to take very much of it.'

'So you don't think you will take her up on her offer?'

Sarah's eyes rested thankfully on the tea tray that was being brought into the room by Rose's maid. 'It was very nice of Eva, but I don't think I am really the right person to accompany her. She needs someone who is used to that sort of life, a sensible woman who can look after her costumes and chaperone her to all sorts of places where I wouldn't feel at home. I explained, and I think she could see my point.'

'She should be able to find some old trouper who hankers after the smell of greasepaint without too much difficulty,' Rose said drily. 'I am sure that she would much rather have had you, of course.'

The compliment touched Sarah, even as she murmured a disavowal. Rose, it was clear, was on her best behaviour. 'Has everything been going smoothly here?' Sarah asked, accepting a cup of tea from her sister. 'Is Michael well?'

Rose's face, beautiful still but with a certain imperious set to the eyes and mouth, relaxed into softer lines. 'Yes,' she said, pausing in the act of stirring her tea. 'Oh, Sarah, if you only knew . . . I never understood what happiness was until now. I don't think I could live without him.'

Sarah sighed. She was only human; the contrast with her own condition was painful.

'Well . . .' Rose said, giving her tea a brisk stir and setting the spoon in the saucer with a businesslike chink. 'If you aren't going to act as Eva's companion, what are you going to do?'

'I don't quite know. Look out for another teaching post, I suppose.'

'You don't have to. You could stay here with us.'

'That's very kind of you,' Sarah said awkwardly, 'but I really think it would be better if I had work of some sort. We would get under each other's feet after a while, you know.'

'Well, that's just it!' Rose said eagerly. 'I've been think-ing. I gave up the lease of the general shop in Ancoats after Simon . . . after I married. Hannah took it on. The bakery has been doing very well, but it outgrew the premises and Michael found a better site further out. He put in a man-ager to run it and really I don't have anything to do with it now. There's still the cook-shop, of course, but it more or less runs itself now. To be quite honest, I've been feeling restless. You know me: at homes and morning visits don't hold much appeal.'

'No,' Sarah agreed, with a growing sense of unease. Rose's energy always left her feeling inadequate.

'The thing is, I've been so used to working that I'm at a bit of a loose end. It would have been different if Eva was at home, of course. I could have taken her around and so forth,' Rose said vaguely. 'But as it is . . . what do you think about a teashop?'

'A teashop?' Sarah echoed nervously.

Rose set down her cup and leaned forward, eyes sparkling. 'A place in the centre of Manchester, nicely fur-nished in an elegant, modern style, where women can go for tea, coffee, scones and cakes, sandwiches and perhaps simple cooked meals. I would have service by waitresses only, and a comfortable, well-appointed cloakroom. What do you think?'

'It sounds very nice ,' Sarah said cautiously, 'but won't it be a lot of work for you?'

'Exactly!' Rose said triumphantly. 'You could help me! You would receive a good salary, of course, but we could share the burden of organising and running the place. What could be more suitable? You need work, and I am looking for an assistant. We understand each other, so there would be no disagreements, as there might be with a stranger. It's perfect!'

'What does Michael say?' Sarah asked, her heart sinking as she realised what Rose meant by *no disagreements*. Rose would be in command, as usual, and Sarah would carry out her will.

'Oh, he thinks it's an excellent idea, so long as Bradley's supply our goods. Well?'

'It has taken me by surprise, dear . . . but I'm sure it would be very successful. It's just that I don't know whether it's the best thing for me to do at the moment. I will think about it,' she added hastily, as Rose's fine brows gathered in a frown.

'Just as you like,' Rose said, the gracious hostess once more. 'If you have finished your tea would you like to go up to see your room?'

Sarah was glad to accept. They were crossing the hall when Rose suddenly stopped. 'Oh, I completely forgot!' she said, picking up a letter from the tray on the chest near the door. 'This came for you at the beginning of the week. There didn't seem much point in forwarding it to you in Hull when you were probably coming back so soon.'

Sarah barely heard her. She was staring at the black-edged envelope, bearing a familiar handwriting.

'They had taken several days to forward it from Miss Lewis's, judging by the postmarks, so I assumed that if it was notice of a funeral you would have missed it anyway,'

Rose said apologetically, as Sarah made no attempt to open the letter. Receiving no reply, she silently led her sister upstairs to her room and, with rare tact, left her alone.

Sarah sat by the window, the letter on her lap. The day was warm and the window was open. A blackbird was singing in the garden, sad and sweet. She closed her eyes for a few moments and, at last, took up the letter.

Sarah stood for a moment to get her breath. The graveyard where her mother and father were buried was not far from their old home, on top of the hill overlooking Warrington. It was a stiff climb for Sarah, and made her unpleasantly aware of her advancing years and comfortable dimensions. She had bought flowers in Warrington, and dressed the grave.

When she had finished she stood a while, gazing at the stone with its simple inscription. It told so little of the lives of those whose last resting place it marked. In another few years, she supposed, all their dramas, their tragedies and scandals would be forgotten. They would be no more than names, growing fainter with every passing day.

Engrossed in her thoughts, she did not hear the steps that hesitantly approached her.

'Sarah?'

She turned, already smiling, and held out her hand. 'How did you know I was here?'

'Old Mr Ramage came by as I was standing at the gate, waiting for you. He said he'd seen you coming up here with flowers.'

'I'm sorry . . . didn't I say in my letter not to expect me until three?' she said, puzzled. 'I thought I would have time to come up here first.'

'I couldn't wait until three, knowing you were here.'

Sarah glanced at him quickly, and looked away. 'Where is Effie's grave?'

'Over there.' Philip gestured. 'Do you want to see it?'

'Yes.' She remained another moment without speaking, gazing at her parents' headstone, before beginning to walk slowly with him to the newer grave. 'I was so sorry not to get your letter in time to come to the funeral.'

'It wasn't your fault.'

'No, but all the same . . .'

There was a pause, which neither of them seemed able to break, until Philip asked, changing the subject, 'So, are you going to stay with Rose?'

'Oh, I don't know. She is very kind, of course, but she will manage me so. I'm sure we should fall out before long, though she really has got the best of intentions.'

'A teashop, didn't you say?'

'She'll make a go of it, I'm sure, but I don't think it's really what I want to do.'

'And what do you want, Sarah?' he asked gently.

'I will teach, I suppose.'

'Around here?'

'Perhaps . . . it's too soon to say.'

He nodded. They had reached Effie's grave. Philip took off his hat and stood bareheaded, his hair ruffled by the breeze that always blew up on the hill. There was as yet no headstone, just the raw mound of earth and a vase filled with copper-coloured chrysanthemums. They stood together in silence, close but not touching and at last, exchanging a glance of unspoken agreement, moved away.

'You didn't say in your letter why you had left Altrincham,' Philip remarked.

'I was asked to go,' Sarah said, smiling ruefully. 'I went to the music hall and the headmistress took exception to it.'

'You went to the music hall?' Philip repeated in surprise.

'Eva was appearing so of course I wanted to go.'

'Of course,' he agreed, taken aback. 'I would never have thought you'd have it in you . . . but good for you.'

'Oh, I think I've changed, over the years,' she said, shrugging, 'in some ways, at least.'

'You're still the same to me, Sarah.'

She smiled. 'Such a lot has happened, all the same. It's bound to have an effect.'

'The most important things about a person don't ever alter, whatever happens.' Philip offered her his arm. She took it, self-consciously, resting the very tips of her fingers on his sleeve, acutely aware of the black mourning band about his arm.

'She was a good wife to me always,' he said, catching the direction of her glance.

'Yes. I could tell from her letters that she was happy with you.'

'I did my best. I don't think she ever guessed . . .'

'Guessed what?' Sarah asked, her voice barely more than a whisper.

'How much I regretted walking away from your father's house without you, that night.'

'It was a long time ago, Philip.'

'But not too long?'

'Who knows?' she asked, slipping her hand a little more closely into his arm.

As they left the graveyard behind them and began to stroll down the hill, deep in conversation, their heads imperceptibly inclined closer together, and the gap between them gradually narrowed until, from the distance, they seemed one being, moving slowly home.

AUSTRALIA LANE

Janet Broomfield

Australia Lane was the place Bridie Graham always came
back to: in her long and varied life, in her memories, in her
dreams. But it was also in the Lane that Bridie's life fell
apart for the first time, when she was separated from her
parents and baby sister Cissie to be brought up by her
snobbish aunt. The early traumas leave their mark, and
Bridie knows she must make her own way if she is to
achieve anything in life. In service with an elderly lady,
she meets the man who will become a source of both
exquisite happiness and anguish. Their affair presents
Bridie with a choice that will shape the rest of her life. And
if Cissie's life has brought her wealth and social standing,
will real reconciliation be possible when fate at last
reunites the two sisters?

Spanning generations from the nineteenth century to the
Great War, *Australia Lane* is a saga of an extraordinary
woman, re-creating with compelling detail a small
northern English town in times of peace and war.

Warner Books now offers an exciting range of quality titles
by both established and new authors. All of the books in this
series are available from:

Little, Brown and Company (UK),
P.O. Box 11,
Falmouth,
Cornwall TR10 9EN.
Fax No: 01326 317444
Telephone No: 01326 372400
E-mail: books@barni.avel.co.uk

Payments can be made as follows: cheque, postal order
(payable to Little, Brown and Company) or by credit cards,
Visa/Access. Do not send cash or currency. UK customers and
B.F.P.O. please allow £1.00 for postage and packing for the
first book, plus 50p for the second book, plus 30p for each
additional book up to a maximum charge of £3.00 (7 books
plus).

Overseas customers including Ireland, please allow £2.00 for
the first book plus £1.00 for the second book, plus 50p for each
additional book.

NAME (Block Letters) ....

....

ADDRESS ....

....

....

☐ I enclose my remittance for ....
☐ I wish to pay by Access/Visa Card

Number ☐☐☐☐☐☐☐☐☐☐☐☐☐☐☐☐☐☐

Card Expiry Date ☐☐☐☐